Marty swooped down on Cavanaugh like a bird of prey. "Where is it?" she yelled, pounding him with pillows. "Where is it?"

Cavanaugh was choking with laughter, but still refused to give in. "I don't know what you're talking about," he managed to get out between bouts of being popped in the face with the velvety cushions.

Suddenly, she noticed something white sticking out from behind the cushion, and reached for it. "Give it up before you get hurt." She tugged at the little silver handle on the box.

With lightening speed, Cavanaugh flipped her onto her back and pinned her to the couch. "I paid for it. It's mine." He looked at her seductively. "And so are you."

He kissed her, and the sweet taste ignited the fire in his soul. He rolled over until his larger body covered hers. Without warning, he felt his manhood responding to the soft warmth of her form. So many nights he imagined what she would feel like beneath him. But nothing he imagined came close to the actual moment. His large hands wrapped around her backside, pushing her up against his quickly rising bulge as he considered the fastest way to get inside her clothes.

LOVE'S INFERNO

ELAINE OVERTON

BET Publications, LLC
http://www.bet.com
http://www.arabesquebooks.com

ARABESQUE BOOKS are published by

BET Publications, LLC
c/o BET BOOKS
One BET Plaza
1900 W Place NE
Washington, DC 20018-1211

All Kensington Titles, Imprints, and Distributed Lines are available at special quantity discounts for bulk purchases for sales promotions, premiums, fund-raising, and educational or institutional use. Special book excerpts or customized printings can also be created to fit specific needs. For details, write or phone the office of the Kensington special sales manager: Kensington Publishing Corp., 850 Third Avenue, New York, NY 10022, attn: Special Sales Department, Phone: 1-800-221-2647.

First printing: January 2005
10 9 8 7 6 5 4 3 2 1

Printed in the United States of America

Dedicated in loving memory to my mother,

BERNICE STEWART
March 25, 1927 – October 12, 2001

Your loving arms, kind heart, and gentle spirit were the greatest gifts ever given to me. Thank you for teaching me that the only real failure is to not have tried.

ACKNOWLEDGMENTS

First, to the source of all things, my Lord and Savior, Jesus Christ. Thank you for the gift of imagination.

To my dynamic one-woman support group, critique partner, and fan club, my beloved big sister, Sue. Your love and encouragement have made me braver than I ever thought I could be. Thank you for saying, "I knew you could do it," and meaning it.

To my brothers, Danny and George, for all the times I've looked back over my shoulder and you were there. Thank you for always having my back and giving me your love. And to all my family and friends for your love and support.

To my son, Stacey, who may not always understand why Mommy spends so much time in front of the computer, but never denied me hugs and kisses when I needed them most. Your sweet love is my lifeblood. Thank you for existing!

And last, but not least, to Demetria Lucas. I expected an editor to have your keen eye and intelligence, but your kindness and humor are worth a thousand bonus points. Thank you for your belief in my work, and for holding my hand through the process.

One

June 5th, Detroit, Michigan

Marty could feel the smoke seeping into her lungs, her nose, and her eyes. She had been exposed to the inferno far longer than protocol allowed. She was starting to get nervous. A tiny coward in the back of her brain was screaming, "No one's in there. Go back. Go back!" But firefighters live by their instincts and hers were telling her the opposite was true. She turned left, then right, trying to see through the mist of gray ash falling around her.

"Help."

Marty froze in place wondering if she had imagined the weak cry.

"Help."

The sound came again, but this time it was strong and forceful, a man's voice.

"Is anybody there?" Swinging her axe in a crisscrossing motion she cut a path in the direction of the voice until she finally came to an opening in the scattered debris.

A man was lying with his legs trapped beneath a large, wood beam that had fallen from the ceiling. He was lying so still she feared she was too late.

As if sensing her presence, he tilted his head back to look at her from an inverted angle. "Help me, please!"

Moving with lightening speed, Marty braced her axe

beneath the wood beam. "Hold on!" she shouted through gritted teeth.

Using every ounce of strength she had, she pried at the wood beam but it wouldn't budge. She scanned the long object and in her mind, rapidly calculated the best possible position for support. She wedged the sharp edge of the axe only inches from the victim's head. She knew what she was about to attempt was dangerous. She would have only one chance to make it work.

"On the count of three, I need you to move out of the way," she shouted over the crackling fire that was quickly becoming unbearable. The man's big, brown eyes were so focused on the object beside his head, he barely heard her.

"Do you understand me?" Marty yelled, hoping to snap him out of his dazed state. Without his help this would never work.

The man shook his head frantically, praying that this was a seasoned firefighter with years of experience in matters such as this and not a rookie trying some untested theory. Marty braced herself hard against the axe. She knew she would need every ounce of her 135-pound, five-foot ten-inch frame to move the fallen rafter.

"One." She watched his eyes.

"Two." He looked terrified. Would he be able to do this?

"Three." She pushed against the axe with all the strength she could muster. As soon as he heard the creaking sound of the wood giving way, the man started scrambling backward. Five solid strokes and he was clear. Seconds later, the wood handle of the axe fractured beneath the weight of the structural beam and both came crashing down hard against the floor. Without missing a beat, Marty had her head beneath the victim's arm.

"Can you walk?" The breathing apparatus she wore

made it hard to hear her words, but he understood her meaning.

"I'll try," he answered, as his rescuer attempted to lift him. He managed to get to his feet, but forward movement was still difficult.

"It's all right. I've got you." Marty half-dragged, half-carried the injured man through the blaze. She led with speed and confidence as the helpless victim lay heavily against her, fighting to stay conscious.

She swallowed hard and breathed deeply when the river of flames opened to reveal the glass doors of the building's entrance. Truth was, she'd had no idea whether they had been moving in the right direction.

Members of her engine team were gathered outside the entrance trying to peer in. Horror-stricken expressions were on every face. The fire had gotten out of control, and everyone had been ordered out. It wasn't until they had cleared the building that they realized Marty had gotten separated from them.

Big Cal was the first to spot the blurred images coming through the blaze. "It's her!" Cal yelled to the group of disheartened men. "It's Marty." He charged for the doors with total disregard for his own safety.

Marty saw someone coming toward her grinning widely. She had never been so happy to see that buck-toothed smile in her life. Cal caught the unconscious man under the other arm, greatly lifting her burden. The trio finally came through the front entrance to a hail of cheers. The news crew that had been standing off to the side came rushing forward, shoving microphones into their faces.

The last things Marty remembered were turning her victim over to the paramedics, the feel of her knees crumpling beneath her, and Big Cal's large hand coming under her back to break her fall.

* * *

Marty blinked hard until she was able to keep her eyes open. What she had believed to be the white light of heaven turned out to be a reading lamp above her hospital bed. She turned her head trying to see out the window. The blinds were open, and from the look of the sky, it was a perfect summer day.

She noticed a square, metallic object on the end of the bed and reached for it. It was heavier than it looked. Marty opened the cover and realized it was her medical record. Some careless hospital staffer had left it lying around. She simply shook her head as she scanned the information. *So that's it.* Smoke inhalation.

The door opened and in came a very attractive nurse dressed in traditional white and carrying a small tray. "Well, look who's awake," the nurse said and smiled.

Marty noted her name badge said Chenault. She tried to smile back but her face was stiff, and she soon discovered, so was the rest of her body.

"Oh." The nurse grinned bashfully while taking the metal file from Marty. "I wondered where I left that." Nurse Chenault did a quick visual scan of her patient. Her years of experience showed in the easy and precise way she checked vital signs. "You must be a very important lady," Nurse Chenault teased while slipping the stethoscope into her ears. She laughed at the look of confusion on Marty's face. "There's a hallway full of firemen waiting to see you." Satisfied with the pulse rate, she tucked the awkward object into her dress pocket. "And let me tell you," she stated, slipping the blood pressure band around Marty's upper right arm, "they are really affecting the efficiency level around here."

"I'm sorry." Marty's caramel-brown complexion did little to hide her blush. She knew firsthand how rambunctious her coworkers could be. She only hoped they hadn't embarrassed her too much. "I'll ask them to leave."

"Don't do that," the nurse said. "I just meant it's hard to concentrate with all those fine black men lounging around the corridors."

Marty held her peace, although she was itching to tell the infatuated woman that after spending the last six years eating, sleeping, and living with twenty nasty men, she just couldn't see them in the same way.

Both women started at the sound of the door swinging open. In walked a six-foot-four-inch giant. Nurse Chenault's mouth fell open.

Calvin Brown, better known as Big Cal for the most obvious reasons, was the equivalent of a chocolate-brown Atlas. His dark skin was pulled taut over his enormous muscles. Even his bucktoothed grin could not scar the image of exquisite masculinity he represented.

"I don't remember seeing him in the hall," the pretty nurse whispered. Marty thought the young woman looked a bit shell shocked.

"He's kind of hard to miss," Marty said. Nurse Chenault never noticed. She was too busy staring up at Big Cal as if he had just stepped out of a dream.

All Marty could think of was the ferocious scent he had left in the latrine last week. Even the thought of it was making her nauseous. The big oaf never even bothered to apologize for leaving their firehouse smelling like a sewer. As if that wasn't bad enough, most of the guys spent the rest of the day trying to determine what combination of foods could create such a powerful fireball. Having had quite enough of both the stench and the god-awful conversation, Marty had finally sought refuge in the back of Big Red. She spent the rest of the day there, curled up with a good book and waiting for the air to clear.

Disregarding the nurse's moon-eyed expression, Big Cal sauntered over until he stood towering over the hospital bed. "Hey, baby girl." He smiled, completely comfortable with the way his two front teeth hung over his bottom lip. "You scared the hell out of me."

Marty twisted her mouth in disdain. "I'm fine, Cal. Thanks for asking."

"You know I love you," Cal teased, and chucked her under the chin.

"Is my *vic* okay?" Marty had been worried about the man from the moment her eyes opened.

"Oh, yeah. They released him yesterday." Cal suddenly remembered something. "In fact . . ." He ran over to open the door, revealing a collage of faces. "She's awake." Cal gestured toward the bed. "But let ole' boy in first."

"Hey, Marty."

"Feel better."

"Love ya, boo."

"Hey, Stilts."

Voices called from the crowd as it parted to reveal what Marty would later describe as the most beautiful face she had ever seen.

"She can have visitors, right?" Cal asked the still-dazed nurse.

Nurse Chenault was so busy studying every inch of Cal's body she never even noticed his lips move. Marty nudged her hard.

"Oh, yes. Yes, she can have visitors. At least for the next hour."

"Remember what we talked about, man," Cal cautioned the handsome stranger before walking out with a thunderstruck Nurse Chenault following close behind. Marty simply shook her head. The girl was lost.

The stranger stood alone just inside the now-closed door, looking completely out of place in his impeccably tailored Armani suit and wing-tipped shoes. His head was covered with tiny, soft, dark-brown curls neatly trimmed. His cinnamon complexion was the perfect compliment to his almond-shaped, deep-brown eyes. Even from that distance, the faint scent of his cologne lingered in the air. Cradled in the crook of his arm was what looked to be a dozen or so white roses.

"I just wanted to say thank you," he said, and smiled beautifully, revealing a slight dimple in his left cheek.

Marty held to the rails fearing she would melt right into the bed. She opened her mouth to speak but nothing came out. At that moment she hated herself, realizing there wasn't that much difference between her and Nurse Chenault.

"From what I understand," the stranger continued, moving closer to the bed, "they called everyone back out and gave up on trying to save the building."

Marty's eyes widened as realization dawned on her. *This* was her *vic.*

His dark eyes slid quickly over her form outlined beneath the sheets. "You weren't even supposed to be in there."

"Really?" The one, simple word was all she could manage.

He extended his arms to offer the roses. "These are for you. Cal told me they're your favorite."

"Thank you." Marty forced herself to smile this time, regardless of the pain. "I'll ask the nurse to put them in some water."

"How are you?" The genuine concern in his dark eyes was touching.

"I'm fine," she lied, finding it very hard to look directly at him for any length of time.

He glanced at his watch. "I'm glad to hear that."

"And you?" She realized that if he were concerned with the time he would be leaving soon.

"Fine, thanks to you."

Marty struggled to smile again, believing it was one of her best features. Then it occurred to her, she hadn't combed her hair in who knew how many days. When properly brushed and styled, her naturally curly hair was quite flattering. But given the time and place, every hair was probably standing on its end. What was the point of having a lovely smile if you looked like Chewbacca from the nose up?

"Well, I assured your friends this visit would be brief." He reached into his pants pocket, pulled out his keys, and stood jiggling the keyring for several seconds. She could tell he had something more to say but was weighing his thoughts.

Then finally he spoke. "There are no words . . . no roses could ever express the depth of my gratitude." He squeezed her hand, and she felt an electric spark shoot up her arm.

Marty had no response. She saved lives every day. It was what she did. But to the person whose one and only life had been saved, it always seemed a miracle. She couldn't comprehend the emotion, although she had seen it a thousand times. But something in the eyes of this stranger as he conveyed his appreciation with such empathy finally gave her some understanding of it. He smiled beautifully one last time, then turned to leave.

Marty felt her heart speed up. *He's leaving.* He was about to walk out of her life forever, and she didn't even know his name. She had to stop him from disappearing like the illusion she half-believed he was.

"Maybe dinner could—" she blurted out.

The handsome stranger turned suddenly, startled by the plea in her voice. "I beg your pardon?"

"You said words and roses could not express your gratitude. Maybe dinner could."

His deep, rich laughter was almost musical. "Dinner it is." He winked and turned to leave once again, this time making it as far as the door before she stopped him.

"Wait. We don't even know each other's names," Marty called after him, feeling every bit as desperate as she sounded.

He stood in the partially opened door. The smug expression on his face told her she was trying way too hard.

"I'm Martina Williams. My friends call me Marty."

"Nice to meet you, Marty." His handsome face suddenly seemed quietly devilish.

"I'm Cavanaugh Saint John. My friends call me Cavanaugh." Then he disappeared behind the door.

Only moments later, it swung open again, and Marty found herself covered in the hugs and wet kisses of her well-meaning friends. Despite the good humor that surrounded her, all she could think about was the handsome stranger with the odd name, the wink of his dark eyes, and that wicked promise on his lips.

Noel covered his brown, soot-covered face as he entered the burnt shell of the building. As always, he stopped just inside the doorway and reviewed the scene of destruction before beginning the collection process. His dark eyes immediately scanned the scorched walls, the carnage of water-soaked furniture, and the many pieces of smudged, dirty paper that littered the floor. Noel understood the importance of first impressions. So much could be ascertained in those first few minutes before his eyes became accustomed to the images of desolation.

"You there. Are you in charge here?"

Noel heard the voice of the angry man before he turned to see him standing in an open office doorway across the lobby.

"I need answers, and I need them now!" The tall, slender white man charged across the marble tile flooring of the lobby toward Noel. His salt-and-pepper hair was in disarray, and his blue eyes were strained with fear and exhaustion. His face was flushed. Noel took a defensive posture, unsure of the man's intentions.

By the time he reached Noel, the man's whole disposition had changed. He stood for a moment taking several deep breaths with his eyes closed.

"I'm Harwood Dowel," the man said, and extended his dirty hand. "I apologize for my tone, but as you can see"—he gestured to the chaos surrounding them—"my business has been ruined by this."

"I understand," Noel said, taking the extended hand. "Noel Lennox. I'm the lead inspector in this investigation. What can I do for you?"

"Do you have any ideas yet? I mean, what could've caused this?" His blue eyes darted back and forth as he spoke. He was watching Gary and Brian, the two investigators under Noel, who were collecting evidence on the other side of the large room.

"Mr. Dowel, we've only just begun the investigation. Unless we find something blatantly obvious, it could take quite a bit of time to dissect the evidence we find here today."

"It's just that my partner was murdered here a few weeks ago by one of our employees. The murderer's in jail right now, but I fear the fire may have been set in retaliation by someone he knows."

"Well, that's somewhere to start." Noel noticed that although Dowel's tone had relaxed, his body was as tense as ever. "But even knowing that is no guarantee we'll put this case to bed any sooner."

"I understand." Harwood Dowel pulled mercilessly at his short-cropped hair, forcing it to sprout out even more than it was. The sound of feet crunching over debris near the door caused both men to turn.

"Please, excuse me." Harwood Dowel moved to greet the two police officers who entered the building. Suddenly, he paused and turned back to Noel. "You'll let me know first, right?" his eyes pleaded. "I mean, if you find out anything?"

"Sure," Noel lied. "You'll be the first to know."

Harwood nodded, seemingly satisfied with the answer. He went to greet the two policemen, then led them into his burnt office space. It was one of the few rooms with all four walls standing, even though the door was hanging partially off the hinges.

"Hey, Noel," Gary called to his boss, after coming out of one of the offices on the other side of the lobby. "You need to see this."

Noel crossed the lobby quickly and followed Gary back into the executive office. The remains of expensive artwork that had decorated the scorched walls and a long leather couch revealed to Noel that this room must have belonged to the other partner.

Gary pulled back a damaged cherrywood desk to reveal a trap door in the carpet beneath it. Noel hunkered down on his ankles and looked at the small pull latch. Since it was a single-story building, he knew the door could lead to anything from a small shoebox-sized hiding compartment to a full-sized basement.

Instinctively, he pushed Gary out of harm's way and pulled the latch open. He chuckled to himself as he reviewed the contents of the small compartment, then turned to smile up at Gary.

"Lawyers," Noel said, emphatically shaking his head. "They've always got a trick up their sleeves."

Two

"Whom does this belong to?" Marty held up the dingy sock with two fingers. The four men sitting at the dining table each looked up briefly.

"Not mine."

"Nope."

"Never seen it before."

"Not me."

Just then, Tommy passed through the kitchen, pausing only a moment to examine the smelly object. "Not one of mine." He hunched his shoulders before continuing on to the common area.

"Well, whomever's it was"—she placed her small foot on the step of the garbage can and the lid popped open—"it now belongs to the Detroit Sanitation Department." She dropped the sock inside and the lid snapped closed just as K. C. rounded the corner.

"Hey, that's mine." He flipped open the can and pulled the sock out. "I must've dropped it on the way back from the shower," he said with a sheepish look.

At the tender age of nineteen, K. C. Renaldo was the baby of their little family and the one most in awe of their Queen Bee. He knew how much Marty hated finding their clothing lying around. He was just glad it wasn't underwear. She had a particularly strong hatred for dirty boxer shorts.

"This is a kitchen, K. C., people eat in here."

"I said I was sorry." He bowed his head and ducked out of the room.

Marty returned her attention to stirring the large pot of spaghetti sauce, missing the serenity of her hospital bed. She had been back at the firehouse almost a week, and things were completely back to normal.

Holding the hot strainer full of noodles, she turned toward the sink. Then she noticed Cal and Dwight leaning on opposite sides of the entryway, grinning like a couple of cats that had tag-teamed a mouse.

"Okay, what are you up to?" She found herself smiling. Their excitement was contagious. There were days when these men truly tried her nerves, but she would give her life for any one of them.

"This just came for you." Cal pulled a white rose with a small note tied to it from behind his back. Marty, recognizing the white rose instantly, carefully placed the strainer in the sink. She rubbed her hands on her pants and with trembling fingers reached for it. By the time she had opened the little envelope and pulled out the card, the doorjamb was brimming with black and yellow T-shirts.

"Marty's got a boyfriend," someone called from the back of the group.

Marty looked up into guilty faces all around her. "What's this about?"

"Go outside and see," someone called out.

Marty reached beneath the counter to find a cover for the saucepan and turned the dial on the stove to the lowest setting.

"Don't worry about the spaghetti," Big Cal said, practically pushing her out the door. "We've got it handled."

Marty tried to stop by the mirror to catch a glimpse of herself. The last thing she wanted was to greet him with red tomato sauce smeared across her nose. But the crowd of men behind her just pushed her along, eager to see her reaction to the surprise they knew awaited her. Once outside, Marty stopped dead in her tracks, not believing what she was seeing.

Set up just south of the large, red firehouse doors were several small tables with checkered tablecloths, each decorated with a single white rose in a small vase. Just beyond the tables were two large drum-sized grills. Both were oozing smoke that smelled like heaven. Marty's eyebrow shot up and her mouth fell open. How could all this have been going on outside her front door and she not hear or smell anything?

Down from the two large grills were three long tables covered with condiments and side items, everything from potato salad to towelettes. Five men and two women dressed conservatively in black pants and white shirts scurried about, all seeming to be in a hurry.

At the end of the second table of condiments stood Cavanaugh, speaking to one of the frazzled caterers. Even in his crème button-up shirt, perfectly pressed jeans, and leather sandals, he still looked like fine china at a picnic.

"Surprise!" the crowd of men yelled simultaneously, bringing Marty's heart up into her mouth and causing one of the female caterers to drop a tray of deviled eggs.

Marty had been so enthralled by the vision before her, she had forgotten they were behind her.

Hearing the commotion, Cavanaugh started toward her, smiling brilliantly. "Are you ready for the best barbecue this side of the Delta?"

"Oh, this is too much." Marty looked around again, still amazed that she'd had no idea this was happening.

"I promised you dinner," Cavanaugh said, taking her hand and leading her to one of the small tables. "I didn't think it was fair to bring you dinner and leave the guys high and dry. I owe you all my life, especially you." He gently tapped his index finger to the tip of Marty's nose. She fought the silly urge to try to kiss his finger as it quickly passed by her lips.

He pulled one of the two small chairs away from the table and gestured for her to sit. She gladly obliged. It wasn't often she was treated with such reverence.

"Thank you," she said, opening her napkin and spreading it across her lap. "I just meant something simple, not this elaborate feast."

"Something small?" He tilted his head to the side, studying her soft brown eyes.

"Yes."

"Something . . . personal?"

"Yes." Marty hated herself for blushing so easily but it was just the way she was born.

He reached across the table, taking her small hands between his larger ones. "We'll get to that." He smiled in that devilish way of his. "Meanwhile . . ." He opened his own napkin just as two heaping trays of food were placed before them. "Eat up before your food gets cold."

Soon the entire company of Firehouse Fifteen was dining on some of the finest soul food they had ever tasted. Laughter was ringing around all the little tables, soda cans were being popped open, and Jill Scott's "The Way" was blaring down from the upstairs window, where someone had placed two large speakers.

Shoshana sat watching her sister curiously. "Either you're on drugs or in love. And if it was drugs, they'd catch you on a piss test, so it must be love."

"Shoshana." Marty shook her head in amazement. "You have *got* to watch your mouth."

"What?" Shoshana said, looking genuinely baffled as she scooped another spoonful of ice cream into her mouth. "I know it's not one of those knuckleheads at the firehouse?"

"No." Marty bit her lip too late. She hated the way her sister baited her. Of course Shoshana knew it wasn't one of the guys, but by presenting the question, she at least confirmed that there was someone.

"Okay. We can do this one of two ways." Shoshana stabbed at her still-frozen scoop of butter pecan. "You can tell me and make it easy on yourself, or I'll follow you until I find out. And considering I'm unemployed right now, I have nothing but time."

"You're not unemployed, you're a housewife," Marty corrected her baby sister.

"Same difference," she sniffed. "What's the point of being a stay-at-home mom if there's no one to stay at home with?"

Marty reached over and rubbed her sister's rounded belly. "My little niece will be along any day now."

"Don't jinx me." Shoshana wagged her index finger. "I'm not due for two months."

"We'll see." Marty gave her a sly grin.

"Un-uh." Shoshana shook her head fervently. "No, no, no. You think you're slick trying to change the subject, but it's not gonna work."

Marty picked another tiny morsel of cookie off the top of her scoop of cookies and cream. "I don't know what you're talking about."

Shoshana peered at her sister over the rim of her glasses. "Who is he?"

Marty sat back in her chair, hesitant about sharing her newfound happiness with her sister. Without the slightest bit of malice, Soshana could ruin paradise. Her pessimistic nature could make anything, no matter how good, seem dangerous and suspicious. Marty hated to admit it, but many times her sister had been right. All Marty cared about was the one time her little sister would be wrong.

"When there's something to tell, you'll be the first to know." Marty chose her words carefully. "But it's still too new to call it."

Shoshana sat for a moment considering her sister's decision. "I guess that means I've got to go *Spencer-for-Hire* on you."

"Shoshana, don't." Marty was deadly serious. "If I see you lurking around any tree, I will never speak to you again."

"Then tell me."

"No." Marty held her ground, something she rarely did with her only sibling. "The last thing I want is for him to think I come from crazy people."

"But you do."

"He doesn't need to know that."

"Okay, at least a name."

"No."

"Please."

"No."

"Pretty please."

"Cavanaugh."

"Huh?"

"That's his name. Cavanaugh."

"What kind of name is that?"

Marty pursed her lips. She was quickly losing her patience and her taste for Baskin-Robbins. "You asked, so I told you. His name is Cavanaugh."

The two women ate in silence. Marty tried to ignore the terse expression on her sister's face, but soon Shoshana looked about ready to burst.

"If you laugh, so help me, I'll sock you right in the arm."

"Marty, we're not ten anymore."

"I don't care. If you laugh at his name I'll sock you." Marty balled her fist. "Right in the arm."

"You'd hit a pregnant woman?" Shoshana placed her hand to her chest in mock indignation.

"In a heartbeat."

Three

Cavanaugh rounded the last bend to his family's ancestral home hardly concentrating on the driving. He'd been down the winding road so many times his BMW-328i could probably find the way on its own.

His mind was preoccupied with a different type of curves. The sensual shape of Ms. Martina Williams. Her caramel-brown skin and soft brown eyes had been ingrained in his mind from the moment he entered her hospital room. With her unique height and regal bearing, she should have been gliding down catwalks, not chasing down fires. But it had been obvious from her appearance at the firehouse that beauty regimens were the least of her concerns. He didn't have the heart to tell her that she still had tomato sauce smeared on her cheek. *Too bad,* he thought, with the right clothes and makeup she could easily go from very pretty to stunning.

His cell phone rang, startling him out of his reverie. He grabbed it off the passenger seat and pressed the *send* button. "Yeah?"

"The final investigation report just arrived." The deep Southern voice of a woman came out of the speaker.

"And?"

"You were right, it was arson."

Cavanaugh felt his jaw tightening. It was one thing to

believe someone wanted to kill you; it was something else to *know* it.

"Are you okay?" After being his personal assistant for seven years, Clarissa Avery understood the meaning behind every finger tap and every lengthy silence. This one was steeped in anger, and considering the news he'd just been given, she thought, rightly so.

"Yeah, thanks, Rees—"

"Before you cut me off," she called out as his finger lingered just above the *end* button, "what do you want me to do with the file?"

"Well, considering the official report has not been released yet. . . ."

"Understood," she said. "By the way, your mother called. Do you want the message?"

"No. I'll see her in a few minutes, anyway." He hesitated before asking, "Any other calls?"

"No. Were you expecting any?"

"Just checking. See you Thursday." He hit the *end* button, cutting off the strange buzzing sound he recognized as the shredder machine warming up.

Cavanaugh pulled his leather tote from the trunk and slammed it shut. He turned to face the large, white, Colonial house. This was the place he had called home for the first years of his life, and where he resided when forced by his business obligations to return to Savannah for any length of time. He would have rather been anywhere else in the world at that moment.

He only planned to be here for the next couple of days to participate in the quarterly board meeting for his family-owned corporation, Saint John Trucking. Then he would be free to return to Detroit and his budding relationship. But first, he had to get past his mother. His door key slid in the lock just as he heard the double beeping sound of his car alarm activating.

"Cavanaugh, is that you?" the soft tremor of his mother's voice called out before the large wood door fell closed behind him.

"Yes, Mother, it's me."

"Thank God." The creaking sound of her wheelchair rolling across the polished oak floor was almost eerie. "I was so worried. Are you all right?"

"Yes." Pressing down the twinge of guilt he felt every time he saw her seated in the metal contraption, Cavanaugh smiled stiffly. "I'm fine." He bent to hug her, careful not to squeeze her frail body too hard.

"Why didn't you call me?" Her deep gray eyes narrowed. "I had to find out from a news report."

Cavanaugh knew it was pointless to defend himself. With his mother there was no defense. "I didn't want to worry you."

He turned and headed for the stairs, hoping to get away from her before the inevitable questions began.

"A news report, Cavanaugh." The frustration in her voice was easily heard. "My friends knew about my son's brush with death before *I* did."

And that, he realized, was her *true* concern. Her friends knew first. He struggled to loosen his tie. The house was already starting to constrict his throat. "Mother, please, I'm in no mood for this." He whispered a string of obscenities in fluent Cajun-French as he climbed the stairs.

"I heard that," she huffed from the bottom of the stairs." We *will* continue this conversation later!" She turned and rolled back into her parlor.

Not if I can help it. Cavanaugh rounded the top banister and headed toward his suite.

* * *

Cavanaugh sat on the side of his bed dreading what was to come. He'd been home nearly four hours and hadn't left his room from the moment he climbed the stairs. He simply didn't have the strength to battle his mother. Had he the choice, she would never have known about the fire. Reline Saint John was a shrewd woman. It had probably taken her calculating mind moments to deduct his purpose for being in Detroit. Especially since he had told her he was going to Puerto Rico for a short vacation.

But now it was six o'clock, which in the Saint John household meant dinner was served. Cavanaugh knew the formal dinners his mother held every night for family and friends were a tradition only God could stop.

He stood and quickly examined himself in the mirror. His black tuxedo was flawless. He double-checked the security of his diamond-studded cuff links. He couldn't bear the thought of them slipping off and becoming lost forever. They were his favorites. They were his father's.

He headed toward the door then stopped. He returned to the side of the bed, lifted the receiver and dialed the number he had memorized the day before. After three short rings someone picked up the other end.

"Hello?" The half-drowsy voice of a woman answered.

"Good evening."

"Cavanaugh?"

He smiled into the phone. "Yes."

"How did you get my number?"

"I wanted it, so I got it." He paused. "I always get what I want."

"Oh, do you?"

He could almost hear her blushing through the phone. "I'm talking to you, aren't I?"

She fell silent, unable to dispute the simple truth.

"Did you get my package?"

"Yes, but really, you shouldn't have."

"Don't be ridiculous," he chuckled. "I did it for me, not you."

"Oh?"

"I saw it in a display window and thought how good it would look on you. Of course, I get the added bonus of seeing you in it."

"Tell me, Mr. Saint John, are you always this forward?"

He hesitated for a long moment before responding. "Only when I see something I want."

The light clicking noise was the only indication he had hung up the receiver. Marty turned on the small lamp next to her bed and sat up. Sleep was no longer an option. Just the sound of the sweet, sexy voice coming through the phone was enough to send her body into overdrive. It had been so long and just the thought, the possibility of a man in her life, was enough to excite her mind.

She picked up the remote control and turned on the television, but her attention was not on the *Law and Order* rerun playing on TBS. In her head, she was replaying every moment of the brief conversation, trying to imagine the expression of pleasure on his handsome face. She didn't care what Shoshana thought. Cavanaugh was a lovely name, and it perfectly suited the handsome young Creole man.

They had spent the barbecue picnic discussing their backgrounds and occupations. It was one of those conversations people have when they are trying to get to know one another without revealing too much about themselves. He was an insurance investigator, and it had been nothing more than poor timing that placed him in the burning building.

Originally from Savannah, he had been in town looking into the death of a lawyer who worked for a law firm with offices in that building. He had been so involved in his work he never heard the alarm or smelled the smoke until it was too late to escape. Oh yes, and to quote him exactly: *"Had he known his rescuer was so attractive, he would never have screamed like a girl."* The thought of that comment still made her laugh.

Marty climbed out of bed and wandered over to the dark green box with the Marshall Field's symbol lying haphazardly on the dressing table. She opened it for the twelfth time that day and held up the mid-length evening gown.

She held it against her and danced slowly in front of the mirror, imagining his long form behind her, his strong arms wrapped around her, his soft lips nipping her neck. She tilted her head to the side and sighed. How could she tell him that this was not something she would ever wear?

The red sequined gown was charming. Everything from the low-cut bodice trimmed in tiny sequined flowers to the triple spaghetti straps that hung just off each shoulder. It was elegant, stylish, and *sooo* not Marty Williams. She tossed the gown across the box again and fell face-first across the bed. What was she thinking?

Everything about this wonderful, magical stranger screamed grace and refinement. Once again, *sooo* not Marty Williams. What was she doing with this man who was obviously out of her league?

Maybe Shoshana was right, she thought. Her little sister had told her long ago to stop kissing frogs hoping to find a prince. Just find a nice frog and be done with it.

Marty turned over onto her back staring at the antique ceiling fan spinning above her head. Having now met a true prince, she had to admit, she was definitely a frog-caliber girl.

* * *

Cavanaugh sat at his father's desk typing away. Sometimes he felt split as if he were trying to live two lives at once. But the alternative, which was moving back to Savannah and devoting his complete attention to the family enterprise, was not an option.

He went to pick up his pen to write down the information that appeared on the computer screen before him. But it flipped out of his hand and onto the floor, which was why he didn't see his cousin Justin entering the library. He only heard him talking into his cell phone as he entered the room.

"I said, I will take care of it," Justin Saint John practically hissed into the phone. It was obvious he was becoming irate with someone.

Cavanaugh, feeling like a spy, sat up suddenly. He startled Justin so badly, he almost dropped his phone.

"Damn, man, you trying to give me a heart attack?" Justin huffed at Cavanaugh. "No, not you," he snapped at the cell phone. "Look, I'll call you back. I said, I'll call you back." He flipped the lid closed hard and tucked it into his pocket without a second thought. Then, flopping down on the long leather couch on the other side of the room, he sighed in frustration.

Cavanaugh sat watching his older cousin for a moment, giving him time to calm down. "What's up?" He settled back into the large chair. It was so rare he saw his mild-mannered cousin in alarm that the incident had startled him.

"Nothing, just a business deal gone bad," Justin said, and ran his hand through his short hair. "I'm surprised to find you still here. I thought you would've been headed back to Detroit by now," Justin said, finally relaxing.

"Yeah, me too." Cavanaugh shrugged in disgust.

"So, what's this I hear about a new lady in your life?"

"That doggoned Candice," Cavanaugh chuckled, not nearly as upset as he pretended to be. He knew his cousin well enough to know she would run right back and tell everyone. Cavanaugh didn't mind; it had been a long time since he'd had anyone worth talking about.

"So what's the deal?" Justin asked, appearing as almost an older mirror image of the other man.

"Her name's Marty. She's a firefighter."

"Wait a minute," Justin sat forward, now even more interested. "Was she that cutie on the news?"

Cavanaugh answered with only a smile.

"She's fine, man."

"Who you telling?" Cavanaugh said, and sighed. The two men fell silent, each lost in their own thoughts of the female persuasion.

"Has she met Aunt Reline yet?" Justin asked.

"Not yet," Cavanaugh said. "We've only been out a couple of times."

Justin silently wondered how many dates would be required of a woman to qualify for an introduction to a psychopath.

"I know," Cavanaugh said, barely above a whisper, as if he had read Justin's thoughts. He had waited all his life for a woman like Marty, Cavanaugh thought, but he dreaded ever having to introduce her to his mother.

"What are you doing?" Justin asked, just then, noticing the papers scattered across the desk.

"Mother wanted me to look over the last-quarter reports."

He laid his head back against the sofa. "Why?"

"She seems to think there's some inconsistencies," Cavanaugh said, scribbling the information.

"Did you find anything?"

"No, everything looks fine to me." Cavanaugh lifted the stack of papers, bundling them into a nice, neat pile.

"Just Mother's way of trying to keep me here a day longer. Another one of the infamous Reline Saint John mind-control games. But I don't care if she's convulsing on the foyer floor, I'm leaving tonight."

"She misses you, that's all," Justin said, sitting forward to study his cousin's face.

Cavanaugh stood and stuck his hands in the pockets of his blue jeans. "You don't know how I wish that were a true sentiment. But missing her child would imply caring, something we both know she's not capable of."

"You're too hard on her," Justin said, in defense of his aunt.

"No harder than she is on me," Cavanaugh called back over his shoulder as he left the room.

Four

Marty took one final look at herself in the mirror. It had taken her almost two hours to pick out the outfit of black jeans and a pink boat-neck knobby sweater. She was trying to appear casual, yet stylish. Fun, yet fashionable. She finally decided that appearing on time was probably the best impression she could make. She grabbed her purse and headed down the circular metal stairs toward her car. They'd agreed to meet at the marina at eight. She only had ten minutes, but luckily, the boat harbor was downtown, just a short distance from the firehouse. She came out of the building and paused. Cavanaugh was standing in front of her car. She didn't know whether to be frightened, flattered, or both.

"What are you doing here?" she asked, approaching the car.

"I missed you. I didn't want to wait another ten minutes to see you." He smiled sweetly, and she decided to be flattered.

"I missed you too," she said, and hugged him. She sighed, feeling his strength and warmth beneath her arms. They had only been out twice before, but she was finding herself thinking about him all the time.

"Ready?" He took her hand and led her to his car. Marty started to protest and insist on driving her own car. But before she could, he had the door open, gesturing for her to get inside his. She allowed herself one quick glance into his dark, sensual eyes. She decided if he were a serial killer, he was the most handsome one she had ever seen. She hopped into the car, sinking down into the soft leather.

They drove to the marina in silence. Only the soft jazz sounds of Yanni's "The Flame Within" coming out of the stereo interrupted the peace. Marty felt so comfortable with him that she didn't feel the need to make idle conversation. That awkward silence that normally fell between people newly acquainted just didn't seem to exist for them.

The light reflected off the glass, and something near the steering wheel sparkled, catching her eye. Marty noticed the beautiful diamond cuff links glittering at each wrist, and felt her first tiny twinge of doubt. *That's a nice little bling-bling for a man of modest means.*

"Here we are," he said, getting out of the car to come around to her side. Marty sat patiently; she'd quickly discovered that Cavanaugh was not a man who needed lessons on proper dating etiquette. No door went unopened. No chair went unoffered. She found herself quickly becoming very spoiled by his Southern gentlemanly ways.

They casually walked along the pier, taking note of the large yachts on either side, each seeming more extravagant than the last. When he had asked her to go sailing with him, she thought he meant a nice little sailboat. She never imagined he meant one of these motorized monsters, which obviously needed no sails to move.

Finally they stopped in front of a large white yacht. It took Marty a few moments to understand that this was their destination. The fancy lettering on the side read *Kid Creole.*

"This is yours?" She tried to hide the awe in her voice, but it didn't work.

"Yes, although I don't get as much time on her as I'd like," he said, enjoying the look of wonder on Marty's face.

She strolled along the planked walkway, running her fingers along the smooth fiberglass hull of the large boat. She liked the way it felt beneath her fingers. She knew Cavanaugh was watching; she could feel his eyes on her. She found she liked that, too.

"She's beautiful," Marty finally said.

"Yes, she is," he said, finding the beauty on land far more appealing than the one in the water.

"So tell me, Kid," she turned to face him, "do you sing and dance?"

Cavanaugh let his eyes roam over her in a way that sent a chill through Marty's entire being. Then he matched her smile with his own. "For the right woman."

Seeing the challenge in his eyes, Marty quickly turned back toward the boat, reminded once again that she was playing way out of her league.

A tall, thin, brown-skinned man appeared on the deck above them. He was dressed in a white hat and shirt, but his youthful appearance made Marty doubt he was the captain.

"I see my passengers have arrived," he said, in a thick Jamaican accent. "Welcome back, Mr. Saint John." The man waved to Cavanaugh.

"Kenny, this is Ms. Williams." Cavanaugh waved back and introduced Marty at the same time.

The man smiled pleasantly and Marty realized that despite his cherub-like appearance, he was indeed the captain.

"Please, call me Marty," she said, lifting herself onto the ladder.

"Un-uh." Kenny wagged a finger at her. "You have to ask permission to come aboard."

Suddenly, Marty felt Cavanaugh behind her, his large hands poised on her waist to lift her up. Marty wasn't sure if Kenny was joking or not. But either way, the feel of Cavanaugh behind her was driving her to distraction, and she needed to go up or down quickly before she spun around and did something really embarrassing like throwing herself into his arms.

"Permission to come aboard, Captain," she said, trying not to visualize the long, elegant fingers she felt kneading her skin.

"Permission granted," Kenny said, reaching down for her.

In one swoop, Cavanaugh lifted her up to the other man and Kenny sat her down beside him. The two men handled her with such ease, it left her feeling delicate and feminine in a way she'd rarely felt before. Once aboard, Cavanaugh excused himself and went off with Kenny, leaving her alone on the deck.

She wandered to the edge of the boat, looking over into the dark water and wondering what was down there. The closest she had ever come to a boat this large was the one that took her family up the river to the Boblo Island Amusement Park when she was a child. Neither the boat nor the amusement park had stood the test of time, but her memories had. She had been a fan of sailing ever since.

She finally settled into one of the lounge chairs and sat enjoying the setting sun. It was early summer and the sun was often high in the sky until late night. A waiter appeared and took her request for an iced tea. She thought about something more relaxing like a glass of white wine but decided against it. Despite his charm and good looks, Marty was still on a boat with a man she barely knew. She needed to keep her wits about her.

After a few minutes, Cavanaugh reappeared and

shortly thereafter the ship set sail. They slowly traveled up the river and back. The city lights on both the American and Canadian sides provided the candlelight for their romantic meal. They enjoyed a pleasant lobster dinner and watched the sun finally disappear beyond the horizon. Marty found herself telling every funny story she knew in an effort to make him laugh. She loved the sound, it was vibrant and genuine. *Just like the man,* she mused.

When they finally pulled back into the harbor shortly after midnight, Marty was disappointed but hid it. The last thing she wanted was for him to think she was the clingy, stalker type.

When he drove her back to the firehouse and gave her one chaste peck on the forehead, she fought the urge to pull him into her arms and kiss him properly, full and lustfully on the mouth. When she slid between her cold sheets and slowed her heartbeat enough to sleep, she promised herself she wouldn't dream about him, but two hours later in the deepest stages of REM, Marty was once again with her magical, mystery man aboard the *Kid Creole.* But this time, he held her in a tight embrace, and passionately covered her mouth with his.

"Wow," Cavanaugh exclaimed as he surveyed one large end of the auditorium to the other. "This place is huge."

This was his fourth date with Marty and she'd insisted on going to the movies.

"Twenty screens of premium movie watching," Marty called over her shoulder, "complete with Dolby surround sound."

"You sound like a commercial," Cavanaugh teased.

Marty laughed as she turned the corner and began climbing the stairs to the top. Cavanaugh followed close behind. He tripped once, and almost lost his bucket of popcorn as a result.

About halfway up, Marty turned down one of the tight-fitted aisles and pushed her way through, holding her snacks above her head. Soon the couple was settled smack-dab in the middle of the large movie house.

Marty watched as Cavanaugh studied everything about the place as if it were a novel experience for him. "When was the last time you went to the movies?"

"Never." He tossed a handful of popcorn into his mouth. "Um, this is good." His eyes widened in surprise.

"There's nothing like theater popcorn." She watched his head swing from one direction to another. "Why not?"

"I beg your pardon?" Cavanaugh was so entranced by the interesting assortment of people entering, he was only half-listening to the conversation.

"I said, why have you never gone to the movies?"

"My mother believed movies and television twisted young minds." *As if she had not done enough damage,* he thought. His dark eyes suddenly sparked with anger, then just as quickly it was gone.

Marty watched the play of emotions on his face and wondered what deep-rooted memory triggered it. She feared she was beginning to care deeply for him, more with each passing day. Yet there was still so much of this man she didn't know. Like, how could an insurance investigator afford a private yacht? "Are you saying you never watched TV either?"

"At least, not at home." He chuckled in an attempt to make light of something that still pained him. Cavanaugh knew his was not a typical childhood, but the last thing he wanted to see in the eyes of the lady next to him was pity.

He took a sip of soda. "Not that it worked."

"What do you mean?"

"I'm warped anyway." He winked, and smiled his perfect smile.

Marty thought, *if you are warped, it's not in any physical way.*

Their eyes met and held as the lights dimmed and a hush fell over the crowd. Cavanaugh reached out in the dark and took Marty's hand, wrapping it in his own.

His feelings were more defined than hers. He knew for certain that he was falling head over heels in love with this extraordinary woman. She seemed to accept him so easily, and yet he knew he could not tell her the whole truth. How accepting would any woman be of a man accused of arson, murder, and embezzlement?

"I hope it's as good as I heard," she whispered as the previews began.

Marty's words triggered a strange reaction. The word *love* sprang to the forefront of Cavanaugh's mind. *I hope it's as good as I heard.* The simple statement took on a new meaning. "Yeah," Cavanaugh said, studying her profile in the dark, "me too."

His cell phone rang and Cavanaugh reached into his pocket. "Hello?"

Marty tried to concentrate on the previews on the screen, and tune out the private conversation. It was the polite thing to do. But some part of her brain refused to be polite.

"Hi, Reesy."

Marty's eyes watched Ben Affleck running through a busy city street, but her ears were focused in a different direction.

Cavanaugh shot to his feet. "What?!"

"Ssshhh," the woman sitting behind Marty hissed.

"Hey, Buddy! What do you think, you're made of glass?" someone in the back called out.

Cavanaugh was oblivious to the reactions of the people. His full attention was on Reesy's announcement that his mother was calling an informal board meeting of the SJT stockholders without his knowledge.

He slumped back down in his chair, having just had the wind knocked out of him. "When?"

Marty struggled to hear with no luck.

"All right, call the airport and have my plane readied. I'll be there tonight."

His plane? Marty tried to hide her surprise. Who was this man?

"Read the sign! No cell phones!" someone called from the back.

Ignoring the comment, Cavanaugh exchanged a few more remarks with his assistant before finally hanging up. He snapped the phone closed and tucked it back into his pocket with the flagrant disregard of a man used to ignoring the reactions of others.

Marty bit back the thousand questions on the tip of her tongue, and asked the most important one. "Are you okay?"

His head snapped around as if he were surprised to see her there. The flash of anger had returned and his eyes shone like black pearls. "Yes, just a family matter than needs attending."

"Do you have to leave?"

He pecked her on the lips. "I'm sorry, but I have to go back to Savannah tonight."

"You must be close to your family." Marty fought the twinge of pain she felt remembering the parents she'd adored.

Cavanaugh's chiseled jaw was set tight. "Not really. It's just that my mother's—she's crippled, and sometimes she tries to do things she really shouldn't."

Ignorant to the double meaning of the statement,

Marty took his hand in hers. "We can leave now if you want."

He lifted the back of her hand to his lips and savored the feel of her soft skin against his lips. "No. I refuse to cut short one minute of my time with you." He paused before adding, "I guess I should warn you, between my family in Savannah and Liberty State here in Detroit, I spend a lot of time in the air."

Marty briefly wondered if family business was all that kept him on the move. The sound of the MGM lion roaring signaled that the movie was about to begin. A theater attendant shone a bright light in their faces moments later, but seeing nothing out of the ordinary, he moved on.

Someone had reported Cavanaugh and his cell phone, Marty thought. In the future, she would have to warn him about movie theater protocol. Then she smiled, realizing there would be a next time.

Five

Marty waved her hand over her head, trying to get her sister and brother-in-law's attention. Erv spotted her first and waved in response. The couple made their way through the crowd and over to the hilltop where their group had spread four large blankets together earlier that evening, staking the land to hold their prime viewing area.

"Hey, everybody," Shoshana said, waddling up the hill. Her round belly made her look like the Pillsbury Doughboy climbing the slightly steep mound.

"Hey, Shoshana," Big Cal called out, reaching over the head of the pretty young woman sitting between his knees. "Hey, Erv," he said, shaking the man's hand. "This is Andrea." He gestured to the woman resting comfortably in the crook of his body.

The late-arriving couple finally found an empty place on the blankets.

"Hey, guys," Dwight's wife, Dina, called from the other side of their expanded pallet. She was unable to move with her husband's head in her lap. Dwight waved halfheartedly, wondering if he could stay awake until the fireworks began.

Shoshana took her foot and nudged the younger man sprawled across the edge of the blanket. "Move over, K. C., and stop hogging the blanket," she scolded.

K. C. muttered something, then moved over. Erv

helped his wife down onto the blanket, and Marty placed a pillow behind her back.

"Will you still treat me so nice after I have the baby?"

"Please, brat," Marty huffed, and settled down beside her. "I'm only thinking of my niece." She rocked against her sister and laughed.

"Forget you, then," Shoshana turned, looking in all directions. "So, where's the mystery man?"

"Don't know," Marty said, checking her watch. "I'm sure I told him the show starts at ten."

"Who's that with Cal?" Shoshana whispered behind her hand.

"Remember my forgetful nurse I told you about?" Marty said, smiling slyly.

"Shut up!" Shoshana exclaimed as a look of understanding came across her face.

Marty was practically biting her nails with nervous energy. Shoshana wanted to talk, but could see from the troubled look in her sister's eyes she was in no mood for casual conversation. They sat in tense silence for a long time.

Shoshana looked around noticing the sparseness of their group. "Where is everybody?"

"Well, we thought we should leave someone behind, you know, in case there's a *fire* or something."

Shoshana sat studying her sister, wondering what prompted that attack.

Marty sighed, feeling her sister's eyes on her. "I'm sorry," she said, looking at her watch again. "I'm just worried about him. He should've been here by now."

A strange hush fell over the crowd as the first spark of light shot across the sky forming a large five-point star against the dark night before fizzling into nothingness. Then another appeared forming a heart. Then another, then another, each making a different colorful design across the canvas of blackness. Soon, they were coming in quick succession.

Marty was too busy watching the three park entrances to be distracted by the show. *Where is he?* She felt the slight vibration of the phone in her pocket, but could not hear the ringing above the sound of the firecrackers popping over their heads and the cheering of the crowd. She put it to her ear, and pressed her hand over the other one.

"Hello?" She spoke loud, but with the booming noises surrounding them she could barely hear herself. The person on the other end sounded far away, but she could still make out what he was saying.

"I'm sorry, sweetheart. I'm not going to make it tonight," Cavanaugh shouted into the phone.

"Are you okay?" Marty yelled out, needing to know he was safe despite her hurt at being stood up.

"Yeah, I'm fine. Just something came up."

"I understand," she lied.

"I promise, I'll make it up to you."

"That's okay, things happen." She tried to sound nonchalant, but her hurt was too deep to be convincing.

"I'll call you tomorrow. Enjoy the show." Then he was gone.

Marty turned off the phone and stuck it back in her pocket. The light show was almost over and she'd missed most of it. She was more disappointed than she would have expected. She hadn't seen him in a week and was truly looking forward to spending the Fourth of July with him.

The fact that he offered no real explanation for the cancellation had not slipped past her. She found herself wondering what could have "come up" that would prevent them from spending the holiday together. Not that it mattered, she decided. Marty wasn't interested in the fireworks anyway. She'd only been looking forward to watching them reflected in his midnight-black eyes, seeing that perfect smile spread across his face and listening to the sweet sound of his laughter.

She felt Shoshana's arm around her shoulder and realized her sister had heard the whole conversation. The two women put their heads together the way they had often done as children to comfort one another. No words needed to be spoken.

Shoshana reached into her handbag and pulled out a Hostess® devil's food cake. Marty gratefully accepted the offering. Shoshana was a firm believer that no matter how big the problem, chocolate would make it smaller.

They split the two-pack and watched the rest of the show. None of their friends around them ever noticed Marty's sudden melancholy mood. She was at least grateful for that.

Cavanaugh turned off his cell phone and tucked it back into his pocket. He turned his attention back to the police officer sitting at the long table across from him. The brown-skinned Hispanic man was scribbling on a pad, and Cavanaugh wondered if he'd been listening in on the conversation.

"Okay, Mr. Saint John," the young officer said, "can you explain how the door came to be locked?" The officer looked to be in his early twenties, but something about his voice revealed his true age to be far beyond that. He had the physical appearance of a rookie, but the commanding presence of a veteran cop.

"I've told you ten times, I don't know." Cavanaugh's head was pounding. Not only with this interrogation, but with having to cancel out on Marty. He had heard the hurt in her voice, but there was nothing he could do about it. He'd promised to make it up to her, and he had every intention of doing that as soon as he could get out of this living hell.

The officer sat back in his chair and twisted his mouth. "I know you said that, but try to see this from my point of view. You were trapped in a small file room for several hours and never bothered to try to get out."

"I told you, I didn't know I was locked in. I was working, I had no reason to leave. How could I know I was locked in until I tried to leave?" Cavanaugh felt himself rising up out of his chair in anger.

"Calm down, Mr. Saint John. We're just trying to get at the truth here." The officer lifted his hands in a gesture of understanding.

"No, you're not." Cavanaugh exploded. "Do I look like a fool to you?"

The man sat watching Cavanaugh's dark eyes flash.

"Mr. Saint John, please, the more you cooperate the better things wi—"

"Am I being charged with something?" Cavanaugh stood suddenly, pushing the chair out from beneath him.

"What?" The officer stood, feeling too threatened being the only one seated.

"I said, am I being charged with something? Because if not, I would like to leave." Cavanaugh was fighting to control his temper.

"Well, if things are as you say, why leave?" The officer's brown eyes studied him accusingly.

Cavanaugh took several deep breaths. The last thing he needed was an assault charge right now. He picked up his jacket and started toward the door.

"Where are you going?" the officer called after him.

"Home," Cavanaugh said, opening the door. "When

you're ready to charge me with something, that's where I'll be."

The officer jumped as the door slammed and shook all the windows along the narrow corridor.

Cavanaugh pulled into the parking lot of the Rattlesnake Club and waited in line for the valet. Since he'd missed celebrating the Fourth with Marty, he'd promised to make it up to her. "Do you see them?" he asked Marty, who was seated beside him.

She stretched her neck to view the group of people standing in front of the restaurant. Then she spotted Erv and Shoshana standing off to the side. "There they are." She waved frantically out the window. Her sister returned the wave with zeal.

Once the car was parked, Cavanaugh and Marty headed toward the couple near the door. Cavanaugh stopped dead in his tracks, recognizing the man as one of his drivers. His mind went into panic mode. With one word of recognition, this man could ruin everything. He only hoped as they came closer to the other couple, that Erv Roper would not remember the one or two times he had met his employer.

Unfortunately, he did. His eyes widened in surprise, and he extended his hand to Cavanaugh. "It's good to see you—"

"Nice to meet you," Cavanaugh spoke over the other man.

Erv felt the tension right away and paused, looking at his boss in confusion.

"Erv, Shoshana, this is Cavanaugh. Cavanaugh, my sister and brother-in-law."

Cavanaugh took Shoshana's hand. "Nice to meet you."

As the foursome headed toward the door, Cavanaugh

tugged at Erv's sleeve and held him back. "Um, Erv, could you not mention to Marty that I'm your boss?"

Erv slowly turned to look at the man he had always thought of as fair and honest. "Why?"

"I just think it would make things . . . awkward." Cavanaugh gave his most persuasive smile.

Under different circumstances, most women would be impressed with his position as chief executive officer and primary stockholder of one of the largest black-owned corporations in America. But Cavanaugh knew that when the truth came out, when Marty learned that he was the Saint John in Saint John Trucking, it wouldn't be long before she heard about the pending investigations and accusations—especially considering that the story updates were playing on the various business news stations at any given time.

Through no fault of his own, his life had become a soap opera. And thankfully, Marty seemed to be oblivious to that fact so far. She thought of him as the insurance investigator who happened to be in the wrong place at the wrong time. And for now, that was just fine with him.

Erv wasn't fooled for a minute. "Awkward?"

"I just need some time to get her to like me for me, not as Cavanaugh Saint John."

Erv nodded. "I understand." He did not, but this was his boss. As long as what he was doing wasn't hurting Marty, Erv decided, he would allow the man to play his strange game. He motioned toward the door.

The ladies were already inside, so engrossed in their own conversation they never noticed their companions lingering behind.

"He's gorgeous," Shoshana whispered.

"I know," Marty said playfully.

"Okay. He's fine as hell, seems like a nice guy, and

given that ride you pulled up in, I would assume gainfully employed. So, what's the deal?"

Marty looked over her shoulder to make sure the guys couldn't hear her. "I don't know, but something's not right."

"What do you mean?"

"That car, for instance. How can an insurance investigator afford that, or a yacht, or an airplane?"

"Did you say a yacht and airplane?"

"You heard me"

Shoshana glanced back over her shoulder and surveyed the man with new eyes. "How do *you* think he affords it?"

Marty sighed heavily. "I don't know."

Just then the guys caught up with them.

Erv winked at Cavanaugh. "Did we give you ladies enough time to gossip?"

Shoshana smirked. "Not quite."

Soon the four were seated at a table overlooking the river.

"Cavanaugh." Shoshana scooted as close to the table as her large belly would allow, and wasted no time initiating the third degree. "Marty says you're an insurance investigator."

Cavanaugh smiled at Marty, realizing his credit was being checked. "Yes, I work for a company called Liberty State." Cavanaugh ignored Erv's startled expression.

"That must be interesting work?"

Just then a waiter interrupted the conversation long enough to take their drink orders, and give Cavanaugh enough time to mentally prepare the proper answers.

The waiter looked at Marty casually as he asked for her order then suddenly did a double take. His smile widened. "And what can I get for you, lovely lady?"

Marty continued scanning the elegant menu, completely oblivious to the fact that she was being examined from head to toe. "Um, let me have a strawberry daiquiri." She smiled at Cavanaugh. "I love fruit drinks."

Cavanaugh never noticed her smile. His attention was focused on the enchanted waiter. He knew how exceptional Marty looked in her black pantsuit. Her curly hair was styled in a French roll, and her light makeup accented her naturally pretty face. He couldn't knock the man for appreciating the view, but did he have to be so blatant about it?

He turned his attention back to Shoshana as soon as the waiter disappeared. "Yes. I enjoy my work a great deal."

Shoshana, in her typical subtle-as-a-freight-train way, went straight for the kill. "Must pay good, huh?"

"Shoshana!" Marty howled.

"What?" The two sisters' eyes met across the table, Cavanaugh coughed into his napkin, and Erv simply shook his head.

"Yes. It pays quite well," Cavanaugh said, once he'd regained his composure. "At least, well enough to keep your sister in style and pampered like the queen she is." He winked at Marty, and she blushed to the tips of her toes. "Is that what you wanted to know?" he asked Shoshana.

Shoshana nodded solemnly. "Yes. That's exactly what I wanted to know."

Shortly after, Cavanaugh excused himself. He returned a few moments later, followed by a young woman who explained she would be their server for the remainder of the evening. Erv and Shoshana exchanged surprised looks, realizing what had happened. Marty, having never noticed the waiter's undue attention to begin with, thought nothing of the sudden change.

The first round of drinks were served, followed by

appetizers and another round of drinks. By the time the main course was served, the foursome were laughing and exchanging jokes as if they had all been friends for years.

Marty knew Shoshana was quite content with Cavanaugh's explanations. Her staunchest ally had been as easily seduced by a pretty smile as she had. But despite Cavanaugh's declaration, something still gnawed at the back of her mind. Something she couldn't quite put her finger on. And her worst fear was that for every day Cavanaugh was in her life that little something mattered a little less, until one day it wouldn't matter at all.

Six

"Marty."

Marty continued to roll the hose without turning around. She knew that voice as well as she knew her own. "Hello, Noel."

"I understand there's a new man in your life."

The cynical tone of his voice made Marty want to throw the remaining line around and trip him with it. "I don't see how that's any of your business." She started walking toward the fire escape.

Dwight and Tommy were still on top, issuing the remaining hose down, but the line was becoming shorter and shorter as she wrapped it around her shoulder.

"I just thought you should know, he's not what he seems."

Having had just about all she could take of the arrogant arson investigator, she swung around to face him. "Noel, when will you get it through your thick head? It's over between us."

"I understand that," he said. "I'm just trying to look out for you."

"Oh, yeah." She twisted her mouth. "I believe that." She whipped the final few feet of the cord around her arm and headed toward the truck.

"Let's go! Let's go!" The sound of someone in the distance called to indicate all the equipment was packed.

Marty lifted the heavy cord up to three of the guys on the back of the truck and sat to take off her soaking wet boots.

She spotted a small group of people huddled together just across the street from the house that was all but destroyed. She knew it was the family who lived there. Luckily, no one had been injured, but more than likely everything they owned in the world was inside that pile of rubble. Her heart went out to them, but she knew just what little consolation that was.

"Noel, just go." Having spent the last three hours putting out a house fire, she was exhausted and in no way ready to deal with a disgruntled ex-boyfriend.

"Cavanaugh Saint John, that's his name, isn't it?"

Marty continued pouring water out of her second boot without so much as a flinch to acknowledge the question.

"Is he bothering you, Marty?" The sound of Cal's baritone voice rang out just inches above her head. Marty looked up to see her mammoth friend standing face to face with her ex-lover. Noel only reached the larger man's midsection, but he stood toe to toe with him anyway.

"No, Cal." She stood, placing her hand against her friend. "I got this. Look, Noel, whatever you *think* you know doesn't even matter. What you need to understand is that no matter who I'm with, it won't be you."

She turned to climb aboard the truck, just as K. C. came running up and slipped past her in the small opening. He glanced at her face briefly to make sure she wasn't crying.

K. C. knew Marty was more than capable of taking care of herself, but he wouldn't stand for anyone making her cry. The horn sounded to clear traffic as the large truck began to pull away.

"Ask him what was he really doing in that building, Marty," Noel called after the truck. "It wasn't what he told you."

Marty held onto the metal rail with one hand and watched her former love become smaller and smaller. She turned, placing her foot more soundly on the running board, and let the wind whip across her face. She removed her large helmet and ran her fingers through her hair with her free hand, hating herself for even considering Noel's words for more than a moment. But she had to admit, she'd had her doubts over the past month.

Cavanaugh was wonderful, thoughtful, and intelligent. He spoiled her to no end and was willing to make whatever concessions were necessary to work around her schedule. But that was just the problem.

His endless stream of money and time went against everything he said. The clothes he wore, the car he drove; he even had his own yacht, for goodness' sake. Only an idiot would believe he lived on the modest income of an insurance agent. Something wasn't adding up. She had known it for some time but didn't want to admit it. It was like forcing herself to awaken from the sweetest dream she had ever had.

"Hey, baby girl." Cal nodded at her. "You all right?"

"I'm fine," she lied.

"You know, if you want . . ." Dwight winked at her and nodded in the direction of Noel. "I could take him out for you." The truck exploded in laughter at what they perceived to be a joke, but some small part of Marty's mind believed Dwight's threat. She knew how protective and loyal her friends could be at times.

"That's all right, Dwight. You don't use an Uzi to kill a fly."

The laughter became even louder, and the driver

sounded the horn announcing their return to the firehouse.

They both heard the light knocking at the same time. Marty climbed over Cavanaugh's half-drowsy form on the couch to get to the door. She handed the deliveryman the money and took the large paper bag from him.

"Keep the change," she said, before pushing her back up against the door to shut it.

"Hmmm . . ." Cavanaugh sat up, suddenly wide awake. "That smells good," he said, peering into the top of the bag. He took out several white cartons while Marty went to the kitchen for plates and utensils. He peeked into each of the tiny boxes and smiled devilishly as he came across one in particular. Checking to make sure she was still in the kitchen, he hid the box behind his pillow.

He had invited her to his apartment believing it was only fair, considering how much time he spent at hers. But because he spent so little time at his place, it had a sterile feel that he could tell made her uncomfortable. Still, she seemed to be finding her way around the kitchen okay, and he hoped, the bedroom as well.

Returning from the kitchen, Marty quickly settled beside him on the couch and began opening the boxes. "I'm starving. This is going to be so good." She opened box after box.

Cavanaugh pretended to watch the TV and ignored her confused expression.

"Hey," she said, once all the boxes were opened, "where's my almond chicken?"

"They must've forgot it," he said, working hard to hide the smile that perched on his lips.

"No way. House of Chung is the best in the city. They always get my order exactly right," she said, now eyeing

Cavanaugh suspiciously. "Humph. You don't look too upset, considering you love it as much as I do."

"It's okay. There's plenty of other food here," he said, avoiding her eyes. One look and he knew he would explode in laughter.

She stood up slowly, staring down at him for several seconds. Cavanaugh tried to ignore her.

He pushed at her legs. "Baby, you're blocking the TV."

Suddenly, she swooped down on him like a bird of prey. "Where is it?" She pounded him with pillows. "Where is it?"

Cavanaugh was choking with laughter, but still refused to give in. "I don't know what you're talking about," he managed to get out between bouts of being popped in the face with the velvety cushions.

She noticed something white sticking out from behind the cushion, and reached for it. "Give it up before you get hurt." She tugged at the little silver handle on the box.

With lightening speed, Cavanaugh flipped her over onto her back and pinned her to the couch. "I paid for it. It's mine." He looked at her seductively. "And so are you."

He kissed her, and the sweet taste ignited the fire in his soul. He rolled over until his larger body covered hers. Without warning, his felt his manhood responding to the soft warmth of her form. So many nights he had imagined what she would feel like beneath him. But nothing he imagined came close to the actual moment. His large hands wrapped around her backside, pushing her up against his quickly rising bulge as he considered the fastest way to get inside her clothes.

"Cavanaugh, I don't think this is such a—"

His mouth covered hers and his hands began sliding the T-shirt up her body. He knew what she was about to say; she'd said it many times before. But he truly did not want to hear it again. Maybe, he thought, if he could bring her to where he was, quickly, then just maybe. But he wasn't quick enough.

She pushed and wiggled until she freed herself of his heavy weight. "Sweetheart, please," she pleaded, still fully clothed. "We've talked about this. I just need a little more time."

He collapsed on the couch, and did what he'd done the last four times they had come this close: he counted backward from fifty. By the time he reached the number one, his lustful body had finally settled down. He said a silent prayer for strength and sat up.

"I know," he sighed, "but you know how much I want you. I can't deny that."

She ran her hand over his curly hair. "Just a little more time," she whispered.

Cavanaugh nodded, knowing he would wait forever if he had to. He leaned in to kiss her neck, but was interrupted by the tickling in his side. She was playing dirty. He curled into a ball, laughing uncontrollably and trying to shield himself from further assault.

Marty darted around him and grabbed the white box of almond chicken. She shook her hips teasingly in triumph. "You said to order what *I* wanted, and I did. So, it's mine."

Cavanaugh sat upright on the couch finally catching his breath. "I'll buy you all the Chinese food you can eat, if you'll do that little hip shake again."

She shook her head in exasperation and sunk down on the couch next to him knowing the threat was gone. "Men," she huffed.

Cavanaugh reached around her waist and pulled her to him. "I think I'm falling in love with you," he said.

"The feeling's mutual." She kissed him quickly and sat

up to eat. Marty didn't want him to see the doubt in her eyes. Not that there was any doubt in what she felt for him, only in what he told her. But it was getting harder and harder to convince herself that this man was the middle-class insurance investigator he claimed to be, while sitting beside him in his riverfront condominium on his leather sofa watching movies on his brand new three-thousand-dollar flat-screen television.

There has to be some explanation for this, Marty thought, *there just has to be.* Otherwise, she would be forced to consider the most obvious choice: that Cavanaugh Saint John was making his money in some nefarious manner.

Before they took this relationship to the next level, she needed to know the truth. This man was slowly digging his way into the very core of her heart. Marty knew that once she allowed him to hold her, to make love to her, no crime or sin would matter.

She watched Cavanaugh as he sat up and dug into the cartons. He never noticed the change in her disposition. He was too hungry, and too happy. How she hoped Noel was wrong. How she hoped her instincts were wrong.

Cavanaugh sat looking over the reports he had received that morning. He had spent most of the day in meetings with the trucker's union, and his head was pounding. He had asked Reesy to track down some aspirin, but that felt like hours ago. The light tap on the door indicated she had returned.

He sat pressing his temples with his forefingers. "Come."

Reesy went charging across the room with her usual speed and efficiency. The long, gray hair flying behind her was the only indication of her age, since her dark brown face was as smooth as a baby's. Dressed in a smart navy suit, she was the epitome of the corporate image. She plopped two tiny white pills and a tall glass of water in front of him. Then she proceeded to take the report out of his hand, tapping the papers against the edge of the desk until they were even again. She placed a neat paper clip on the top and set them in his "in" box.

Cavanaugh glared at her over the top of his water glass. "I was reading that."

"Not anymore." She took him by the hand and led him to the long leather couch on the other side of the large executive office.

"What are you doing?" he asked, even as she pushed him down onto the couch.

"Putting my child to bed." She lifted his long legs onto the couch and walked over to a cabinet in the corner. Opening it, she took out a soft, yellow cotton blanket and shook it out.

"Reesy, I've got too much to do to take a nap now," he yawned.

"I know," she said, smiling in her usual appeasing manner and spreading the blanket over him.

Cavanaugh watched her beneath his quickly falling lids, wondering how much of what he told her she actually listened to.

She pressed the volume button on his phone to the lowest level and gently closed the door behind her. As soon as she returned to her desk, she reached for her ringing phone.

"Hello, Clarissa." The cold voice of the older woman came through the receiver loud and clear. Reesy hated the way she insisted on calling her by her formal name.

"Mrs. Saint John, how are you today?" she asked sweetly. Reesy's ability to feign affection was one of her greatest attributes.

"Fine, dear. Is my son in?"

"No, I'm afraid he's stepped out for a while. Can I take a message?"

The woman on the other end of the phone fell silent for a long time. Reesy knew it was just an intimidation tactic.

"No, just tell him I called." The phone sounded a light click, and then it was dead.

Reesy shook her head. *So that's where he gets it.* Reesy knew better than to ever mention to Cavanaugh any similarity between him and his mother. He would probably fire her on the spot.

She silently wondered how much longer he could keep up such a grueling pace. His attempts to live between Detroit and Savannah were wearing him out, and with the added weight of a murder investigation hanging over his head, it was amazing that he managed to get as much done as he did.

She sat down to finish typing out the letters Cavanaugh had spent the morning dictating, and considered what she wanted for lunch. Her little tabletop radio was set to the local R&B station, and the smooth sounds of Luther Vandross's "Take You Out" drowned out the soft snoring coming from the other office.

Seven

Cavanaugh pulled up outside Marty's small apartment building. He grabbed his overnight bag off the passenger seat and got out of the car. He hoped Marty wasn't home yet, and he would have time for a quick shower. He had taken to stopping by the gym on his way to her apartment. An hour-long workout was the only way he could get through the night curled around her warm, soft body.

He opened the door with the key she had given him a week earlier, and from the sounds in the apartment, she was already there. The bedroom TV was on, although he couldn't make out the program. The sound of the microwave humming meant she was probably in the kitchen, but when he got there, she was nowhere to be found. He poked his head in the bedroom but didn't see her. He decided as he tossed his bag on the bed that she must have stepped out for a moment.

During the past several weeks he had become very comfortable in both her apartment, where she resided only a few days a month, and the firehouse, where she spent most of her time. Her apartment had none of his expensive artwork and decor, but it did have the lived-in, well-loved feeling of a home.

He had once asked the guys if they had a problem with him hanging out at the firehouse so much. The group answer came from Tommy. "Man, with a woman like Marty, it's understandable." The statement was supported by a few fervent "you know it"s, and "sho'nough"s. He had to admit, it was kinda cool watching them go out on runs and feeling the adrenaline that continued to pump around the large building for hours after their return.

Cavanaugh went into the bathroom planning to get his shower before she returned. Being wet, naked, and close to her was simply too much temptation. He had undressed and was about to step into the shower when he heard the TV turn off. Wrapping a towel around his waist, he went back into the bedroom.

Marty was sitting in the far corner of the room with her knees drawn to her chest and a vacant expression on her face. The remote dangled from the tips of her fingers. *Had she been there all along?*

"Babe, are you all right?"

She continued to stare at the blank screen in silence.

"Sweetheart, what is it?"

Marty stood to face him, and swallowed hard. She knew she had to keep it short and simple. The longer she was exposed to him the weaker she became. Especially with him standing there with that towel barely concealing him. His taut shoulders and muscled torso looked molded from some kind of marble stone. He was breathtaking, plain and simple. She just wasn't that strong.

"This isn't working."

His dark eyes pleaded with her. "Whatever I did, I'm sorry."

Marty had to look away. This man had a stronger hold on her heart than she realized. "You didn't do anything, Cavanaugh," she said. "It's just me."

"What are you saying? You don't feel anything for me?"

"It's not like that." She struggled to find the right words. "We just aren't compatible."

"Not compatible?" Cavanaugh's eyes widened. "Baby, I don't know any two people more compatible than you and I."

She made the mistake of looking up at that moment, and found his full pink lips perched in a crooked grin that could have melted an ice queen. He was weakening her resolve. How easily she could remember the taste of those lips.

"Cavanaugh, it's best this way." She fought to hide the hoarseness in her voice.

He was slowly moving toward her. "Best for whom?"

She had to do something quick. If he touched her she was done for.

"Not best for me." He held out his hand to her. "And I don't believe it's best for you."

Her heart was pounding. What was happening? She'd prepared two hours for this and he was shutting her down like a flame under water. Marty had finally accepted the most obvious conclusion regarding Cavanaugh's mysterious background and secretive, pampered lifestyle. And that conclusion had led her here.

"I can't deny the truth anymore, Cavanaugh."

"What truth?" His heart sped up until it was beating against his chest. Had she somehow found out about the investigation, that he was a murder suspect? Is that what this was all about? "What are you trying to tell me?"

She quickly cleared her throat deciding there was no easy way to say this, except to simply say it. "I know you're dealing drugs."

His eyebrows crinkled in confusion. "What are you talking about?"

"Well, how else can you afford the lifestyle you have?" She opened his gym bag and took out the first thing her fingers touched. "This watch, for instance," she said, holding it out to him. "I'm not crazy, Cavanaugh. I know this is a five-thousand-dollar watch. How can you afford this on your salary?"

Something about the look on his face was making her feel very stupid. "Is that what this is all about? You want to know where my money comes from?"

She tilted her chin up trying to appear more confident that she felt. "Yes, I want to know."

"Baby, why didn't you just say something, instead of scaring me like this?"

"You still haven't answered the question," she said, folding her arms across her chest to match his pose. She hadn't come this far to be hustled so easily.

Cavanaugh sighed heavily. The time had come to tell her the truth, at least a partial truth. He could only hope she wouldn't connect his name with the Saint John Trucking in the news reports. "My family."

"Your family?"

"In Detroit the name Saint John means nothing, but in Savannah . . ." He shook his head. "Let's just say we wouldn't even be having this discussion."

Marty watched his eyes for any hint of deceit. There was none. He was telling the truth, and that confident half-smile on his face only confirmed it.

"I don't know what to think, anymore." She sank down on the bed, suddenly very tired. He came to kneel before her. She turned her head away knowing how easily he could sway her.

"Look at me," he commanded.

When she didn't respond, he took her chin in his hand, and turned her face to his. "Please, Marty, look at me."

Marty looked into his dark eyes. They were like bottomless pools. Who was she kidding? She loved him. She had foolishly thought keeping the relationship nonsexual would somehow steel her heart against him. But it hadn't mattered, he was in her blood now.

"I'm not a drug dealer. Do you believe me?" But before she could answer, he slowly covered her mouth with his. Careful and patient, he wanted to savor every ounce of her sweet taste. He pulled her against him. She was so soft and tender. He could feel his manhood hardening in anticipation.

He had wanted her for so long, craved her, ached for her. He had to have her, he simply had to. "Come with me," he stood, lifting her with him.

Cavanaugh held her hypnotized with his dark, seductive eyes as he led her back to the bathroom, letting go of her only long enough to turn on the water in the shower.

Checking the temperature for warmth, he reached to pull her Old Navy sweatshirt over her head. His heart paused for a second. Many nights they had gotten this far, but only this far before she'd pulled back and refused to love him. This time, she lifted her arms and allowed the cotton shirt to slide over her head. He reached around and released her bra, then slid it down her arms enjoying the sight of her full breasts.

"You're more beautiful than I imagined," he said, before filling his mouth with her soft flesh.

Marty fell back into his strong arms, allowing him to brace her weight against his own body. She could feel him now beneath the cotton towel, throbbing against her thigh. Pressing her to him, he kissed her hard, prying her mouth open even farther. In that instance he wanted her, all of her, fast and furious, and he thought of taking her right there on the bathroom floor. But when he felt her trembling against him, he forced himself to slow down.

He had waited so long for her, it had felt like an eternity already. The thought of having to wait another night would have killed him, he was sure. But even more certain than that was it had to be her choice. As desperately as he needed to be inside her, he would not take from her what she was not ready to give. Taking a deep breath to steady his hands, he patiently unbuttoned and unzipped her fitted jeans taking in every inch of her as she was exposed to him. In some absurd urge to conceal herself, she hid the patch of red silk panties with both hands.

His heart skipped a beat. Was she having second thoughts? "Please, Marty," he pleaded as his hands covered hers, "please, let me love you." Cavanaugh felt ready to fall to his knees and beg if he had to.

After a few very tense moments, she finally let her small hands slide away and she allowed him to lower the jeans and panties down her well-toned legs. Lifting each bare foot, he removed them completely and stood to face her. Embarrassed by her nakedness, she moved closer to him. But he held her off at arm's length, needing to see her in her full glory. He stepped back and let his eyes rake over her long form. It seemed he had waited forever for this moment.

"You were made for me, Marty," he said, as his towel slid to the floor. He reached into his pants pocket and pulled a condom from his wallet. Quickly, he donned it and returned to her arms, whispering loving endearments into her mouth as his soft lips covered hers. "This is what's meant to be." As he murmured all the things he wanted to do to her in a strange mixture of English and Cajun-French, he bit along her neck and shoulders.

Marty hardly spoke a word of French, but his tone and fervor made his meaning perfectly clear. She was convinced most of it was probably obscene and oh-so-wonderfully arousing.

They stood toe to toe, chest to chest, and hand to

hand. The rest of their bodies were barely touching, but the electricity in the room could have short-circuited a city.

Cavanaugh stepped back into the onslaught of warm water, guiding her with him. Turning her, he pressed her back against the wall and kissed her once. Then again and again, the way he had kissed her in his dreams. All the passion and longing he'd felt for so long finally came gushing forth like an ocean that had been dammed for a century.

Marty found herself stimulated by both the feel of the cool tile against her naked flesh and the passionate kisses of her loving man, who touched her with such caring and hunger. She could clearly feel how aroused he was in his heated breath on her flesh and the strength of his hold, but still he handled her with a tenderness she had never experienced, almost . . . reverent.

He reached over to take down the massaging showerhead, slowly covering her in the warm water, taking the time to let the pulsating bubbles touch every inch of her. She closed her eyes, simply enjoying the effect on her skin. How she loved this man. She thanked whatever force had brought them together.

The strange, slippery feel of his other hand against her bare skin startled her. It took a moment for her mind to realize that his hands were covered in soap. He slid his nimble fingers over her body, caressing, moving in and out of every crevasse, and bathing her with a sensual ease. Placing the bar of soap between her palms, he moved her hands over it until they too were lathered. Cavanaugh placed her soapy hands against his own chest, smiling sinfully as if the rest needed no explanation.

She closed her eyes and saw him only in her mind. The rounded contour of sculpted muscles, the isolated soft places, the smoothness of his perfect, flawless flesh as his demanding tongue continued to wreck havoc on her mouth. He was magnificent, and he knew it, standing before her with the regality of a noble prince. Then suddenly, his hands covered hers, again taking them places they would never have had the audacity to go alone, and he returned the affection tenfold, touching, caressing, exploring until every part of both their bodies were covered in the white foam.

Marty felt her heart pounding against her chest and the warm moisture forming between her legs. She sensed the primal woman in her coming alive under his guidance. He played her body like an expert conductor bringing a hundred-piece orchestra to life. Unable to control her own desire, she found herself writhing against his hand as he massaged and explored places that hadn't been touched in what seemed like forever. All she could do was shake her head to convey the mania he was causing inside her hungry body.

He worked her as if he had known her body a thousand times, touching her with some all-knowing wisdom. In desperation, she reached for him, groping clumsily for his protruding vine, trying to bring them together quickly. But he shifted just in time, slipping through her wet hand.

"Oh please, please," she cried out, unable to say any more, but it was enough.

Dropping the showerhead to the floor, he slipped one of his long fingers inside her, then another, then another, massaging her swollen cleft, stimulating every nerve in her body. Then, just as quickly, he pulled back.

Without warning his slender fingers returned, plying her tender flesh with lightning speed, lifting and gliding in and out. Then they disappeared again, leaving her struggling to regain control of her erratic breathing. Again they returned, shooting tiny bolts of lightening throughout her body.

Slow torture. It was the only way her mind could describe what he was doing to her. He continued the assault on her senses until Marty was certain her sanity was at risk.

She fought the urgency building inside her, the undeniable need for release, never wanting the feeling to end. She bit into his shoulder in anguish, so determined was she to hold back the tidal wave coursing through her. And still he pushed her and pushed her further, until, finally incapable of denying her urges any longer, Marty cried out as her body gave up its sweet nectar. She shuddered against him, hating herself for the selfish reaction. She tried to stop the quickening tremors, but he continued to torment her mercilessly claiming every ounce of the honeyed liquid.

Marty's whole being quaked at his demand, powerless against his need until he was certain she had nothing left to give. She lay against him for several moments, simply trying to breathe again. Looking up at him with drowsy eyes, she half-laughed. "But what about you?"

His devious smile distracted her mind, and she never noticed his hands wrapping around her thighs, not until she felt him inside her. Holding her hips, he brought her down on him, slowly forcing himself inside the tight orifice. She shivered at the feel of him.

Cavanaugh simply held her against him for several long moments in a joining of soul mates. Staring into her eyes, saying so much without a single word. Then, pulling her further down on him, he forced himself deeper and deeper inside her until the whole of him was buried within her walls.

Marty could feel him becoming one body with her. They fit together perfectly, everything about it seemed right. She knew in that moment he was right. He was made for her, fashioned just for her body. She wrapped her arms around his muscular shoulders and allowed him to take her wherever he would.

Sensing her surrender, he began moving against her with slow deliberate motion, rotating his hips in such a way as to explore every inch of her inner being. He probed her, learning her deepest secrets. The only evidence of his restraint was the hard breath she felt against her neck. Then the rotation shifted to become glides, then thrusts, until he was pounding his body against hers.

"*Rendez-vous-moi, mon amour, rendez-vous-moi,*" he whispered, in a mantra. *Surrender yourself to me, my love.*

Marty was amazed by her own body's immediate response to his insistence, the aching pressure she felt forming as her sheath closed around him.

"*Ma chérie,*" he cried, against her neck as his want for her overrode his self-control. He battered her lithe body hard against the wall, unable to hold back a moment longer. Their union, which had been forged in fire and bound by love, was now sealed in passion as his long fingers clawed into her tender flesh.

Holding her tight against him, he felt the release of everything he had wanted to give her for so long: himself, wholly and completely. He continued to hold her tight, burying his head against her warm neck as his body erupted in spasm after spasm after spasm.

Eight

"Noel, I don't want to hear it!" Marty slammed the phone down. Distressing as it was, she had come to realize over the past few weeks that Noel had to be spying on her. He seemed to know where and when she saw Cavanaugh, and on those days he would call and harass her constantly, insisting that her boyfriend was not the man she thought he was. Under some foolish notion that she could deter him, she had confessed that Cavanaugh told her the truth about his family. But Noel had only laughed at her feeble attempt, still insisting that there was so much she didn't know. Yet, he never bothered to fill her in.

She took a deep breath and went back into the common area, hoping Cavanaugh could not see the anxiety written so clearly on her face. She had to step over scattered bodies to reach him where he sat in one of the four large recliners. His liberal use of the La-Z-Boy®s was proof to Marty that the guys truly liked him, and didn't just put up with him for her sake. A guest had to be pretty special to be allowed to sit in one of the sparse recliners. She knew it was Cavanaugh's unique ability to flow easily from boardroom to basketball court that endeared him to the group. It was one of the things she liked most about him too.

"Did I miss anything?" she asked as she snuggled down into his lap.

"Nah, just a lot of pregame stuff," he answered, offhandedly.

Dina, Dwight's wife, came strolling into the common area with a large bowl of mixed munchies in each hand. She gave one to Cavanaugh, who set it down on the short table just beyond his reach, and the other to K. C., who lay sprawled across the floor. The group of men descended on the bowls like bees on a honeycomb.

"Hey Baby, can you grab me a cold one while you're up?" Dwight called, before popping a couple of Doritos® from a nearby bowl into his mouth. Dina shot one eyebrow up and gave her husband a wicked look, but still turned and headed toward the kitchen.

"Here, I'll help you." Marty hopped off the chair and quickly climbed over the guys to catch up with the other woman. She was feeling the need to get away from Cavanaugh's disconcerting silence.

Strange as it was, Cavanaugh's lack of interest was far more unsettling than if he had asked a thousand questions, which was his typical way. "Who was that? Is everything okay?" He was a jealous man, a trait he'd revealed early on in the relationship. So, for her to disappear for several minutes to take a call, and he not say a word, was unusual. She wondered if he had possibly heard the conversation with Noel, and was just waiting to confront her later.

Marty stood at the can opener listening to the soft humming as it cut into the large can of salsa dip. "Dina?"

Marty had been considering doing this for several days, but was unsure of whether or not to go through with it.

"Yeah?" Dina was bent over the cooler scooping ice into a large container.

"Dwight says your firm does a lot of pro bono work?"

"Is that your way of asking for my legal services?"

"Just a favor." Marty was feeling guilt-ridden down to her toes. Dina stood and turned to face her friend, hearing the seriousness in her voice.

"Can you look into a law firm called Stanton and Dowel? They were in that building that burned down about two months ago."

"Isn't that the building you met Cavanaugh in?" Dina Johnston wasn't voted one of Detroit's up-and-coming top legal minds for nothing.

Marty avoided the other woman's eyes. "Yes."

"Cause of the fire?" Dina asked.

Marty knew in her heart this was wrong. Hadn't Cavanaugh already proven himself to her time and again? But something just wasn't right. It wasn't so much what Noel said, just a feeling in her gut. "Yes."

"Sure." Dina was already calculating what angle to approach it from. Considering she had known Kenneth Stanton since college, she decided to start there. "I'll look into it." She pulled a long tray from one of the cabinets. "Is Dwight this helpless when I'm not around?" Dina reached into the refrigerator and pulled out several cans of pop and beer, knowing the instant she walked back into the room someone else would want something.

"Please, girl." Marty was pouring the salsa into a large glass dish. "Do you think *I* would wait on him hand and foot? Humph, not even." The two women were laughing as they reentered the common area.

Later that night, curled in Cavanaugh's arms, Marty fell asleep in her little twin bunk as she had so often. Usually, he left shortly afterwards, fearing what he would do if he stayed. She had made it perfectly clear from the beginning that making love in this bed was out of the question. He understood that for her the job came first, and given the importance of her job, he had no problem accepting that stance.

But tonight, he could not seem to bring himself to let her go. It was well after 3:00 AM, and most of the guys had gone to bed. But the strange telephone conversation was still working on his brain. *Who was Noel?*

He tried to remember as much of the conversation as he could, but even that was only fragmented. When she had returned to the common room, her anger was still palpable, although she tried to hide it.

Cavanaugh yawned sleepily. No need to rack his brain over a question he could answer with a couple of phone calls tomorrow. Kissing the soft skin on her neck one final time, he forced himself to release her body and slip from the bed.

Marty stood working with the tangle of white cord around her hand. Cavanaugh stood patiently by, watching her try to unravel the long knotted string of the kite. He had nothing to offer. In this endeavor *she* was the expert.

Cavanaugh was in his mid-thirties and had never flown a kite before. Somehow, in passing, the topic came up and he mentioned it to Marty. From that moment to this one, she had set out on a mission.

"Marty," he said. "I don't think it's supposed to be wound up like that." The cut of her eyes told him he should have kept his mouth shut.

Seeing her trembling, he took off his pea coat and slung it around her shoulders. Enjoying the feel of her soft body beneath the wool material, he kept his arms wrapped around her. It was an unusually cool day, the wind was whipping around them in swirling funnels. According to Marty this was perfect weather for kite flying.

Cavanaugh appreciated the effort, but the only Sunday morning games he wanted to play with her were conducted indoors. He nibbled at her neck. "Can't we just go back to your place?" He knew he was treading on thin ice.

"Not until we have fun," she hissed, before pulling hard on the line, causing the knot to tighten. Her mind was split between the task at hand and the feel of those oh-too-soft lips on her neck.

"If it's fun you're interested in"—he tilted his head to look at her—"I can think of much better ways to have it."

Marty only spared a slight glance in his direction. That smile of his could melt her quicker than anything else. And she was bound and determined to fly a kite before the day was over.

It had hurt her deeply to learn of all the things he had missed as a child, the simple things she had always taken for granted. He managed to explain his extravagant lifestyle, but there were still many mysteries surrounding him. Like why he gave little or no information regarding his background, including a reason or explanation why so many monumental moments had been denied him. She came up with the idea of kite flying only wanting to give him everything he had missed, although she knew that experiencing the pastime as a man was completely different from that of a child.

Marty could feel her frustration building and was tempted in every part of her being to rip the kite to shreds.

Feeling the tension coming into her body Cavanaugh wisely released her and walked to the edge of the water. He stood staring out at the river he had seen a thousand times. Somehow, it was different now, the greenish blue coloring seemed deeper. Strange as it was, he realized the colors in everything seemed more vivid since he had met her.

Marty was muttering and cursing the kite when the contraption slipped through her fingers and quickly sailed away on one of the strong swirling currents. They both ran after it, but it climbed higher and higher at such a speed, it was soon beyond their reach. Marty was crushed and Cavanaugh fought to stifle a laugh.

His good humor disappeared when he noticed real tears in her eyes. "What's wrong?" He lifted her face to his.

"I really wanted to fly a kite with you." She tried to choke back the tears, but it was too late.

"I'll buy you a thousand kites, please don't cry." He pulled her against him. "You name it, any kind of kite you want, it's yours."

"No, it's just . . . you deserve to fly a kite." She wiped at her face with the back of her hand. "I had such a great childhood, I just wish you had too." Wrapping her arms around his muscular torso she took comfort in the strength of his embrace.

"Marty, my childhood was what it was. You can't change that," he said over her head. "I don't really regret it. It's all I know."

She looked up into his handsome face. "But why?"

Stepping back away from her, he pulled his peacoat tighter around her. "Life is what it is, please accept that as an answer," he pleaded. "I'm just not ready to talk about the details yet. I know it was twenty years ago, but it feels like yesterday to me."

She nodded against his chest and snuggled closer, enjoying the subtle smell of his cologne. On several occasions she had tried to get him to talk of his childhood, but had only gotten bits and pieces—his distaste for his mother, his intense love for his father, and how his world came to a crashing halt the day his father died. They just stood there in the cool summer grass enjoying the breeze whipping around them, and the warm cocoon they had created with their body heat.

"I promise, our children will all be expert kite flyers," he chuckled, and kissed the top of her head.

Marty didn't say a word, her mind was still wrapping around the only two words she heard, *our children*. She sighed into his lightweight sweater, enjoying the sweet thought. She wondered whether she would ever know enough about this man to consider such a lifelong commitment.

"Tom, you have been doing business with SJT for forty years. First with my father, and now with me." Cavanaugh leaned against his desk, his arms folded over his chest. This was the fifth major client he had lost as a result of the murder investigation.

"I don't like this any more than you, Cavanaugh," said the Southern voice coming through the speaker phone. "I know you didn't do it, but it's bad PR."

"This isn't about public relations. We're talking about two hundred thousand dollars in lost profits between the two of us. Do you think a few media lies is worth all that?"

"I'm sorry, Cavanaugh. But the board's vote was unanimous."

"I understand, Tom," he lied. He didn't understand, as he watched his business crumble around him. He didn't understand anything at all. He hung up the phone and went to stare out the window.

Cavanaugh knew SJT could survive this investigation, even if they lost more clients like Tom Maxwell. SJT was well-insulated with its holdings and subsidiaries. But the trucking division was his father's first endeavor, the root of the Saint John tree. And Cavanaugh was determined to do everything in his power to save it.

He glanced at his desk clock. It was already 2:05 AM. He cursed under his breath. He was supposed to be on his way back to Detroit by now. Accepting that he was too exhausted to fly, he picked up the phone and dialed Marty.

"Hello?"

"Hey, baby. I won't be back tonight."

"Oh? Is everything okay?"

"Yes. My meetings ran later than expected, but I'll be there for brunch—in bed."

She laughed. "Just make sure you bring it with you."

"It's a date. See you then."

After he hung up with Marty, Cavanaugh stretched out on his leather sofa, planning to relax for a few minutes before heading home for the night. Within seconds, he was sound asleep.

Cavanaugh was having a nightmare. There was fire everywhere. The room was becoming hotter and hotter. He had tried to open the door, pulling hard, then ramming his shoulder against it, but it wouldn't give. He pulled at the handle again, but was forced to release it when it became too hot.

He ran back to the other side of the room to pick up a chair or anything heavy enough to smash the only window in the small office. There were flames all around him. He was bending to pick up a desk chair when he felt the wood beam fall across his back.

The pain. Oh, the pain had been unbearable! Then there was nothing but blackness.

When he opened his eyes again he was trapped. The fire still raged but now he didn't even have the ability to help himself. His whole body hurt like nothing he had ever felt. He fought to stay conscious, hoping that someone would come.

The room was so hot even the floor beneath his trapped body was heating up. He knew he was going to die. The thought wasn't so bad, really. At least he would once again be with his father. But some deep-rooted need to survive forced him to cry out.

"Help!" His eyes darted around the room. There had to be some way to lift the beam. "Help!" he cried out again.

The door fell, and there stood a blur of yellow and black. The apparition lifted the axe high and brought it down, shredding the remnants of the door and lifting him to safety.

Cavanaugh's sleep settled, as the horrible images were replaced by pictures of Marty's face. Her flirty smile, her sweet laughter. Her soft, brown body slowly gliding beneath him as she cried out his name. Cavanaugh moaned softly again, but this time there was no nightmare.

Nine

Marty sat playing with the desktop pendulum. She had talked herself into and out of this appointment several times over the course of the morning. Finally she decided she had come this far, why not go all the way. She nervously shifted one way then another in the chair, trying to get comfortable. The guys in the firehouse thought she went out for lunch so she couldn't be gone too long.

The door swung open and Dina came strolling across the room. Marty noted how different the woman looked in her beige double-breasted pantsuit compared to the jeans and T-shirt she sported when visiting the firehouse.

Marty found herself unable to resist teasing her friend. "My, my, don't we look fancy."

"Shut up," Dina said with a smile, then reached into her desk drawer and pulled out a long file.

Marty sat staring at the manila folder. The information in there would change her life forever one way or another. She looked to Dina for some evidence of what was in the folder. She was simply unable to open it.

"Good news or bad?"

"You asked me to discover the cause of the fire." Dina settled into her high-back leather chair, picked up the folder and opened it. "But because it's an ongoing investigation the police won't release the details. Although I did discover that Cavanaugh was there that day in the capacity of an insurance investigator for a company called Liberty State. Which is exactly what he told you, right?"

"Yes," Marty sighed, glad she'd chosen to come, until the look of concern on Dina's face stole her elation away as quickly as it came. "But?"

"Marty, how much do you know about the attorney who was murdered there?"

"Just that it happened a couple of months before the fire," Marty said, a bit confused. "Why?"

"Well, I knew the man personally. In fact, I went to school with him. I had no idea that he'd died or that he was—" Dina stopped suddenly.

"What?" Marty asked, growing more alarmed with every word coming from her friend. She'd never seen Dina Johnston anything but cool, calm, and completely in control. Now, she was looking more than a bit troubled.

Dina flipped through the pages of the file. "Apparently, before he was murdered, Kenneth was investigating a large corporation he believed was involved in corrupt activities. You know, things like paying off local politicians to get information to underbid the competition, cooking the books, the typical stuff. The corporation was the parent company to one of the small subsidiaries Stanton and Dowel represented. That's how he came to know about the illicit activities."

"I'm confused, what does any of that have to do with Cavanaugh?"

"The corporation he was investigating was SJT."

Marty wondered if she had clearly conveyed her intention to her friend. The things Dina was talking about had nothing at all to do with Cavanaugh or the fire at Stanton and Dowel.

"The man in prison for the murder still insists that he

didn't kill anyone. He says that he was framed by the same boss that he supposedly killed, Kenneth Stanton."

"Let me get this straight. Some guy in prison is saying that he was set up by a dead man?"

"That's his story."

"He's obviously delusional, Dina." Marty rested her elbows on the arms of her chair. "But, what does any of this have to do with Cav—"

"SJT is Saint John Trucking, Marty." Dina leaned forward, needing to be certain her friend understood her. "Kenneth Stanton was investigating Cavanaugh's business dealings at the time of his death. A man's who's obviously mentally incompetent is accused of murdering him under very questionable circumstances. Then a month later, Cavanaugh shows up to *investigate* the death."

Marty shot up out of the chair. "Are you trying to say Cavanaugh is somehow involved in the murder of that attorney?"

"I don't know," Dina shook her head. "But apparently the authorities do. He's under investigation, has been from the night of the fire."

Marty felt the room spinning. *This is not happening! This is not happening!* She turned and headed toward the door, but the floor seemed to be moving under her feet. She leaned against the wall to steady herself and felt Dina's arms come around her.

"Are you all right?"

"Yes," she lied, as her face flushed crimson red. "I'll be fine." But Marty knew if what Dina was saying was true, she would never be fine again.

As Erv Roper waved good-bye to his ride and headed up the walkway to his house, he was whistling to himself. Today was a good day.

He had scored almost a hundred percent on his annual evaluation and gotten a 25 percent increase to boot. Before he left that morning, he had seen Shoshana preparing his favorite dish, lasagna, for dinner. And best of all, by some strange twist of nature, being pregnant seemed to be making his wife more lustful by the day. At that moment, Erv was a man truly happy with his lot in life. Yes, he thought, swinging open the front door, today was a good day.

That was until he saw his sister-in-law standing in front of the couch, looking like Satan himself, and his wife sitting on the couch glaring with equal repulsion.

Later than evening, after having confirmed everything Dina told her with Erv, Marty returned to the firehouse. Most of the guys were still up playing cards and Play-Station®, but she just wanted to be alone with her thoughts. She feigned exhaustion, which was only a partial untruth, and went to bed early. She had to make a decision, a painful one at that. One she already in her heart knew the answer to.

Marty now understood what had been troubling her all along. From day one, she had sensed there was more to Cavanaugh than he revealed. Even after he told her about his wealthy family, she still felt something was—missing. Now she knew what that something was.

Like everyone else who watched the six o'clock news, she had heard that the CEO of SJT was being investigated for murder, arson, and embezzlement. But never did she imagine that she was dating that very CEO, or that her own brother-in-law would knowingly keep that information from her.

When she confronted Erv, his only explanation was that no one who knew Cavanaugh Saint John believed the charges against him, and most people, including himself, simply believed it would all blow over. But that still did not answer the one question that troubled Marty the most, the one question she could not rectify. Why would an innocent man lie?

Cavanaugh had plenty of opportunities to come clean over the past months, and yet he had said nothing. He had even gone out of his way to make sure she did not find out. Why? Was it a trust issue? Or guilt issue? Or . . .was it that he just didn't expect her to be in his life long enough for it to matter?

She knew from the first that Cavanaugh Saint John was out of her league. As much as it pained her to consider it, maybe he had not told her the truth because he didn't feel she was important enough to him to warrant the explanations.

The light knock on the door was nothing more than a formality as Tommy poked his head around the corner. It took a moment for his eyes to find her prone form in the small storage room, which had been converted to a private bedroom for their only female counterpart.

"Telephone, it's Cavanaugh."

Marty never moved, just pulled the cotton blanket closer around her slender form. "Tell him I'm sleeping."

Tommy's eyebrows shot up. "You sure?"

"Yes. Just tell him I'm sleeping."

After a long uncomfortable silence, Tommy finally slid the door closed.

Cal saw the familiar, slender man stepping out of the silver BMW as he exited the firehouse on his way to his truck. He shifted his weekend bag, slinging it over his right shoulder. "It's about time you showed up."

"I was out of town. What's going on?" With his frequent

visits to the firehouse it hadn't taken Cal and Cavanaugh long to discover they had much in common. A love for fine cars, fine jewelry, and fine women. The two men greeted each other with a handshake.

"Don't know, she won't talk about it." Cal dropped his duffel bag and took a pack of chewing gum from his jacket pocket. "But whatever you did, man"—he glanced over his shoulder at the firehouse—"you messed up bad." He half-chuckled, unwrapping a stick of gum.

"I didn't do anything," Cavanaugh said, as he waved away the gum Cal offered.

"I beg to differ, my friend." Cal tucked his hands in his pockets. "My girl ain't one to go off about nothing. You had to do something." Cal picked up his bag again. "Maybe you just don't realize it yet," he said, then headed toward his pickup truck. Cal shook his head while unlocking his door. This was exactly why he remained single.

Cavanaugh looked up at the large brick building and wondered what had gone wrong. Everything was going great, she was vibing him, he was vibing her, and then all of a sudden, without any notice, she stopped taking his calls. No justification given.

Unfortunately, by the time he realized what was going on, he was entrenched in negotiations with the truckers' union. The union leaders were threatening to strike, and with the murder investigation hanging over his head, SJT stock was already taking a beating. A strike would have been disastrous, so the group had stayed at the negotiation table almost day and night for three weeks, finally coming to a mutually satisfying conclusion early yesterday. Up until then, it had been impossible to get away. In fact, it was Thursday, and he had to be back by Monday to sign the finalized contracts.

Cavanaugh's first instinct was to go charging in,

demanding an answer as to why she'd blown him off for the past two weeks. Then he thought that maybe that was why she was avoiding him. She had told him once that he was too forward; he'd thought at the time she was joking. Maybe he was coming on too strong. But he was finding it hard not to. He liked everything about her.

The light whispers and strange tension in the air that suddenly came over the room told Marty he had arrived long before she heard his sultry voice behind her. She stuck the dirty mop back into the bucket of water and turned to face him. One look at him and her legs became weak. She toyed with the mop handle. He smelled so good, she was finding it hard to stay focused on the task at hand. How was she supposed to do this?

"I deserve an explanation for why you've stopped taking my calls."

Marty's head shot up to search his eyes. She had never heard him sound so stern before. "I think you already know the answer," she said.

"No. You're going to have to say it."

"I didn't want to believe it," she whispered. "When Dina told me you were under investigation, I didn't want to believe it."

"Hold up! Dina told you I was under investigation."

"Only because I asked her to look into your background, to—"

"You what?!"

"I needed to know the truth, Cavanaugh. The truth *you* refused to tell me."

The silence that fell over the room was stifling.

"The point is," she continued, "that despite what she told me, I still didn't believe it. I didn't want to believe it."

"So, what now?" Cavanaugh began to pace. "First, you

accuse me of being a drug dealer, and now what? An embezzler, and arsonist?" He raked his fingers through his hair while continuing to pace.

"A murderer." She spoke the word so softly he barely heard her. But he did, and it stopped him dead in his tracks.

He felt as if all the air had been taken out of his lungs. "A what?"

"I know about the attorney at Stanton and Dowel. I know about your involvement. I know everything," she said.

"So what? You think I killed a man?" Cavanaugh was feeling heated. This investigation had cost him many nights of sleep, several millions of dollars in lost profits and the respect of many of his peers. He refused to allow it to take Marty away from him too.

He stood with his legs parted, his fist balled at his side. All the frustration and anger of the past few months had culminated into this moment, into the faith of this one woman. Her answer would determine his fate. Would he continue to fight or give in to the guilt the world had assigned him?

"Answer me, Marty. Do you think I killed a man?"

She allowed herself to look on his handsome face once more, knowing it was probably one of the last times she would be able to enjoy the elegant beauty of his features. Of course, he was no murderer. She had been insane to even consider it.

"No. I know you didn't kill anyone."

He sighed in relief, feeling as if a ton had been lifted from his shoulders. Her trust, her confidence were the only weapons he needed to battle the demons that would come for him.

He leaned forward to kiss her, pausing with his lips just inches from hers. He looked into her soft brown eyes, so open, so loving. There was peace in those eyes, and he desperately needed that.

"What do you want from me, Cavanaugh?"

"I want you," he slid his large hands along her soft face, "that's all I've ever wanted."

Marty felt the room spinning as his large hands came against the small of her back. She found herself pressed hard against his rock-solid chest. The feel of his warm mouth on hers was electrifying, awakening every nerve in her body. He kissed her with a passion as intense and vibrant as life itself. It was demanding, and revealed all the hunger and desperation he had fought to hold back over the past few weeks.

This was the real Cavanaugh, the one who scared her to the bone. The Cavanaugh who haunted her dreams. She would awake breathless and in a pool of her own sweat. This was the Cavanaugh she feared losing herself to completely, and she would, if she allowed him to get inside her soul any deeper than he already was.

"You have no idea how much I need you," he whispered against her skin.

"No." She pushed hard against him, but he held tight. The strength of his hold frightened her. She pushed again. "Please, Cavanaugh. Let me go."

"I can't," he cried against her neck. "I wish I could, but I can't."

"Let her go, man," Tommy called from the doorway. When Cavanaugh had arrived, Marty's team scattered to give the troubled couple some time alone, but hearing her cry out had brought every one of them back.

Cavanaugh turned to find himself facing a wall of flesh. Ten or more men stood shoulder to shoulder, fully prepared to protect one of their own. For only an instant, he considered dragging Marty out of there with him, unable to accept leaving her behind and possibly lost to him forever. Seeing the insanity of his idea, he finally released her.

"I love you, Marty." His dark eyes were fiery with his unspent passion. His chest was pounding with the beating of his erratic heart.

Marty realized she had never really seen him before, this savage part of him that he reined in so well. Heading toward the entrance, he pushed his way through the wall of men.

Marty watched him go before collapsing in the nearest chair she could find. The guys crowded around, all eager to be certain she was physically okay. Her whole body was trembling, but not with the kind of fear they thought. This was a different fear. This was like the moment an addict realizes she's addicted to her drug of choice. She was fully and completely strung out on Cavanaugh Saint John, and far worse was that he knew it too.

She saw it in his eyes, a kind of possessiveness. And she knew he would return to collect what he believed belonged to him. She put her head in her hands, terrified that she would never have the strength to push him away again.

Ten

Marty was packing her bag to leave when Cal walked in with an armful of white roses. She looked up briefly and shook her head.

"Right on schedule," Cal chuckled, placing the wrapped bouquet on the small table next to her bed. There were already two vases full on the tiny nightstand.

"Take those to Andrea. I don't have room for them," she said, folding her favorite nightshirt and shoving it down into the bag.

"I've already taken her two dozen this week," he laughed. "In fact every wife or girlfriend in this unit has received flowers this week. Why don't you just talk to him?"

She zipped her bag, and slipped her long arms into her leather jacket. "There's nothing to say."

Cal grabbed both her hands forcing her to stop and face him. "This is me, remember?"

She avoided his eyes. Her friend knew her too well. "Cal, it's over. That's all there is to it."

"If you didn't feel anything for him, you'd throw these things away, not give them away. And you only give them away because you ran out of room yourself."

Marty couldn't help being amused. Cal was so rarely serious. She pulled her hands away, and placed them firmly on her hips. "Well, thank you, Dr. Freud."

"Yeah, yeah, you got jokes, but you know I'm right." He turned to walk out.

"Hey," she called after him. "Speaking of romance, how's things with Andrea?"

He slid his foot across the floor, embarrassed by his feelings for the pretty nurse. "She's all right," he said, unable to hide the small smile that formed on his lips. "It's only been a few months, it's still new."

Marty picked up her overnight tote, as her eyes took on a dreamy state. "You'd be surprised what could happen in a few months."

Shoshana turned the vacuum cleaner off and listened. She heard it again, the faint knocking at the front door.

"Coming," she called, setting the still-warm machine to the side. She opened the door to see Marty standing with a small tote hanging from her shoulder.

"Can I crash here for a few days?" She was already pushing past into the house.

Shoshana closed the door behind her. "Forget to pay your rent?"

"Ha, ha," Marty said, flopping down on the chenille-covered couch.

Shoshana came over and sat down next to her sister, regretting it the moment she did. She hadn't been able to rise from the couch unassisted in over a month.

"He just won't stop calling."

Shoshana sat watching her sister, knowing this was not the time for one of her flippant remarks. Marty just needed some support. She sat back, deciding that if she had to be trapped on the comfortable couch, she might as well enjoy it.

"Talk to me," she yawned.

Marty felt a small smile in the corner of her mouth. "Am I disturbing your nap time?"

"As a matter of fact you are, but since you're here, talk." Shoshana interlaced her fingers across her wide stomach.

"I don't know what to do," Marty confessed. "I know he's no good for me, but I still want him. Am I crazy?"

Shoshana held up her hand. "Okay, let's start at the beginning. Exactly what did he do to be thrown away so quickly?"

Marty furrowed her eyebrows in confusion. "Shoshana, the man is being investigated for murder. He could go to jail."

"I know you're not believing that crap on the news, are you?"

"Of course not. I know he didn't kill anyone, but he lied to me from the beginning. What kind of future can I have with a man who would hide something like that from me?"

"That depends on why he lied."

Marty shook her head furiously and held to her own convictions. "No. There is no excuse, no reason good enough to explain that."

"Okay. What if it was the other way around?" Shoshana decided to try a different approach. "If you were a suspect in a murder, and you'd just met this great guy. You really liked him, and wanted to keep the relationship going. Would you have told him?"

"Of course," Marty answered without hesitation.

"How?"

"What?"

"Exactly how would you tell him?" Shoshana's mouth twisted in cynicism. "Hello, I'm Marty, nice to meet you. By the way I'm being investigated for embezzling money from my company, killing the attorney who discovered it, and then starting a fire to cover it up. Would you like to go out to dinner sometime?"

"Don't be ridiculous."

"I could say the same to you."

"Wait a minute." Marty was feeling more than a little silly under her sister's scrutiny. "You're supposed to be on my side."

Shoshana sat up. "Don't ask my opinion if you don't want the answer."

"He could've told me, Shoshana. He could've trusted me." Marty found herself doubtful for the first time in a week. "He didn't even give me the chance to try and understand. He just assumed I couldn't handle it!"

Shoshana sat watching her sister's temper tantrum like a patient parent. A light went on in her head. "That's what this is really all about, isn't it?"

Marty swung around, still glaring. "What are you talking about?"

"You're hurt that he didn't trust you enough to tell you the truth." Shoshana knew how important trust was to her sister. Being a firefighter, Marty's very life depended on her confidence in her team members. It defined the level of a relationship. For Marty, Cavanaugh's trust was essential to their future, and his lack of it was like a death sentence.

Marty sank down beside her sister on the couch, and laid her head against her shoulder. "Why didn't he tell me?"

"Here's a crazy idea: how about asking him?"

Cavanaugh sat in his car watching the children playing in the park. His fingers tapped nervously on the leather-covered console. The melancholy sound of Maxwell's "This Woman's Work" was coming out of the CD player.

Then he noticed it, the first drop of rain falling against the window. Then another, then another, until they were coming down in a steady stream. He watched parents scurrying to get their children back into the cars before they were soaked. How he wanted that life, and during his brief relationship with Marty he had started to hope for the impossible.

And he had thought they were moving that way until she stopped talking to him completely. Being raised in the shadow of his mother's insanity, he had always thought normality was something he would never experience. But those few short months with Marty had been nothing but pure bliss. The simplest things could bring a smile to her lovely face. Everything from a grand night out to the tiniest trinkets. Tokens that would have made other women turn up their noses.

It had been embarrassing to admit to Marty that the first time they went to the movie theatre was the first time he had ever been inside one of the large auditoriums. So as a gift to her, he had the tickets mounted and framed on a small silver plaque to commemorate their date. She absolutely loved it. The women he had known before wouldn't have wanted the simple plaque unless it had been trimmed in jewels.

He looked up briefly as a light blue Dodge Caravan pulled into the now-empty parking lot, but he paid no real attention to it. Marty drove a white Volkswagen Jetta. When she had called and asked him to meet her, he couldn't believe it. After almost three weeks of trying, he had almost given up hope, although, he realized the fact that she wanted to meet in a public place still did not bode well.

The blue van pulled in a few spaces away from his BMW and the window rolled down. Cavanaugh saw a woman who looked a lot like Marty sitting behind the wheel, but it wasn't her. It took only a moment for his mind to understand. He reached behind the seat and grabbed his spare umbrella, then hopped out and ran over to the mini van.

"Hi, Shoshana," he greeted the woman behind the steering wheel.

She nodded sternly, and he realized Marty had brought a chaperone.

"I know you wanted to talk in the park, but considering it's raining, can we sit in my car?" He looked around Shoshana to Marty, hoping she couldn't see through his deception. The rain had little to do with his reasons for wanting to get her into his car. He was still certain that if he could just get close to her again, light the spark that they both felt in the firehouse, she would come to her senses and realize they belonged together.

Marty hesitated, knowing full well what he was up to.

Shoshana squeezed her sister's hand for reassurance. "I'm here."

"I guess that's all right," she said.

Before she could finish the statement, Cavanaugh was already coming around the van. He pulled open the door while holding her umbrella for her. Within seconds they were back in the warmth and safety of his car.

Marty turned in her seat to began stating her long list of complaints, but before she could utter a word he had her in his arms. He wrapped his strong hands around her waist and pulled her to him. He sucked up the air in her mouth, drinking her in. The sensation was almost too much. Her scent, her taste, her feel, the richness of her was overloading his senses.

"I've missed you so much," he whispered against her lips. Cavanaugh felt his heart lighten with every tiny ray of light that peeked through the clouds. Outside, the rain had stopped. And inside, the woman he loved was back in his arms where she belonged.

Marty fell back against the seat, trying to get away from his soft mouth and busy hands, but they followed. "We need to talk," she managed to get out between kisses.

His large hand slid inside her partially unbuttoned blouse, lifting the wet fabric from her skin. Her breath caught in her throat as his fingertips closed around her hard nipple through the thin, silk fabric of her bra.

"No, Cavanaugh." She pushed hard against him, and finally got his attention.

Dragging his eyes away from her exposed cleavage, he forced himself to listen. "I'm sorry, you're right." He took a deep breath and pulled back.

"I need to know why you lied to me."

"I never lied to you."

"You never told me the truth either, and as far as I'm concerned that's the same thing."

"And for that, I'm sorry. I never intended to hurt you."

"I need to know why. Is it that you don't trust me?"

"Baby, no. It's not like that. It's not about trust, Marty."

"Everything is about trust."

"I was afraid I would lose you."

She sat up suddenly. "Don't you get it? That's all the more reason why you *should've* told me."

He just stared at her in confusion.

She sighed. "Cavanaugh, you can't wait until you're in the fire to find out who's got your back. You need to know that going in. If you had any doubts about where I stood, you should've told me the truth, and you would've known for certain."

"Look at what happened when you did find out. You did exactly what I feared you would, you turned away from me just like everyone else."

"That wasn't because of the investigation! That was because you didn't trust me enough to tell me about it."

"So, what now?"

Marty wrapped her arms around herself to brace for the answer to the next question. "Do you love me?"

"I've loved you from the first moment I laid eyes on you, and have never stopped loving you since."

"Love and trust, Cavanaugh. They're the same things. If you want to be with me, you've got to understand that."

"I've made my feelings for you clear from the start, Marty. But I've got to know." He stared into her eyes. "Do *you* love *me*?" he asked in a voice barely above a whisper.

Her heart melted. Marty could feel his vulnerability as if it were something palpable. She leaned forward until her lips hovered above his. "With my life."

His arms came around her again, as he pulled her down on top of him. "I want you so bad," he said, against her soft flesh as his mouth found its way inside her shirt. He nipped at the tawny cleavage, pulling her blouse open even farther with his teeth.

"Cavanaugh, we can't do this here." Marty suddenly became very aware of how exposed they were. "This is a public place." Her heart was pounding as she remembered her sister was sitting only a few feet away.

"I don't care," he groaned, "I need you." His hand slipped down to the bend of her body trying desperately to find the one spot that could change her mind.

She caught his hand and pulled it away. "Not here."

The hungry look in his eyes reminded her of the intense feelings they shared in the firehouse. She knew if she didn't put a stop to this now, she wouldn't be able to.

Thump, thump, thump!

They both were startled at the sight of Shoshana standing just outside the passenger side window. Cavanaugh growled under his breath even as he pushed the button to let the window down. Marty wondered frantically about just how much her sister had witnessed.

"Umm . . . I don't mean to bother you." Shoshana's eyebrows were furrowed. "But I think my water just broke."

Because of the calm manner in which she spoke it took a moment for the comment to register on the brains of the two people in the car. But once it did, Cavanaugh was out of the car in a flash and beside the woman. He opened the back door to his car and helped her in.

"My van!" Shoshana had only come seeking help, not expecting to be hijacked as a result of it.

"Do you have your keys?"

"Yes."

"We can come back for it later." Cavanaugh slammed the door closed and ran back around to get in. Marty was up on her knees looking at her sister over the seat.

"Why do you look so terrified?" Shoshana teased. "I'm the one having a baby."

The two women were laughing as Cavanaugh settled back into the driver's seat and started the car. Marty flipped over and sat down, then she quickly reached into her pocket and pulled out a cell phone.

Turning it on, she called over the seat to her sister. "Where's Erv?"

"He's on the road. Just call his dispatch, they'll find him." Shoshana was struggling to breathe.

Marty dialed the number and left a message for her brother-in-law to meet them at the hospital. What seemed like seconds later, Cavanaugh pulled into the emergency entrance of the hospital and helped the nurse get Shoshana out of the back of his car.

Marty stood torn for only an instant. "I've got to go with her."

"Of course," he said. "I'll meet you inside."

Cavanaugh watched her jog down the hallway after the nurse-driven wheelchair her sister had been placed in. He felt his groin harden at the sight of her soft, rounded form bouncing along. How clearly he could visualize her, straddling and bouncing on him. He shook off his lust and slipped back into the driver's seat, knowing he couldn't stay in the red zone for long.

Eleven

Marty looked both ways to be sure the hallway was clear before pushing her shoulder against the coffee machine. It had stolen her forty-five cents, and refused to give her anything in return. She pushed against it hard, knowing she would pay the price for her assault in the form of a sore shoulder come morning. But it would be worth it, she decided, not to let another one of these thieving machines get away with extortion. And she was certain that's what it was, that the oddly shaped contraption had been constructed, even designed, to steal the money of innocent bystanders like herself.

"Lift the right side just a little." A familiar voice rang out behind her.

"What?" Marty spun around like a guilty child caught with her hand up the candy machine slot. "Girl, you almost gave me a heart attack," she sighed, obviously relieved to see Andrea propped against the wall behind her, smiling in amusement.

"Here, let me show you." Andrea sauntered over to the machine and carefully lifted the thing barely a quarter inch off the ground. The paper cup slid into place, and within seconds it was being filled with the good-smelling, brown liquid. "Sometimes the cup gets stuck, and without the cup nothing will happen." Andrea handed the filled cup to Marty and put her own coins in the machine.

"Thank you," Marty said, and sighed into the steam drifting off the top. "You just don't know how I needed this."

"What are you doing here?" Andrea asked, taking her own cup from the dispenser.

"Shoshana's in labor," Marty said proudly.

Outside of a few distant relatives, all the two sisters had in the way of family was each other until a few years ago when Shoshana married Erv. Now there would be a baby to love and spoil. Marty was very happy that their little family was finally growing.

"Oh, how wonderful. I'll stop by maternity later and check on her."

"Uh . . . you may want to wait a while," Marty said. "I'm supposed to be one of her coaches. She just cussed me out and sent me on my merry way."

"Oh," Andrea said, now a lot less enthused about the idea. "Yeah, maybe I'll wait."

"Erv will be here soon. It's his baby and his wife," Marty said, taking another sip. "Let him deal with her."

Andrea chuckled, only half-listening. She was considering whether to broach a subject she had been wanting to discuss with Marty for some time. But it was very rare the two were ever alone together without Cal. This seemed like the perfect opportunity, and she decided not to pass it up.

"Marty," she started, still unsure how wise this was. She knew how close this woman was to Cal; it was why she wanted to talk to her. But at the same time she feared Marty would run back and tell Cal they had discussed him behind his back.

"Yeah?" Marty's soft brown eyes were shining with satisfaction as she sipped at the paper cup.

Eyes that warm and caring had to belong to a good-hearted person, Andrea thought, as she decided to take a chance. "Can I talk to you about Cal?"

Marty hesitated for only a second, wondering if this was something she should be hearing. "Uh . . . sure."

"Well, we've been going out for a few weeks now, and I'm developing real feelings for him, but—" She paused, looking for the right words.

Marty shook her head, already understanding. Given Cal's wonderful abs and other attributes, he tended to draw his fair share of female companionship, but unfortunately things always became sticky after the initial attraction.

"When you first started dating you seemed to have a lot in common, but lately you can't seem to agree on anything. Whatever you say he seems to have the opposite opinions or idea, right?" Marty's mouth twisted in frustration.

"Yeah," Andrea practically shouted, happy to finally talk to someone who understood the man.

"You say left, he says right, right?" Marty asked, just to further confirm her suspicions.

"Exactly," Andrea slumped down in a nearby plastic hospital chair. "What's up with that?"

"Andrea . . ." Marty started slowly, not knowing exactly how to phrase the statement. "He's trying to ditch you."

"What?" Andrea sat up, stunned and amazed by the simple statement.

"Okay," Marty rubbed her chin. "How can I explain this?" she thought out loud.

"But he likes me, I know he does. I think he may even love me," Andrea dared to hope. She'd seen it in his eyes, in the way he touched her. She was certain it was not her imagination.

"I'm sure he does," Marty confirmed, "which is why he's trying to ditch you."

"Huh?" Andrea said, now more confused than ever.

"Cal has some . . . commitment issues." Marty chose her words carefully. "When he feels himself getting close to someone, caring too much, it scares him, so he—"

"Ditches them?" Andrea said in utter amazement, but at the same time the pieces of the puzzling behavior of the past few weeks were finally fitting into place. It made sense.

"You got it," Marty said, finishing off her coffee.

"Wow." Andrea sat back, feeling more powerless than she ever had. She had fallen in love with a man who was terrified of love.

Marty saw the hurt and disappointment in the woman's eyes, and decided to do something she never had before: interfere. "Do you love him?"

"Yes," Andrea whispered, admitting it for the first time out loud.

"Then fight for him," Marty said, gripping the other woman's forearm. "No one has ever fought for him."

"What do you mean?"

"If you say left and he says right, say okay, right it is."

Andrea felt a small smile forming in the corner of her mouth. "Beat him at his own game."

"I don't know if it will work, but I can promise you, no one's ever tried it."

Andrea squeezed Marty tight, feeling hopeful again for the first time in weeks. Then the two woman parted as Andrea returned to her department, and Marty headed back toward Cavanaugh in maternity. She was almost there before she realized she'd had her coffee, but had forgotten his tea. She turned and rushed back to the machine and this time the machine gave up the goods without a fight. She headed back toward Cavanaugh. She was thinking about Andrea and Cal and anxious to see if love had finally trapped her friend.

By the time Marty returned to the Maternity ward, Cavanaugh informed her that Erv had arrived minutes before and was already in with his wife.

"Good." Marty laughed. "Let him feel her wrath for a while."

Cavanaugh studied her face. "So?"

She sipped her second cup of coffee. "So, what?"

"Are we cool?"

"Yes." She hesitated for one second. "Love and trust, Cavanaugh. They're the same."

Cavanaugh toyed with the rim of his paper cup. "Marty, do you ever think about having children?"

She shrugged. "Sometimes, but in my line of work . . ." She let the thought trail off.

He nodded sadly. "I understand."

She touched his arm. "No, I don't think you do. I would love to have your child. It's just—we would have to be sure." *You* have to be sure, she thought, I already am.

Cavanaugh contemplated his thoughts for several seconds, before deciding to simply go for it. "Marty, I've been—"

"Ms. Williams?"

Both their heads turned at the sound of the cheerful nurse.

"Yes?" Marty stood.

"Would you like to meet your niece?"

Marty beamed from ear to ear. "Absolutely."

"This way." The nurse led the way down a long corridor and around a corner.

Cavanaugh followed at a much slower pace, realizing the opportunity to make Marty a permanent part of his life was lost for the moment. There would be another time, he told himself, but found little comfort in the thought.

Twelve

"Cavanaugh Maurice Saint John?"

Cavanaugh turned at the use of his full name. "Yes?"

Two men were standing a few feet behind him, a tall, muscular white man and a short, stocky black man, both dressed in dark blue uniforms.

"I'm Officer Brown and this is Officer Pulaski." The black officer made the introductions while the white officer stood by. "We would like to have a few minutes of your time, if you don't mind," Officer Brown continued.

Cavanaugh dropped the leather attaché case he'd been holding into the open trunk and slammed it shut. "In regard to?"

"We're investigating an arson fire that occurred approximately three months ago."

Cavanaugh didn't so much as flinch; he knew they were watching his every movement looking for any hint of guilt.

"At a law firm downtown by the name of, uh . . ." Officer Brown flipped through the pages of the small notebook in his hand. "Stanton and Dowel."

Cavanaugh didn't buy it for a moment. He knew the man probably knew the name and address of the law firm by heart. This was their poor attempt to lighten the seriousness of the matter.

"How can I help you gentlemen?" He glanced at his watch. He was meeting Marty for dinner in twenty minutes.

Officer Pulaski interjected. "As I'm sure you know, sometimes we have to collect samples from the victims to compare against evidence we find at a crime scene."

Cavanaugh felt the hairs on the back of his neck stand up. This was the first time they had ever asked for a sample of anything. "What do you need?"

"We need you to give us a fingerprint sample to exclude yours from the others we found on the scene."

"I see." Cavanaugh stood rattling his keys as his mind was working overtime. "Do we have to do this now?"

"Well, that would get it over with," Officer Pulaski said.

"How long do you think this will take?"

"Just a few minutes," Officer Brown said. His attention was on the car. He was examining it with the keen eye of a reseller who'd found something of value, not at all like an investigator looking for evidence in an investigation. Cavanaugh wondered briefly if maybe Officer Brown had a sideline business.

"Okay." Cavanaugh walked around to the driver's side. "I'll follow you to the precinct."

"No need for that." Officer Pulaski ran his hand through his blond hair. "We'll take you."

Cavanaugh's eyes narrowed and an alarm went off inside his head. "But how would I get back?"

"We'll bring you," the kind-looking Officer Pulaski continued. Officer Brown was studying the tires on the car now.

"I think I would feel more comfortable taking my own car." Cavanaugh was trying to get the key in the lock and watch the two men at the same time.

Officer Pulaski's face suddenly twisted into a snarl. "I

said, we'll take you," he practically hissed between his teeth while moving closer to the car.

Cavanaugh pushed the second button on the alarm activation device and the loud piercing noise filled the air. Two young women coming out of the building turned to see where the noise was coming from, along with an older man sitting in his car outside the office building, apparently waiting for someone.

The two officers both took a couple of steps back. Without another word, Cavanaugh slid into the driver's seat, turned his key in the ignition, and peeled away. He could still see the two men standing where he'd left them, as his BMW rounded the corner.

He had tried to talk her out of coming, fearing for her safety. Cavanaugh had only called Marty to explain the situation and assure her that he was okay after standing her up for dinner. The run-in with the policemen had rattled him more than he cared to admit.

If the men were whom they claimed to be, then whomever wanted him dead obviously had some serious connections. He headed straight for the airport and boarded his private plane for Puerto Rico, not knowing whom to trust, or where was safe. He sought out the most secluded location he could, his family's island villa.

During one of their numerous telephone conversations, he had mistakenly revealed his location, and she insisted on following him there. Marty assured him that with or without his help she would be in San Juan shortly. It didn't take him long to realize there was no way to stop his headstrong woman. So, after making her promise that she would only stay a few days, he purchased a round-trip ticket for the following week.

* * *

Carefully, Marty circled the thruway twice, watching her mirror to be certain she was not being followed. Once she felt secure, she pulled into the parking lot quickly, paid the attendant, and took the first opening she could find. She checked her watch. She had less than twenty minutes to board her flight.

Unfortunately, there had been a false alarm that came into the firehouse dispatch just as she was packing to leave, which took almost two hours of her time. Not to mention all the security measures Cavanaugh insisted she take, which took up another large portion of time.

She grabbed her bag and ran into the terminal, sighing in relief to find only four people waiting in line for United. The line moved quickly, and she found herself standing before an overweight Hispanic woman.

"Name?" The woman spoke with a thick accent.

"Martina Williams," Marty answered, still scoping the crowded terminal. She was new at this whole spy thing, and wasn't at all certain she was not being watched.

"Yes, Ms. Williams, I have your reservation right here." The woman's plump fingers clicked away at the keyboard for several very long, very tense minutes.

Marty noticed a bald man near the coffee shop who appeared to be watching her. She felt herself begin to tremble, until she saw another man approach him and the two walked away together. She looked all around her, and it seemed like other people were watching her as well, but she knew her paranoia was just getting the best of her. Why was it taking so long to print a boarding pass?

Finally the woman behind the counter spoke. "Aisle or window?"

"Whatever!" Marty snapped unexpectedly. This whole

situation had her nerves a bit frayed. She closed her eyes and took a deep breath. "Window, please."

The woman's eyes narrowed and her typing slowed down. Marty pursed her lips, realizing she was being punished for her outburst. After several seconds, a long ticket came out of a machine sitting to the side of the computer.

"Any bags to check?" The woman's tone was much less friendly.

"No, just one carry-on."

"Here you go," she said, handing Marty the ticket. "Have a nice flight."

Marty smirked tightly and turned away, knowing the woman didn't mean it.

The line of people boarding in front of her was moving very quickly, and she was thankful for that. She had walked up and down the narrow aisle several times, and did not see seat 4F. She showed the ticket to the flight attendant, seeking direction.

"Up the stairs and down to the front." The woman pointed, then quickly moved on to the man standing in line behind her.

Marty climbed the circular stairwell and felt as if she were walking into a different world with wide aisles and spacious seats. Even the air smelled better.

"So this is first class?" Marty said, not realizing she had spoken her thought out loud.

"Hello." A redheaded woman noticed her standing in the aisle looking lost. "First timer?" The pretty woman chuckled and tossed her hair over her shoulder.

"Is it that obvious?" Marty asked, still looking for 4F.

"Yes, but trust me honey . . ." The woman took a sip from the wineglass she was holding loosely between her fingers. "You'll get used to it."

* * *

Marty stood looking in both directions as hoards of people dressed in radically loud clothing and big floppy hats moved about her. Expensive cameras hanging from the neck of every fifth person practically screamed "tourist" to the local con men.

She felt a bit underdressed in her white jean shorts and hooded Fubu pullover. She'd been in such a hurry to get going, she forgot to ask about the type of vehicle Cavanaugh would be picking her up in. The thruway was bumper to bumper with everything from Fiestas to Hummers.

Unfortunately for her, Cavanaugh was the kind of man who could look comfortable in either. Led by some internal instinct, she looked to her left and saw him standing a few feet from her on the sidewalk. As always, her whole body reacted to just the sight of him.

He looked like a native in his plain gray T-shirt and cutoffs. His normally light mocha skin had darkened to a deep bronze, and his dark brown hair had lightened. How had she managed to go four weeks without him?

She ran toward him and he swept her up in his arms, holding her so tight she felt as if she would suffocate.

"I'm so glad you're here," Cavanaugh said, and kissed her before she could respond. Taking her by the hand, he took off in a light jog. "Come on, I'm double-parked." He opened the passenger door of an Expedition and enjoyed every moment of watching her climb into the raised vehicle. Tossing her bag behind the seat, he got in, and at the first opening pulled out into traffic.

"Welcome to Puerto Rico," he said.

Marty couldn't speak, her mind was too preoccupied with studying every inch of him. She just needed to assure herself that he was indeed okay. He had told her as much in their many conversations over the past month, but she needed to see it for herself.

Sensing her thoughts, he winked at her. "See, I'm fine," he lied. He hadn't been fine since the moment he left her behind in Detroit.

Before long they were pulling into his family's island estate. The long drive leading to the large rose-tinted villa was lined in palm trees. Marty tried not to show her surprise on her face. Cavanaugh had told her long ago he came from money, but she was only beginning to understand just how much. He turned the ignition off, but made no attempt to move.

Marty sensed his hesitation. "What?"

"Please understand." He covered her small hand on the console between them. "I love having you here with me, but if there is the slightest sign of trouble, I want you to promise me you'll leave without a fight." He watched her eyes dart back and forth. She was trying to find a way around it. "Promise me, Marty," he insisted, squeezing her hand tight.

"Okay, okay," she said, sweetly.

Cavanaugh tilted his head to the side and studied her. He wasn't the slightest bit convinced.

Cavanaugh looked at the small clock on the nightstand. It read 11:30 PM. They'd spent the entire afternoon making up for lost time, saturating each other with the pent-up passion they had been unable to share for over a month.

He turned over and felt his heart tug at the sight of her closed eyes and open mouth. She was sound asleep and completely exhausted. He sat up on his elbows, grinning down at his handiwork. "I wore it out, didn't I?" he boasted, more to himself than her.

He kissed her cheek lightly, swung his legs over the side of the bed, stood, and slipped back into his shorts.

Deciding there was no more loving to be had, he headed toward his study.

Sitting in the large leather chair, he studied the walls covered in diagrams and pictures. His mahogany desktop was covered in stacks of police investigation reports and other information.

Cavanaugh had spent the last month not enjoying an island vacation, but trying to get to the bottom of exactly what happened that fateful day that brought him and Marty together. He had found a way to finagle almost every piece of information pertaining to the fire, the dead lawyer Kenneth Stanton, and the investigation into his family's business. But still the pieces did not fit.

That day outside his office, although he still had not discerned whether the two men who approached him were real policemen, he had realized that whoever had tried to kill him in the fire had not given up.

He was certain someone still wanted him dead, but *who* and *why*. He considered it might have something to do with his investigation into the death of the lawyer, but his reasons for being at the law firm that day were exactly what he told Marty: standard followup. There was nothing unusual about it.

According to the official record, a jealous coworker who discovered his boss was sleeping with his wife had killed the man. The murderer, Greg Toberson, was serving a life sentence in Jackson and the case had been closed. He was just finishing up the paperwork, dotting the I's and crossing the T's to ensure Stanton's spouse received her full compensation.

He bit the top of his pencil, deep in thought. Apparently, that was not all there was to it. No, he decided, he must have stumbled onto something he didn't even realize was important. But whomever was trying to kill him did. Now, he had to find out what he knew. Somewhere buried in the back of his brain was the key to this whole thing.

"Have I ever told you how sexy you are when you're thinking?"

He turned to see Marty standing in the doorway, wrapped in the bedspread.

He rose to meet her. "No, you haven't."

"Well, you are," she smiled seductively. "*Absolument irrésistible.*"

"Your French is getting better," he said, as his dark eyes slithered over her. He could see the curves of her long form clearly outlined in the bedspread.

She began backing away from the doorway and Cavanaugh followed easily. Whatever was in the back of his brain would have to stay there for now.

Thirteen

Marty snuggled against his warm, bare chest, just soaking him up. She hadn't realized how much she had missed him, or how completely head over heels in love she was until he was gone. Now she was here lying in his strong arms again, and regardless of whatever unreasonable promises he forced her to make, she had no intention of leaving him anytime soon.

In her six years with the department, she had taken only half of her vacation allotment, so she had more than enough time to help Cavanaugh work out whatever nightmares were haunting him. He had only told her bits of what had happened. She knew he felt he was protecting her by keeping her in the dark. But she'd decided there was little comfort in ignorance when the man she loved was in mortal danger.

"Cavanaugh?"

"Hmm?" His half-groggy answer indicated how close to sleep he was.

"Why did you become an insurance agent instead of going to work at SJT?"

"Long story," he murmured.

"I've got time," she prodded and shook him.

He cracked one eyelid and saw she was wide awake. If they didn't learn to synchronize their sleep schedules this was never going to work, he thought, before rolling over to face her.

"Mostly, my mother," he said, hunching his shoulders. "I just wanted to get as far away from her as I could."

"I know you aren't close to her from what you've said, but to that extent?" Marty furrowed her eyebrows. "She can't be that bad?"

Cavanaugh chuckled lightly. "Obviously, you don't know my mother."

"So, what happened?" She was now more interested than ever. "What brought you back to the family biz?"

Cavanaugh's eyes took on a faraway look. "My father died when I was a kid, but the final stipulation of his will went into effect on my thirtieth birthday."

"Let me guess," Marty said. "He left you the company."

"Controlling interest. Although several of my cousins each have smaller shares of the stock."

"So, that's why you fly back and forth between Detroit and Savannah so much?"

"Yes. Being the primary shareholder I sit on the board, and I try to remain active in the day-to-day business, contract negotiations, acquisitions, and so forth. I feel like I owe at least that much to my father."

Marty watched his handsome face, trying to visualize "corporate Cavanaugh," the level-headed businessman as opposed to the islander who looked incredible wearing only a pair of cutoffs.

"But I like the insurance business, so I still do independent investigations and consulting for different companies in my spare time," he said and yawned. "It gave me a kind of release . . . until I met you." He smiled crookedly. "Now, you give me all the release I need." The words trailed off as his heavy lids finally fell shut.

* * *

"Hello?"

"So, what does he know?"

"Nothing, really. I think the fire was a waste of time."

"So do I, considering he's still alive."

"No. I meant, I don't think we need to kill—"

"I know what you meant. But luckily, you're not the one who does the thinking for us, now are you?"

"So, you still want him dead, I suppose?"

"Of course. Unlike you, I don't leave loose ends."

"I told you, I'll take care of that."

"If you'd done what you were told to begin with, there wouldn't be anything to 'take care of.' Quite frankly, I'm getting a little tired of cleaning up your messes."

"Is that a threat?"

"What do you think?"

"I'm quite capable—"

"No, you're not—but it's okay. You serve other useful purposes. And for those, I forgive your ineptness in this particular area."

"It'll be done right the next time."

"See that it is."

Cavanaugh was trying desperately to concentrate on the white board sprinkled with times and dates. The sight of Marty sitting cross legged atop the large desk, her long, toffee-colored legs peeking from beneath the powder blue silk fabric was proving too great a distraction.

She tossed a kernel of popcorn from the bowl in her lap into her mouth, completely oblivious to the effect she was having on him.

"You know . . ." he began, swiveling around in the leather chair to face her. "I got a lot more done before you arrived." He reached into the bowl and grabbed a handful.

"Hey, don't blame me for your laziness," she laughed, and tossed a kernel at his head.

"Just don't get any butter on that shirt," he frowned. "It's my favorite."

"If you want," she said, toying with the top button of his shirt she was wearing, "I could take it off."

Cavanaugh ran both hands through his hair, trying to shake off the desire she so easily incited in him. "Please don't do that," he pleaded, knowing the silk shirt was all she had on. "I've got to get something done today."

She motioned to the scribbling on the board. "What is all that?"

"Significant dates and times," he said, rising to go to the board. "For instance, March 15th, Kenneth Stanton got into an argument with Greg Toberson, who'd discovered Stanton was having an affair with his wife. The argument escalated until the two men came to blows. Greg Toberson hit his boss over the head with a sharp-edged bookend, and the man was killed instantly. But I don't think any of that is related to the fire or the men that tried to grab me."

"Wow," Marty said, in amazement, "this is starting to sound like something off the 'movie of the week.'"

"Tell me about it," Cavanaugh muttered, before moving on to the next exhibit.

"This is when I arrived and began my investigation into Stanton's death," he said, pointing to another date written in red marker. "At the time I had no idea of Stanton and Dowel's connection to my business, or that Kenneth Stanton was investigating my dealings in Detroit."

She tossed another kernel into her mouth. "How's that possible?"

"They're not listed in the professional services directory at the corporate headquarters in Savannah. And

SJT, which is our primary holding company, is handled out of our corporate office. Stanton and Dowel are only responsible for one small subsidiary, an investment company called Genesis Investments. Apparently it was a pet project of my father's. It never really turned a profit until recently. I never knew it existed before all this began." He turned and leaned against the wall.

"After the fire, I called and asked Harwood Dowel to provide me with the records for the company, thinking that maybe whoever started the fire was trying to cover up the investigation that Kenneth Stanton began into SJT."

"And?" Marty sat the bowl aside. Cavanaugh's recitation was becoming more interesting with every word.

"Nothing. Just the usual stuff. The company is profitable but nothing above and beyond what you'd expect in this economy. Harwood said he had no idea why his partner was investigating SJT."

"Do you trust what this Dowel guy said?"

"I have no reason not to."

"So where does that leave you?"

"Back at square one," he said, and sighed in disappointment before sinking back down into the chair.

Marty could hear the frustration in his voice. She scooted to the edge of the desk and began massaging his tense shoulders.

Cavanaugh turned his head, and kissed the back of her hand. "I feel like it's staring me right in the face and I just can't see it."

"You'll figure it out." She tried to sound reassuring as she played with a lock of his curly hair. Marty paused before continuing. Her mind was on a totally different topic, one she knew he would not be nearly so receptive to. "Have you spoken with your mother since you've been here?"

His silence was answer enough.

"Cavanaugh!" Marty couldn't believe her gentle, loving man could be so callous. "She's probably worried sick about you."

He shot up out of the chair, nearly flipping her back over the desk. "Stay out of this, Marty." His dark eyes were hard and cold. "You don't know anything about it."

Marty felt herself trembling in the wake of his fury. He kept his temper so well hidden, she often forgot he had one. But when it surfaced, it did so with a vengeance.

"Okay, you're right," she said, while coming up on her knees. "I *don't* know, so tell me."

Cavanaugh shoved his hands down hard into the blue jeans causing his chest muscles to ripple as he began pacing the large room.

Focus, girl, focus. Marty scolded herself for being temporarily aroused by the subtle sensuality of his lean body.

"Do you remember telling me that you and your sister always knew you were loved, right up until the day your parents died in the car crash?"

"Yes," Marty said softly, reminded of those two loving faces.

"That's how I felt about my father. He was always there for me no matter what, right up until the day he died." Cavanaugh continued to pace, each step moving him closer to some small dark place inside. He stopped suddenly as if just remembering something. "He helped me start a butterfly collection the summer he died."

Marty could clearly see whatever was going on in his head being reflected in those deep, dark eyes of his. She waited for him to continue, but he was silent for several minutes before speaking again.

"My mother," he huffed, "now she's a piece of work. I swear, I'll never understand how she and my father came to be together."

"Your father must've seen something in her." Marty tried to defend the woman she didn't know, not believing that any woman who spawned a man like Cavanaugh could be all bad.

"Whatever he saw in her cost him his life."

Marty's eyes widened in alarm. How could he make such a simple statement with such a horrific implication, and never even slow his pace?

"What do you mean?" She asked the question, but was unsure whether she really wanted the answer.

He finally came to rest before the large bay window that ran the length of the wall. Marty wanted to go to him, but something about the set of his shoulders told her not to.

"My father committed suicide when I was twelve, Marty."

"And you blame your mother?"

"She may not have pulled the trigger, but she may as well have."

"Cavanaugh, you can't mean that."

"No?" He turned to face her. All the compassion and warmth seemed drained from his face. "You don't know what it was like growing up in that house. Everything had to be perfect. Only the best for Reline Saint John." He started toward Marty and she fought the urge to bolt. "It's a classic tale," he continued, cynicism dripping from every word. He paused in the center of the room. "Boy meets girl, boy works his ass off to give girl the lifestyle she's accustomed to, boy is punished for the rest of his days and eventually understands that despite his financial success, he's still not good enough for girl." He started walking toward her again.

Marty's heart was breaking. Cavanaugh was close enough for her to see the tears in his eyes.

"Don't you see, Marty? He wasn't good enough, and neither was the child he gave her."

Marty felt the sorrow coming off him as if it were something tangible.

"If I died tomorrow, she'd cry because it was what was *expected* of a grieving mother, not because she loved her child."

He finally came to a stop before her and Marty opened her arms, taking him inside. Cavanaugh clung to the woman he loved desperately and allowed his tears to flow freely for the first time in his life.

Fourteen

Marty sat atop the large desk, waiting and watching, but not daring to interrupt his tears. Cavanaugh sat in the middle of the large room, his knees pulled up to shield his face, and his slumped shoulders trembled with the release of twenty years of repressed pain.

Marty knew instinctively that this was the first time he had ever let his guard down enough to mourn the death of his father. Finally his head came up. The surprised look in his eyes said he had forgotten she was there. He bounded to his feet with the limber ease of a cat, as if the past thirty minutes had not happened. He walked to the windows to stare out at the deep blue ocean and dark night sky. Still, Marty waited in silence. However long it might take, he needed this time and her understanding.

"A black and orange monarch butterfly." When he finally spoke it was so softly Marty had to strain to hear him. His broad back was to her, but the trembling had finally ceased.

"What?"

"I was chasing a black and orange monarch butterfly when I heard the shot that ended his life."

Marty swallowed hard, not knowing what to say in response. So she said nothing, and he continued to talk with his back to her. Even from across the room, she felt the painful memories flooding his heart and mind.

"I heard the shot, but I didn't know what it was." He paused again, replaying the events in his head. "I'd never heard a gunshot before."

"Where were you?" Marty's heart was breaking for the man she loved. She wanted to know what he knew, see it the way he saw it.

"A small pond near our house. I used to play there during the summer. There was this really huge willow tree right beside it." He chuckled lightly, remembering. "I used to touch it every day for good luck." He breathed deeply and sighed. Then he turned to face her, leaning against the window. "I heard the sirens of the ambulance, but didn't think anything of it until I reached the road and saw where it was headed."

He lifted his bloodshot eyes to meet hers. "I jumped on my bike and raced home. I knew it was him, Marty. Somehow I just knew."

"How?" She wanted to go to him, take him into her arms and comfort him. But at that moment he needed her ears, not her touch.

"He was always so unhappy. There was . . ." He struggled to find the words. "Something in his eyes."

"How did you find out what happened?"

"When the adults talked, I listened." He hunched his shoulders in a way that suggested the answer was obvious.

To Marty's understanding, it was not. Someone should have taken him aside, tried to explain. A child should not have learned of his father's suicide through eavesdropping.

His dark eyes took on a faraway look. "I remember everything so clearly."

Marty wanted to ask a question, but feared the answer. "Did you see th— Your father?"

"Just the black bag they carried him out in," he said, then lay his head back against the cold window pane and faded back in time, back to a fateful night in August of '78. The memories were so vivid he felt as if he were standing in the driveway reliving the events over again.

As he rode up to the house, he spotted his mother at the other end of the driveway. She was on her knees in a prayer position. There was a police officer standing over her, a large dark-skinned man. The man looked toward the house, then toward Cavanaugh.

Cavanaugh was a visitor from another time watching the events unfold before him. With all the people meandering around no one acknowledged his presence or spoke directly to him. Had the officer standing over his mother not looked at him with such pity, he would have doubted anyone's ability to see him.

His mother looked up only as the paramedics carried the stretcher out with a black, plastic, zipped bag strewn across it. His mother jumped up and raced toward the stretcher trying to reach the bag. And she would have, had the police officer not grabbed her around the waist, and hauled her backward. His petite mother swung viciously at the officer, and pounded against his chest. The man was nearly three times her size, but he just held her and took the punishment in silence.

Once the ambulance was loaded, the officers gathered around and talked to his mother, where she sat once again slumped on the gravel horseshoe drive. Cavanaugh wondered if the sharp stones cutting into her knees hurt much.

He guided his bike to the house, and laid it against one of the large balustrades that ran the length of the front porch. Then he sat on the top stair and waited.

The officers finally loaded into their two cars and drove away. The ambulance was long gone. Still his mother sat there with her knees bearing into the small white rocks.

The servants all seemed to disappear. The sun was beginning to set and the hot summer day was giving way to the coolness of the night. Still she sat. The blanket of darkness covered the city of Savannah, and Cavanaugh wrapped his arms around his body feeling the chill off the lake.

Finally his mother rose and came toward the house. Cavanaugh watched her, studying her storm gray eyes for answers. They were as coolly vacant as always. She passed by him without a word and went into the house.

Cavanaugh chose to stay outside, preferring the cool night air to the coldness of his mother. Besides, he reasoned, his only motivation for ever returning home at night had just been taken away in a body bag. He curled his thin adolescent body against the other side of the balustrade and fell asleep.

He never heard his Uncle Warren drive up, or felt the man lift his slight weight in his arms. He never felt himself being tucked into his bed or the covers being pulled around him. The next morning when the bright sunlight came streaming across his face, he awoke to the nightmare reality he'd escaped for a few precious hours. Cavanaugh resolved in those moments to never feel anything again.

He opened his eyes, and saw Marty studying him intently, love and concern shining brightly in her light brown eyes. She'd hopped a plane without a moment's hesitation to come to him, knowing that she did so at great risk, and putting herself in imminent danger.

How easily she accepted him, he thought. Was she aware of how badly he needed that acceptance? For so long, he'd hid these painful memories, unable to share them with anyone, partially because of pride, but mostly due to shame.

He always felt the only one who could have truly understood him had chosen to place a Colt .45 in his mouth and end his suffering in the only way he knew how. A tormented little boy would always wonder why he was left behind.

Cavanaugh had accepted his solitary existence long

ago, never imagining that someone like Marty would ever come into his life. But just like an avenging angel, she'd appeared through the fire, rescuing him, body and soul.

Suddenly, he stood straight, and quickly crossed the room. Sensing his need for her as he knew she would, she opened her arms instantly welcoming him into them once again.

Quickly, he came out of his jeans, pulling the small square packet from his back pocket. Living with Marty, he'd learn to keep one handy. His mouth covered hers as his long fingers worked to unbutton the silk shirt she wore. Laying her back against the desk, he stopped as suddenly as he began, contemplating this caramel-colored miracle God had given him. He covered himself with the plastic shield.

"I felt so alone, Marty," he whispered. His large hands ran up the length of her body causing the shirt to fall open and reveal her full breasts. "So alone," he whispered again, lost in his own pain.

"I know," she answered, feeling every ounce of his hurt.

"Then you came." His hot mouth closed over one of the upturned mounds and he entered her simultaneously.

In sharing his torturous past with her, he'd somehow freed himself of the demons that had haunted him most of his life. The intensity of his lovemaking was catapulting her as he propelled himself deeper inside her with every powerful thrust. She held to the edge of the wood top and wrapped her long legs around his waist. Lifting her body to allow him easy access, she gave herself over to his savage lovemaking. His body spoke to hers in that secret language shared by those bonded in love, and Marty understood every word.

She pressed his head to her breast, feeding his emptiness with her love. He drove himself deeper inside her, his being stiffening as it consumed her throbbing heat. His whole body quivered with the feel of her body closing around him. Grabbing her by the shoulders, he impaled her on his iron rod, forcing her to take him into the very center of her being, hammering her against the polished wood surface in celebration.

After living in near peril most of his life, having no sense of belonging to anyone or anything, somehow, inside of her, her beautiful, troubled man had finally found his safe haven.

Marty counted cadence in her head to keep rhythm. The cool wind on her heated face felt wonderful. The gritty sand shifting beneath her Air Jordans made every step more difficult, and she loved every minute of it.

Seeing the salmon pink house up ahead brought a cheer to her heart. This was always the best part of the run, seeing the finish line, knowing it was so close. If she could just push a little farther, take her endurance to the limit.

She began taking longer strides to build forward momentum and it worked. Soon, she was breezing right by the large white boulder she'd indicated as the starting point. She stopped short, but her heart kept right on thumping so loudly she could almost hear it.

Marty bent in half to regain her equilibrium, then stood looking out over the ocean. The enormous, orange globe was sitting just on the edge of the widest expanse of blue water she'd ever seen. All her life she'd wondered why people made such a big deal about the ocean. Now she understood.

Feeling grimy but victorious, she stepped into the

kitchen, pulling the glass door closed behind her. For one brief moment, she despised her lover.

There he stood at the stove, stirring a large pot, dry as a bone and smelling like soap. He had the slender, well-toned physique of a swimmer, yet she'd never seen him swim a lap or do any other form of exercise for that matter. His red, cotton shorts molding to his perfectly rounded buttocks sent her mind places she knew her body was in no condition to go.

"How do you do that?" Marty asked, making no attempt to hide her envy.

"What?"

"Eat the way you do, and still look like that." She took her towel off the back of one of the dining chairs and wiped her face.

"It's a gift," he said, and winked.

"You know, I hate you." Her playful tone said the opposite as she wiped down her sweaty arms and neck.

"You won't once you taste this."

"What is that?" She tried to peek into the large kettle, but the steam oozing over the top made it impossible to see in.

"Tonight, you get your first taste of gumbo."

"I've had gumbo."

"No, you haven't," he said with smug satisfaction.

"Yes, I have," she retaliated. "In fact, we had it together month before last at that soul food restaurant downtown, remember?"

"I'm not talking about that watered down Northern imitation," he said, with his soft mouth twisted in disgust. "This is *real* gumbo."

Taking a spoonful of the scalding hot mixture, he held it to her mouth. Marty had only taken a tiny sip before her eyes lit up in surprise.

"Hmm . . ." The muted adjective was all she could

manage to describe the sweet, salty taste that felt like pure joy on her tongue. She quickly grabbed a bowl from an overhead cabinet, holding it out in front of her with both hands. "More, please." She stood beaming like a child who'd just discovered candy.

A hot shower, three bowls of gumbo, and a half bottle of red wine later, Marty sat slumped in the chair looking every bit the sloth she felt like. She covered her mouth as a tiny burp escaped, understanding her well-meaning run along the beach had been no more than a waste of time.

"That was good," she said, realizing that in her greed she had forgotten to compliment the cook.

"I got the impression you liked it, after your second bowl," he teased, still scribbling in the notebook that had become his constant companion during his time on the island.

Marty noticed that his first and only bowl still sat half-eaten, and his wineglass was full. She feared that what started as an investigation was quickly becoming an obsession. It seemed he was forever scribbling new ideas and questions in the spiral-bound book. Yet he was still no closer to the answer than he had been a month ago. And what was worse was that he kept his thoughts to himself. He answered any direct questions she had, but made no attempt to share his findings or theories. She knew she would stay on the island with him forever if he asked, but she wasn't even certain that was what he wanted.

"Anything new?" She attempted to open the dialogue on his most recent notes in hopes that he'd share something with her.

"Afraid not," he said, dropping the pen on the table and souping up a spoonful of the cold broth.

Marty hesitated for a long moment. This was where

their recent conversations usually ended. *Should I push?* she questioned herself. *It's not like he doesn't have enough grief without you hounding him,* her conscience scolded. She decided to leave it alone. *If he wants me to know, he'll tell me.*

"I'm sure you'll find something soon," she said, taking another sip of her wine. "Sometimes, the tiniest bit of information can change everything."

Marty could tell by his upraised eyebrows that she'd said something very important, although she didn't have the faintest idea what.

"That's it," he whispered, before bolting out of the chair and heading toward his study.

Grabbing a couple of crackers from the basket in the middle of the table, she trailed after him, feeling like the unlikely hero. "What'd I say? What'd I say?"

Ignoring her pleas, Cavanaugh went straight to the white board and began connecting lines. To Marty, the elaborate display looked like a giant connect-the-dots puzzle.

"Genesis is it." He swung around to face her, his brilliant smile had returned. "All this time I've been looking into SJT, but Genesis is the key." Just as quickly as his euphoria came, it went.

"I've got to get ahold of my father's files, which means going back to Savannah." His sparkling dark eyes suddenly dimmed. "I've got to send you home."

Marty felt her whole body begin to tremble in revolt. Bringing her hands up to rest firmly on her narrowed hips, she stared at the man she loved in pure defiance.

"Oh, I don't even think so!"

Cavanaugh swept her up into his arms. He knew he should send her back. It was the right thing, it was the safe thing, and all the while in the back of his mind he was praying she wouldn't go.

"We'll turn in your ticket tomorrow," he said, still holding her tight.

Marty's eyebrows furrowed in confusion, thinking that even if she was going to Savannah and not back to Detroit she'd still need a ticket. Still, she held her peace.

It didn't matter, she thought, laying her head against his broad shoulder. She sighed in contentment, certain she would follow him into hell, even if she had to walk there.

Flipping the ignition switch, Cavanaugh couldn't hide the mischievous grin that played across his face. The way Marty was clinging to the dashboard paneling of the tiny Cessna reminded him of a desperate kitten clinging to the branch of a fifty-foot tree.

"Are you sure you know what you're doing?" she asked, with terror in her voice.

"Sweetheart, I've been flying since I was fifteen. I think I've got a handle on it."

Within seconds, the single propeller on the front of the airplane started turning, gaining momentum with every rotation until it was moving at full speed.

"Are you ready?" he smiled, fully enjoying her obvious trepidation.

"What do you think?" she howled, over the roar of the engine.

"Marty," he called to her almost musically as the tiny plane started down the runway.

"What?" she snapped, not at all amused.

"I love you," he said through his laughter as the plane lifted off the ground.

"Morning, Reesy." Cavanaugh strolled through the doors with such a casual demeanor, Reesy barely recognized him. Seconds later, as the extension to his arm appeared, she understood why.

Reesy quickly took in the woman she'd come to call "The Miracle Worker." The young woman's long form was perfectly suited for the rust-colored, wraparound skirt and matching body suit. Her long, curly hair was slighted tinted with auburn highlights, and although it was evident her fresh, girlish face needed no makeup, she wore it conservatively.

Reesy smiled inwardly at the well-worn handbag slung over her shoulder. It matched nothing she was wearing, not to mention being covered with scuff marks. But the young woman carried it proudly anyway. Reesy sensed that even though it was beaten up and obviously overused, it was probably her favorite. She decided that instant that she liked the girl.

"Well, you must be Marty." Reesy extended her hand when the couple came to a stop in front of her desk.

Cavanaugh made no effort to introduce the women. He simply picked up the pile of mail stacked neatly on the end of the desk, and began rummaging through it.

"It's nice to finally meet you, Reesy." Marty took the offered hand. The two women had spoken many times over the phone, but had never met in person.

"Any calls?" Cavanaugh asked, while tearing into an envelope.

Reesy handed him a stack of message book pages. Then, taking Marty's hand again, Cavanaugh headed toward his office. Suddenly, Marty pulled back, slowing his stride only enough to draw his attention.

"Why are you being so rude?" she asked, not caring that Reesy heard.

He was still flipping through his messages. "What are you talking about?"

To Marty's surprise, she realized he really didn't know

what she was talking about. She'd sensed the change in him the moment they walked through the front door of the lobby. There was an air of intense purpose about him; he was all business now.

Marty looked into his dark eyes, so serious and somber. Gone was the twinkle of mischief she adored, or that sultry look that could bring her to her knees.

She was beginning to understand: he was in the zone. She recognized the look because she'd been there herself. That place she went when she was working, when it seemed nothing else mattered accept slaying the flaming red monster.

He was no longer her carefree Cavanaugh; there was simply no room for that man here. No, she thought to herself, *Mr. Saint John* lived here.

"I think I'll just hang out here with Reesy," she said. "Besides, I'll just be in your way in there."

"Suit yourself." He hunched his shoulders and headed toward his office again. Shortly afterward, the door slid shut, and that was the end of it. Marty sighed in exasperation.

"You should see what he's like when you're not here," Reesy said.

"He gets worse?"

Reesy stood studying the woman with her arms across her chest. "Actually, thanks to you he's getting better."

Marty accepted the compliment graciously. "I won't be in your way, will I?" she asked, just realizing she'd practically forced herself on the woman.

"Are you kidding?" Reesy came around the desk, and led Marty to the long leather couch. "I've been dying to meet you."

Marty settled onto the couch, and turned to the older woman. "Okay, I need dirt," she blurted out. She felt an almost instant kinship to the other woman.

"Like what?"

"Well, the family, for starters."

"Girl, there's just simply not enough time." Reesy fell back on the couch. "Let's just summarize it by saying, Pugsly Addams probably had a more normal childhood."

Marty's eyebrows shot up as she wondered, how bad would a home have to be to have someone compare it to the Addams Family? Her mind quickly flashed back to the images Cavanaugh had painted of his father's death. But for some reason, she still could not bring herself to believe everything was as he remembered it. *Things look different through the eyes of a child*, she thought. Somewhere in the back of her mind Marty still harbored the hope that Cavanaugh was exaggerating his upbringing.

The two women spoke like old friends, and knew they would be future ones. Reesy gave Marty a little background on the company, the types of services they offered, and some of their heavy-hitting clientele. She explained that Cavanaugh served as CEO, but each of his first cousins headed a department. The upper level of the building was primarily SJT, but there were many subsidiaries. *Such as Genesis*, Marty thought.

Reesy also gave her the name of a stylist in the area that took walk-in clients, information that Marty was most grateful for.

The sound of Cavanaugh barking Reesy's name through the intercom system quickly broke up their powwow. They agreed to have lunch together later as Reesy picked up her notepad and hurried into the office, and Marty went off to try to find the stylist Reesy had told her about, and maybe, if she had time, do a little sightseeing. She had a feeling she wouldn't be seeing *her* Cavanaugh for the rest of the day.

Fifteen

Toying with her ear, Marty felt a wisp of hair on the back of her hand. She pulled down the vanity mirror just to be sure not a single strain of her freshly relaxed hair was out of place. She patted at the corner of her mouth, seeing a tiny smudge of lipstick that had somehow strayed outside the outline of her lips, then flipped the mirror back up.

That's when she noticed the tiny string hanging from the top button of her houndstooth jacket. She carefully cut the string with her fingernail, then thought to check the collar of her turtleneck sweater to be certain her makeup had not smeared it. She pulled down the vanity mirror again.

"Will you stop fidgeting," Cavanaugh said, with more annoyance than he meant.

Marty didn't respond, just turned her focus to the scenery outside the window. She could feel the tension radiating off him like a furnace generating heat. She knew instinctively this was not the time to pick a fight.

He rounded the last bend leading up to the large estate, at the same time struggling to find a CD in the flip-up console between the bucket seats.

"What are you looking for?"

"My *Billie Holiday's Greatest Hits.*"

"Feeling a little blue?" she teased, hoping to lighten the mood. His darting, coal-black eyes told her just how poorly received the joke was. "Here, let me." She pushed his hand aside. "You just drive."

He placed both hands on the steering wheel, squeezing it so tightly the veins were standing up on the back of his hand. Marty found the CD and slipped it into the player. The melancholy sound of "Good Morning, Heartache" flowed from the speakers.

Marty wanted to talk to him, to hear his sweet voice. But his stern profile told her there would be no light conversation to pass the time this day. Instead, she gave her attention to the forest of kaleidoscopic colors that lined the two-lane highway, everything from deep emerald green to flamboyant orange yellows. Even though it was late autumn most of the trees were still well-covered with leaves.

The winding road had a strange way of shifting directions with little or no warning. Only someone as familiar with it as Cavanaugh could have driven it with such practiced ease. They drove in silence for several minutes before he suddenly turned off the road onto an adjacent path. The elegant sports car handled the bumpy terrain with no problem, but it didn't take Marty long to realize they were not still on the way to his home.

"Where are we going?" Given his reserved composure on the long ride from the hotel she found herself a bit concerned by the change in course.

"A place I used to play at as a child."

The sentiment was nice, but something about the way he said it bothered her. "Why?"

"Because, it's deserted. No one ever goes there." He turned the wheel hard to avoid hitting a tree.

"Okay, and again I ask the question, Why?"

"Because I want you." He turned to look at her straight on for the first time since they had left the hotel that morning. "I need you."

Seeing the lustful look in his eyes, Marty began to panic. "Cavanaugh, we can't do this now." Marty was mortified at the thought of meeting his family for the first time in rumpled clothes and tousled hair. Considering Cavanaugh was not a constrained lover, she knew the evidence of their act would be written all over her.

"Your family is waiting for us," she pleaded desperately, seeing that he made no attempt to turn the car around. "Cavanaugh, don't do this to me," she pleaded again. "Do you know what I had to do to get this just perfect?" She pointed to her neat hairstyle.

Cavanaugh said nothing as he pulled in beneath a large, low-hanging willow tree. He came to a stop, turned off the ignition, and turned in his seat to face her.

Looking out at the small pond Marty knew instantly where she was. A small chill ran through her body as she visualized a little boy with brown curly hair racing across the grassy field in front of her, hot on the trail of a black and orange monarch butterfly. She could clearly see him stopping suddenly at the foreign sound of a gunshot.

Once again, her heart went out to him. She turned, and looked at this man she adored. Searching his eyes for that little boy, she wondered if he would ever find peace, or whether he would be left there to haunt the pond forever.

"Do you have any idea how much you mean to me?" His dark eyes pleaded with her. "You're the only thing of substance in my life, Marty."

The pain in his eyes was enough to melt stone. Something was troubling him, something more than what he'd told her so far. She could feel it like a third body in the car with them.

He watched her eyes carefully. "Do you love me?"

"Of course, I love you," she said, reaching to touch his face. "Baby, what's wrong?"

"Things are different here, Marty. Not like in Detroit. I'm just so afraid meeting my family will change how you feel about me. Everything that goes into that house gets ruined."

Marty could feel his torment in every word. She took his face between her hands looking into his eyes. "Nothing in this world can change the way I feel about you."

His jaw was set in a determined line, his eyes roamed over her face as if he were trying to memorize every detail. Suddenly, he turned the ignition on and slowly pulled from beneath the shade tree, back onto the tiny trail and finally back onto the main road.

Marty sat stroking his thigh as if she thought in some way her touch would provide a small measure of comfort. But if it did, he never acknowledged it. For the remainder of the ride not another word was spoken.

"Hello, mother." Cavanaugh bent to kiss her cheek.

"Cavanaugh," Reline Saint John answered coolly, her attention fully focused on the tall woman at his side.

She smiled, but there was no warmth in it. "And who is this?"

"This is Martina, the young lady I told you about." He guided Marty, toward the wheelchair.

"My friends call me Marty," she said with a smile, and reached for the woman's hand.

"Nice to meet you, Martina." She ignored the hand, turning the wheels on the chair in the direction of the library. "Cavanaugh, I don't know what you expected to find here, but quite frankly, your father had very little information regarding Genesis. The company was never anything more than a ghost corporation." Reline Saint John spoke over her shoulder, using all her attention to push her chair forward.

Marty wondered why a woman with her wealth would not have invested in an electric wheelchair instead of the antiquated steel trap she obviously preferred.

"Whatever you found will be helpful, Mother." He took Marty by the hand. She kept falling behind, looking around at the artwork and elegant furnishings of the eighteenth-century home. The intricate carvings along the walls and the high cathedral ceiling that spanned the large foyer were enough to occupy the mind for hours.

"Honestly, Cavanaugh." Reline stopped her chair just outside the library, and turned to face her son. "First, that ridiculous insurance business and now attempting to revive a long-dead company." She sighed. "If you invested half the time and energy in SJT that you put into hopeless ventures, you might bring the company back to its full potential."

Marty listened quietly. He'd told his mother he was trying to *revive* Genesis.

"Well, for whatever it's worth, here they are," Reline said, gesturing to the stacks and stacks of boxes that covered the plum carpeting of the large library. She turned to roll away, then paused. "I assume you're staying for dinner?"

"Sure." Marty blurted out quickly. When she turned to Cavanaugh, the terror-stricken expression on his face told her she'd answered far too quickly.

They sat sifting through the stacks of rectangular boxes. Cavanaugh had given her a list of documents he needed to find in order to confirm his suspicions. Marty rubbed her eyes. After several hours of staring at the tiny print, the endless rows of letters and numbers were beginning to run together.

Cavanaugh was sitting with his legs crossed in front of

him, his cable-knit sweater pushed up to his elbows. He was gnawing on a yellow pencil as he sifted through manila folders.

"Have I told you how sexy you are when you're thinking?" She watched his reaction over the top of a bound ledger of computer generated financial reports.

Cavanaugh couldn't hide the smile that formed on his lips, remembering the last time she had made that statement to him and the sweet session of lovemaking that followed.

Marty stood up, leaving a faint imprint on the soft leather sofa. "This is your mother's idea of not much information?"

He leaned back on his forearms. "She has a way with understatement, doesn't she?"

She bent backward to stretch. "Why don't you want to stay for dinner?"

"Like I told you," he said, taking the top off another box. "Things are different here."

"Mr. Saint John." A pretty, brown-skinned girl stood just inside the doorway. "Your mother thought you might like some tea?"

"Thank you, Penny," he said, with his head buried in the most recent box.

The girl crossed the room quickly to set the tray down on a mahogany side table, never once taking her eyes off Cavanaugh. She stood beside the table so long Marty wondered if she were waiting for a tip.

"It's good to have you home," Penny said, smiling dreamily at Cavanaugh. Then she turned, casting a steely glance at Marty before leaving the room as quickly as she came.

"Someone has a crush," Marty sang.

"I know," he muttered into the box. "I've been trying to shake her off for three years."

Marty got down on her knees, and crawled across the floor to straddle his waist. "You're not an easy brother to let go. I know *that* first hand."

His impish smile was like a breath of fresh air drifting across the stuffy, overdone room. His soft lips came up to hers as his large hands closed around the small of her back.

"You know . . ." Marty was looking around the walls lined floor to ceiling with rows of books in every size and shape. "This place is not at all what I expected, and neither is your mother."

"Oh, really?" Cavanaugh kneaded the small of her back. "And what did you expect?"

"You made it sound like the place would be off the hook, wall-to-wall Saint Johns. And your mother, she seems nice enough."

Cavanaugh's pleasant expression changed instantaneously. "You spend two minutes with her, and you think you have her all figured out, huh?"

Marty wanted to slap herself. When would she learn his mother was not a topic open for discussion? Remembering what happened the last time she ventured an opinion of the woman, she suddenly kissed him, slowly, passionately, hoping to wipe his mind clear of the past few minutes of conversation. She finally pulled away with a smile. The sudden feel of something solid and hard against her thigh confirmed her plan worked.

When he leaned in to kiss her again, she pulled back, placing both her hands firmly against his strong chest. "What if your little girlfriend comes back?"

"Then I guess she'll get an eyeful," he said while swatting away her barricade of hands. He kissed her as sensually as she had him, but with a lot less patience, feeling his need for her grow stronger with every breath. His large hand came up to caress her breast, his thumb brushing the outline of her beneath the fitted turtleneck. She felt her small tips hardening instantly, and hated her body for so easily betraying her.

"Stop," she said, fighting a seemingly pointless battle against his magical hands. As quickly as she removed one, another appeared on some other more vulnerable part of her anatomy.

"Starting something you can't finish?" His hungry eyes locked with hers in an undeniable dare. Why did this man make her consider things she never would have dreamed of before?

Fortunately, the sound of his mother's wheelchair in the doorway answered the question before she was ever forced to.

"Sorry to interrupt you, I just wanted to see if Martina had any allergies or diet restrictions before my cook puts the finishing touches on dinner." The woman's thoughtful gesture was overshadowed by her disapproving grimace.

Marty jumped up like a guilty schoolgirl. "No, ma'am," She tugged at her turtleneck collar. Although she was still fully dressed, having being caught in such a compromising position left her feeling more than a little exposed.

"I can eat just about anything." Marty laughed nervously. She realized how ridiculous she was acting, but for some reason she couldn't seem to stop. Why did she so desperately want this woman's approval when her own son didn't care for it one way or the other?

"Very good," Reline Saint John nodded, seemingly pleased. Marty couldn't help feeling the slightest bit vindicated.

"You know," the older woman continued, "Cajun foods are very spicy, but that's what makes them work," she said, shaking her frail finger. "Dinner is served promptly at six. I understand you weren't expecting to stay so I will excuse your attire." With that she turned and rolled away.

Marty watched her leave before turning to face Cavanaugh, who still sat with his legs crossed on the floor, resting back on his palms.

"What does she mean, she'll excuse my attire?" Marty looked down at her turtleneck sweater and houndstooth slacks.

"My mother's dinners are a formal affair," he said, rising to his feet without any stiffness.

"You don't mean ball-gown-and-tuxedo formal?"

"That's exactly what I mean." Taking her around the waist he pulled her against him, then kissed her quickly more out of habit than desire. "Let's go wash up," he said, already leading her out of the room. "Unless you want to show up at the dinner table smelling like mothballs."

Sixteen

Marty placed another spoonful of rice to her lips, trying to ignore the piercing stare of the woman at the head of the table. Reline Saint John had spent most of the evening scrutinizing her every movement. Everything from the way she sat to the way she held her utensils to whether she even knew which shiny piece of silverware was the salad fork.

As she was told, all the guests were dressed in formal attire. Beautiful sequined gowns and tuxedos with tails, no less, giving the family dinner the feel of a holiday celebration at the White House. The elegant, rectangular table was beautifully decorated, and alive with chatter. Most topics, Marty could not participate in: family affairs, local gossip. Cavanaugh blended right in to the mixture of brown faces without the slightest bit of effort.

Marty and Cavanaugh had spent almost every available moment of the past four months either together or trying to get together. Her world now revolved around him, and she just assumed the same of him. Of course, she knew he had a life before her, she'd just never stopped to wonder what kind of life it was. But from the light banter that flew back and forth across the table it was a very vibrant one.

Cavanaugh had chosen to stay in his casual clothes—dark navy Dockers and a button-up, charcoal-colored, cable-knit sweater, although Marty had seen a closet full of clothes when they went to his bedroom to wash, including several tuxedos and everything from scuba gear to Gucci loafers. The large box on his dresser was filled with shiny baubles. She felt a slight tinge of jealously. Her man had more jewelry than she did.

She studied his handsome profile as he spoke with his cousin Justin, who was sitting directly across the table from him. There was apparently a lot more to Cavanaugh Saint John that she realized.

"So, Marty," Angelica Saint John began, "Cavanaugh says you're a firefighter." The young woman smiled in a way almost identical to Cavanaugh.

Always eager for new gossip, everyone at the table turned their attention toward the visitor. The pressure was too much.

"Yes," Marty managed to choke out, feeling as if she'd gotten a lump of rice stuck in her throat.

"That's how we met." Cavanaugh squeezed her hand. "She saved my life."

"How romantic." Priscilla, the youngest Saint John, practically screeched with pleasure. She looked to be no more than fifteen, but was already showing signs of great beauty, a trait that seemed to be common amongst the group.

Seven of the ten other guests bore a striking resemblance to one another and were all unusually attractive. They were all first cousins, the descendants of four siblings, they explained. Looking at the husbands of Nicole and Candice, Marty thought, *we're the three ugly ducks in a pond of swans.*

"A firefighter?" Candice Saint John-Pippin's eyes seemed to light up as she finally caught up with the group. She was pregnant, from what Marty could tell, about four or five months, and she seemed to be having a great deal of trouble following the conversations of the table.

"You know, Marty, I do a lot of work with the Make-A-Wish Foundation, and I received a letter just last week from a ten-year-old boy in Ann Arbor who wanted to spend the day as a firefighter. That's near Detroit, isn't it?"

"Very." Marty was already gearing up to say yes.

"Do you think you could—"

"I would love to!" Marty sounded off.

The table exploded in laughter at her eagerness. Marty loved what she did, but the endless stream of misery was sometimes almost too much to bear. The thought of being able to bring joy to a child was an opportunity she would never have passed up.

"Just tell me when and where."

"Cavanaugh," Candice said, smiling at her younger cousin, "I think she's a keeper."

The laughter began again, and for the first time all evening Marty felt comfortable in her surroundings, despite the glaring old woman at the end of the table.

After dinner, everyone moved into the large parlor. Young Priscilla went straight to the piano as if trained to do so, while the adults found seats around the room.

Cavanaugh sat on the end of one of the two long sofas, and motioned for Marty to sit on his knee in the manner of the other two couples. But she could still feel the eyes of the family matriarch boring into the back of her skull, so she chose to squeeze in beside him on the crowded couch instead.

"Priscilla has a lovely voice, Marty," Justin, Cavanaugh's oldest cousin, boasted about his daughter while lighting a cigar. Looking at him, Marty could clearly see Cavanaugh in twenty years.

From what she'd been able to surmise at dinner, the older man was a widower and single, as were most of the Saint Johns. Although Angelica and Tabitha were both in their mid-thirties, neither had ever been married. Marty found it a bit odd that such an attractive group of wealthy, young African Americans would all be unattached.

Soon the haunting sounds of the piano filled the room, and they were all enthralled by the pretty girl with the soprano voice.

Marty never heard the well-oiled wheelchair until it pulled alongside her. She tried to ignore the older woman and focus on Priscilla's music, but found that nearly impossible, given the way Reline openly glared at her.

Never being one to run from a challenge, Marty turned in her tight corner of the sofa. "Is there a problem, Mrs. Saint John?"

Reline continued to stare, taking in Marty's casual appearance and proud demeanor. "Nothing time won't fix."

"I beg your pardon?"

"Surely you don't think you're the first little tramp Cavanaugh's dragged home?"

Marty was on her feet in an instant. "What did you call me?"

Priscilla was the first to notice the scene taking place, and the shock of it was heard in her sudden inability to hit the right keys. Her flawless recital became choppy and strained.

Cavanaugh stood quickly and crossed in front of the wheelchair. "How dare you! Apologize, now!"

"No need to be offended, dear," Reline smiled evilly. "I understand men have their"—her gray eyes quickly roamed over Marty's long body—"urges."

Slowly, everyone turned to look toward the commotion. Priscilla stopped playing. Cavanaugh's handsome face was drained of all color, leaving a contemptuous expression smeared across the stark pale canvas. Almost everyone in the room came to their feet in a defensive posture.

"Aunt Reline!" Angelica gasped. "How could you be so cruel?"

"I'm not being cruel, I'm being honest. I'm sure Martina understands the situation."

Marty placed her hands on her hips preparing to do battle. "And what situation would *that* be?"

"Mother, I'm warning you," Cavanaugh growled low.

Candice came up behind Cavanaugh, placing her hand on his shoulder. "Don't do anything rash," she whispered.

Everyone was aware of Reline's unique ability to bait and conquer. It was the strongest weapon in her arsenal of verbal poisons. She'd used it to control her family for years. She'd used it to destroy her husband, and control her son through guilt.

Everyone in the room except Marty remembered the fateful day Reline fell down the main staircase, and the awesome guilt Cavanaugh had carried around since. Although Reline continued to bait her only child relentlessly, Cavanaugh had survived intact as long as he had by not allowing himself to be drawn in by her.

"Cavanaugh is a Saint John," Reline continued, tearing into Marty, "and along with that name there are certain responsibilities."

Cavanaugh fought to ignore the metal throne his mother used to manipulate him. She could have upgraded to a much-easier-to-control, more-maneuverable chair years ago. But this one was the original, and it served as a reminder of his part in her paralysis.

He fought to control his temper. "Mother, stop this. Now."

Reline ignored her son, and continued to speak directly to Marty. "When the time comes for him to choose a wife, he will require a woman of a certain social standing that you obviously do not possess."

"What the hell do you think you're doing?" Cavanaugh leaned over his mother, fighting the urge to strangle her.

It took Marty a moment to realize the voice she heard was Cavanaugh's. It sounded cruel and biting, nothing at all like him.

Reline sat up straight in her chair. "This is still my house, Cavanaugh, and I am still your mother. It is my duty to protect you from gold-digging—"

"You may be my mother, but that does not give you the right to insult my friends."

Reline's mouth twisted in a leer, and her eyes cut to Marty. "Is that what she is? Your—*friend?* Well." She sat back in her chair. "It seems my concerns were unfounded."

Marty wanted desperately to disappear at that moment. The implication of the word "friend" was undeniable, and it gave voice to all the things Marty herself had considered. He hadn't called her his girlfriend, or even his woman; nothing so permanent.

Marty felt the room spinning. The carvings along the wall fell in and out of focus. The image of Cavanaugh's sweet smile as he ran along the beach in Puerto Rico played like a movie in her head. She could see the sun reflecting off his tanned body as he bent to splash water on her. She could hear his wonderful laughter as he dodged her attempt at revenge. And she knew she would never be that happy again.

"She may be your mother, Cavanaugh, but she's not mine." Marty stormed toward the doorway with Cavanaugh right on her heels.

Right behind him were Nicole, Justin, and then Angelica, until the entire Saint John clan was moving down the corridor behind Cavanaugh.

"Marty!" He caught up with her as she rounded the corner leading to the front foyer, but she simply pushed him aside. "Don't you see? This is exactly what she wants to happen."

Marty understood that by leaving she was playing right into Reline Saint John's cruel hands. But how could she stay, knowing what she had believed to be the love of a lifetime was nothing but a passing fling for him? Marty had her doubts all along, but to have them spoken aloud, and then confirmed by Cavanaugh himself. . . . She could no longer live in denial. In one fell swoop the evil woman had destroyed the best thing that ever happened to her. Somewhere in the back of her mind, Marty had always known she wasn't good enough for him, but going to his mother's house proved it.

"You were right, Cavanaugh, about this place, your mother, everything." Marty fought to hide the tears swelling in her eyes. "Ruined. Isn't that the word you used?"

"Please, let's just go somewhere and talk." He hated the way his voice cracked, but he'd never been so terrified in his life. All his life, his mother had managed to destroy the things he loved most. And it looked as if her perfect record would stand.

"Cavanaugh, let her go, man," Justin said, trying to block the other man's path. "Maybe she just needs some time alone."

Cavanaugh ignored his cousin and pushed forward. Time. *Time for what?* Time to decide she wasn't in love with him? Time to realize that marrying him would be attaching herself to his insane mother? No, Cavanaugh decided, the last thing he would give her was time alone with her thoughts.

Thanks to Justin, Marty had managed to get a few feet away from him again. "Marty, wait!" For some unknown reason, it was critically important that he catch her before she reached the front door. Through some inborn knowledge, Cavanaugh understood that this was a turning point in their relationship. This moment would make or break them forever.

In the background, he heard his mother howling his name. She seemed to be making some kind of demand, but he couldn't have cared less. He would deal with her later. Other than catching Marty, he was oblivious to everything around him, even the scurry of the staff as they rushed to clear a path, yet stay close enough to witness the show.

The only thing that slowed him was the faintest cry of Candice as she bent over holding her rounded stomach. Cavanaugh rushed to his cousin's side, but her husband, Tony, was already there.

"Are you all right?" Cavanaugh's dark eyes were sparking with the heated emotions coursing through his body. Rage and fear battled inside him. Everyone gathered around Candice to be certain she was okay.

Candice straightened again. "Yes, I'm fine," she said, after several tense moments. "Go," she whispered to her cousin, "catch her before it's too late."

It already was. The heavy, wood door stood gaping. Cavanaugh shot out onto the horseshoe drive as quick as a bullet, but it was still too late. Just as his foot hit the gravel road, his BMW peeled away. All he could make out in the haze of dust was the faint impression of the taillights disappearing into the night.

A strange hush fell over the room as Cavanaugh reentered the house. He simply reached into his pocket and took out his cell phone. He turned his back to the crowd of sad faces, and dialed the number to Marty's cell phone.

He continually tried to reach her from the moment she drove away until well into the night, knowing she was probably still too angry to answer. But in repeatedly typing her name, he used the caller ID on the phone to convey the only message he could send to her. *I love you, Marty.* He knew she would understand his code. He only hoped she would respond.

Cavanaugh paced his bedroom floor fighting the urge to confront the woman sleeping only doors from him. He paced the length and width of the large suite, fighting to tamp down his anger and frustration. Reline Saint John had moved her family members around like pieces on a chessboard for most of their lives. But he'd always believed that once he became a man, turned twenty-one, and had access to his trust fund, he'd finally be free of her. But clever, resourceful Reline didn't think that way. What she couldn't control through money, she controlled through guilt. If he didn't know better, he could believe she fell down those stairs on purpose.

And now, she'd managed to take away his one chance for happiness, the one woman in the world who could accept and love him with all his troubles. If he didn't stop her now, he never would. He swung open his bedroom door, and found Tony standing on the threshold.

"What are you doing here?" he asked, startled by the man's appearance.

Tony folded his arms over his chest. "Stopping you from doing something you'll regret."

Cavanaugh's jaw set in a determined line. "I have to stop her now, Tony. I can't let her keep making a mess of my life."

"Man, don't you get it! Marty's gone. The house is in chaos. This is just what Aunt Reline was going for. Don't play into her hands any more than we have. Just let it go for now. I promise you'll feel differently in the morning."

Cavanaugh, being too broken-hearted and too tired to fight, simply conceded, knowing his cousin-in-law had a point. They had indeed played right into his mother's hands.

Not being born a Saint John, Tony Pippin had a unique perspective on the whole family situation, including the maternal head. He had seen right through Reline from the moment he met her, and like every other outsider, she'd tried to chase him off.

But Reline had misjudged Tony's love for Candice, and the miscalculation had almost cost her a relationship with her favorite niece. Realizing the man was a permanent part of Candice's life, she finally welcomed him into the family, as if the yearlong war she had declared on him had never happened.

Much the same had occurred with Donald, Nicole's husband. Tony considered himself and Donald survivors of the "Reline Plague." With such a rare collection of single beauties, such as Angelica and Tabitha, he'd watched victims come and go. They were all eager young brothers, who thought love would be enough to sustain their relationships with the young women.

Tony had known the moment he looked into Reline's stormy gray eyes that he was in for the fight of his life. He took up his battle stance, and seven years later, he was still standing. Not only standing, he was flourishing, and so was his growing family.

Poor Donald had not faired as well; Reline was still well able to get under his skin. Tony guided the younger man as much as he could, but being the only non–Saint Johns, they were constantly treated as outsiders. Both men had fought to hold their marriages together in a family controlled with an iron fist by their chair-bound ruler, and neither had any intention of giving their women up.

Tony's heart constantly went out to Cavanaugh, who seemed to be the greatest victim of the Reline Plague. Tony had only been a part of the family seven years, and considering what he'd seen in those years, he could only imagine the torment the young man must have suffered growing up under her. It seemed every time he came close to finding the slightest bit of happiness, she would blow her dragon's breath on it and scorch it to hell. Just as she'd done tonight.

After everything settled down, Reline had the audacity to try and claim no responsibility in Marty's decision to leave earlier that evening, stating the girl's own insecurity forced her to flee. But Tony knew only a fool would believe that, and Cavanaugh was no fool.

Tony was right. By morning, Cavanaugh was feeling much different. Through his untimely death, Graham Saint John had made his son one of the most powerful black men in the country. And now, it was time to stop being a victim and start wielding some of that power.

He had awakened at the crack of dawn and began researching the questions he needed answers to. A few hours later, he showered, shaved, and dressed, feeling much better than he had the night before.

By the time he entered the hallway outside his bedroom, the house was alive with activity. He heard someone knocking at the front door below, but wondered only briefly who would be calling at such an early hour.

"Morning, Cavanaugh," a cheery voice called.

He turned to see Priscilla looking fresh and vibrant as only a fifteen-year-old could at eight in the morning.

The events of the previous night were already forgotten, relegated to their status of less importance. Her mind was already on to new things, clothes, boys, and driving lessons, which was the concern that drew her to Cavanaugh's door so early.

Cavanaugh kissed his younger cousin on the cheek. "Morning, sweetheart," he said, heading toward the stairs. "How'd you sleep?"

"Better than you, I'll bet," she huffed.

Cavanaugh glanced to the side and found a pair of dark brown eyes watching him sympathetically. "I'm okay, really."

"I can't believe Aunt Reline would say all those cruel things."

"I'm used to it."

"So you're okay? Really?"

Cavanaugh smiled to himself hearing the request for confirmation. She needed to be sure he was okay before she asked whatever selfish thing she wanted from him.

"Yes. Really. What do you want?"

"Want?" Her eyes widened in offense, but her playful smile gave her away. "I just wanted to be sure you were—"

"I'm leaving for Detroit today."

"Teach me to drive!" she blurted out.

He spun on his heels. "What?"

"Not drive, really, just parallel parking and highway merging."

Coming down the stairs just then with Priscilla trailing on his heels in the same manner she'd trailed after him from the time she could walk, Cavanaugh saw Tony speaking with a sheepish-looking courier at the front door. Cavanaugh knew this must have been his first stop of the morning as he watched Tony sign for the small envelope.

"Please!" Priscilla batted her eyelashes shamelessly, and used every feminine wile at her disposal.

"If and when I get my car back . . ." Cavanaugh paused on the step wondering if he was insane to commit to what she was asking. "I'll consider it."

"Please, Cavanaugh!" Priscilla continued, not satisfied with the vague answer. "I've already been practicing on Daddy's jeep, and I have almost everything down except parallel parking and highway driving."

"Maybe," he continued, watching Tony examine the envelope.

"Why not?!" Priscilla whined, practically stomping on the polished wood stairs.

"If your own father won't take you on the highway, I'm inclined to believe maybe I shouldn't either."

"That's just because Daddy's a big chicken!" she huffed.

"Hey! Watch that, missy!" Justin said, coming up behind her on the stairs.

"Cavanaugh, I want you to teach me, you're the best driver in the family," she cooed.

Cavanaugh wasn't the slightest bit impressed by the flattery. "We'll see," he said, heading toward Tony. Cavanaugh caught a glimpse of the bulky envelope with his name on it. "What's that?"

Tony handed him the envelope. "This just came for you."

Tony and Justin exchanged a knowing look, but Priscilla, who was oblivious to anything but her own desire to find a driving instructor, continued to berate her cousin.

"Think of me as the daughter you'll have someday. This is just practice for you, too!" she said, in a voice that was part girl, part woman.

"Uh, come on, honey, let's get some breakfast." Justin maneuvered his daughter toward the dining room.

"But Daddy—" Priscilla tried to protest, but her father

already had her moving through the doorway. Tony followed behind, casting one backward glance.

Cavanaugh opened the envelope quickly, and took out the letter and his car keys. He tucked his keys in his pocket, and unfolded the note:

Cavanaugh,

Your car is in the hotel parking lot near the front entrance. I've enclosed your keys, but removed my apartment key. Please do not make any attempts to call me or see me. Consider this good-bye.

Cavanaugh felt as if a bucket of cold water had just been poured over his head. The harshness of the short note said much about what she was feeling. There was none of the sentiment he expected. Marty wasn't asking any questions, nor seeking an explanation.

The note made it perfectly clear. She didn't want to know why. She quite frankly didn't care. Their relationship was over, and that was all there was to it.

When Cavanaugh entered the breakfast room and saw his mother sitting in her usual place at the head of the table, it took every ounce of his strength not to confront her immediately. Instead he went to the buffet table and began piling a plate high with food.

Reline watched her son over the rim of her teacup, waiting as he added scrambled eggs and Canadian bacon to his platter. Then he buttered his two slices of toast. By the time he began surveying the fruit bowl, the anticipation had become too much.

She neatly placed her cup on the saucer and wiped her mouth with her linen napkin. "Surely, that woman did not think you were going to marry her?"

Cavanaugh was strong willed, Reline decided; it was up to her to make him understand that his free-wheeling ways could only be tolerated to a point. He was still a Saint John, the head of the family, no less. She meant every word she'd spoken the night before. The young woman had obviously developed a potentially dangerous relationship with her son. It was her duty to put a stop to it. She rolled her chair back from the table. He may be angry now, she thought, but eventually he would understand.

Everyone else seated at the table continued to eat, as if they did not see the storm brewing on the horizon.

Finally, Cavanaugh turned to face his mother. "This is the only warning I will ever give you." He crossed the room to stand over her. "If you ever do anything like that again in *my* house, you will be moving shortly afterward."

Reline sat up straight. "I beg your pardon?"

"Last night, you said this was your house, but it's not. I checked father's will this morning. The house is one of the SJT holdings. And since I inherited all of father's holdings, I am the legal owner of this house and everything in it. He sneered evilly. "And you, Mother dear, are very close to being evicted."

"You—you can't. I'm your mother—"

"You're also a pain in the—"

"Cavanaugh," Justin warned.

He took a deep breath. "Just so you're straight, Mother. I have every intention of marrying Marty, if she'll have me. But first, I need to get the rest of my life in order, starting here—today."

"You'll choose that whore over your own mother?"

Cavanaugh set his jaw. The key to getting through this was not to allow her to play her head games. "You have one more opportunity to call her something other than Marty, and you'll be moving out today."

She pounded her small fist on the arms of the chair. "I'm your mother, for God's sake!"

Cavanaugh slowly leaned forward until they were almost touching noses. "I'm glad you've finally realized that. But unfortunately, it's thirty-four years too late." With that statement, he turned and carried his plate out of the dining room.

Seventeen

Marty sat flipping the remote control from channel to channel, barely bothering to notice the different programs that flashed across the screen. She felt hungry but wasn't sure what to eat; she had no appetite for anything in particular.

"You know, you could do that at your own place." Shoshana crossed in front of her carrying a full basket of clothes. She sat down next to her sister and dumped the clothes out on the couch between them. "Here, earn your keep," she said, offering Marty a fresh-smelling onesie, before flipping the control to her favorite soap opera.

"I don't like being in my apartment anymore. Everything smells like him," Marty said, knowing it was pointless to seek comfort from her sister. Shoshana had made her feelings on the matter perfectly clear.

"You are about as pathetic as it gets," Shoshana said, holding a towel beneath her chin to fold it in half.

"So you've told me." Marty could only blame herself for continuing to walk into the insults.

"Well, you are." Shoshana continued the attack in her uniquely ruthless way. "Sitting here all, '*I don't want to be in my apartment, it smells like him,*'" she squealed in a terribly mocking tone. "Correct me if I'm wrong . . ." she continued, holding up her hand to silence any rebuttal. "But it was *you* who left *him*, right?"

Marty only sat watching numbly as her sister did what she did best, rip her apart.

"I mean, I don't know what's up witchu." Shoshana kneaded a tiny pink sweater until it was as smooth as having been ironed. "The brotha was fine, and rich."

"Looks and money aren't everything." Marty wondered if she was trying to convince herself, or Shoshana.

"Yeah, but you loved him. I know you did, don't lie." Shoshana was pointing her silk-wrapped fingertip at her sister. "How you just gon' walk off and leave your man is beyond me."

"That's the point." Marty shot up off the couch having had all she could take. "He's not *my* man. I'm just a fill-in until a *real* relationship comes along."

"Whatever," Shoshana continued, not the slightest bit put off. "You were together for over five months. If that doesn't qualify as a relationship, I don't know what does."

The sound of the door opening and closing over their heads startled both women. The sound of heavy footsteps came across the basement ceiling.

"Hey, baby, what's for dinner?" Erv called down the stairs, already opening the oven to peer inside. "Umm, umm," he muttered in approval, "that roast is jumping."

"Get out of my oven," Shoshana called from below.

Erv started to walk out of the kitchen, then paused. "Hey, Marty." He knew she was there because he'd seen her white Jetta out front, but he could've assumed it anyway. She seemed to be there a lot lately.

"Hey, Erv." Marty fought the temptation she felt every day her brother-in-law came home. *Did you see him? Is he okay? Did he ask about me?*

Marty slipped into her leather jacket. "I've got to get going, anyway."

"I thought you were off duty?" Shoshana asked casually, trying to conceal her concern.

"Yeah, but one of the guys asked me to work part of his shift."

"Marty, you can't keep this up, you're working too much. You need to take some down time."

"I need the money," Marty said, already heading toward the stairs.

"For what?" Shoshana called after her sister, but received no answer. Shoshana narrowed her eyes as she heard the footfalls over her head fade into nothing. For the first time in her life Marty was doing something she'd never been able to do: keep secrets from her sister.

Cavanaugh stood staring up at the elegant curved staircase that lead to the second-level balcony. He was thinking how much nicer Harwood Dowel's new office space was compared to the small cramped office he'd shared with his deceased partner.

The large foyer was tastefully decorated in eighteenth-century antiques that perfectly suited the renovated historical home. Only the boxes of files and the office equipment that lined the hallway indicated the true use of the building.

"Cavanaugh." The tall, thin, gray-haired man came strolling out of the office at the end of the hallway with his hand extended in greeting. "It's good to see you again."

"Harwood." Cavanaugh took the man's extended hand. "Thanks for seeing me on such short notice."

"Not at all." He stepped aside, allowing Cavanaugh to pass into the large executive office. "Please excuse the mess. I'm still trying to get settled in here." He cleared a large stack of folders from one of the two leather chairs facing the desk.

"Please have a seat. Can I get you something to drink?" He settled in behind the desk. "Hopefully, I'll be able to start interviewing for a clerk soon. I really need some help."

Cavanaugh remembered the young legal clerk serving life in Jackson, the one who'd murdered Kenneth Stanton. Harwood swung around in his chair to the coffeepot sitting on the window ledge behind him.

"Coffee?" he offered, holding up the pot.

"Thanks, but I'm a tea man myself," Cavanaugh said.

"So, what can I do for you?" Harwood reached into his desk drawer and pulled out a box of cigars. Cavanaugh realized he liked the man more every time he met him. He reached inside the box and accepted the rare treat.

"I found some new information regarding Genesis, and I was wondering if you could decipher it for me."

"What kind of information?" Harwood asked around the cigar he was attempting to light.

Cavanaugh opened the long folder and began pulling out newspaper clippings. The piles of crumpled papers were shredded around the edges, and the smudged print was hard to read in some places. Some were smaller than others, but all had similar subtitles: "Million believes Murphy's Law" and "Genesis – Beginning to End."

The articles spoke of a company on the edge of bankruptcy, and a disheartened millionaire who thought he could do the impossible, only to find out it was worse than he thought.

Harwood took each of the articles and let his blue eyes drift over every word, neatly returning each to the pile. Cavanaugh watched the man in silence, hoping to read something in his body language. But if he knew about any of the dire predictions, it didn't show on his face.

"I don't know what to tell you, Cavanaugh." Harwood sat back in his leather chair shaking his head. "This is all news to me. When I got the account the company was clearly in the black."

"Here . . ." Cavanaugh reached under the pile and pulled out another large article. "This one says there was a class-action lawsuit filed by many of the investors who felt their money was being mishandled."

Cavanaugh extended the article to Harwood. "Say's here Stanton and Dowel were legal counsel for Genesis in the suit. Do you remember this?"

Harwood took the article and quickly skimmed over it. "That's not possible. This article was written in 1989, and we didn't begin representing Genesis until 1992."

Cavanaugh's eyes narrowed. Someone was lying. "How did a major newspaper make that kind of a mistake?" Cavanaugh was suddenly suspicious of the man.

"Believe it or not, mistakes like this happen all the time," Harwood said, puffing away on his cigar. "There are very few firms in Detroit that specialize in corporate law. We're one of them. Every local business writer knows our name. Trust me, it happens."

Cavanaugh sat back in the chair, wanting to believe him. "Maybe . . . I don't know," he muttered.

Harwood Dowel leaned across the table. His face had sobered. "I had a great deal of respect for your father. I would never have done what you're thinking. You reviewed all the records for Genesis yourself. Did you see anything suspicious?"

"No," Cavanaugh said, mostly frustrated because he seemed to have hit another dead end.

Harwood sighed. "I wish I could help you more, but all I know is all I know."

Cavanaugh studied the man for several seconds, deciding to trust him. "Do you have any idea who represented the company before you? I didn't see any indication of another firm in the boxes my father had."

"I believe it was a private firm, Andy Carpenter Esq. That's just an intelligent guess, mind you. I once heard your father make some less-than-flattering comments about ole' Andy. I assumed it was based on past business dealings."

"Andy Carpenter." Cavanaugh made the mental note while packing up his folder. "Well, I appreciate your help, Harwood." He stood to leave.

"No problem." Harwood rose with him. "The client always comes first."

"By the way. " Cavanaugh took a pen from his inside jacket pocket and looked around for a piece of paper to write on. "Can you give me driving directions to the Genesis office?"

"Why do you want to go there?"

"Just to verify a few details I found in the records."

"Okay, but I really don't think anyone there can help you."

"Just the same, if you will." Cavanaugh found a Post-it® pack on the edge of the desk.

Harwood grabbed his Palm Pilot from the top desk drawer and quickly pulled up the address of the company, then proceeded to give Cavanaugh instructions based on his best recollection. Cavanaugh thanked the man again for his time, before seeing himself out.

A few minutes later, Cavanaugh was behind the wheel of his car. His mind was split between the tasks of carefully guiding his way through traffic and the conversation he'd just had. He wanted to believe Harwood, but if he were right, then what did the information in the folder mean? He decided he would move forward under the assumption that Harwood was being up front, but still keep his eyes open for any discrepancies to what he was told.

Unfortunately, at this point in the game, he didn't know whom to trust, and the only person he knew he could for certain wouldn't even return his calls.

Marty stood hosing down the ladder truck. Washing Big Red was one of her favorite things in the world, although her cherished chore gave her no joy today. Most of the guys just thought her affinity for the engine truck was a *woman thang.* She never bothered to explain that Big Red was the reason she wanted to join the department in the first place. She remembered as a child watching the big, red trucks come rushing through traffic, the loud siren blaring long before she saw the crimson red torpedo. Cars would hurry to get out of its way because they knew wherever it was on its way to, it was going to save lives.

Marty and her sister grew up in a pretty tough neighborhood, and had it not been for the love and devotion of their parents, they both could have chosen very different paths. By the time she was thirteen, Marty clearly understood that corruption was everywhere from the pulpit to the police department, leaving her little faith in anything. Anything except Big Red, whose dedication to its purpose was clear cut and simple. Get to the scene as fast as you can and save as many lives as possible. By the time she was fifteen, Marty knew for certain what she wanted to do for the rest of her life.

"Hey, baby girl," Cal said, coming up behind her. "I got *Cast Away, Forrest Gump,* and *Saving Private Ryan.*" He tossed the bag of videos on the table.

Marty felt a little smile forming in the corner of her mouth. *Faithful Cal,* she thought. He had to be the biggest Tom Hanks fan in America. Since she met him, she'd watched everything the actor had ever made, at least twice. She could always depend on Cal for a Hanks-A-Thon when she was feeling blue. She turned off the hose and came over to the table to review the selections.

"I see we have *The Hurricane,* also?" she sighed, remembering how well Mr. Washington had toned up for the movie.

"Yeah, that one's for Andrea," he said, unaware of the way his eyebrows furrowed in concern. "She's into him."

"Understandably so," Marty teased, seeing the first sign of jealousy ever in her best friend.

"Let's not forget . . ." He spun around and snatched the video out of her hand. "Denzel Washington may get her all hot and horny, but I get the payoff."

"True, that," she said, laughing, while she wound up the water hose.

Shortly thereafter, the pretty nurse showed up with two large pizzas, which was just enough gluttony for three.

"Hello, all," Andrea called, coming through the large red doors.

"Hi, Andrea," Marty called from where she was squatting, collecting her cleaning brushes and rags.

"Hey, baby," Cal greeted Andrea with a passionate kiss. "I got the movies—"

"The Hurricane?" Andrea asked, her eyes sparkling with excitement.

Marty fought to hide a small smile at the concern that flashed through Cal's eyes.

"Yeah, but I thought we would watch *Cast Away* first," he said, with a touch of defiance in his voice.

Marty continued cleaning up her mess with her back to the couple, but she didn't need to see them to know what was going on. After a long silence, Andrea's soft voice was heard.

"Okay," she said, handing the pizzas off to Cal. "Hey, Marty, doesn't Tom Hanks have the prettiest eyes?"

Marty almost dropped her bucket, realizing the soft-spoken little nurse had gotten clever.

"He sure does," Marty said, trying to ignore the way Cal's two eyebrows had almost crimped into one line, "and *Cast Away* is a one-man show," she added just for good measure.

Cal carried the pizzas up the stairs without saying another word to either. Once all three had a heaping plate of food and drinks, they settled into the common-area recliners. Neither woman was surprised to see the credits for *The Hurricane* begin to flash across the screen. Marty had to admit, she was impressed. She bit into a slice of pizza thinking that maybe Cal had finally met his match.

The trio spent the afternoon watching movies and laughing about everything. Although she never acknowledged it, Marty was extremely grateful. Her best friend and his woman had dedicated their entire Sunday afternoon to trying to help her forget that today would've been her and Cavanaugh's six-month anniversary.

Cavanaugh pulled up outside the small office and looked up at the sign over the door. The simple burgundy and gold plaque read "Genesis Investments, Inc."

He pulled the door open slowly and stepped inside, finding himself in the center of a small room bustling with activity.

A young blonde woman behind the front desk smiled pleasantly. "Hello, may I help you?"

"Hello. I'm Cavanaugh Saint John. Can I speak to your manager?"

The woman's suntanned face turned stark white. "Did you say Saint John?"

Cavanaugh heard the hesitation in her voice. "Yes."

"Just a moment," she said as she quickly dialed a three-digit extension.

Within seconds, a balding, middle-aged white man appeared with his arm extended. "Mr. Saint John." The man was beaming from ear to ear. "What a pleasure to finally meet you."

Cavanaugh shook his hand. He was not the least bit surprised by the man's over-zealousness. How else would a barely competent manager of a ten-man office react to a surprise visit from the owner of the company? Especially considering the owner had never bothered to visit before.

Cavanaugh had done his research on the small investment firm, and knew that up until a few years ago the company had barely turned a profit. It was only a chance turn of the economy that caused that sudden boost. He had looked over the books and corporate notes, and was not impressed by the office manager, Tom Richards. But he hadn't come to clean house today; that task would be saved for later. Today, he needed information.

Cavanaugh leaned close to the man. "Is there someplace we can speak privately?" The young receptionist was actually straining across the desk to hear.

"Yes, yes, of course," Tom Richards said, leading Cavanaugh back to his office. Once they were inside and the door was closed, Tom Richards came around to the front of the desk and propped himself up on one corner. "I must admit, it is quite a surprise finally meeting you in person this way."

"In person?" Cavanaugh asked a bit taken a back by the statement. The man spoke as if they were acquainted in some manner.

"Yes. I mean after three years of telephone conversations it's nice to finally have a face to put with the voice."

"We've spoken on the phone?" Cavanaugh sat straight

up, more confused than ever. He found the slight blanching that passed over the man's face a bit alarming.

Suddenly Tom Richards stood and went behind his desk. Watching Cavanaugh carefully, he sat in his high-back desk chair. Cavanaugh's mind was scrambling. He could feel the other man closing up as surely as watching a door being slammed shut.

"I just mean, you sound as if we've spoken today." Cavanaugh tried to sound casual, but Tom Richards was still watching him warily.

"Oh, no, I just, I never expected you to just show up here this way." Tom Richards continued to eye him suspiciously.

In desperation, Cavanaugh decided to take a chance. "Did you handle that matter we discussed?" Cavanaugh thought the generic question was a safe bet, since most offices of this sort always had some *matter* that needed to be *handled*.

Tom Richards's face relaxed considerably. "Yes. In fact, I thought that was why you were here."

"Well, yes; that, and I have another issue I'd like to discuss." Cavanaugh chose his words carefully, certain that any one of them would betray him for the fake he was.

Tom Richards reached into the desk drawer and pulled out a ledger book. He slowly pushed it across the table toward Cavanaugh, watching his eyes for a reaction.

Cavanaugh fought to hold his blank expression in place. He was dying to see what was inside the ledger, but the expression on Tom's face said he should already know.

"First, let's discuss the other matter that brings me here," Cavanaugh said, feeling ridiculous for having to pretend to be himself. But what had become painfully clear was that someone had been communicating with the man across the desk from him. And that someone had obviously told Tom Richards that he was Cavanaugh Saint John.

"What would that be?"

"I would like to get access to the archive files for the past ten years."

Tom Richards tilted his head to the side. This was not the strangest request his employer had asked of him, but it was right up there. "Sure, but those records are in the basement. I'll have to have them brought up for you." Tom Richards leaned over and picked up his phone.

"No need." Cavanaugh put up his hand to still the man. "I'll just go down there." Cavanaugh wasn't sure he'd fooled the man, and didn't want to risk having him pilfer the files before he had access to them.

Slowly standing, he said a silent prayer before lifting the ledger book up off the desk and tucking it under his arm. When Tom came around the desk and headed for the door, Cavanaugh sighed in relief. He wasn't sure if he was supposed to take the book with him or not, having no idea what instructions the *other* Cavanaugh had left. But *this* Cavanaugh had no intention of leaving the office without it.

Cavanaugh spent almost four hours in the basement of the small building sorting through box after box of files and financial records. There was absolutely nothing that looked the slightest bit out of order. He was further disappointed when he discovered that the ledger book under his arm was nothing more than the internal monthly financial report. Apparently the other Cavanaugh kept a close watch over the office spending. He was embarrassed to realize the other man had done a better job of managing his company than he had. He had left the small firm in neglect for years, believing it to be nothing more than a tax write-off. But someone else had known it was more than that, and had stepped into the job he hadn't. Once again he was left with the same two questions that had haunted him for the past several months: who? And why?

Cavanaugh sighed as he lifted his jacket off the chair and began climbing the stairs. If there had been any evidence of wrongdoing, someone had done a fine job of covering it up.

Harwood Dowel saw her before she saw him. He tried to dart out of her way, but she was coming straight toward him.

"Well, hello there," Dina Johnston smiled, and offered her hand to the man. She fought to hide the confusion she was feeling, not knowing exactly how to say, *"Surprised to see you here, thought you were dead."* So, she decided to say nothing.

"Dina, good to see you again." Why tonight of all nights would he meet someone who had known him for so long?

"Good crowd tonight," she said, looking around at the roomful of lawyers. She hated these associations, but understood the importance of networking in her business. She planned to stay only long enough to make an appearance and then rush home. Dwight would be off later tonight, and their time together was spare and precious as it was.

"Sorry to hear about your firm." She sipped at her wineglass trying to make small talk while scanning the room for potential connections.

"Thank you," he said, pulling at his collar, obviously uncomfortable.

Before long the two stood like a shackled pair of chain-gang criminals not particularly wanting to be bound together, yet neither knowing exactly how to get free. Dina considered it too rude to simply walk away.

"Oh, look, there's Bob Lyon. I've been meaning to speak to him," Harwood said, and looked over her shoulder. "Bob! Bob!" He waved over his head, frantically.

Dina just stood watching his strange behavior.

"Well, Dina, it was good seeing you, but I want to catch Bob before he leaves," Harwood said, then hurriedly moved past her and across the room.

Dina just hunched her shoulders and took another sip of her wine. If he wanted to go, why didn't he just go, she thought, instead of making up that lie of seeing Bob Lyon whom Dina knew was out of the country for the next four months. *I never did like that man,* she thought, as she continued scanning the crowd.

Seeing one of her other old classmates who worked for the prosecutor's office, she moved through the crowd. This woman was considered a serious contender for the next attorney general, and Dina thought those were the kinds of friends she needed.

"Jen!" she raised her hand and waved. The man she'd just being speaking with was already a vague memory.

Eighteen

Cavanaugh stood holding the nightgown in the light, thinking how good Marty would look in it. He could still clearly see her copper skin against the powder blue of his silk shirt; it was the perfect color for her complexion. But he knew she would never accept it. Even if he sent it anonymously, she would know it was him. She'd probably shred it into a thousand pieces, and happily return to sender.

"Can I help you, sir?" The eager saleswoman practically had dollar signs twinkling in her eyes. She'd been watching him from the moment he entered the store, everything from the top of his curly head to the tip of his well-made Italian boots. If she handled it right, this commission could set her up for the next two months.

Cavanaugh toyed with the thin fabric. It was so sheer he could almost see Marty's long, smooth legs beneath it. He rubbed it over his hand, imagining the feel of her soft body against him. He was tempted to buy it just to hang in the back of his closet. To see it every day and let his mind believe for one insane moment that she was still in his life.

"No, thank you," he said, then turned and walked out of the store, still unsure of what had lead him inside in the first place.

"Merry Christmas," the woman called after him, hoping

if he ever returned he'd remember her. She sighed heavily, and returned to her post behind the counter, thinking of the new washer and dryer she'd almost had.

"Merry Christmas, boo-boo." Marty spoke in perfect baby babble, lifting her five-month-old niece above her head. The happy gibberish noise and dribble of saliva that ran down her face was the equivalent to a *Right back atcha, Auntie.*

The sound of Donny Hathaway's "This Christmas" was oozing out of the stereo. Shoshana had disappeared into the kitchen to check on a meal whose wonderful smell had every mouth watering. Erv's middle brother, Paul, and his wife, Janice, were there from Atlanta, along with Marty and Shoshana's great-aunt, Josephine. Erv had gone to pick up a coworker who had no family to share the holiday with, and the snow had started only that morning. Christmas had come to Detroit.

The sound of the doorbell forced Marty to put her niece back into the playpen. She opened the door to a quartet of carolers. Although well-intended, their stoic hymns were completely drowned out by the rhythm and blues Christmas album playing in the background. Marty found it a bit annoying, but smiled appreciatively until the small group moved on.

"Merry Christmas," Janice called to the group, just before Marty closed the door. Marty flopped down on the crowded couch. Somehow the carolers had darkened her mood instead of lightening it. She peeked into her aunt's face, realizing no one had checked on the elderly woman in almost an hour.

"Everything okay, Auntie?"

They'd discovered early in the evening that Aunt

Josephine had left her hearing aid in her small apartment on the east side of town.

The eighty-seven-year-old woman frowned, upset at having her nap disturbed. "What?"

"Is everything okay?" Marty sounded her words slowly.

"What do you mean what's today?" Aunt Josephine had often wondered about Katie's oldest girl. She'd always seemed a bit odd. "Today is Christmas."

Marty smiled to herself, deciding that was answer enough.

"So Marty, what's new?" Paul tossed a handful of table nuts into his mouth.

"Not much," she said, settling back onto the couch.

"I understand you've been stomping in our neck of the woods." Janice's sly smile revealed just how much she knew. The dumb expression on Paul's face revealed just how *little* he knew. Marty made a mental note to talk to Shoshana about her big mouth.

"No," she said, trying to hold on to some semblance of dignity under the scrutiny of the young woman's eyes. "Nothing worth speaking about."

"Who's sneaking out?" Aunt Josephine yelled, startled out of her fifth nap of the evening.

"Nobody, Auntie." Marty sounded the words slowly to calm the older woman.

The door opened as Erv walked in with another man. "Hey, everybody, this is Frank," Erv said, pushing the man in front of him. He whispered in his ear, "Just remember, no cursing."

Erv made all the introductions, taking Frank's coat. When he went to hang it up, Frank stood in the middle of the room, looking like a man condemned.

"So Frank, are you a driver, too?" Marty asked, trying to make light conversation, and at the same time wondering if the sad-eyed man knew Cavanaugh.

"Yep," he managed to say, pulling hard at the collar of his sweater.

"Hey, man, don't look so stressed, we don't bite," Paul said jokingly, but the look on Frank's face said he wasn't convinced.

He took a seat anyway, turning his attention to the broadcast of the Macys's Christmas Day Parade and stealing sidelong glances at Marty every chance he got.

Soon Shoshana reappeared looking flustered and rushed. Only then did everyone realize Erv had been gone a lot longer than it took to hang up a coat. When Erv entered the room moments after his wife, Marty twisted her mouth and shook her head, thinking if they weren't careful little Kendra would have a sibling in no time.

Realizing what she was doing, Marty closed her eyes and breathed deeply. Just because she was miserable didn't mean everyone else should be.

Slowly but surely, Frank began to relax until he was finally making conversation with everyone, especially Marty. He quickly discovered that Erv's fly sister-in-law was a muscle head. She loved fast cars and knew almost as much about them as he did. Soon, they were huddled in a corner swapping stories about the fastest cars they had ever seen, and arguing over the greatest car ever made.

Shoshana continued to disappear off and on throughout the night, insisting that she didn't need any help. Marty was the only one who knew the truth about her control freak sister. Shoshana was like a crazed dictator, and her home was her little kingdom.

Finally, Shoshona appeared in the doorway announcing dinner was served. The small group practically ran over each other rushing to the table.

They took one another's hands and bowed their heads in prayer. Marty took a closer look at the group and almost laughed out loud, comparing her family dinner to a Saint

John affair. Well, she thought, at least the devil's not sitting at the head of our table. Then she closed her eyes and thanked God for another year.

The table conversation was lively as gossipy Janice continued to pick at Marty for information about her torrid love affair.

Shoshana kept her eyes glued on her plate, avoiding her sister's eyes. She'd known it was a bad idea to tell Janice, but at the time she thought her sister's relationship was permanent. How was she to know they would break up two weeks later?

"Come on, Marty." Janice finally tired of trying to be discreet. She wanted information and she wanted it now. "Even in Atlanta, the family is well known. How could you have not known who he was?"

Marty jabbed her fork into her turkey dressing. "Not that it's any of your business, but I just didn't, that's all."

"Oh, come on, Marty." Janice had the tenacity of a bulldog. "Your own brother-in-law works for him."

The table went silent at the sound of Frank's wineglass spilling over. Shoshana and Marty both rushed to help him, but the man just sat there dazed as red wine poured over his faded jeans.

"Erv," he finally said, "can I speak to you?"

Everyone at the table watched as the two men went into the back pantry and pulled the sliding door closed.

"That's her?" Frank asked, practically screeching. His sad brown eyes were now wide in terror. "That's who Saint John was kicking it with?"

Erv quickly looked over his shoulder and attempted to cover his friend's mouth at the same time. "Keep it down, man, they'll hear you."

Erv knew what concerned Frank more than the fact that Cavanaugh Saint John was his employer. It was all the stories they both had heard of Cavanaugh's riotous youth. Unlike Frank, who hadn't met the man in person, Erv was certain most of the rumors were just tall tales.

"Are you crazy?" Frank continued, wondering how he let himself get into situations like this. "Are you trying to get me killed?"

"Shh." Erv was getting more nervous by the moment knowing just how thin the door was.

"Why, man?" Frank pleaded painfully. "Why would you bring me here on Christmas Day, and offer me the one woman who's off limits?"

"I was trying to do you a favor, help a brother out." Erv had never been so embarrassed in his life. He had never imagined his friend could fall apart so pitifully.

"Help me out? Why didn't you just strap a time bomb to my ass? That would've been just as helpful."

"Shut up, man, they can hear you."

"You don't know Saint John, man. He's crazy as hell!" Frank grabbed his head with both hands to still the sudden pounding. "I got to go," he said, still muttering under his breath as he approached the door. He stopped suddenly as another terrifying idea ran through his frazzled brain. "Did you tell anyone about this? That you were hooking me up with Saint John's woman?"

"She's not Saint John's woman," Erv tried to make the man understand one final time.

"Did you tell anybody?" Frank's voice was dripping with desperation.

"No," Erv said, shaking his head. He knew if Shoshana heard even a fraction of the conversation he wouldn't be unwrapping anything tonight.

Frank swung the door open and stopped dead in his tracks. Every eye at the table was firmly trained on the door, dumbfounded expressions on every face. Even Great-Aunt Josephine had heard. Frank felt bad. He'd only come hoping for a good meal, and possibly a hookup that could lead to something solid. And somehow ended up with his butt in a sling.

"Shoshana, please forgive me for interrupting dinner, but I just remembered something urgent I gotta do," he sputtered, all the while moving toward the door. He swung open the front door, then paused, turning back to the table.

"Marty, I'm sorry. I mean, you're fine as hell, but you're just not worth my life." With that statement, Frank Meadows pulled the door closed behind him, and disappeared from the Roper home—and Marty's life—forever.

Cavanaugh circled the block a second time, watching his rearview mirror. Sure enough, a few seconds later the black car rounded the corner. He'd noticed it for almost a week, waiting for the occupant to make a move. But the car just followed him, always careful to keep its distance. It was almost as if the other car was waiting to be led somewhere. Cavanaugh had decided that tonight he would find out exactly who was inside the vehicle with the tinted windows.

He doubled back around to the parking structure and pulled in as he did every night. Entering his secret code, he watched as the black car stopped just outside the structure. He pulled inside and parked in his assigned spot, then reached beneath the seat to pull out a small leather pouch he'd begun carrying ever since he realized his life was in danger. He doubled back on foot to the parking entrance, and sure enough, the car had pulled up to the front of the building.

The black car sat waiting for him to come across the glass catwalk that led to the condominiums. But the person in the car never saw him until he heard the sound of a .45 being cocked near his head.

J. J. Palmer felt his heart stop for one flitting moment and knew his cover was blown. A small part of him was very impressed. No one ever snuck up on him. Not unless he wanted them to, and he most certainly did not want this.

"Don't move!" The deadly, serious tone of the man's voice told J. J. he would have to play this close if he expected to get out alive. This was a man who felt he was in danger, and probably wouldn't hesitate to remove what he perceived as a threat.

J. J. berated himself for cracking the window. He'd only opened it to let in a little night air, but it had been enough to slip the barrel of the .45 in. This was his own fault, he'd gotten too comfortable with the assignment.

Slowly the man with the gun opened the door and motioned for him to scoot over. J. J. knew this wasn't good, but he still hoped he could talk to the man, try to reason with him. Soon the two men were sitting inside the car, neither knowing exactly what would happen next.

"Who are you?" Cavanaugh asked with the pistol still pointed at the stranger in the passenger seat. He studied the middle-aged man's face and tried to identify him. He was not one of the two officers that tried to pick him up or anyone else he recognized.

"A friend," J. J. said, taking the fact that he was not already dead as a good sign.

"Whose friend?" Cavanaugh said, his handsome mouth twisted in doubt.

"Yours, believe it or not."

"Sorry," Cavanaugh said, knowing this was just a desperate attempt of a man who believes his life is about to end, "I make a point of meeting all my friends."

"J. J. Palmer, nice to meet you," he said, secretly toying with the door handle. Of course, this was the one day he'd remembered to lock the door.

Cavanaugh watched his failed escape and decided this had to be the clumsiest criminal he'd ever seen. The man couldn't even find his way out of his own car. This was no hired gun. "Why are you following me?"

"I'm paid to," J. J. answered, honestly.

Cavanaugh sat up feeling he was finally getting somewhere. "By whom?"

"Sorry, I can't reveal that," J. J. said, knowing what a mistake it was even as he spoke the words. But that's why his client paid him well, he thought, to keep his mouth shut.

"I'm sure your employer will eulogize your loyalty at your funeral." Cavanaugh lifted the gun, holding his hand steady.

"Okay." J. J. folded, firmly convinced this one would do what he threatened. "M. Williams is how she signs the checks. That's all I know."

Cavanaugh felt suddenly lightheaded. Why would Marty have him followed? He felt another layer of darkness blanket the night as his heart sunk a little lower. He'd allowed himself to believe that for once in his life he'd experienced real love. He was prepared to carry that love in his heart for the rest of his life, even if he couldn't have the woman. And now to find out even she was up to something . . .

"Why? What does she want?" He tried to sound strong and forceful, but the pain was apparent in his voice.

"Nothing," J. J. said, watching the procession of emotions play across the younger man's face, but he was still unsure what he was witnessing.

Cavanaugh was more confused than ever. "Then, why are you following me?"

"To protect you."

"To protect *me*?"

"Yes. You see . . . I'm your bodyguard."

Nineteen

Marty was the last one to sit at the dinner table, and the first one up when the phone rang. Not one of the guys made a move to get it. She'd been getting to the phone faster than lightning since the New Year began.

"Hello?" She realized she was still holding her fork; she'd jumped up so quickly, she'd forgotten it was in her hand.

"Uh, Ms. Williams?"

She recognized the scruffy voice on the other end right away.

"Yes?"

"There's been a slight hiccup."

"A slight hiccup?"

"Uh, yes, I was well . . . discovered."

Marty felt her heart skip a beat. "I thought we talked about that, Mr. Palmer."

"Believe me, Ma'am, it wasn't by choice."

Marty was suddenly terrified. She was so certain the experienced detective could do his job undetected, she never considered the consequences of him being caught. "Are you all right?"

"Yes, but of course, this little problem changes everything. He made it perfectly clear he did not want, nor need, my protection."

Marty twisted her lips in frustration. "I'm sure."

"I was hoping we could get together to discuss the situation."

"Yes, of course."

"Tomorrow, around 4:00 PM.?"

"Yes, that's fine."

"Okay, I'll see you then."

Marty returned to the table and her half-eaten food. Apparently someone thought it would be funny to take most of her fries while she was away. She never noticed though. Her mind was preoccupied with the thought of Cavanaugh being out there all alone with some unknown shadow trying to kill him. And now, he was without even a guardian angel to watch over him.

Marty parked quickly and went into the building. Having been there so many times before, she pressed the third-floor button without even looking at the elevator panel.

Soon she stepped out onto the third floor and saw the sign that read "Palmer Investigations" written in gold lettering on the door at the end of the hall.

"Hi, Mary," she said to the elderly receptionist.

"Mr. Palmer's expecting you, dear," the woman said with a smile. "Go right in."

Marty always thought she looked like one of those television grandmothers who were always overdone. Everything from her multiple strands of imitation pearls to her carrot orange, color-treated hair screamed "blast from the past." But despite her outdated appearance, she was always pleasant.

"Thank you," Marty said, as she bypassed the counter and went into the first door on the left.

She stopped suddenly, feeling like her feet were magically rooted to the spot where she stood. Her erratic heart was pounding madly against her chest. Instinctively, she turned to run.

In a flash, Cavanaugh was on his feet, and between her and the doorway. Marty's eyes darted around the room as she tried to think of a way out of the trap.

Seeing no other choice, she charged him, but only managed to get swept up in his arms. Slamming the door shut, he spun her around and pinned her back against it. She struggled hard to free herself, but had forgotten just how strong he was. It didn't take her long to realize her resistance only made matters worse. The more she struggled, the more of his body he used to hold her in place until the whole of his lean form was pressed hard against hers.

"You are gonna talk to me whether you like it or not," he hissed against her neck.

"This is what you're good at, isn't it?" Her anger had taken hold of her brain. "Pushing people around?" Her sudden freedom surprised her until she saw the look of devastation on his face.

His dark eyes were filled with some unidentifiable emotion. "I would never hurt you."

Marty struggled to put her clothes right again. Although she regretted her harsh words, her pride still had a firm hold of her senses. "You already have."

"I simply wanted to talk to you, that's all." Cavanaugh hated the pleading tone of his voice. He'd promised himself he wouldn't beg for her love, but now seeing her, touching her again, he knew he would cut off his right arm that instant if she asked him to.

"We have nothing to say." She folded her arms across her chest. It was the only camouflage she could muster against her treacherous body. With one touch, he'd activated her *on* switch. She knew it would be emotional suicide to let him know her trembling was caused by lust, not fear.

"Why did you hire J. J.?" He decided to cut straight to the chase. This reunion was getting off to a very bad start. Maybe, if he could get it back on track, he could make her see she still cared for him.

"J. J.?" she said, with contempt. "Oh, so it's like that. You're on a first-name basis. Did you pay him off?"

"No, I just told him the truth."

"What truth?"

"The truth about two people who love each other very much, but like every couple, have some problems to work through."

Marty heard herself laughing before she felt it, a coarse, bitter sound. "Apparently, your mother's not the only one with the gift of understatement."

"Sometimes, Marty, things are not what they appear. If you'd given me a chance I could've explained."

"I bet you could've," she snarled in disbelief. "Sorry, but where I come from, if it walks like a duck, and quacks like a duck, it's a damn duck."

Before he could respond, she had slammed the door shut in his stunned face.

She turned the full wrath of her fury on the pleasant-looking receptionist who'd cheerfully led her into the trap. "Where's Palmer?" she howled at the woman, no longer fooled by her simple expression.

"Hiding in the storage room," the woman said, not the least bit ruffled. She turned back to her computer and continued her typing.

Marty threw open the door to find the man practically crouching behind a large shelving unit. Seeing Marty, he stood straight, knowing his gravy train had ended.

"I know. I'm fired," he said.

"No, you're not fired." She was still fuming, but the

walk to the end of the hall had begun to calm her. "I don't care what he says, he needs somebody to watch his back."

She turned to leave, then paused. "If you ever try a stunt like that again, getting fired will be the least of your problems. I know a fire marshal who would be very interested in inspecting this building. Do we understand each other?"

J. J. nodded, studying the woman with a newfound respect. He came out of his hiding place, and watched as she stormed out of the office. He opened the door to his office to find Cavanaugh standing at the window watching her cross the parking lot to her car. She slipped into the white Jetta, and within seconds pulled out of the lot.

"I take it things didn't go very well," J. J. said.

"You could say that."

"She loves you, you know. Why else would she have hired me?"

"I know," Cavanaugh said. *But how do I make* her *see that?*

K. C. came bounding around the corner with his usual energy. Poking his head into the laundry room, he tapped on the doorjamb. "Marty, there's a weeble wobble downstairs looking for you."

"A weeble wobble?" Marty asked, still loading the washer.

"Yeah, you know . . ." He stretched his shirt to imitate a pregnant woman. "They weeble and they wobble, but they don't fall down," he sang, pleased with his own humor.

"You're lucky you never called Shoshana that when *she* was pregnant."

"I did. She just never heard me," he said, before disappearing back the way he came.

Marty came around the spiral staircase, and paused, not believing her eyes. There in the entry of Firehouse Fifteen stood a very pregnant Candice Saint John-Pippin. She looked very businesslike in her neat, eggshell-colored suit. Her long brown hair was pulled back away from her rounded face. Even seven months pregnant, the family resemblance was undeniable. This woman was most certainly cut from the same cloth as Cavanaugh. She was carefully studying the pictures of each member of the firehouse, and the long list of commendations that lined the brick wall.

"Candice?" Marty asked, still not certain. If it was Candice Saint John, she was a long way from Savannah, Georgia.

Candice turned smiling. "Marty!"

The woman looked so genuinely happy to see her that Marty was a bit startled. Was this a social visit? Had Candice somehow missed the memo on her and Cavanaugh's split?

Candice opened her arms, pulling Marty into a tight embrace. "It's so good to see you."

Marty hugged her in return, thinking she smelled like fresh flowers.

"Let me look at you." Candice held her at bay, looking Marty up and down.

Marty blushed, suddenly embarrassed by her homely appearance. Around the firehouse, she wore nothing but ratty sweats and oversized T-shirts. It wasn't like the president was going to drop by any moment, but it was becoming apparent that Saint Johns weren't as predictable.

"Have you lost weight?" Candice's face showed more concern than she meant to.

So, Marty thought, seeing the pity in her soft brown eyes, she did get the memo after all. "Yes, a little." Marty tried to say it with pride, but it didn't work. She had lost weight but it wasn't for trying. She simply had no appetite for food, or life for that matter. The pregnant woman standing before her was one of the few people in the world who knew the true reason why.

"Well, you're looking good," Candice lied, quickly finding something else to focus her attention on. "So, this is a firehouse."

"Firehouse Fifteen," Marty said, this time with honest pride. "The best in the city."

"Are you the only female?"

"Yeah, but you couldn't sell that to these guys."

Candice could see the twinkle in her eyes when she spoke of her team. "You like what you do, don't you?"

"No," Marty said, "I *love* what I do."

"That's what's important, Marty," Candice replied, reaching out to touch her arm. "Not everyone is lucky enough to find a passion in life."

Marty's eyebrows shot up. *Was this going to be a "you-two-were-meant-to-be-together" speech?*

Marty decided to get this over with before Candice said something they would both regret. "What brings you to Detroit?"

"You," Candice said, gingerly. Reaching into her bag she pulled out a letter.

Marty sighed heavily, never noticing the piece of paper in the other woman's hand. "Candice, I think you should know, it's over between Cavanaugh and me. Please don't try to play matchmaker."

"Quite frankly, I could care less about you and Cavanaugh," Candice lied again. "I'm here for my own reasons."

She handed Marty the letter. The sloppy handwriting was written in red crayon and trimmed in perfect tiny fire engines. Marty felt her heart sink to her feet, realizing that this was the letter from the little boy Candice had spoken about at that fateful dinner so long ago. She carefully read over every heartfelt word, feeling like a heel the entire time.

In her own pain, she'd forgotten all about the "Make-A-Wish" child who wanted desperately to become a firefighter. Finishing the letter, it took her several seconds to muster the nerve to meet Candice's eyes.

"You made a promise to me and a very sick little boy." Candice Saint John's pretty face turned stone cold. "And I have every intention of holding you to it."

Twenty

Cavanaugh struggled to see in the dimly lit room. The desolate atmosphere of the place was in everything from the sounds of The Eagles "Desperado" playing on the jukebox to the stench of beer to the sticky substance that caked the floors.

He ignored the hungry look from a half-drunken barfly and continued searching the dark booths that lined the back wall. How different this place was from the clubs he frequented with his friends. Cavanaugh recognized the man before he reached him. He looked exactly as the bartender had described. His long, thin form was clearly visible, even slumped over the table with his stringy dark brown hair partially shielding his face.

"Andy Carpenter?" Cavanaugh said.

Slowly, the skinny man lifted his head. He carefully surveyed the stranger who wore neatly pressed Khaki pants and a brown leather bomber jacket. Even his well-made leather loafers screamed money. Andy knew instantly the man was not a potential client. He watched him unzip the jacket to reveal a stark white polo shirt beneath. He knew this guy could probably afford much better.

"Maybe, who wants to know?"

"I'm Cavanaugh Saint John. I'd like to—"

"Save it." The man staggered to his feet, then braced

himself against the table. "I've had enough of you Saint Johns to last a lifetime." Looking at him up close, Andy could clearly see the family resemblance.

It took Cavanaugh a moment to recover. He'd not expected a warm welcome, but certainly not the vehemence he heard in this man's voice.

"Mr. Carpenter, I understand you and my father parted in less than favorable circumstances, but I assure you—"

Andy Carpenter's coarse laughter was so loud it caused heads all over the dingy room to turn in their direction. "Less than favorable circumstances?" He shook his head and circled Cavanaugh, still looking him over. "You fancy Southerners sure have a way with words."

Cavanaugh felt his jaw tighten. Being a Saint John had shielded him from many of life's injustices, but not all. He heard the infliction when the man said the word "Southerners," and Cavanaugh understood full well the meaning behind it. His first instinct had been to punch him in the face, his second was to turn and leave before he lost his temper. But this man had information he needed and, bigot or not, Cavanaugh fully intended to get it.

Cavanaugh leaned over the table and picked up the glass of beer, his mouth twisted in disdain. Without warning, he slammed it against the hardwood floor.

"What are you doing?" Andy screeched, grabbing the man's arm seconds too late.

The bartender immediately headed toward the table. "Hey, you can't—" the bartender started, his already flushed complexion turning fire red.

Cavanaugh turned and stilled the man with one look. A dangerous warning was evident in his dark eyes, but he cooled his temper as quickly as it rose and nodded toward the bartender. The man accepted the silent promise, and returned to his place behind the bar.

Andy's drunken eyes bugged in disbelief. "What'd you do that for?"

"To get your attention," Cavanaugh said, and pulled free of Andy's hold on him.

"You got it, you got it!" He looked at the splatter of liquid and glass chips around his feet knowing it represented his last four dollars.

The bartender continued to watch them. The well-dressed stranger didn't look like the type to stiff the bar, but he couldn't be sure. He kept his rifle at his side just in case.

Since the start of his investigation, Cavanaugh had taken to carrying a large amount of cash on him for those whose cooperation could be purchased. As he pulled the wad of money from his pocket, he could see Andy's eyes widen and his mouth begin to water. Feeling others regard him as well, Cavanaugh was glad he had the foresight to remember the small piece of steel tucked in the back of his pants.

"I need to know what happened between you and my father," Cavanaugh said somberly, thumbing through the money as if counting it.

"Wha—huh?" Andy said, only half hearing. His mind was completely focused on the large roll.

Deciding on a hundred-dollar bill, Cavanaugh peeled it off and dangled it toward the thin man. Based on the look of him, Cavanaugh decided his cooperation shouldn't cost much.

Andy tilted his head to the side, suddenly wary of the generous offer. "That's it? You just want to know what happened?"

"Yes," Cavanaugh said, still offering up the money. "What made my father leave you for Stanton and Dowel?"

Andy quickly snatched the bill and tucked it into his pocket, fearing the owner would change his mind once he heard what he needed. "Stanton and Dowel used to be Carpenter and Dowel." Andy slumped back down in the booth. "Harwood Dowel was my partner before he hooked up with that Stanton guy. When he left he took most of my clients, including your father. When I fought back, Dowel and Stanton started a smear campaign against me, telling my clients that I was cooking the books. It got so bad, even the press got hold of the stories. Once the news media got involved, I was finished."

Cavanaugh was unaware of the stunned expression on his face. Only the look of confusion reflected in Andy's bloodshot eyes signaled him.

"You mean Harwood Dowel and you were partners?"

Andy was now a bit curious himself. "Yeah, why does that surprise you so much?"

Cavanaugh ran his fingers through his curly hair trying to make sense of it. "It's just when I spoke to him about you, he acted as if he'd never met you before."

"Well, if I screwed a guy over the way he did me, I wouldn't want to 'fess up to it either." Andy hunched his shoulders. "Tell you the truth, I don't much blame him. Harwood always had his eye on the prize, he wanted to play in the big leagues. When he met that Kenneth Stanton, he thought he was finally on his way. I tried to warn him about the guy, but he wouldn't hear it."

"Warn him about what?"

"The guy's a shark. He'd sell his mother to make a dime. I tried to warn Harwood that doing business with a guy like that could only lead to trouble."

"Well, you don't have to worry about that anymore. Kenneth Stanton was murdered last year."

"Really? How?"

"Killed by an employee who found out Stanton was sleeping with the guy's wife."

Andy's coarse laughter resounded again. "Sounds about right."

"Thanks for the information." Cavanaugh peeled off another fifty and tossed it to the man. He turned to leave, having learned more than he expected from the disheartened barrister.

"Hey." Andy shrugged his shoulders again. "Sorry about the way I treated you earlier. It's just been a long time since I heard that name. I guess I always kind of blamed your father for my business failing."

"Why?"

"Well, once he went over to Stanton and Dowel, many of my clients took it as an omen and followed him. Genesis was just a little company, but the name Saint John carries a lot of weight, you know?"

"Yeah," Cavanaugh said. "I know."

As he paid the bartender for his losses on the way out the door, Cavanaugh's mind was still reeling with new information.

When Greg Toberson entered the courtyard, everyone went on alert. His arrival had been the only missing piece of the plan. The four prison guards assigned to watch the yard had all been paid off. Razor-sharp knives had been fashioned from the plastic utensils smuggled out of the cafeteria. Everyone was in position.

Greg headed straight toward the weight bench, the way he did every time he came into the yard. He seemed to be obsessed with pumping iron, believing brute strength was his only hope for survival in the savage environment. Seeing him approach, the two men using the weights finished the set they were working on, and gave up the bench without the slightest hesitation.

That was the first sign something was wrong. Greg

looked around the yard. His blue eyes searched for anything out of place. He watched for new guys, he watched for anyone showing a unusual amount of interest in him. Nothing seemed out of place.

He adjusted the weights, taking only the two smaller dumbbells off the ends of each. Two-fifty was a respectable weight, and it would allow him to hold his own. That was all he needed, to hold his own until someone discovered the truth. His lawyer promised to keep working on it, but he didn't trust him. After the kangaroo court trial he'd been given, he didn't trust anyone. He knew without a doubt that if the truth were ever to come out, it would be by his efforts and his alone. That was why he split his personal time between lifting weights and studying in the law library.

He lay back, taking one last look around before lowering his head beneath the bar and leaving himself completely vulnerable. He reached above his head and took a deep breath, preparing to lift the heavy load.

He closed his eyes to muster his strength, and when he opened them again, three men were standing over him. Greg Toberson knew he was dead long before he ever felt the makeshift knife pierce his abdomen.

"Can I get a number two with a Diet Coke." Cavanaugh went to reach into his pocket, then stopped. "Super-size that."

"Will that be all?" a tired voice said through the intercom.

Cavanaugh turned to his passenger, who was still studying the menu board.

"Make mine a number five with an iced tea," J. J. said. "Super-size it, too."

"Did you get that?" Cavanaugh asked the intercom.

"Will *that* be all?" The voice in the box was becoming increasingly annoyed.

"Yes. Can you repeat that?" Cavanaugh asked, not the slightest bit perturbed by the exaggerated sighs.

"A number two with a diet, and a number five with an iced tea, both super sized." Without confirming the order was correct the intercom box shut off.

Cavanaugh slowly rolled forward, waiting until the two cars ahead of him drove away. Pulling to the window, a tired-looking young girl turned to collect his money. Her mouth was already twisted in disapproval when she turned to look at the driver who'd placed the order. Her sour disposition turned to sunshine under the magnetic charm of Cavanaugh's smile.

"Sorry to give you a hard time. It's just they get my order wrong so often." His smile deepened, allowing the slight dimple in his left cheek to show.

"Oh, it's all right." The girl's laughter bordered on giddy. "I'll check it myself to make sure it's okay."

She hurried away from the window, and after a few minutes, returned with two large bags. She opened her hand, allowing Cavanaugh to place the bills in it, but he could've been giving her a handful of rocks for all the interest she paid. Her eyes were firmly trained on his dark eyes and unusually lush lashes. The young cashier counted the change twice, seemingly unable to focus on the simple task. She finally gave him the correct change, his bags, and drinks.

"There's a little something extra in the bag for you," she whispered, handing it out the window.

"Aren't you sweet." Cavanaugh winked before pulling away.

J. J. immediately began rummaging around in the bag. The girl had added two additional cheeseburgers and two more large fries to the order. J. J. sat studying the younger man's profile, a look of disgust clearly written on his face.

Cavanaugh fought to hide the grin he felt forming on his lips. "What?" he asked, doing his best to feign ignorance.

"It must be nice being you," J. J. said, biting into a french fry.

Cavanaugh's rich laughter resounded throughout the car as it turned into the freeway on-ramp. After Marty's visit, Cavanaugh had still insisted to J. J. that his services were not needed. But J. J. had also insisted that he had a job to do, and a very angry, black woman to answer to if he didn't.

Realizing that neither would get exactly what he wanted, they agreed to a compromise. Since they were both inevitably headed to all the same places, why not go together. Over the past two weeks they had developed a camaraderie that neither saw coming, since they were as different as night and day.

J. J. was a middle-aged, retired policeman whose hair loss forced him to shave his head. He told everyone who asked that he just liked the look. His deep cocoa skin was crinkled and creased with too many hours of stakeouts in the elements. His rounded form and wrinkled look were the complete opposite of Cavanaugh's slender physique and neat appearance. Yet the men found they liked each other very much, and each had something to add to the hunt for an arsonist. J. J. still had a lot of friends on the force who occasionally provided them with hard-to-find information, and where friendship didn't work, Cavanaugh's checkbook did.

Together they discovered that due to a breakdown in communication within the department, an autopsy on Kenneth Stanton's body had been done against the wishes of his family. The autopsy revealed that had a jealous husband not bludgeoned the man to death, he would have died from the traces of poison the coroner found in his system. Apparently someone wanted him dead long before his affair was discovered.

After his visit to the Genesis office, Cavanaugh had begun to second-guess his theory that Genesis was at the center of the puzzle. Although he knew it played some part, given that someone was pretending to be him and managing the small office, he was now more concerned with finding his doppelgänger than anything else. Which left him with only the suspicious death of Kenneth Stanton as a lead.

"Do you have it yet?" Cavanaugh asked, slowing almost to a stop along the busy avenue. He was peering through the windshield at each individual address along the tree-lined street.

"Yeah, here it is." J. J. pulled a small notebook page out of the stack of folders he held on his lap. "It's 1412."

Cavanaugh slowed as the numbers began to descend quickly into the thirties, then into the twenties, until they finally reached the elegant brick home with the address of 1412 Maple Lane. They pulled into the driveway and stopped the car.

Cavanaugh reached for the folder titled Stanton. "Wait here," he called over his shoulder, stepping out of the car. Cavanaugh rang the bell twice before the door finally opened.

"Hello, Mrs. Stanton?" Cavanaugh noted the woman's reluctance to open the door more than a crack.

"Yes?"

All he could see was half a face. One green eye peered at him through the small opening.

"My name is Cavanaugh Saint John. I'm the agent investigating the death of your husband for Liberty State."

The door closed softly, he could hear a chain rattle,

then it opened all the way revealing a middle-aged woman with graying blond hair.

"Yes, I remember you," she said, noticing J. J. in the car for the first time. "We spoke on the phone."

"I was hoping to get a few minutes of your time to discuss some of the details surrounding your husband's murder."

Her green eyes dimmed briefly, but her stoic expression never changed. "Is there a problem?" She rubbed her arms.

Cavanaugh knew she was cool standing in the open doorway in the short-sleeved knit sweater in the middle of winter. But he was almost certain the rubbing was more out of nervousness than cold. Her eyes swept up and down the tree-lined street.

"No," he said. "Just some things that need clarification."

"Please, come in." She stepped aside to allow him in, taking one final look both ways along the sidewalk and then at J. J., sitting oblivious to her uneasy stare as he lifted his second burger to his mouth. She led Cavanaugh into a living room covered in plush pink floral designs.

"Mrs. Stanton, what I'm about to say is sensitive information," he said, sitting down on the sofa and opening the file. "But I believe it is crucial to what happened to your husband." He pulled out the coroner's report.

She came to sit across from him on the sofa. Her full attention focused on him as the words *sensitive information* came off his lips.

"We believe Mr. Stanton was being poisoned before his actual murder." He watched her reaction knowing she was as much a suspect as anyone. Her green eyes widened in terror as her hands came up to her mouth.

"My God, they were telling the truth," she said.

"Someone's been here already?" Cavanaugh was not as surprised as he pretended to be. He had assumed someone would've been there—in fact, two someones. His assumption was correct.

"Yes," she said, standing as if to go somewhere but instead she just stood there. She wrung her hands nervously. "Two officers were here about a month ago. They believe that since I requested no autopsy be done I was trying to hide something. They actually suspected me of poisoning Kenneth."

She began pacing rapidly. "But why? Who would do such a thing?"

"Well, I was hoping you might be able to help us with that." Cavanaugh took out a notepad. "Do you have any ideas at all? Did Kenneth have any enemies?"

"He was a corporate lawyer." She became livid as the reality of the situation began to hit her. "His enemies wear three-piece suits and sit on the boards of fortune five hundred companies. I doubt the lot of them would even know how to poison someone." In the climate-controlled room, she began rubbing her arms again.

"Well, nevertheless, I would appreciate it if you could give me those names." Cavanaugh slid the notepad across the coffee table toward her.

Beth Stanton stood looking down at the empty pad, her eyes narrowed suspiciously. "What does any of this have to do with Kenneth's insurance policy?"

"I'm sure you understand that the cause of death is—"

"Get out," she snapped. Her worn face was red with rage or fear. Cavanaugh wasn't sure which.

"Mrs. Stanton, please—"

"I don't know why you're here, but it has nothing to do with Kenneth's life insurance policy." She stormed across the room to the cordless phone. "Get out, or I'll call the police."

"Please, just hear me out," he pleaded, even as she turned the phone on, and dialed the first digit. "Someone tried to kill me, too," he blurted out, as she dialed the second one in nine, one, one.

Without a second of hesitation she turned the phone off. "What?"

"The day of the fire I was there finishing up my investigation. Someone locked me in the back file room right before the fire started."

"You think it was intentional?" Beth asked, coming back to his side of the room.

"About two months ago, two men approached me claiming to be police officers. One was a tall, thin white man and the other was a medium-complexion, short, burly black man. Are these the two men who came here last month?"

"It sounds like them." Beth slumped down on the couch. The past seven months had been exhausting both emotionally and financially. And now, to find out it was far worse than she thought. . . . "Do you think they were trying to finish the job?"

"Let's just say I don't think they wanted to take me on a joy ride."

"What was Kenneth into?" She was feeling that she didn't even know her own husband.

"I don't know, but he seems to have made some powerful people very angry. You see, I believe those men really were police officers."

"But why you?"

"I think I may have inadvertently stumbled onto something during my investigation."

"What?"

"That's what I have to find out."

"What do you want from me?"

"Those names, if you will," he said, then looked over

his shoulder at the sliding wood doors. "And if I could look through some of his files."

"I'm sorry, I can't."

"Mrs. Stanton, every day I remain alive I'm in someone's way. If I don't find out what this is all about soon, whoever is behind it will eventually find a way to remove the obstacle."

"No. I mean, I can't," she said, rubbing her arms feverently. "Harwood took all Kenneth's files."

"Harwood Dowel's been here?" Cavanaugh said, this time genuinely surprised.

"Yes. He said the information in those files was critical to an important account."

Cavanaugh sat back on the sofa feeling winded. He'd wondered if he could trust the man. Now he had his answer.

Twenty-one

"Wow." Henry Romaine stood staring up at the raised ceiling of the firehouse. He'd been inside one of the newer ones in Ann Arbor, but it was nothing like this. This was like stepping back in time. Everything about it was like something out of one of his books.

Candice stood with her hand held loosely on his shoulder, partially to hold him in place, lest he touch the wrong thing and get them both thrown out. Or worse, he might have a seizure, causing him to be rushed to the hospital and lose the opportunity to live his dream.

"Is this what you meant by a real firehouse?" She knew the ancient building with all its red brick charm was exactly what he was looking for.

"Yeah, this'll work." His wide grin revealed the gap where a molar had fallen out the week before.

"Hi, guys." Marty came up behind them. She'd been out running. "You're early." Looking at her watch she sighed in relief. It wasn't as early as she first thought. If the guys followed the plan everything should be in place by now, including them.

"You're lucky I was able to hold him off this long," Candice said, rubbing her hand across his cornrowed hair. "He wanted to show up at dawn."

Henry had been too enthralled in his surrounding to notice the sweaty woman until she smiled.

"This is Henry," Candice said, pushing him forward a bit. She knew he was shy.

"Hi," Henry said, while unconsciously stepping back into Candice.

"Nice to meet you, Henry," Marty held out her hand. "I'm Firefighter Williams, but you can call me Marty."

Henry stared up at her as if she were flapping wings, instead of reeking of a five-mile run. Marty took his hand, signaling to Candice that it was okay to let him go. Candice hesitated, knowing this is what he'd come for, to be drawn into the world he loved. But still, she was very protective of her heart-adopted children, especially when they were as special as Henry. Candice held on a moment longer before finally releasing him. Her only comfort was knowing Marty had the training to deal with seizures.

"Well, now, Officer Henry, if you're going to be putting out fires, you've got to get geared up."

"Huh?" Henry asked, a bit bewildered. He'd thought this would simply be a tour, leaving him with pictures to add to his scrapbook. What was she talking about, 'putting out fires?"

Marty led him up the metal stairs to the living quarters. There on the dining table was a miniature set of turnout gear, complete with helmet, boots, and gloves.

"Whoa." Henry's brown eyes lit up as he went from item to item. "They look so real."

"They *are* real. The same company that makes our suits made this one special order."

"Really?"

"Really." In that moment, Marty was extremely thankful that Candice hadn't let her out of her promise. She stood with her back against the double doors leading to the common area, toying with the brass handles.

"A good firefighter knows that his equipment is onl
half the equation to fighting fires. Do you know th
other half, Henry?"

"That's easy," he blurted out, while trying on one c
the rubber gloves. "The other firefighters."

Just then, the double doors swung open, revealing th
full engine team of Firehouse Fifteen. The twenty me
stood in the center of the colorfully decorated room
The big-screen TV and recliners had been pushed aside
In their place was a long table with party foods, incluc
ing a twenty-foot sub.

Seeing the snake-like monstrosity, Marty regretted gi
ing them free reign with the menu. This was supposed t
be a party for a ten-year-old boy, not a super-bowl event.

Henry's eyes widened even further seeing the crow
of men who embodied everything he dreamed of bein
one day.

"Guys, this is Henry," Marty said, feeling elated at the e
pression of pure joy written so clearly on his small face.

"Hey, Henry."

"Hey, Little man."

"Hiya, shorty."

The guys called out greetings as the group's unoffici
spokesman, Big Cal, sauntered over to the boy. Henry li
erally leaned back to look up at the giant.

"Hey, man," Cal held out his hand. "Welcome to Fir
house Fifteen."

Henry placed his tiny hand in Cal's palm. "Hi," h
managed to squeeze out.

"This is Big Cal." Marty made the introduction
"That's Dwight, Tommy, over there is K. C.," she contin
ued, until she'd introduced everyone in the group
Henry stood patiently taking it all in, but still obvious
uncomfortable in the roomful of giants.

Thirty minutes later, Marty left him sitting swallowe

ıp by one of the large recliners with a half-eaten sandvich in one hand and a soda can in the other. His artially full mouth was wide open as he laughed at the ight of Cal trying to slip into his miniature jacket.

Marty disappeared long enough to get a shower and lip into a pair of fresh jeans and a hooded sweatshirt. he was combing her hair when she noticed out the athroom window that Candice's rental car was still in he parking lot. She went back downstairs and found the voman exactly where she'd left her.

"I thought you left a long time ago," Marty said apoloetically while bounding down the stairs.

"I should've, but I'm always wary about leaving them n foreign environments," Candice said, knowing it was nly part of her reason for staying.

"Come with me." Marty led her up the stairs to the oomful of men.

The stereo was playing an identifiable rap song, and Ienry was trying to show the guys how to do some new lance that bore a striking resemblance to the robot of he seventies.

Sliding it closed again, the two women fell against the loor in a fit of hysterical laughter at the sight of the roup of men trying to twist their stiff bodies into the ontorted movements.

"As you can see, he's fine," Marty managed to say, wipng a tear from her eye and regretting not having the oresight to bring a camera.

"Yes, I guess he is," Candice said, still laughing.

"Later, we're taking him on a ride in the truck, and ve've got a few other surprises in store." Marty was quite leased with the day she had planned for their guest.

Candice smiled to herself, thinking how little it took o make a child happy. She rubbed her rounded belly, hinking of the life inside her.

"You're going to be a great mother." Marty could se
Candice's thoughts written in her eyes.

"I hope so," Candice confessed. "So, what about you?
This was the opportunity she'd been waiting for.

"What do you mean?"

"You ever think about the whole husband and babie
thing?"

"Once," Marty confessed, turning her head away.
wouldn't take a rocket scientist to figure out which ma
inspired that thought.

"He's a good man," Candice said, deciding it was silly t
keep tiptoeing around the subject. Cavanaugh was as pre
sent in the air as if he were standing right before them.

"He's a weak man," Marty snapped, releasing the an
guish she'd felt for the past two months. "He stood b
and let his mother call me a gold-digging tramp."

"No, Marty, you don't understand."

"Candice, please don't try to fix this." Marty had los
all her earlier enthusiasm. She should've known this wa
coming. She'd seen the closeness between Candice an
Cavanaugh during her one-day stay in his family home
Of course the woman would try to defend him.

"Just hear me out." Candice held up her hand to sti
any response. "There are things you don't know abou
reasons why he did what he did." She bowed her head
"My Aunt Reline's not an easy woman."

"Tell me about it." Marty was holding the door handl
so tight her palms were sweating. She could still clearl
remember the sadistic smirk on the mouth of the elderl
woman.

"Quite honestly, we're all surprised Cavanaugh's no
more screwed up than he is." Candice was speakin
more to herself than Marty. "He's come a long way."

"From what?" Marty said, refusing to believe the ma
who broke her heart could be an improvement.

"Cavanaugh turned thirty-four on his last birthday, but there was a time I didn't believe he would see twenty-four. The night his father died, something inside Cavanaugh died, also.

"My father found him that night sleeping on the porch. Dad used to say he'd never seen a human being as defeated as Cavanaugh looked that night, his little body slumped on the porch like a discarded bag of garbage. After his father died, Cavanaugh changed.

"By the time he reached his early twenties, he seemed determined to follow my uncle into the grave. He would go on these binges and disappear for days. When he did return home, Aunt Reline would only make matters worse. She practically blamed him for what happened to his father." Candice stroked her belly. "The way she blamed him for everything."

"What do you mean?" Marty found herself fascinated by the image Candice was painting. This was the stuff he would never share with her, the pain she always saw just beyond his deep brown pupils.

"She's never come right out and said it, but she implies that he is responsible for her being in the wheelchair."

Marty's curiosity got the better of her. "How?"

"She was arguing with Cavanaugh when she fell down the main staircase." Candice's jawbone set in a tight line so like Cavanaugh's. "She's never let him forget it, either."

"But that doesn't explain—"

"Yes." Candice nodded her head emphatically. "It does. It's how she controls him. How she manipulates all of us. She finds your weaknesses and homes in on them like some kind of stealth bomb." She tilted her head to look into Marty's eyes. "She must've sensed that you were insecure about your relationship with Cavanaugh."

"I'm not insecure," Marty lied.

"Marty, Aunt Reline attacked you because she picked

up on your feelings right away. She could see you were different, that Cavanaugh loved you. And unfortunately, you did exactly what she hoped for. You left him."

"How was I supposed to stay there with her saying all those horrible things?"

"I understand why you left, I just want you to understand why he's stayed all these years. He's carrying the weight of the world on his shoulders, so much pain, so much guilt." She shook her head. "First, Uncle Graham's suicide and then Aunt Reline's accident. He blames himself for it all, and it's cost him so much. I know it just sounds like a copout," Candice said, turning to face the other woman. "But, he truly is a victim of circumstances."

The two women stood in silence for several moments, both lost in their own thoughts. Finally, Marty spoke. "Okay, you asked me to hear you out and try to understand," Marty said. "Now, it's your turn."

"I'm listening," Candice said.

"I love Cavanaugh like I have never loved another. There were days I felt like I couldn't breathe without him, he became my everything. And then just like that . . ." Marty snapped her fingers. "It was gone. Over with. Wiped away like it never happened. All that time, I thought he felt the same way about me. But how can I believe I mean anything to him when he just stood there and watched his mother walk all over me?"

Candice held her peace. She loved her cousin, but as a woman she completely understood. When she and Tony first started dating, Aunt Reline had done everything in her power to scare him away, but Tony had matched the older woman blow for blow. She could not fully understand why Cavanaugh had put up with his mother's cruelty for so long.

"Candice, it's been rough getting over him. It's taken me a long time to get to a place where I even feel like getting up in the morning. I can't afford to let him into my heart again."

"Marty, I've been married to Tony for seven years now, and every day has been a struggle in one way or another. But the pleasure has far outweighed the pain, and that's what you have to ask yourself."

"What's that?" Marty studied the face of this woman who looked so much like her beloved they could've more likely been brother and sister, rather than first cousins.

Candice lifted Marty's chin with her index finger until they were eye to eye. "Is your life better with or without him?"

"Reesy," Cavanaugh called to his assistant while pulling file after file out of the metal cabinet.

She appeared in the doorway. "Yes?" Reesy sighed heavily and shook her head, knowing she would be the one cleaning up the mess.

"Where's my copy of last year's returns and financial statements?" he asked, feeling completely helpless. He'd had no choice but to enlist an ally. Since his meetings with Beth Stanton and Andy Carpenter, Cavanaugh had made a point of saying very little to anyone, having come to the conclusion that only someone inside his camp could pull off the elaborate scam.

But he needed Reesy's help. That was undeniable. Besides, he reasoned, if she'd wanted to ruin him, he'd given her the means years ago. She had every password and secret code he possessed tucked in her tiny organizer, and could sign his signature better than he could.

She was his very efficient right hand, but more than that she was his friend. No, he felt certain that Reesy was not the traitor. But until he discovered who was, he had to be careful in his search, lest the culprit become suspicious.

"I keep those locked up in my desk," she said, then disappeared from the doorway and returned a few seconds later with a manila folder.

"Thanks," he said, settling in behind his desk. He opened the file and began studying it fastidiously. The information he was looking for practically jumped off the page. Once again, he became angry with himself for having been so careless in the handling of his business affairs to this point. Had he been a better guardian to his father's legacy, none of this could have happened.

Cavanaugh picked up the phone and began dialing a long-distance number. He couldn't change the mistakes of the past, but he could most definitely correct the future.

Twenty-two

Noel stood slowly, fearing if he moved too suddenly he would frighten her away. "What are you doing here?" He came toward her, wiping the grease from his hands.

"I need to talk to you." Marty felt a bit uncomfortable being back at the small ranch-style house.

"So, you're finally ready to hear the truth about Saint John." Noel hated himself for the pleasure he was deriving from her pain, but he had made no secret about his feelings for her.

"No, that's over," she confessed, and regretted it the moment she saw the spark of hope in his eyes. "I see you're still trying to get the Charger running," she said, trying to change the subject.

Noel looked back over his shoulder at the beat-up jalopy. He'd bought it for pennies at auction, believing it could be restored to its former glory. That was three years and two relationships ago. And of the two relationships, Marty had been the only one willing to crawl beneath the metal dinosaur beside him and attempt to breathe life into it.

"Yeah, but I think I'm about ready to pull the plug." He took the wrench from his back pocket and tossed it into his toolbox.

"Have you tried the rebuilt engine we talked about?" She quickly moved past him. The intense way he was studying her long form was making her nervous. "I really think that was the problem."

"Why are you here?" Noel knew whatever it was had to be pretty important to bring her to his front door.

"The Stanton and Dowel fire. I need to know the cause." She stood with her back to him, but could feel his suspicious eyes boring into her back.

"That fire is part of an ongoing investigation," he said. "You know I can't talk about the details."

She finally turned around. "I'm not asking for details, just the cause."

"Why?"

"It's just important to me."

"Important to you, or Saint John?" He tried to hide his jealousy, but it didn't work.

"I've got news for you, Noel," she said. "With his connections, he probably already knows."

He was now more suspicious than ever. "So, what's it to you?"

"Are you going to tell me or not?" Marty was quickly tiring of going round and round. She felt she had swallowed enough pride in just coming here.

He walked across the room to his workbench and stood toying with his table saw. "What's in it for me?"

"Never mind!" She threw up her hands, and turned to leave. She was suddenly mad as a bull seeing red, and feared what she might do to him if she stayed a moment longer.

"No, Marty, wait." He chased after her down the long driveway back to her car parked on the street. "I'm sorry, really I am," he pleaded, getting in front of her.

"Have you come to this, Noel?" She was still on fire. "Blackmailing women into your bed?"

"That's not what I meant," he lied.

"Yeah, right," she huffed, pushing past him. "We both know exactly what you meant."

"Arson," he blurted out.

She stopped with her car door partially open.

"It was an electrical fire. Someone tampered with the wiring."

"But why?" Marty asked, more confused than ever.

"The police believe someone wanted to cover up a very damaging investigation Stanton was conducting." The satisfied smirk on his face said exactly whom the police suspected the *someone* of being.

"Cavanaugh didn't do it," she said, unsure why she still felt the need to defend him.

"Are you so sure, Marty?" He stood with his arms crossed over his chest. "I have some very damaging evidence to the contrary."

"Like what?" Something about his stance held a confidence that shook her from the top of her head to the tips of her toes.

"Come by the station tomorrow, and I'll show you," he said, taking a cigarette out of his pocket.

"I thought you gave those up." Marty clearly remembered the long two months of cranky moods and endless eating that finally led to the conquering of his worst habit.

"I only did that for you," he smiled crookedly, before shielding his mouth to light the cigarette.

Cavanaugh sat slumped in the chair across from J. J. while the man tapped away on his desktop computer. He listened to the muted curses and occasional fist-pounding for several minutes.

"Gotcha," J. J. shouted in triumph. "We're in."

Cavanaugh came around the desk quickly and found

himself staring at the Web page of the Detroit Police Department criminal databank. "You know, if we get caught, I'm going to pretend I don't know you," he said, still not believing the man had done what he said he could do.

"Don't thank me, thank my delinquent grandson. He's the one who taught me how to do this." J. J. laughed. "Okay, let's see what we got here . . ."

The phone rang, and J. J. picked it up without missing a beat. It was midday and Mary was out to lunch. "Palmer Investigations," he said, in his most professional voice.

J. J.'s eyes quickly darted to Cavanaugh before he turned away. A sly smile came across Cavanaugh's face. J. J. had the worst poker face he had ever seen. That guilty expression could only mean one thing. With J. J.'s back to him, he slipped out of the room unnoticed. He went to Mary's desk, and very carefully picked up the only blinking line on the phone. Sure enough, the voice on the other end was the sweetest sound he'd ever heard.

"Just checking the progress," Marty said, into the phone.

"Well, to be truthful, it's like peeling an onion." J. J. chose his words very carefully, believing Cavanaugh was standing just a few feet behind him. "The more I learn, the more there is to it."

"Is he okay?"

"Yes. Everything's fine."

She could hear the uneasiness in J. J.'s voice. "Is he there now?"

"Yes, that's exactly the case." J. J. continued to speak in code.

"Well, just keep me posted," she said, fighting the urge to ask more personal questions of the detective. Because of her frequent inquiries she knew the two men had been spending a lot of time together.

"I'll do that, good-bye now," he said, returning the receiver. He turned in his chair and discovered he was alone in the room.

Marty held the phone a moment longer as she struggled to unwind the long tangled cord, which is how she heard the second click in the line.

"Hello," she said into the empty silence. "Hello, is anyone there?" After several seconds, the automated operator came on the line, and she hung up. She leaned against the wall, knowing someone else had indeed been on the line.

Did J. J. know he was on the line? she wondered. Probably not, given his nervous conversation. But Cavanaugh had been there; even through the phone line, she felt his presence. For a few brief moments she thought she heard him breathing, that slow, steady breathing she felt on her neck whenever he fell asleep in her arms.

She turned and headed back to the common area, realizing that despite what she told Candice, she wasn't nearly as over him as she pretended.

Noel spotted her before she saw him. He was up high on the second level and he saw her talking to one of his men asking for directions. Even in her work pants and department-issued T-shirt, she was still a beauty.

Noel thought, if he could've made it with anyone it would've been her. But he now understood that was impossible for him. After two failed marriages, several failed relationships, and a shrink, he'd finally figured out that he had some serious trust issues.

The shrink attributed it to his mother running out on him and his brother Leon when they were five and eight, respectively. They'd gone to school one morning and come home to an empty house. Only the bunk beds he shared with Leon, a few boxes of their toys, a small black and white TV, and a couple of bags of clothes remained. Too young to understand, they waited patiently for her return.

Later that evening, after all the cartoons had gone off and their bellies began to growl, they went next door to the neighbors. Luckily, the neighbors knew their family and called their grandmother instead of children's services.

Even as a child, Noel understood that things could've gone much differently than they had. They had a loving grandmother who took them in without question and gave them both the best she had. Their father had abandoned the family before Noel was old enough to remember him, but the mark of how his mother left would always be a part of him.

He'd missed a lot of opportunities because of it, including the opportunity to love Marty the right way. But that was water under the bridge; he understood that a week ago when she showed up at his house out of the blue.

She felt nothing for him anymore; he saw it in the emptiness in her eyes. He would have to accept that, but he didn't have to accept her hooking up with a man he was certain was a murderer.

"Marty, up here," he called out to her.

She looked up, spotting him. She thanked the guy she was talking to and headed in his direction.

"I thought maybe you'd changed your mind," he said, turning to greet her as she bounded up the stairs, her long legs easily taking them two at a time.

"Sorry, just got tied up last week," she lied. Truth was, she had changed her mind, believing he may have actually had something on Cavanaugh. Something she didn't want to know.

But after spending the last four nights lying alone on her small bed thinking about the Cavanaugh she knew, she decided the idea of him being involved in anything corrupt was preposterous. Whatever Noel had, no matter how bad it may look, it could not be proof of murder. Cavanaugh simply was not capable of something like that.

"So, where's this damning evidence?" she asked, looking in all directions.

Noel realized how hard she was working at trying to appear confident, but he knew her better than that. "Right this way, Ms. Williams," he said, stepping aside for her to pass him on the narrow catwalk.

She instinctively headed in the direction of his office. The evidence room was at the other end of the catwalk, but she knew Noel would never keep anything he truly valued in there. Not where anyone could walk in and walk out with it.

He unlocked the door, and they moved through the glassed-in outer room and into the second, more private office. There in the middle of the floor sat a beat-up wall safe. It was badly scorched, but for the most part undamaged.

"After the fire, I found this in the office of Kenneth Stanton. Apparently he had this installed without even his partner's knowledge of it."

"Why didn't you give it to his partner?" She was beginning to realize that this was more than just evidence.

"From the moment I walked into the building, I made it for arson. And given the strange set of circumstances, I liked his partner as the doer."

"But Noel, this isn't right," Marty said, realizing Noel had all but stolen the metal box. Her mind wandered for a moment, wondering how many of his other cases had been solved through questionable means.

"Do you want to know what I found inside or not?" He

was regretting his decision to share this with her. He had forgotten what a goody two shoes she could be.

Marty tried to block the theft from her mind; she had to know what he found inside. "Okay, what was it?"

"This," he said. He handed her a small stack of manila folders from his desk. She sat down on his beat-up couch and began thumbing through the stack of files. Each contained labels: SJT Financial Statements '91–'98, Saint John, Cavanaugh—Cayman Islands Acct., Saint John, Cavanaugh—Personal, SJT—Genesis.

In each file was document after document, listing all the financial accounts and holdings for SJT, including several offshore accounts that held several millions that were not accounted for in the financial statements; e-mails and memos from a well-known senator and city officials; letters sent to what she recognized as Cavanaugh's e-mail address; letters regarding business dealings that even to a novice sounded shady.

"Face it, Marty, your boy is dirty," Noel said, leaning against the wall to light a cigarette.

"How do you know that any of this is legitimate? I mean, anyone could've forged these documents to frame him."

"You don't really believe that, do you?"

"I believe in Cavanaugh, and I know he didn't do those things." The words were a surprise, even to her.

Noel just watched her carefully, studying every detail of her face. "You're in love with him, aren't you?"

"I told you, my relationship with Cavanaugh Saint John is over." She quickly turned her attention back to the files.

"You didn't answer my question."

"And I'm not going to," she said, flipping through the rest of the thin folders. "This is not a subject I feel comfortable discussing with you."

Noel crossed the room and sat beside her on the sofa. "Do you love him, Marty?"

She paused a long moment, finally realizing he wasn't going to drop it. "If you must know." She took a deep breath. "Yes, I do." Her heart broke seeing the sadness that passed quickly through his brown eyes.

"You're certain he didn't do this?" Noel asked, not believing what he was about to say.

"Absolutely." She batted her eyes hard, fighting the tears brimming in them. She'd once cared a great deal about this man and in no way wanted to cause him any more pain than she'd caused in leaving him. But she couldn't deny what she felt either, even though she could tell that her words were cutting him deep.

"Well, if you believe he's innocent, then you've got to find out where this money went."

She wiped carelessly at her eyes. "What do you mean?"

"If he didn't embezzle this money, who did?"

"Marty, telephone," Dwight called around the corner.

She turned the burner down low on her skillet full of half-cooked chicken, and rounded the corner to the phone. She'd picked it up and placed it to her ear before it occurred to her that Dwight had not said who was on the line.

"Hello?" she said, seeing the grin on Dwight's face a moment too late as he slid around the corner at the end of the hall.

"Marty, it's me." The sensuous voice came through the line like a sweet love song from her memory. "Please, don't hang up."

Her mind was torn. She knew she should slam the receiver down before he had a chance to even begin working on her, but it was just so good hearing his voice again.

"What do you want?" There was a long pause, and she knew the answer to her question. He wanted her.

Finally, he said, "I just wanted to wish you a happy Valentines Day."

Marty cocked an eyebrow, realizing the holiday had all but slipped her mind. She mentally calculated the date; it was Wednesday the thirteenth.

"You're a day early," she said, still holding to her steely tone.

"Not where I'm at, "he chuckled. "It was February fourteenth almost an hour ago."

She fought the urge to ask where that was. "Thanks," she said, not knowing what else to say.

"I wrote you a poem. I wanted to send it to you, but I was afraid you'd burn it."

"You wrote poetry?" Her even pitch faltered in her astonishment.

"Hey." He laughed, "I'm a man of many talents."

She closed her eyes and breathed deeply, thinking how well she knew that.

"Anyway, I'm not going to hold you up long. I just wanted to say that."

"Well, same to you," she said, not wanting the conversation to end. "How's J. J.?"

"Still in my way, but fine."

She could feel him smiling into the phone. Those soft pink lips curled around two rows of perfect white teeth. She tried to shake off the thought, but it was hard when she could see him so clearly in her mind's eye.

"Well, good night," he said in a whisper.

She looked at her watch; it was 6:30 PM. "Good night." She held the phone until she heard the light click on the other end.

She asked K. C. to watch the chicken while she went to her room and pulled out her heavy dictionary with the almanac in the back. Her long forefinger perused the pages, looking up all the places where it could be later than midnight already. Finally, she found it. She cocked her head to the side, wondering what he was doing in Europe.

"Hello, gentlemen. I'm Mr. Maesa, the bank manager. How can I help you?" The short, rotund man's expression edged on suspicious.

"I'm Cavanaugh Saint John, and this is my associate, Mr. Palmer." J. J. tipped his brand-new English bowler.

"I wanted to talk to someone regarding my account." Cavanaugh handed the man a small card, and the man's suspicious expression became friendly.

"Oh, yes, Mr. Saint John." He touched Cavanaugh on the shoulder. "We've been expecting a visit from you for some time now."

"Oh?"

"Oh, yes. It's very unusual for someone to open an account of this nature and not come to verify everything is in order."

Cavanaugh exchanged a knowing glance with J. J., but Mr. Maesa didn't notice.

"Please, come with me," Mr. Maesa said.

He led the two men through the large open lobby, up a flight of marble stairs to the second level, and down a long corridor to a private office.

"Have a seat. I'll be right with you," he said before leaving the room and pulling the door tight behind him.

"So, no one's been in to care for my little nest egg," Cavanaugh said to J. J. He examined the various pieces of crystal and china that decorated the office. He wondered how much interest was charged to pay for such an office.

"Apparently not," J. J. said, as he yanked the tiny hat off his head. He scratched painfully at his itchy, sweaty scalp.

"I told you that thing was ridiculous when you bought it." Cavanaugh chuckled, leaning against the wide window.

"Yeah, but it's sharp," J. J. smiled, still pleased with his European trophy.

The door opened again, and Mr. Maesa returned with a young Asian woman who made no attempt to hide her curiosity about Cavanaugh.

"Mr. Saint John?" She went directly to him.

"Yes?" Cavanaugh said, standing upright. Something about the intent way she studied his face told him she wouldn't be as easily fooled as Mr. Maesa.

"I'm a bit confused," she said, looking back at her manager. "When we spoke on the phone you were emphatic regarding the point that no one would ever make a personal appearance, including yourself."

"Yes. Unfortunately, that stipulation had to be changed," Cavanaugh said, fighting the uneasiness he felt in every part of his being. Her blank expression gave nothing away as to her thoughts. "I'm dealing with some legal conflicts and the discovery of wiring such a large sum of money would be, well . . . questioned." Cavanaugh let his dark eyes flash on Mr. Maesa, briefly.

Mr. Maesa, having many years of experience in matters such as these, understood perfectly. Men in Mr. Saint John's position were not to be questioned, only accommodated.

"Thank you, Baylou." He scooted her toward the door. "I'll assist Mr. Saint John from here."

Four hours and twenty minutes later, Cavanaugh and J. J. walked out of the Union Bank of Switzerland carrying a large briefcase containing twenty-five million, seven hundred and fifty-five dollars and loose change.

Catching a cab, they went back to the hotel along Lake Zurich where they'd stayed the previous night. Cavanaugh deposited the large briefcase in the hotel safe and the two men went upstairs to their room to make preparations to go home the next day, believing they were finally putting the last pieces of the puzzle in place.

Cavanaugh lay across the small bed, staring at the ceiling. How he wanted Marty with him at the moment. Not only for the most obvious reason, but simply to share in his discovery.

"What if he calls the bank and finds out?" J. J. asked, picking through the plate of baked salmon he'd ordered from room service.

"So what?" Cavanaugh said. "As soon as we're back on American soil, I'll notify the authorities. They'll have him in custody before he can ever retaliate."

"I'm not so much worried about him as his associates," J. J. said. The wariness was evident in his voice. Cavanaugh said nothing. What was there to say? He had the same fear. He still had not found his impersonator, and was led to the bank by nothing more than a hunch.

It had occurred to him after visiting the Genesis office that the only way a person could transfer money to and from the business was through the SJT accounts. That's why he'd asked Reesy to dig them out. And right there in plain view was the unexplained Swiss bank account information.

His accountants would have never questioned it as long as the numbers added up, which they did. His lawyers wouldn't have questioned it since his signature was in all the right places.

No, his shadow was far too clever to move unusually large amounts of money at one time. The transfers had all been no more than a few thousand at a time until it reached several million, twenty-five million to be exact. All of which was now sitting in the safe of the hotel.

He and J. J. were hunting for a murderer, and now the trap had been set. The only question that remained was whether their prey would take the bait. Cavanaugh yawned and stretched. The events of the past few days were crashing down on him fast. The last sound he heard was J. J. snoring across the room.

Twenty-three

Marty came downstairs to find Candice standing in the firehouse garage for the second time in a month. She looked very casual in the silk pantsuit that pulled mercilessly at her expanding belly.

"Hey, girl." Candice held out her arms. Marty embraced her easily, wondering how such warm, loving people could be related to such a dark, wicked woman like Reline Saint John.

"Didn't expect to see you again so soon," Marty said, leading her to the bench of the picnic table. Her flushed face was alarming to Marty.

"Didn't expect to see you either, but I need a favor."

"Anything," Marty said.

"I was in town for the 'Make-A-Wish' annual fundraiser banquet. I purchased two sets of tickets in advance, gave one set away, and Tony and I were using the others. Unfortunately, I had some Braxton Hicks contractions this morning. It was nothing, really, just enough to terrify Tony," she said, taking a deep breath.

Marty studied her with concern, seeing she was having difficulty breathing.

"We decided to return home. In fact, we're heading to the airport right now."

"Do you think you should be flying in your condition?" Marty asked.

"Uh-huh." Candice nodded her head fervently. "I'm having this baby at home. Angelica's been training for weeks to be my midwife. If we leave now, I should be fine." She touched Marty's hand seeing the genuine concern in her eyes. "I just don't want to have my baby in a strange city," she continued as she struggled to get up.

"But still, Candice," Marty cautioned.

Candice turned to face her suddenly. "Do *you* want to be my midwife?"

Point made. "Have a safe trip," Marty said, pushing her toward the door.

"I stopped by to ask if you wanted one of my tickets for the banquet. Henry will be there, and I know he would love to see you."

Marty thought about it for only a moment. She was in no mood for a party, no matter how good the cause. "I don't know, Candice. I'm not in a very festive mood lately."

"The donations are calculated by the number of ticket stubs returned. I would hate for even two tickets to not be counted." Her soft brown eyes were pleading.

"Okay. How much are they?" Marty said, taking the tickets.

"Nothing," Candice said, and started moving toward the door again. "They're already paid for. Just go, so you can turn them in to be counted, and have a good time."

"Thanks," Marty said. "Call me when you drop your load," she teased. The two women hugged briefly, and then Candice waddled back to the waiting truck. Marty waved to Tony as she stood in the doorway watching him help his large wife up into the rented SUV.

Then something occurred to her. "Candice," Marty called, just as the SUV was pulling away. "Who got the other ticket?"

Candice leaned out the window. "My biggest contributor, of course." She winked. "Cavanaugh."

The light rumble of the engine was all that was heard as the large lumbering vehicle pulled into the street and quickly meshed with the oncoming traffic. Marty stood in the large entryway of the firehouse, realizing all too late that she'd just been duped.

Cavanaugh came through the door just as the phone began ringing. Quickly, he tossed his small, leather tote on the couch, and grabbed the cordless phone off the sofa table just beyond it.

"Hello?" he said, pulling off his heavy peacoat.

"Hey, Cuz," Candice's airy voice rung out.

"Hey, what are you doing back in town?" He was genuinely pleased to hear a comforting, familiar voice. After such a disconcerting week, Cavanaugh was happy to be home again.

"The banquet, remember?"

Cavanaugh physically flinched. "Oh, yeah, that," he said, as his mind tried to calculate a proper excuse.

"Oh, no, you don't," she hissed into the phone. "You promised me you'd be there."

"Just tell me how much, and I'll write you a check."

"No, Cavanaugh. You won't buy your way out of this," she said. "You made a promise, and I'm holding you to it."

"All right." He gave in, knowing how persistent his cousin could be. "When and where?"

"I sent you an e-mail earlier; all the details are in it."

"Okay," he sighed heavily. "I'll see you there." The phone clicked and then she was gone.

Cavanaugh pulled his sweater over his head, moving blindly toward the refrigerator. He hated flying long distances; they never gave you enough food. He popped a Hot Pocket® in the microwave, and headed toward the shower.

Shoshana stood leaning over the ironing board looking at the tickets. "Where did you get these?"

"A friend," Marty answered vaguely, while pushing Kendra in the baby swing.

"So, why are you giving them to me?"

Marty hunched her shoulders, settling into a chair to continue pushing her niece from a more comfortable position. "I just don't feel like going."

Shoshana watched her sister suspiciously. "Make-A-Wish?" Shoshana said. "Why is that so familiar?"

"Remember that little boy who came to the firehouse a few weeks ago?"

"Yeah."

"He's one of the children they help."

Shoshana's mouth twisted as understanding came. "Wasn't that hooked up by Cavanaugh's cousin?"

"Yeah, so what?"

"Is that where you got these tickets?"

"She's pregnant, actually about to burst. She asked me to go in her place."

"So, why don't you?"

"I told you, I don't feel like it."

"Is Cavanaugh going to be there?"

"How would I know?" Marty snapped, giving her sister a confirmed yes.

"I don't *even* believe you." Shoshana bent to pull the iron cord from the wall. "You've been pining over that man for almost three months, and now you get to spend an evening of dining and dancing with him, and you pass."

"I have not been pining."

"*I miss Cavanaugh, oh, woo, woo.*" Shoshana's imitation looked more like a wounded bear than a broken-hearted woman.

"For your information, I am completely over him." Marty tried to sound confident, but feared her sister could see right through her. Which she did.

"Oh? So, you're over him?" Shoshana said, placing her hands on her hips.

"Absolutely."

"Prove it."

"What?"

"Go to the banquet.

"I don't have to prove anything to you."

"Just what I thought, chicken."

"Who are you calling chicken?"

"You—chicken." Shoshana danced just out of her sister's reach, flapping her arms furiously and making a horrible, squawking sound.

"Cut it out."

"Boak, boak!"

"Cut it out." Marty finally caught her as she rounded the pool table for the second time. Wrapping her in a headlock, she playfully pulled her to the floor.

Little Kendra sat watching with her mouth gaping open in glee, wanting to get in on the fun. The two women tumbled across the carpeted floor until the sound of someone on the stairs stopped them cold where they lay.

Erv just stood looking down at the sight of his wife and her sister entwined in a position that would have qualified both women for the World Wrestling Federation.

"Hey, baby, you're home early," Shoshana said, embarrassed by the look of utter exasperation written on his face.

"When will you two grow up?" He shook his head as he turned and headed back up the stairs. "What's for dinner?" he called back over his shoulder. The comical image was already forgotten.

Realizing what they must look like tangled on the floor, the two fell over on each other laughing out loud. Marty thought when it came to her sister the answer to Erv's first question was, probably never.

Marty stood posing in front of the mirror, wondering how Shoshana could get her to do things no one else could. She straightened the belt on her leather pants and turned, checking her derriere in the glass. Tonight there could be no panty lines. The phone rang, startling her out of the close examination.

"Hello?"

What are you wearing?" Shoshana's voice came through the phone.

"None of your business."

"The red dress." Shoshana sang into the phone. "You have to wear the red dress."

Marty shook her head, regretting ever telling her sister about the green box. "I don't think so."

"If ever there was a time to wear that dress, it's tonight!" Shoshana sounded almost desperate.

"Shoshana, please leave me alone."

"Who are you fooling? We both know you want to knock his designer socks off."

"How many times I gotta tell you, I'm just doing this as a favor for a friend."

"Whatever," Shoshana continued. "Look, he saw that dress on a dummy, and he thought of you." She laughed, realizing her accidental pun.

"Get to the point."

"The point is, the thought of you in that dress did

something to him." She paused for a long moment. "And we both know what that *something* was."

"And?"

"You wear that red dress, and he'll be thinking about that *something* all night long."

Twenty-four

Cavanaugh handed his keys to the valet, while looking in every direction for his cousin. She was a member of the fundraiser committee, so he just assumed she would be near the door to greet her guest. He moved through the crowd easily, never noticing the many female heads that turned in his direction.

"Cavanaugh." Winslow Niigata came toward him with his arms extended. As always, Cavanaugh was startled by the appearance of the large, African man. Dressed in a bright turquoise-colored dashiki that perfectly accentuated his dark skin, he looked the very embodiment of regality.

"Winslow," Cavanaugh said, taking the man's extended hand.

"How are you, my friend?" Winslow asked, taking a champagne glass from a passing server.

"I'm good, and you?"

"Wonderful. We've had a much better turnout than we ever expected."

"That's terrific," Cavanaugh said, continually looking around for Candice. "Have you seen Candice?"

Winslow looked at his friend oddly. "She's not here. Didn't she tell you?"

"Tell me what?"

"She left for Savannah this morning. Apparently her little one is close to arriving."

Something about Winslow's sublime smile told Cavanaugh that the glass he held was not his first of the evening.

"No. She didn't tell me." Cavanaugh frowned, wondering why she didn't mention that when they spoke earlier.

"Well, enjoy yourself." Winslow patted his back, then, moving toward the entrance, he greeted the latest arriving guest.

Cavanaugh didn't think anything of it. Winslow was the consummate public relations guy. He always made sure the biggest contributors were given the most personal attention, but with such a worthy organization there were many large supporters. SJT was just one of many, and Winslow was on to the next.

Cavanaugh ordered a glass of red wine from the bar and settled at an unoccupied table. He decided since he was here, why not enjoy a good meal, and a bit of people watching?

Tipping the glass to his lips he nearly choked on the stream of liquid flowing down his throat. He coughed hard, trying to regain his normal breathing pattern, and struggled to see around the plumpish gentleman who had suddenly stepped into his line of vision. It seemed if he leaned right, the man stepped to the right. If he leaned left, so did the man. Finally, he gave up, deciding that what he thought he saw was nothing more than a figment of his overactive imagination. He wanted her so badly, he was seeing her in places she couldn't possibly be.

Marty quickly ducked into the ladies room. Her heart was pounding wildly against her chest.

She caught sight of herself in the mirror over the sink, and was a bit startled by her own image. She wasn't a vain woman, but even she had to admit she was looking good. What was it about the color red that could make any woman look striking?

She tried to steady her weak legs. How could she have forgotten how mind-bogglingly fine he was. Who was she kidding? This man was so out of her league it was nothing more than freakish luck that she had stumbled into a relationship with him the first time. She breathed deeply, trying to muster enough strength to sneak out the back entrance before he spotted her again.

A well-dressed, elderly woman touched her on the arm. "Are you okay, sweetie?"

"Yes, ma'am," Marty replied.

"What a lovely dress," the woman said, studying Marty's troubled eyes.

"Thank you," Marty said, wanting to toss some cold water on her face but not wanting to smear her makeup. It was the first time in recent memory she'd gotten it exactly the way she wanted it.

"Are you here with someone? Is there anyone I should call?" the woman said, genuine concern shining in her brown eyes.

"No, thank you. Really, I'm fine."

"All right." The woman turned to leave, then paused. "So there's no one?" she asked again, but the tone of the question was different this time.

"No, ma'am," Marty understood the hidden meaning. "No one."

"Such a shame," the woman said, shaking her head softly. "It really is a beautiful dress."

Marty heard the door close lightly, and stood erect, looking at herself in the mirror. She turned slightly to the side, quite pleased with the view. The older woman was right, the small piece of red, silk fabric was something special. It did something to her overall appearance. It was special, she decided, and so was the woman in it.

She felt herself growing stronger even as she stood there. She was a good woman and Cavanaugh was a fool. If he couldn't appreciate what he had, then he deserved to lose her. She wasn't the first woman to make the mistake of loving the wrong man, and unfortunately, she wouldn't be the last.

She felt rejuvenated as she silently counseled the woman in the mirror. She studied herself, from the top of her perfect spiral curls to the tip of her bright red stiletto heels. She had given him her heart, open and trusting. And he had offered her nothing but lies and deceit in return.

She took her ruby red lipstick out of her small handbag and carefully reapplied. She dabbed a touch of her Chanel No. 5 behind each ear and her wrists. She closed her small bag, threw back her shoulders, and stoned up her face.

She turned to open the bathroom door, reentering the large room full of celebrating people. The time had come to make him pay.

Cavanaugh yawned and prepared to leave. His unoccupied table had become full, and the uneven distribution was causing him the unwanted attention of almost every man in the room.

There he sat, now with six apparently single woman, although he wasn't really certain about the last two that had joined them. He could have sworn he'd seen them both earlier, each on the arm of a different man. But now they seemed completely alone and crowded around as if his was the only table in the room. Worse yet, they pretended to ignore him.

He turned in his seat, putting his back to the table and contemplating whether the plate of roasted chicken and baby potatoes was worth the headache, when two small red objects moved into his line of vision. His eyes moved up past the shoes to the smooth caramel skin that seemed to stretch upward unendingly. The long, slender legs finally disappeared beneath the hemline of a crimson red dress. His eyes continued their upward climb over sumptuous hills and curvaceous valleys until they landed on the face of an angel.

"Good evening," she said.

Cavanaugh sat there, both deaf and mute. Unable to speak or move, he was suddenly paralyzed with desire. He finally stood to face her, but was unable to do anything more.

"Marty?" He just needed to confirm that it was truly her and not some phantom created by his lonely heart.

She only smiled in response.

"What are you doing here?" He was unaware of anyone else in the room, only the soft, brown eyes that watched him evenly.

"Candice offered me her tickets at the last minute."

The statement was met with dead air.

"And you?" she continued, seeing he was unable to respond.

"I got mine from her a while back," he answered dumbly. "Wow," he whispered, unable to hide the hungry lust in his eyes, "you look . . . um."

"Um?" She chuckled. "Is that a compliment?"

"Most definitely," he said, carefully studying every inch of her, and silently congratulating himself on his good taste. She was absolutely stunning.

Then something occurred to him. It had been almost

three months since they separated. In that time, he'd only seen her once, the confrontation at J. J.'s office, which left plenty of time for her life to have changed.

"Are you here alone?"

"With a friend," she said.

"I see." His dark eyes flashed with poorly hidden jealousy.

"Well, I just wanted to say hello." She turned to leave.

He quickly took her hand before she had a chance to move away. "Care to dance?" He smiled in that way she loved.

Marty felt her legs melting beneath her, and she wondered again exactly what she was doing here. "Well, actually . . ." She glanced over her shoulder. "My friend will be back any minute."

Cavanaugh's throat constricted as if she'd just cursed him.

"But I'm sure I have time for one dance." She allowed him to lead her onto the dance floor and slid easily against his solid chest. Their bodies fell into rhythm with the sounds of Earth, Wind & Fire's classic "That's the Way of the World." She sung the lyrics in her head: "Hearts afire."

She tried to gauge the space between them, allowing just enough closeness for familiarity but not enough for intimacy. Cavanaugh wasn't having it, pulling her hard against him until their two bodies merged into one moving spirit.

He closed his eyes and allowed himself the simple pleasure of holding her. It had been so long since she had been this close to him. How he'd missed her sweet smell, her softness, everything that was Marty. He adored her. Why couldn't she see it?

Marty held her peace and tried not to breathe him in. *Remember, he's addictive,* she cautioned herself. She pressed her eyes closed, determined to not enjoy the feel of his large hand pressed against the small of her back. She wouldn't lay her head against his paisley vest, although she could easily remember how warm and comforting it had been to fall asleep against the silky smoothness of his bare chest.

He moved her across the crowded floor as if they were the only two people in the world, swaying her as easily in dance as he had in every other aspect of their relationship.

Her whole body stiffened at the feeling of his soft lips ever so lightly grazing her exposed shoulder.

"So, how was your trip?" She tried desperately to change the course of events. One more kiss like that and she was headed for disaster.

"My trip?" He was distracted by a tall, handsome man moving their way.

"Yes. Remember, you called to wish me Happy Valentine's Day?"

"Oh, yes. It was fine," he sighed, relieved when the tall man moved past them, barely noticing Marty. He hadn't realized until that moment that he'd been secretly watching every man in the room trying to determine which one was the mysterious friend.

"Can we sit down?" he asked, close to her ear, so she could hear him better. Her sweet fragrance drifted into his nose.

Sit alone with him in a quiet place? She considered it for less than thirty seconds. Having been his lover and constant companion, she knew him too well for that. How easily he could convince her that everything she'd seen and heard three months ago was not what it seemed. Looking into those mesmerizing black eyes, all reason would be lost, and all her efforts would have been in vain. She knew in her heart the only way she could hold this love in her heart forever was to walk away.

"No, I've really got to be going," she said, looking in all directions. "I wonder what could be keeping him?"

"Just a few more min—"

She abruptly but gently broke free of his hold and blended into the crowd. She turned left, then right, trying to disappear in the maze of people. But he wouldn't be deterred so easily.

"Marty, wait," he called, moving through the crowd. He quickly worked his way toward her, placing his hand on the backs of those unaware of his approach.

"Excuse me," he said. "Pardon me." Until, finally, he came to an opening, and she was gone as if she'd vanished into thin air. He turned in a complete circle trying to spy even the faintest glimpse of red. There was every other color imaginable in the sea of happy faces. Cavanaugh stood in the middle of the room staring in every direction like a child who had lost his way.

Marty stood hidden behind a small plant that was barely wide enough to conceal her on the far side of the room. She had wanted to tease and torture him, and from the pained expression on his handsome face, it had worked like a charm. So why, she wondered, didn't she feel any better?

A tiny tug on her hand caused her to turn around.

"Here's the program you asked for." Henry stood beside her, holding up the small brochure. He never questioned why she was hiding behind the tree.

When she'd decided to approach Cavanaugh, she'd sent Henry on a small errand just long enough to play out her little game.

Henry begged her to go to the activity room and see some of his drawings. She decided it was better than the alternative of watching Cavanaugh suffer. To her surprise, the room was filled with activity and children not interested in the grown-up party.

Her little fireman, who apparently had some serious talent with the paintbrush, very quickly impressed Marty. He showed her picture after picture of everything from animals to buildings.

"Henry, you may want to consider a change in career paths." She laughed, looking at his canvas-sized drawing of her firehouse. He'd drawn everything from the partially chipped stones along the north side of the building, the result of Dwight making a slight miscalculation in distance four years ago, to the deep red color of the bricks. The detail was amazing, from a boy so young.

It was almost two hours later when she returned to the party. Marty slid back into the room, staying against the back wall as she carefully scanned the area for Cavanaugh. She finally found him sitting with an attractive couple, and from the way they interacted, it was clear he knew them well. She sighed, half relieved and half disappointed. He seemed to have gone on with his evening, completely forgetting about their little encounter. The woman said something that made both men laugh out loud. The sweet, musical sound reached all the way across the room.

She stayed against the far wall and worked her way around to the front entrance. Once outside, she handed the valet her ticket, and waited patiently for one of the drivers to bring her car around. She lifted her face, enjoying the feel of the cool evening air across it. She contemplated the evening; all things considered, she'd had a good time. She got to see Henry again and spend the evening with some interesting people. And best of all, she got to be held by Cavanaugh one last time.

A few minutes more on the dance floor and he would have broken her down. She knew for certain now it would never work. She simply wanted more than he was able to give her, and she loved him too much to settle for less. She had to let him go.

Cavanaugh felt the slight tremor of his cell phone before it sounded the musical alarm.

"She's leaving," the timid valet whispered into the phone.

"You're sure it's her?" Cavanaugh said, turning his back to his friends.

"Yes, this time I'm certain," the young man said, in as confident a tone as he could muster.

Cavanaugh had already been to the parking lot twice that night looking for white Jettas preparing to leave the party. One contained an elderly white couple, and the other a single man.

"Trust me, Mr. Saint John," the young man tried to reassure his benefactor. "This lady is all that. It has to be her."

"Is she alone?"

"Yes."

Cavanaugh paused, hesistant to leave his friends for another false alarm. Where was the mysterious friend?

"And, man." The young valet was unable to hide his appreciation for the tall beauty standing only a few feet from him, completely oblivious to the secret call he was making regarding her. "That is one kick-ass red dress—"

"I'll be right there," Cavanaugh said, before turning off the phone. He said his good-byes to his friends, and moved quickly toward the door.

He stood in the shadow of the doorway for several seconds waiting patiently for her companion to arrive. He wasn't sure why, but he needed to see the man.

He stood watching her as she repeatedly checked her

watch and peered around the corner for her car. Fearing she would go in search of it, he finally made his move.

"Are you leaving already?"

Was it the wonderfully familiar feel of his hand rubbing against her back that caused her to jump, or the spark of electricity that ran up her arm? She would never know.

Marty turned to face him, unable to hide her wide-eyed surprise. "I thought you'd gone," she lied.

"I was waiting for you," he said, still carefully studying every man who came through the door.

"Oh, really?" She nervously watched him watch the crowd. Marty knew instantly whom he was looking for.

"I wanted to meet your friend," he said. "You know, introduce myself, compare notes, that sort of thing."

"Don't be petty, Cavanaugh." She looked toward the parking lot again wondering why her car had not arrived.

"What did you expect?" He was barely able to conceal the malice in his voice.

"A little maturity would be nice," she snapped. Marty was only now seeing the improbability of Cavanaugh showing up, and her car not.

The thought of her with another man was eating him up inside, but he had to do a better job of hiding it if he expected her to talk to him. "I'm sorry, you're right. That was childish."

"So was bribing the valet to hold up my car," she glared at him, accusingly.

His guilty silence was all the confirmation she needed.

Just then, the car came around the corner. Marty moved quickly to approach it. She wanted to get away from him before he figured out there was no other man.

"What about your friend?" He looked back toward the door. Cavanaugh wondered what kind of man would leave her alone for so long.

"He already left."

His dark eyebrows furrowed. "When?"

"Quite a while ago."

"Then let me follow you home. It's not safe, you being out here all alone."

Marty twisted her mouth in disbelief, knowing the only wolf in the woods tonight was the one standing before her. "I don't think that's such a good idea."

She smiled, and it took his breath away.

Cavanaugh was on her before she realized it, pulling her against him as he covered her mouth, plunging his tongue deep inside. She felt wonderful, so real and solid beneath his strong hand, her soft, warm body next to his.

Marty wrapped her arms around his neck, holding him to her as his tongue explored her hungry mouth. Running her hands over his hard chest, his muscular shoulders and arms. She ran her fingers through his wonderful curly hair. He tasted so good. God, how she'd missed him.

Suddenly, her senses came to her. What was she doing?

"Cavanaugh, you have no right!" Pushing against him she stumbled backward. Dizzy with her own lust, she struggled to regain some composure.

"So, it's like that?" His dark eyes were bright with passion. "You're just going to move on to the next brother like I never existed?"

"I don't know what you're talking about." She feigned innocence, and tried to hide the sweet satisfaction she felt in every part of her being. Marty became alarmed at the determined glint of his dark eyes. That one kiss had quite effectively set off the fireworks. There would be no stopping the show now.

He moved toward her and she moved back just as quickly. He felt as if he would die if he couldn't get her back in his arms at that moment. She wanted him; he felt it in the way she kissed him, and the way she touched him. Why was she denying it?

"I love you, doesn't that count for anything?" He was livid and completely careless of the stares of the other guests as they came out looking for their vehicles.

"You're causing a scene," she tried to whisper, but it was pointless.

"I thought you loved me, too," he baited her, looking for any sign of the woman he knew.

She bit into her bottom lip to keep silent. She would not let him have his way in this.

"Wearing my dress for another man," he said, his soft mouth twisted in disdain. "Who is he, Marty?" Unexpectedly, he grabbed her arms, squeezing her tight. "Is it Noel?"

The look of pure terror in her eyes and the grief in his heart was enough to extinguish the fire in his brain. Finally exhausted, he released his hold on her and hung his head.

"It doesn't matter, does it?" he said, with his soft mouth twisted in a thoughtful expression.

The crowd of people had grown. They mingled around, pretending not to listen, but Cavanaugh didn't care. The only thing he was conscious of was the loss he felt in his heart at that moment. He touched his index finger to her sealed lips remembering the taste of her lipstick.

"Whoever he is, I hope he's good to you." With that, he turned and walked away.

Marty felt her heart breaking with every step. But why should it? This was what she wanted, wasn't it? To hurt him like he'd hurt her? And she'd done just that with so few words and a couple of kisses.

All she had to do was give him the vaguest impression that there was someone else and let his tortured mind do the rest. It had worked like a charm. So why did she feel so bad?

She watched his back disappearing into the building, leaving her very embarrassed, and very alone. She climbed into her car and slowly drove away, realizing how poorly she had handled the situation, once again.

Twenty-five

Cavanaugh, unable to endure the company of cheerful people, left the party shortly after Marty. He rounded the narrow road that ran along the river. He sped along at top speed, constantly checking his mirror. This was not the night to get pulled over, but he needed the speed. Focusing all his attention on the task of driving always cleared his mind of all other thought. But tonight, try as he may, he couldn't get her out. Her long, luscious form could've been sitting beside him in the passenger seat. Her beautiful smile, her sweet smell. He got excited just thinking about her in that sexy dress. He knew the moment he saw it in the window, it would look *that* good on her. He huffed loudly. There wasn't a mannequin in the world with curves like that.

He struggled with his discordant thoughts. She said she was there with someone else. But how could she be with someone else when he saw what he saw in her eyes?

She wanted him as badly as he wanted her. He could feel the sparks off her the way he always did when they were in close proximity and passion was high. She beckoned him like a watchtower to a ship, drawing him in to her. How could she be with another man when she so obviously loved him still?

At the next median, he turned the car around and headed back toward the city. He knew Marty like he knew himself; she was a part of him. She would come to him. She simply had to. They needed each other too much for her to stay away. New boyfriend or not, she belonged to him. The silver BMW moved along the two-lane highway with frightening speed as he raced back.

Marty stood outside the door feeling every bit the fool. She'd won. Anyone else would've taken their victory and gone home. What was she doing here? Standing at his door like a beggar? She started to knock, then noticed the door was standing ajar. Fearing the worst, she pushed it open.

The elegant apartment was fully intact; not so much as a chair was out of place. Slowly she entered, picking up a small statuette of a black Madonna near the door, praying that what she intended to do with it would not be considered sacrilege.

She moved as light-footed as possible from room to room. Her heart was racing at the thought of her beautiful Cavanaugh laying dead in one of them. The apartment was completely still, there was not even the faint whisper of his beloved tea kettle. Standing just beyond the doorway she peered into the master bedroom. It was as empty as the others.

She started to move away when something caught her eye. Someone was on the terrace. She edged along the wall until she could make out the silhouetted figure of a man. But not just any man, she realized, sighing in relief. She knew every mold and contour of that exceptional body all too well.

"Do you realize you left your front door standing wide open?" she said, not caring how she exaggerated the situation. She was trying to make a point.

"How else would you have gotten in?" He never moved

from his position bent over the railing. His silky, cocoa-brown skin was taut across his shoulder blades and his navy slacks were unbelted as if he'd stopped in the middle of undressing to gaze out over the lake.

"Were you that sure I would come?" she said, stepping out of the shadows.

"Yes."

"You think that much of yourself, do you?"

"No, but you do." He turned to face her. "You're the only one who doesn't see what this is." He gestured to the air between them.

"And exactly what am I missing?"

"Us, Marty," he said, as his dark eyes pleaded. "You don't understand what we are to each other. You don't see *us.*"

Marty knew the moment he started moving toward her she had stayed too long. She turned to flee, but his strong arms came around her waist before she reached the door.

"Don't you realize we belong to each other?" He breathed in the scent of her skin. "You're my Eve."

Marty fought to hide the trembling that began any time he touched her. She couldn't let him do this to her again. Everything in her mind and heart told her he would only hurt her. She pushed away and turned to face him, summoning courage she didn't even know she had.

"I can't— I won't let you—" She fought to hide the tears that were quickly forming in her eyes.

"Baby, don't do this," he interrupted, pulling her tight against him. He couldn't let her finish what she was about to say.

"I can't let you keep doing this to me." She sealed her eyes shut, but not before a drop of water fell onto his hand.

He lifted her head, wiping away one tiny tear that hung precariously from her bottom eyelash.

She pried herself free of his strong hold and moved toward the front entry. Every step felt as if she were dragging lead weights around her ankles.

He followed slowly a few steps behind her. An empty feeling in the bottom of his stomach told him she was serious this time. He knew he couldn't let her walk out, yet he was powerless to stop her.

"Stay the night."

She paused in the middle of the room. "What?"

"Stay the night. In the morning I'll let you leave and never bother you again. But for everything that could've been, just be with me tonight."

Her mind told her to keep walking, but her heart was begging to stay. He closed in behind her, pressing his unfair advantage against her trembling body.

"Please, just once more." He lifted her head up, and his mouth closed over hers.

Marty moaned a pointless rebuff, even as her arm came up around his neck. She whispered refusal, even as her fingers wound their way through his loose curls. Feeling the slight shift of her world, she found herself cradled in his arms as the front door began drifting farther and farther away, and she found herself being carried back to his bed.

Nothing else mattered as she felt herself falling helplessly onto his soft mattress. Not the unanswered questions or the feeling of betrayal that scarred her heart. Only the caress of his muscular arms around her, and the feel of his warm mouth on hers.

Cavanaugh propped himself up on one elbow to look down at her in the red After Five dress he'd given her so long ago. "You look so beautiful tonight."

He'd tried to get her to wear it on several occasions, but

she always insisted it was simply too formal. His midnight-black eyes seemed to darken even more. "Why tonight?"

She hesitated, unsure whether to share the truth or not. She finally decided tonight there would be no inhibitions. She would speak her heart and damn the consequences. "I knew you would be there."

His lips separated, revealing his perfect smile. He fell on her again, burying his head in her neck and pulling her tight against him. He wanted to hold her there forever, closed in the safety and warmth of his embrace. He wanted to wipe away all the hurt and mistrust he'd planted between them, and begin again. He wanted a lot of things, but feared all he had was tonight.

"Do you remember the shell we picked up on the beach that day in Puerto Rico?"

Marty thought for a moment. "You mean the one that turned out to be a crab, and bit you?" She fought the urge to laugh, wondering what would bring that isolated thought to mind.

"Yeah, that's the one," he chuckled, feeling good for the first time in a long time.

"Why do you ask?" she said.

"I just wanted to know if you remembered." He tried to hide the loneliness in his voice. For the past few months, he'd relived every moment they shared over again in his head a thousand times. They comforted him in the dark, empty night. He often wondered if she were lying alone in her bed thinking of him as often as he thought of her.

"I remember everything," she whispered, now understanding the question completely.

He kissed her again, determined to give her with his body what he had not with his actions, complete honesty. Slowly he rose over her, covering her long form.

Marty parted her legs as the silky material fell back,

and she welcomed him into the canyon of her body. She loved the feel of him, his large bulging arms, his perfectly rounded buttocks, his scent, and his taste. Everything about him.

"Tell me you love me," he said, sliding into that grove of her body he felt was designed just for him.

"I love you," she confessed, not caring how vulnerable it made her. She did love him, and she needed him to know. It was the one pure thing between them, what they felt for each other.

"Say it again," he whispered behind her ear, completely aware of the erotic sensation of it.

"I love you." She reached up taking his face between her hands and kissed him.

"Again." He breathed heavy against her flesh peeling away the spaghetti straps. He kissed every inch of skin as it was revealed. He pulled the thin fabric down exposing her perfectly rounded, copper-colored breast. He slid the satiny silk fabric of her dress up to expose her equally velvet-skinned legs.

"I—I love you." She struggled to focus on his words, but her mind was on the warmth of large hands, touching, caressing, stroking.

"This is the way it was always supposed to be, Marty," he said, stroking her darkened tips with his thumbs. "This is the way it was always supposed to be."

"I know." She turned her head away to hide her pain. She could not tell him what she knew in her soul. That tonight would be all they could have. Despite her craving for him, or the empty ache she felt in every part of her being when they were apart, Marty knew she could not bear to live in doubt of his love or his heart. She would not live in the shadow of his internal pain.

"I need you," Cavanaugh said, as his body involuntarily began grinding against her center place. Even with the shield of silk fabric between them, the feel of her beneath him was thrilling. His hips were thrusting hard against her, pinning her lithe frame to the bed. He had been without her too long, his need was too much, and his body responded instinctively to a want he could no longer deny. Marty felt her pelvis reacting to his demand, reaching up to him with each thrust. She felt his large hands molding around her thighs through the material.

He pulled away from her, and then in what seemed like seconds to her scattered mind their clothing was gone. Other than the condom he'd donned with lightening speed, they were skin to skin. Cavanaugh was on her again. The heavy weight of his body was a welcome burden as he squeezed her flesh hard, pulling her up against him.

Marty went eagerly into his web of passion, unable to fight the strength of her desire. She was certain this man had the ability to crush her heart, commanding her body in ways no one ever had. His insatiable hunger pushed her beyond any imaginable limit. She knew he could destroy her, and she would gladly die in his arms. Just to be one with him, one body, one soul. To have him completely would be worth any price.

In a single but sudden motion, he lifted her hips off the bed and they were united again, moving in rhythm as if they had never been parted, understanding each other in ways known only to them. With lips and hands they spoke their secret tongue, a language that went beyond words: body poetry as ancient as man himself.

Cavanaugh could read the message in her passionate lovemaking. The sheer desperation was in her kiss, her tight hold on his shoulders, the water from her eyes that smeared against his smooth, bare chest. He felt it in the thrust of her hips as she gave herself over to him. With every upward lunge she was saying good-bye. He knew with certainty this was the last time he would ever be inside her. Once she parted from him tonight, it would be forever.

He shook his head frantically, struggling with his conflicting emotions. This is what he'd asked for, just one more night of love. But it was not enough. It could never be enough. *I can't lose her again.* His conscience battled itself as he pressed her against himself again, holding her so tight she found it hard to breathe. In that instant, his course was set and the decision was made.

"Marry me, Marty," he cried out, even while continuing to ravish her, unable to slow his starving body. "Please, please, marry me!" Cavanaugh surrendered to his passion, abdicated his pride, and begged for her love.

Marty's eyes widened in amazement, not believing her ears. She shook her head from side to side, even as she gave her body over to him completely. "No!" she cried out.

"Yes, just say yes," he coerced, more focused now. This was no longer an act of passion, but a deliberate conquest. He shifted the weight of his body just enough to glide along her tender cove. Her fervent groan was her answer that the movement had served its purpose.

Her mind was racing with doubt and disbelief. Even as she wrapped her long legs around his waist pulling him deeper, her heart rejected his mournful plea. "I can't," she whimpered, melting under his expert touch. He could manipulate her body like it was nothing more than soft clay beneath his clever fingers.

"Just say yes," he whispered into her hair as he continued his assault. She shook her head again trying to hold to her quickly slipping sensibilities. How could he do this to her? She would've said anything he wanted at that moment, done anything to maintain the sweet torture he was lavishing on her.

In the instant when she was certain her whole being

was about to shatter he suddenly pulled away. Not far, but enough to punish her for her disobedience.

"Say yes!" he demanded, staring down at her with unbelievable restraint.

"Yes," she surrendered, "yes, yes!" She had to have him, no matter the cost, and was instantly rewarded as he plunged into her deepest depths, filling her with everything that he was. "Yes." His body convulsed madly, fastening her beneath him. "Yes. Yes."

Even as he exploded, spilling his seed inside, she continued to cry out fearing that he would deny her the fruition of his love.

"Yes. Yes. Yes!"

In utter, trembling bliss they carried each other to the highest heights of ecstasy, and back to earth again. Not until his strong hands relaxed against her thigh did she finally quiet her cries.

Not until those final moments before falling into a deep, satisfying slumber did Marty realize that in her zeal to be loved, she may have forfeited her heart.

Twenty-six

Marty opened her eyes and slammed them shut again as the bright sunlight came streaming across her face. She covered her head with the pillow, wondering how the sun could shine so brightly so early. She peeked from beneath the pillow to look at the clock on the nightstand. It was only 7:20 AM. She turned to see if she were alone in the bed. Of course she was. Cavanaugh rose with the roosters, one of his seemingly few faults.

"Good morning." His deep voice rang across the still air, cheerful and lively.

She pulled the pillow tighter around her head. It was insane for anyone to be so happy that time of the morning.

Cavanaugh placed the tray at the end of the bed and stood staring down at her exposed back. Her velvety caramel skin begged to be kissed, so he did.

She only grunted in acknowledgment.

"I made you breakfast," he practically sang. "And coffee," he added, knowing the magic words to get his lover moving.

Her head popped out from beneath the pillow. "Coffee?"

"Brazilian blend." He reached for the cup and handed it to her.

Taking a long gulp, she finally mustered the strength

to smile. Some people needed miracles and sunrises as proof there was a god. All Marty Williams needed was coffee.

"Thank you," she said, taking another gulp.

"You're welcome." He sat watching her drink. She looked like a contented cat sipping on a warm cup of catnip. He fought the urge to yawn, knowing Marty would recognize it right away for the telltale sign it was. He had been up most of the night, fearing that if he slept, he'd wake up and find her gone. She hadn't so much as stirred all night.

"So, I was thinking . . ." He crossed his long legs and leaned back against her still-folded body. "How's June?"

"What?"

"Our wedding. June's a popular month for weddings, isn't it? And in June, the weather would be good enough to have it outdoors, if we like."

"Cavanaugh, you can't be serious?" She avoided his eyes, knowing just how serious he was.

"Why can't I?" All the good humor had disappeared from his voice.

"That was said in the heat of passion." She took another sip, not knowing which she enjoyed more, the taste or the smell.

Suddenly, her sweet wake-up call was snatched from her hands. Cavanaugh stood staring down at her, his whole body seeming constricted. The half-empty coffee mug dangled carelessly from his finger. "So, what are you saying? You don't want to marry me?"

"I'm saying, it was unfair to ask while we were *doing it.*" She was up on her knees now, holding the sheet around her naked form with one hand, and reaching for the coffee mug with the other.

He lifted the mug over his head, intentionally keeping it out of reach. "Okay." He nodded patiently before kneeling down beside the bed. "Marty, will you marry me?"

"Cavanaugh, please," she sighed heavily, wondering how such a wonderful night could lead to such a bad morning. "It's too early for this nonsense."

"Nonsense?" His voice was deeply calm as he stood.

Marty sorely regretted her choice of words.

"Is that what my love is to you?" His deep brown eyes were bright with fire.

"We were making love," she pleaded, trying desperately to salvage the wreckage of the shattered morning. "You didn't mean it, and neither did I."

"I meant it." He pushed his hand down into his pants pocket. "And in my heart I know you did too, but I can't hold you to that."

"Let's just eat this beautiful breakfast you prepa—"

"No. You don't have to patronize me." He took a deep breath. "I told you, if you wanted to leave in the morning, I would let you go and not bother you again."

"What are you saying?" Marty had a sudden migraine as her brain tried to wrap around what was happening.

"I'm saying that I love you and want to spend the rest of my life loving you. But if you don't want the same thing, I don't see any future in this."

The room fell silent as they each stood waiting for the other to make some heroic move and save the day, but neither did.

Marty climbed out of the bed still clutching the sheet. She picked up her discarded clothing along the way to the bathroom. She paused in the doorway wanting desperately to run back to the bed, throw herself at his feet, and beg him to love her, but her pride wouldn't allow it.

A few minutes later, when she came out fully dressed, he was gone. Not just from the room, but from the apartment. She stood in the living room looking around at the place so like him, elegant, refined, and barren. She returned the black Madonna to her mantle by the door. Touching her cheek lightly, Marty prayed that the Holy Mother would watch over him.

She let herself out, slowly pulling the door closed behind her, knowing she would never see the condominium again. She only wished it were that easy to cut the man out of her heart.

"You'd better have a good reason for being at my house at 8:00 AM on a Sunday morning." J. J. stood staring down at his friend, seeing defeat written all over his body. Cavanaugh sat with his forearms resting on his thighs and his head hung low. "I had nowhere else to go." He regretted his joking words, now that he was able to see Cavanaugh's bowed head and hear the sadness in his voice. Pulling his ratty bathrobe closed and knotting the belt, J. J. sat down at the table.

"Here you go." Evelyn Palmer came in carrying a tray with two mugs, a fresh pot of steaming hot tea, and a small plate full of pastries.

"Thanks, Evelyn," Cavanaugh smiled, knowing the woman probably served tea twice a year, but had scrounged some up on his behalf.

"Tea?" J. J. looked at his wife like she'd just sprouted a second head. "Where's my coffee?" he said, then turned and found himself startled by the ferociousness of Cavanaugh's stare. "What?" He wondered what he'd said to offend his friend.

"Nothing," Cavanaugh shrugged, "I've just developed a strong dislike for that particular beverage."

"Hey, don't punish me for your prejudice." He reached out, grabbing the end of his wife's housecoat as she passed. Without a word the message had been passed.

The unspoken language of closely related people had always impressed Cavanaugh: twins who shared each other's pain, or a husband and wife who could communicate without speaking. The way a mother could sense when her child was in danger, or the way a man would hear his best friend call his name, only to learn later that he'd died at that exact moment in some distant place.

For the first time in his life, he had experienced that closeness, with Marty: the way she would always call just when he needed her the most. That she seemed to be the only person in the world to get his offbeat sense of humor. The way he knew all the things she loved long before she ever told him. He had meant what he told her the night before, they were *supposed* to be together. He'd only wanted to make her understand that, but instead just forced her away.

When Evelyn returned with the single cup of coffee, J. J. tooted his nose. "Oh, I see. He gets a pot of tea, and I get a *cup* of coffee."

"He's a guest." Evelyn said, sauntering away. "You know where the kitchen is."

"That woman's cold," J. J. chuckled, while spooning sugar into his coffee mug. "So, what are you doing here?"

"I saw Marty last night," Cavanaugh said, taking a sip of his tea.

"How'd that happen?"

"I ran into her at a banquet." Cavanaugh avoided J. J.'s eyes as he cut into a cheese strudel.

J. J. saw the guilt on his face right away. "You did something stupid, didn't you?" He had a great deal of respect for the younger man, but his temper was most certainly his weakness. "What'd you do?"

"Nothing," Cavanaugh said, feeling every bit the idiot

J. J. was making him out to be. "I just told her to decide whether we had a future together or not."

"You propositioned her?"

"No." Cavanaugh was offended by the vulgar sound of the word, but once he stopped and truly considered his actions, he realized the word applied.

"Okay, maybe," he said. "But it wasn't like you make it sound."

"No?"

"No, it was just—you see—" He stuttered terribly, feeling worse with every word. "I asked her to marry me," he finally blurted out.

"What'd she say?"

"Yes."

"Great."

"Then she changed it to no."

"What do you mean she changed it to no?"

"Just that. She said yes. Then in the morning, she changed her mind."

"Wait a minute—in the *morning*?" J. J. scratched his bald head. "You didn't ask her during—"

"Why does that matter?" Cavanaugh jumped to his feet. "A yes is a yes."

"The hell it is," J. J. said, completely dumbfounded by his friend's actions. "Evelyn could ask me for a new car while we're making love, doesn't mean she's getting one."

"I heard that." The woman's voice came from the other room.

"Listen, Cavanaugh, you can't just go through life manipulating people into doing what you want."

"What's that supposed to mean?" he said, genuinely hurt by his friend's coarse description of what he thought was a heartfelt proposal.

"Okay, think back to the girl in the restaurant," J. J. said, before biting into a chocolate chip cookie.

"What girl?"

"The one who gave us the extra food."

"What does that have to do with anything?"

"It's the same thing," J. J. said, blowing cookie crumbs in every direction. "You smiled and winked and got exactly what you wanted. Maybe instead of a wink and a smile, it's a pat on the back, or a hearty laugh at a bad joke. You do the same thing with everybody, but Marty's not the type of woman who's going to be manipulated by anyone."

Cavanaugh considered his friend's words carefully and realized there might be some truth in it. After all, he thought, he was raised by the queen of manipulation.

"What about you?"

"Me?"

"Yeah, why are you my friend?"

"I'm just a sucker for a sob story." J. J. said, and gulped down the rest of his coffee.

Marty had pulled on her Jordans and was beginning her stretches when she noticed Cal coming out of the latrine.

"Didn't you run this morning?" he asked, surprised to see her back in her work-out clothes.

"Yeah, but I've been getting a bit flabby around the middle," she lied. "I'm doubling up my routine."

Cal hunched his shoulders absently, and headed back to his quarters. Marty charged out the door and down the long sidewalk at top speed, hoping that after the five-mile, forty-minute run she would be ready to collapse across her bed in exhaustion and sleep, something she hadn't been able to do in the past three nights. Not since she'd been with him again, felt him inside her, tasted him on her mouth.

Just when she thought she had gotten him out of her system, she'd gone and contaminated herself again. Marty knew instinctively that this time the detoxification process would be much more difficult.

She ran, allowing the cool air to whip across her face, trying to wipe away the feel of his strong shoulders gliding back and forth beneath her hands. She stretched her legs out, trying to run away from the sensuous feel of his breath on her neck. She pumped her arms ignoring the pumping of her heart at the memory of his hands in places that only his hands should ever be.

She ran and ran, until five miles became seven, and forty minutes became sixty. Still she ran, until her legs were so weak they quivered beneath her and threatened to fail. Only then did she stop, realizing she'd run almost ten miles from her firehouse.

After bending and stretching to slow her erratic heartbeat, she sat down on the curb and watched the sun set just beyond the tall buildings that outlined the downtown skyline.

Folding her head across her legs, she allowed herself to cry. Alone on an empty street just after dusk, she cried for the little girl who'd finally kissed the right frog, yet was farther away from her happy-ever-after than she had ever been before. And for the handsome prince, whose dark past would forever haunt him.

Twenty-seven

"I'm sorry, honey, but that sea hag just brings it out in me." Donald fumed across the well-polished oak wood foyer. Nicole was trailing behind, trying in vain to calm him. They both stopped dead in their tracks at the sight of Cavanaugh standing at the bottom of the staircase.

Donald bowed his head, feeling guilty for however much the other man may have heard. Sea hag or not, she was still this man's mother. And considering the depth of love he had for his own mother, Donald could never imagine hearing anyone speak of her in such derogatory terms. But then again, he thought, his mother was nothing at all like Reline Saint John.

"Sorry, man," he muttered.

Cavanaugh nodded, not truly offended, but feeling he should show some indignation, if just for the sake of appearance. There were days when he felt exactly the same as Donald was feeling right then toward his own mother. She took almost as much pleasure in belittling her nephew-in-law as she did in demeaning her son.

Donald took off toward the west wing. He was insisting for the umpteenth time to Nicole that they should move out and get their own place. Of course, Nicole was agreeing for the moment, as she always did to calm her husband when he began one of his tirades about her aunt. But by morning, the discussion would be nothing more than a vague memory. The Saint Johns stayed together. It was the way it had always been, and if Reline Saint John had any say-so, it was the way it would always be.

Cavanaugh entered the busy library and started toward the large desk that took up the far corner. Priscilla and one of her girlfriends from school were working on the computer terminal stationed on a smaller writing desk on the other side of the room. They were so engrossed in what they were doing they barely noticed him enter the room.

Candice was sitting on the large leather couch with her newborn baby curled in the crook of one arm, while the other hand held a half-empty bottle of formula to his mouth. Cavanaugh paused long enough to kiss her on the cheek and look at the baby nestled in the soft, blue blanket. A male child, which was a rarity in their family. He already knew the infant would be spoiled to no end, starting with his older cousins, and moving out into the extended family.

"And how is Mr. Marshall today?" Cavanaugh saw the tiny ball of peach-brown flesh was already sprouting blades of brown fuzz on his bald head.

"Just fine," Candice looked up and smiled, but the exhaustion was clearly written on her face. It had been a long, difficult birth. She had been in labor nearly forty-two hours before the doctors finally decided to do a C-section. And then there was more heartbreak when she discovered her milk was no good, and she would not be able to feed the baby naturally, something she'd wanted desperately to do. But as turbulent a birth as it might have been, little Marshall had fought his way into the world kicking and screaming, and brought his mother and father endless moments of joy since then, albeit not much sleep.

"Are you okay?" She could see the dark shadows under his eyes.

"Yeah, I'm fine," he lied, and smiled, but the false gesture did nothing for the sadness in his eyes.

"How long do you plan to hide out here?" She carefully lifted the baby over her shoulder and began patting his back.

"I'm not hiding out," Cavanaugh said. He slumped down on the sofa, completely forgetting about the large stack of contracts he needed to review on the desk across the room.

"What do you call it?" she said, watching his face.

"Visiting with my family." He reached for the sleepy infant. The baby curled against his shoulder as easily as he had his mother's.

Candice sat back on the comfortable couch, thankful for the short reprieve. "Please, boy, who do you think you're talking to?"

He sighed, remembering exactly whom he was talking to. This was no-nonsense Candice, the most fearless and honest woman he knew.

"Well . . ." He hesitated as his mind flashed to the image of Marty's smiling face, the second most fearless and honest woman he knew.

"I think I've lost her for good this time," he said, while his large hand stroked the baby's back.

Candice watched him for several long seconds before responding.

"Maybe," she said, "maybe not."

Cavanaugh tilted his head to the side, studying her with mild amusement. "Wow, thanks. That was enlightening."

She prodded him. "I just meant that she's the only one who can answer that question for you. You won't find it here in Savannah. Go talk to her, Cavanaugh. Ask her to marry you again. Show her you think she's worth fighting for, even at the risk of your pride being hurt."

Cavanaugh felt the tiny body ripple against his shoulder as the gas bubble finally escaped. "And what if she says no again?"

Candice reached over and stroked his cheek. *My little cousin,* she thought. His goods looks and charm had brought him the companionship of many women over the years. And yet, he knew nothing about them. "Trust me, Cuz, she won't."

Cavanaugh had never told anyone, but he had discovered the root of his mother's animosity toward him long ago. He had felt it as a child, but didn't understand it until well into adulthood. The underlying, manipulative control that his parents' union had been built on had ended with his birth. His father had someone to love and be loved by in return, and no longer needed to grovel at the feet of his wife for affection—although Cavanaugh knew for a fact that his father bowed to his mother until his dying day. He assumed his father's love must have overridden his senses, despite what he knew about his heartless wife. And Cavanaugh would always believe that love was his downfall.

Then, with his father's death, the animosity grew. In the stipulation of his will, Cavanaugh's cousins were all dependent on their aunt for their inheritance, and she doled out every penny with the malicious nature of a power-lusty overlord. In contrast, Graham Saint John had designed his son's trust in such a way that Reline not only had no control over it, she had no access to it. His father's foresight had given him the ability to live his life the way he wanted, not depending on his mother for every morsel of food that entered his mouth.

So when he saw her as she was now, sitting in her beloved parlor entertaining a group of her women friends as though she were the Queen of Sheba, he fought the urge to call her out, to reveal her for the fake she was before her peers. He knew it would devastate her, maybe even crush her. He could never have done it. For all her wickedness she was still his mother. The woman that gave him life and had been trying to snuff it out ever since.

"Is something wrong, dear?" Cavanaugh knew her friends only saw the sweet smile of concern on her lips. He alone saw the silent challenge gleaming in her gray eyes.

"I was just coming to let you know I'm leaving now," he said, and smiled to her circle of friends, ever the dutiful son. He had played the role almost from birth, and wore it now as naturally as a well-worn suit.

She held up her arms and gestured for him to come give her a farewell hug. The women around her cooed at the sentimental gesture, thinking of their own children spread across the country and how they wished they could see them more. Reline was so lucky, most thought, to have the bulk of her family right under the same roof.

Cavanaugh crossed the room and embraced his frail mother, breathing in the faint scent of orchids. He was certain it was the first smell he had ever been conscious of.

Without warning, she tightened her hold and squeezed him hard and solidly. Cavanaugh's eyes widened in surprise, realizing the act of a hug had somehow become a genuine one. He pulled away and looked into her familiar eyes. There was something there, not love, but it wasn't hatred either. And for his mother that was an improvement.

He pecked her on the cheek, excused himself from the company of the other ladies, and strolled out of the room with a regal air well-recognized as the movement of a Saint John. The whole lot of them moved with the grace and elegance of stallions prancing, or so it was said.

For Cavanaugh his proud countenance was as natural as breathing. It hid well the silent leap his heart was doing inside his chest at the moment, and the possibility that at the age of thirty-four, he may have just received his first genuine hug from his mother.

But what did it mean, he wondered. And more importantly, would there be more to come?

Cavanaugh passed through the glass enclosure, walking quickly toward the parking lot. He only mildly noticed the rain drizzling against the clear tunnel. He was more interested in the messages being recited by Reesy on the other end of the phone.

"Got that?"

"Yeah, got it." He tapped away at the Palm Pilot cradled in the palm of his hand.

He shifted left, just in time to miss a head-on collision with a fellow tenant charging in his direction. The man didn't even bother to acknowledge his rude behavior.

"Is that it?" Cavanaugh asked, pressing the button to disarm his car alarm while still several feet away from his vehicle.

"Yes. That's all I have for now. And by the way, thank you," she said, holding up her wrist to look at the shimmering gold bangle bracelet that had arrived earlier that afternoon with the tiny card that read "Happy Birthday to the best assistant in the world."

Cavanaugh smiled. "You're welcome. I gotta go."

Reesy didn't bother saying good-bye, she simply hung

up the phone. In almost seven years of working for the man, she'd never once heard him say the word.

Cavanaugh slipped behind the wheel of his car and started the ignition. There was much he wanted to do today. He and J. J. had discovered there were only a few stores in the Detroit area that sold the type of accelerants used to start the fire at the law firm. A cop friend of J. J. had gotten a lead on a store that reported selling a few cans of it just days prior to the fire. Picking up J. J. and checking into that was the first order of the day.

Later, he needed to check out two used trucks he'd been considering buying for SJT. Personally inspecting and procuring trucks was not necessarily his responsibility, but with everything that had been happening lately, he'd decided to learn as much about the inner workings of the business as he could.

He'd also decided to try to talk to Marty again, to broach the subject of marriage with a little more finesse than he'd used the first time. He knew she loved him. It was just a matter of presenting that love in a more appealing manner, not as a take-it-or-leave-it proposition.

Ten minutes later he pulled up to J. J.'s house and blew the horn. He decided to wait in the car. Cavanaugh loved Evelyn Palmer like a favorite aunt, but every time she saw him lately she was trying to stick food in his mouth. She personally thought his svelte physique bordered on skinny, and felt some type of compulsion to fatten him up. Luckily he didn't have to wait long before he saw J. J. running toward the car with his jacket lifted above his head. The man slipped in beside him, shaking off the water.

"Hey, man," J. J. said, while reaching inside his jacket pocket.

"Hey," Cavanaugh responded, and turned to check for oncoming traffic.

"Here." J. J. offered him a small, square, tin-foiled package. "She thought you may not have had lunch yet."

Cavanaugh just sighed and pulled into the busy lane. He and J. J. had talked about his wife's disdain for scrawny men, and her mission to save Cavanaugh from such a fate.

J. J. didn't have the heart to tell her he was the one who ate the bulk of her love offerings. He waited just long enough to be certain the other man didn't want it, then tore into the foil and smiled to see it was his favorite, corned beef with Swiss cheese on rye, and just a dab of mustard.

"Mmmm, mmmm," J. J. shook his head in delight. "You just don't know what you're missing."

Cavanaugh just chuckled lightly, watching his friend chomp away happily. His attention was focused on the rain that was now pouring down in sheets against the glass. He maneuvered through traffic with caution, making sure his speed was reasonable for such driving conditions.

He and J. J. were discussing the reliability of the latest bits of information they'd obtained when Cavanaugh noticed the brake lights across the three lanes in front of him. He pumped the brake, but the car did not slow down. He pumped it harder, but it continued to cruise along. Cavanaugh stopped talking and pumped it again. The motion did nothing to impede the speeding car.

By now J. J. had noticed what was going on, and was instinctively bracing himself against the dashboard while watching his friend. He knew there was nothing he could do, and questioning the man now when he needed to concentrate more than ever wouldn't help. Instead, he just watched and waited.

Cavanaugh continued to press on the brake, holding it down and finally accepting that his brakes had gone out and that they were about to crash into the back of the stationary traffic in front of them if he didn't do something fast. His mind was quickly calculating the possibilities as he looked left and right up the embankments on both sides.

"Hold on," he called to J. J., and turned the steering wheel hard, forcing the car to move across two lanes and onto the curb of the highway. Cavanaugh continued to press the brake even as he worked to transition the car out of harm's way.

If anything, the car had picked up momentum with the sudden jerking move. J. J. sat back and accepted the inevitable. They were about to crash; it was just a matter of when and where. Cavanaugh worked hard to control the movements of the car even on the slippery gravel of the curbside. They floated along the shoulder of the highway, the cars they quickly passed becoming blurs of color. Cavanaugh was still looking for a grassy knoll or some kind of soft trench to run onto, but there was nothing.

The cars alongside them, not understanding what was happening, began blowing their horns at what they perceived as aggressive behavior. But all Cavanaugh heard was the sound of metal against metal as he accepted the reality that he had no brakes whatsoever.

Suddenly, out of nowhere, a white sedan shot out in front of the silver BMW, cutting it off at the pass, and forcing it further up onto the embankment. The car tipped up onto the side, then rolled back down the hill and into the still-unmoving traffic.

Marty stopped in the gift shop to buy a nice card with a fluffy puppy on the cover, and a few small games to pass the time. She wanted to take him some candy too, but knew he would not be allowed to have it in the hospital. After picking out a "Get Better Soon" balloon, she bent over the counter and filled in the card:

Henry,
Hurry up and get well.
Your engine team needs you.

She tucked it into the envelope, paid for everything quickly, and turned to leave, humming to herself. In the few months she'd known Henry Romaine, she'd only visited him twice in a hospital. Both times, his enthusiasm and positive attitude had left her feeling silly for whatever mild grievances she may have had. She knew little about multiple sclerosis, except that it was considered the disease of young people. She understood that most lived long lives with it, but unfortunately, hospital stays were a common part of that life. Luckily, none of Henry's episodes that she knew of had been severe, and he'd fully recovered from every attack.

She was standing with four other people waiting for the elevators, when she saw the doors leading to the ambulance entrance swing open, the stretcher plowing toward the small group of pedestrians. They all moved back against the wall to give the trauma unit the floor, and she felt her heart go out to the unfortunate person on the white table.

The group of doctors and nurses crowded around the bed were moving quickly through the crowded corridor. But not so quickly that Marty could not recognize her very own heart and soul laying like a mass of rubble across the stretcher.

The bag of games and balloon slipped from her hands as she felt a numbing sensation run through her body. Quickly she regained her senses, and went running down the long hallway, her long legs pumping hard as she chased after an unconscious Cavanaugh.

Twenty-eight

"Marty."

She slept so lightly, the soft whisper of her name combined with the gentle stroke of her face was enough to wake her. She smiled before opening her eyes, certain that the hand touching her was Cavanaugh's. The smile faded when she looked up from the bed to find J. J. standing beside her.

His smile remained firmly in place, offering what solace he could to the bleary-eyed woman who'd held vigil for the past seven nights.

Marty turned her head quickly toward the bed where Cavanaugh lay sound asleep, his brown skin in stark contrast to the snow-white linen sheets. His brown curls nestled against the fluffy pillow. He looked like an angel resting on top of a cloud.

"Any change?" Using the back of her hand, she wiped at the saliva that had formed in the corner of her mouth.

"Afraid not, sweetheart," J. J. said, looking over her shoulder at his comatose friend. How he wished it were him lying in the bed, instead. Or better, that neither of them were there.

"Here, I brought you some lunch." He offered it to her with his right hand, while unconsciously rubbing the arm where it was supported by a nylon sling.

"Thanks." Marty watched the action, feeling a bit

guilty. For the past week her attention had been so focused on Cavanaugh, she'd all but forgotten the other man who'd been in the car with him.

"How are you doing?" Marty asked, as she stood and stretched.

Better than him," J. J. said soberly, using his one good arm to unpack his own Burger King lunch bag.

"Here, let me," Marty said, taking the bag away from him. She unwrapped the burger and poured the fries onto the open liner while J. J. pulled up a chair.

The end of the hospital bed had become a makeshift table, used for everything from a desktop for signing important release papers, to a game board on which they played checkers, to a dinner tray. And through it all, the much-beloved man lying beneath the covers never so much as stirred.

"Hey, guys." Andrea came through the doorway.

Marty had thought it a wonderful blessing that if he had to be here, at least Cavanaugh had ended up in the care of someone who knew, and truly cared for, him. Cal's new girlfriend had quickly become a member of their firehouse family, and a friend to both Marty and Cavanaugh. On those rare occasions when Marty decided to leave the hospital for a hot shower and change of clothes, she made sure it was during Andrea's shift.

The nurse rounded the bed and came alongside Cavanaugh. Marty knew anyone else would have chased her out days ago for bringing in food and eating on the bed like it was a countertop.

Andrea exchanged the empty IV pouch for a new one, checked Cavanaugh's vitals, and charted the findings, all the while going on about the conversation she had overheard the doctors having regarding their friend. Marty knew the information being given so freely had to be confidential. But she wasn't about to chastise her friend regarding her ethics. Anything she knew or heard about Cavanaugh was welcome news, considering the doctors themselves gave her little or no information.

". . . anyway, suffice it to say, they're clueless." Andrea shrugged her shoulders before tucking her stethoscope back into the pocket of her pink scrub shirt.

Marty looked down at her precious man once again. She was as clueless as his doctors were. She'd learned two days ago that according to the medical profession's diagnosis he should be awake by now.

Fortunately, he had not sustained any internal injuries or broken limbs. He was banged up a bit, with a few scratches and bruises, but nothing to explain this deep trancelike state of being. Having done all they could, the doctors were left in the same place as Marty, J. J., and everyone who loved this man: mental purgatory.

After they ate, J. J. stayed for another two hours before he headed home, promising to return the next day. Marty knew he would. She also knew Evelyn, his wife, would stop by later that afternoon on her way home from work, the way she had every day for the past five days. In fact, it seemed that at some point during the past week everyone they knew had been by to see him.

At that moment, Candice and Tony were on a plane headed to Detroit. Tabitha Saint John called to get updated reports for the family every day promptly at ten AM. Marty wondered why Reline Saint John had not hopped the first flight available to be with her child. Cal had stayed there with her most of the previous night, and the rest of the guys from the firehouse swung through when they could. No, the lack of companionship and concern for him were not the problem.

Marty watched back-to-back episodes of *Jeopardy* before going to stand and look out the window. The sun was setting, and the streetlights were just beginning to come on. The faint knock on the door caused her to turn around.

"Hi, Evelyn." Marty hugged the woman.

"Hey girl, any news?" Evelyn Palmer asked, setting her purse down to take Cavanaugh's limp hand between her own. Being a firm believer in touch therapy, Evelyn was certain that Cavanaugh could feel the touching of his skin. She also thought he could hear them, and had told Marty as much, trying to encourage the girl to touch him more. She knew it was painful for her to see him in this condition, but he needed the human contact, and what man could not find comfort in his woman's touch

"Have you rubbed his arms down today?" Evelyn tilted her head to the side and studied Marty.

Marty leaned against the window sill, and nodded "This morning."

"Good," Evelyn said. "Just remember, he can still hear you even if he can't respond. I read this story once about a man who'd been in a coma for almost a year, and when he finally woke up he remembered almost everything that had been said to him."

Marty's heart skipped a beat at the thought of Cavanaugh being like this for a year. "Don't worry, I talk to him all the time." Marty said, but didn't add that the conversation consisted mostly of begging and pleading for his forgiveness.

"Well, I need to get home and see about J. J." Evelyn lifted her purse. "But I'll see you tomorrow."

Marty waited until the other woman left the room before approaching the bed. This was their alone time. Those few precious hours in the evening after all the visitors had come and gone. Marty knew she wasn't supposed to be there either, but Andrea never said a word to her.

She stood looking down on his exceptionally handsome face, studying every inch of him, from his lush brown eyelashes to his full perfect mouth. Even the sprinkling of partially healed cuts and bruises did nothing to take away from his fine features.

"There's so much I need to say to you," she said, rubbing his arm. Marty knew she would give her last breath to hear him wake up and answer her. She quickly looked up at the door to make sure no one was in the hallway, then bent to press her lips to his. Her one daily indulgence, stolen kisses. It had become her source of strength.

Like something out of a fairy tale, this time the kiss caused her beauty to stir from his deep sleep. He shook his head left, then right on the pillow. He looked as if he were struggling to escape from some dark, cerebral dungeon. His features twisted in pain as he wrenched back and forth on the bed.

Marty rung the buzzer over his head and Andrea appeared almost instantly. Seeing the movement on the bed, she quickly went over to Cavanaugh and pulled his eyes apart, looking into them with her slim penlight.

"He's trying, girl. He's trying." Andrea hugged Marty tight, then released her suddenly. "I'll find the doctor." Then she was gone.

Marty was beside the bed again, tears of joy in her eyes. He was going to be fine, he was truly going to be all right.

"Cavanaugh? Baby, wake up," Marty encouraged lovingly. She stroked his hair, and pecked kisses on his face. "I'm here, right here beside you. Wake up for me."

He twisted his body on the bed making hard, jerky movements. His mouth opened, but Marty could not make out what he was saying.

"I'm here, it's okay. I'm right here with you," she cooed.

He tried to speak again, and this time she pressed her face close to his mouth to hear his words. Marty listened once, then twice, not wanting to believe what she'd heard. Once she was certain, she stood upright, and immediately went to collect her small travel bag. She packed up a few of her toiletries, and other personal items that had become scattered across the room over the past few days. She grabbed her light jacket off the back of the door, walked out of the hospital room, and never looked back. She left Cavanaugh still contorting on the small bed, his face flexed in pain as his voice finally strengthened enough for the words to be heard clearly. "Go away! Why won't you just leave me alone?"

Cavanaugh stormed down the hall away from his mother. He had just turned twenty-one earlier that week, and she was giving him another of her many lectures on maturity and responsibility. She followed close behind, her heels clinking on the polished wood floors.

"It's time for you to take your place at the head of this family, Cavanaugh. You've ignored your responsibilities for far too long now."

"Leave me alone, Mother!" He headed toward the library, intent on devouring one of his father's best bottles of brandy, then veered for the staircase at the last moment. He had no desire to add his excessive drinking to her list of grievances. He just wanted to get away from her.

"You're just like your father, worthless!" She hounded his heels.

He paused on the bottom step, his dark eyes burning with fury. "I hate you. Why won't you leave me alone?" He turned and headed up the wide staircase, his long legs taking the stairs two at a time. Reline followed close behind, but halfway up, her plastic heel became tangled in a piece of the carpeting that had come unraveled. The last sound Cavanaugh heard was his mother's cry of terror. He turned to grab for her, but it was too late. Moments later, her small body lay unconscious at the bottom of the staircase.

Cavanaugh stood terrified, looking down on the crumpled body of his mother. He rushed to the bottom, calling for help. When one of the maids appeared, Cavanaugh instructed her to call 911. He refused to leave his mother's side, fearing her shallow breathing would fade to nothing. Cavanaugh had prayed so many times, asking God to rid him of his tyrannical mother, but this was not what he wanted. This was not what he'd meant!

"Oh, Mama." He whispered the childhood name he'd given up the night his father died. He sat rocking her body and begging God not to punish him this way.

J. J. stood in the doorway with a small bag containing personal items and a change of clothes Cavanaugh had requested tucked under his arm. He was beaming from ear to ear. "It lives," he said, coming to hug his friend.

Cavanaugh leaned forward to receive the hug, although his body was still extremely stiff. "Hey man," he said, putting his spoon down. He'd only taken five small bites of the unidentifiable thing they called Salisbury steak, and that was only at Andrea's insistence.

J. J. just stood thanking God and staring at the man he'd been certain would not survive when he watched him being pulled from the crushed car by the "Jaws of Life."

"How's my car?" Cavanaugh asked, pushing the tray away. He had a good idea, but still needed to hear it.

J. J. paused for a long moment. "You got good insurance, right?"

"Yeah," he answered slowly.

"Good, your gonna need it."

"Damn." Cavanaugh laid his head back against the pillow feeling like a cowboy whose horse had just been put down. "I loved that car."

"Well, at least it died for the greater good," J. J. teased.

"I guess you've got a point," Cavanaugh said, running his fingers through his hair.

"I never liked those little foreign numbers, but that one was tougher than it looked." J. J. crossed the room and put the bag he'd brought onto the window ledge.

"Andrea said Marty was here all week." Cavanaugh was hoping J. J. would turn to face him. J. J. had a very expressive face; if he knew anything it would show there.

Cavanaugh still didn't know what to make of what he'd been told. According to Andrea, Marty had been by his side all week, day and night. So why would she disappear just as he began to awaken? Unless, he thought, she'd only come out of pity for a former love, and had no desire to be near the recovered version.

"Yes, she was." J. J. stood looking out the window, keeping his back to the other man. How he'd hoped this would not come up, but he should have known better. Andrea had brought him up-to-speed in the hallway only minutes ago about how Marty had stormed out the night before, offering no explanation to anyone. J. J. had no more idea about it than anyone else.

She'd seemed so concerned about Cavanaugh and perfectly content to stay by his side no matter how long it took for him to recuperate. Seeing Marty's rededication to the man, everyone had just assumed that the couple would be able to work out their problems when Cavanaugh woke up. If Cavanaugh woke up.

"I tried to call the firehouse, but I got no answer," Cavanaugh said.

"I'm sure she'll be by later, probably went home to change clothes." J. J. turned to face Cavanaugh.

Cavanaugh's heart sank, knowing J. J. didn't believe his own words. But what had happened? If she cared enough about him to stand by him through his coma, surely she'd come to realize they belonged together.

"Yeah, maybe you're right," he said, trying to shake off the melancholy mood he'd had ever since he opened his eyes and found himself alone in the hospital room.

J. J.'s face sobered into a hard line. "I know you just woke up, and probably don't need to hear this right now, but there is something you should know."

"What?" Cavanaugh could hear the sudden change in his tone.

"Apparently, someone cut the brake lines."

Cavanaugh looked at his friend, not very surprised. He'd assumed as much. He turned in the bed, and swung his long legs around to the floor.

"What are you doing?" J. J. asked, watching him pull the IV from his arm.

"That's the third attempt." Cavanaugh paused. "That I know about. I'm not going to just lie here and let someone put a pillow over my head while I'm sleeping, or inject poison into my IV."

"You watch too many movies, man," J. J. chuckled, trying to lighten the seriousness of the situation. He'd only meant to make his friend aware that he was still in danger; he had not expected this reaction.

"Look, someone wants me dead." Cavanaugh stood, then grabbed ahold of the bed. After being in a prone position for a week, his legs were weak. When he regained his composure, he came to collect the fresh clothes from the windowsill.

"I can't just lie in this hospital bed and pretend like everything's rosy. I need to find out who is behind this."

"And just where do you think you're going?" Andrea stood in the doorway with her hands on her hips.

"Just go back out the door, Andrea, and pretend you didn't see this," Cavanaugh said sternly.

But Nurse Chenault was not about to be bullied by her own patient. "Cavanaugh, you've only been awake one day. We still don't know if there will be any long-term effects."

Cavanaugh looked from J. J. to his nurse. "So, if I go, I could die from some unknown complication."

"Exactly." Andrea sounded off, loud and strong.

"And if I stay, I could be murdered in my bed."

"Well, I doubt . . ." This time, her voice faltered, realizing she'd been tricked.

He took the bag into the bathroom and changed quickly. Andrea continued to plead with him. J. J. didn't say a word one way or the other, he just followed the determined man out of the hospital room, and out of the building.

Twenty-nine

"It seems our man has more lives than a cat."

"Don't worry, it'll be taken care of once and for all."

"You're damn right it will, since I'm doing it myself."

"What are you talking about?"

"If you want something done right, do it yourself."

"Hey, wait just—"

"No, you wait just a minute. You've been screwing this up from the start, and need I remind you that our employers are not the most forgiving people? Now we need to get this matter settled, once and for all. Cavanaugh Saint John must die."

"But, this was—"

"Do you really want to challenge me on this?"

"How will you do it?"

"That's the easy part. I'll use bait."

Marty entered the common area, and Cal turned to look at her. He jerked his head to the left causing her to look toward the man sitting in the large brown recliner on the other end of the crowd of spectators. He sat intently, watching the basketball game on the big-screen TV. The guys scattered across the floor and in the other chairs all seemed completely comfortable with his presence, as if he had not been absent for the past three months.

Seeing her enter, Cavanaugh rose and crossed the room quickly. "Can we talk?" The statement was spoken quietly; still, every head in the room turned in their direction.

"Come in here," she said, leading him into the kitchen, and away from the room full of prying eyes. She knew he would come eventually, and she had mentally prepared herself. She set the two large bags of groceries on the counter and turned to face him.

Without warning, she felt his hands close around the small of her back, and his lips closed on hers, causing her breath to catch in her throat. She wanted to push him away but she simply couldn't. He felt so good, so right. Her arms came up around his neck as she parted her mouth to his warm tongue.

He took the offering eagerly, plunging his tongue deep. How he wanted to lift her up on the counter and make love to her right there. He needed the healing effects of her warmth, her embrace. He needed her body. His large hand came up to cup her breast. The soft tissue rolled between his fingers.

Marty closed her eyes and let her head fall back as his kisses turned to tiny nibbles on her cheek and neck. He pulled to lift the cotton T-shirt, wanting to put his mouth where his hands were, but Marty refused. She had not forgotten the roomful of her crew members who were so very close.

"No, we can't," she said, and pushed him away. The momentary break in their passionate display had been enough to clear her mind. As much as she loved him, as much as she wanted him, she knew he didn't feel the same. He may want her physically, but he didn't love her, something she would never have believed, had she not heard him speak the truth in his delirium.

"Cal said you're off duty in a couple of hours. Let's go back to your place," he whispered, fighting her resisting hands. He had felt her passion, her hunger for him, and he wasn't about to just drop it.

"No," she insisted, knowing she had to get away from his hands if she wanted to hold to her senses. Marty moved away from the counter, and began unpacking the bags as though the last few minutes had never happened.

"What's going on?" Cavanaugh asked, his head swirling in confusion. "I know you were at the hospital almost up until the time I woke up. I know you still want me by what just happened here. So why do you keep fighting it?"

"Keep your voice down," she said, placing a finger to her lips.

"No," he snapped. His deferred lust had him bordering on anger as his scrambled mind still struggled to make sense of her erratic behavior. His whole body was aching with his need for her, and all she cared about was who heard.

"I love you," he continued, intentionally raising his voice. He turned and went to the doorway. "Hey guys, I love this woman. Does anybody have a problem with that?"

The group of men all shook their heads from side to side, and muttered seeing the threat in those black eyes of his.

"Naw, man."

"Not me."

"Hm-um."

And so it went, as every man in the room had felt the same overwhelming emotion at one time or another. Objecting would've been like getting between a lion and a fresh carcass. Just simply not very smart.

Cavanaugh turned back to face Marty who'd come up

behind him. "See, they understand." He gestured to the group of guys. "I—love—you," he continued at the top of his lungs and grinning from ear to ear. "I—love—you."

"Well, I don't love you."

The silence that fell over the room was only interrupted by the sound of two sports announcers, discussing an impressive rebound by Kobe Bryant.

Cavanaugh leaned against the wall to brace his suddenly limp body. He hadn't fully recovered from the accident, and the sharp verbal blow had been nothing less than a knife slicing into his heart. As he struggled to breath, he looked into the eyes of this woman he adored, and shook his head fiercely, refusing to believe the words she'd just spoken. It couldn't be true.

"That's why I left the hospital, so I wouldn't have to deal with just this kind of scene," she said, but even in her fury, the tears were quickly forming in her eyes. Her pride had taken charge again, and the words were all coming from a deeply hurt place inside her.

"You don't mean that," he whispered, his heart thudding madly against his chest.

"Oh, yes, I do," she said, drawing out each word for stinging power. "I mean, it was fun while it lasted, but it was over a long time ago. You just don't know how to take no for an answer, and I didn't want to deal with your drama, so I left."

"So why did you come to begin with?" His whole body braced for the blow he was certain was about to come. But if he were wrong, and how he prayed that he was wrong, she would finally see they belonged together.

Marty's mind raced as she struggled to come up with an answer that would end this discussion once and for all. She had to send him away from there and know that he would never return. One more encounter, one more embrace, and her paper-thin wall of resistance would fall.

"Pity," she said. "I felt sorry for you."

Cavanaugh's heart fractured like fragile glass. Why couldn't he have been wrong? Cavanaugh stood straight, and turned facing the group of guys. Then he looked away quickly as he made his way toward the doorway, unable to bear their sympathetic stares. He stumbled down the metal stairs and out to his rented sedan. He started to open the door, then fell against the hood pounding on it with his fist.

For so long, he'd successfully shielded his heart from this kind of pain, not letting anyone inside his shell of indifference. But Marty had gotten in, and look at what she'd done to him. Cavanaugh had vowed after the death of his father to never feel anything again.

He turned and looked up at the brick building once more, and thought about the beautiful woman who'd captured his heart. For her, he'd too easily broken that vow.

He climbed into the car, and pulled away, wondering if there would ever be a time when loving someone didn't cost him everything.

J. J. pulled up outside the empty warehouse and looked up at the tall building. Then he turned and looked up and down the street. There was no sign of the rented sedan.

He had received a call less than an hour ago from Cavanaugh asking to meet right away. He'd sounded so frantic, not at all like himself, and it had instantly alarmed J. J. Whatever was troubling him, Cavanaugh refused to discuss it over the phone.

J. J. had come as quickly as he could. And now, he was here, but where was Cavanaugh? There was no sign of him, at least none on the outside. He stepped out of his pickup truck and looked around once more. Something about the whole scene didn't sit well with him. But if Cavanaugh was in trouble inside the building, then J. J. knew he had to get inside. He decided to disregard the missing car, knowing there could be a thousand reasons why it was not there.

He slowly approached the building, carefully inspecting everything from the window ledges to the edge of the doors. He was looking for signs of tampering, or maybe even the settings of a trap. Twenty years of instincts were hard to ignore. Not feeling completely confident that he wasn't walking into a trap, he opened the door slowly. The large, metal door swung open with a creak.

J. J. looked around the large empty room. Sunlight was streaming in from the many large, highly-placed windows. Dust covered everything including the large crates stacked haphazardly in all four corners. He stepped inside and moved carefully toward a shadow on the floor in the far left corner. It appeared to be coming from behind one of the large crates, but the size and shape of the shadow did not coincide with the crate. As J. J. came closer, he recognized the shadow for what it was: a human shadow.

He reached into his holster and slowly drew his weapon, still moving toward the crate. The only sound was the faint crunching sound of his soles crushing the tiny grains of gravel on the floor. He quickly glanced back over his shoulder, making sure no one was behind him. Whoever was standing behind the crate obviously didn't want to be seen. He knew instinctively it was not Cavanaugh.

He cocked his pistol, and slid alongside the crate until he was just short of the corner. He braced himself, preparing to swing around the corner suddenly and surprise whoever was standing there.

But the real surprise came when he heard a scrambling noise above his head. He suddenly looked up, his eyes widened, and his pistol fell to the floor as the weight of a fully grown man came down hard on him.

Cavanaugh grabbed a Pepsi out of the fridge on the way to answer the front door. He heard the light knocking again and assumed it was Candice. She'd called earlier and said she would be by to check on him. His eyes widened in surprise to see Big Cal's massive frame filling his doorway.

"Hey, man," Cavanaugh said, taking the other into a light embrace. "What are you doing here?"

"I need to talk to you," Cal said, feeling like a stool pigeon. Had it not been for Andrea's insistence, he would never have done this.

Cavanaugh stepped aside, allowing the other man in. There was no need to ask what Cal needed to talk to him about. They both knew there was only one topic of discussion that would have brought Cal to his door.

"Want something to drink?" Cavanaugh said, offering up the Pepsi.

Cal shook his head no, while pulling off his jacket. He took in the elegant living room. "Nice crib." He slumped down on the leather couch.

"Thanks." Cavanaugh took a seat on the matching sofa across from him. He'd had little to do with the decorating of his condo. He had hired professionals, and they had done their job well. But having spent time in Marty's small apartment, he just couldn't see his own in the same light.

There were no pictures of loved ones covering every ounce of empty wall space. No badly done fifth-grade clay model touting a gold plaque that read "Second Place." No mismatched pillows impulsively bought from a resale store that strangely enough went together perfectly. No dingy pink throw cover that once belonged to a grandmother. In short, there was no love in his home, especially since the woman who'd brought it into his life was gone.

"First of all, let me say that I don't like doing this," Cal said, looking more uncomfortable by the minute. "But Andrea seems to think your knowing this will somehow make a difference."

"Knowing what?" Cavanaugh said, leaning forward.

"I love Marty like a sister, and if she thought I was here giving up her busi—"

"Cal, just say what you gotta say," Cavanaugh said, fighting to hold his impatience.

"Well, Andrea thinks she knows what happened at the hospital."

Cavanaugh scooted to the edge of the sofa, desperately wanting to hear what Andrea thought.

"She thinks it may have been something you said in a dream," Cal said, watching his friend suspiciously.

Cavanaugh's face turned pale and his mouth fell open. He suddenly remembered dreaming of that terrible accident so long ago, and instantly understood. He covered his face and shook his head, then stood and went to face the window. He needed to see the sky, the way he always did when he was distressed.

Seeing he would get no answer, Cal continued. "Andrea said Marty was there when you started waking up. Andrea went to find the doctor, but when she got back Marty was gone and you were whispering, "I'm so sorry, I'm so sorry."

Cal sat for a long time staring at the other man's back. He didn't like the tone of his body language. He looked guilty.

"Man, tell me you weren't messing around on my girl."

Cavanaugh heard the veiled threat and smiled, wishing he had a friend as loyal as Cal was to Marty. "No."

"So what's the deal?" Cal said, standing to go toward the kitchen, having decided to take Cavanaugh up on his offer of something to drink.

Cavanaugh, feeling more like himself again, returned to his position on the couch. "Before I woke up at the hospital, I remember having a nightmare about an accident that happened to my mother years ago. She fell down a flight of stairs, and I was right there, so close. And still, I couldn't catch her. That's what Marty heard, me reliving a nightmare."

"What happened?" Cal finally decided on a Sprite, and returned to the living room.

"I was drinking a lot back then," Cavanaugh said. "Mostly beer, but lots of it. I guess I blamed myself. My reflexes were too slow."

"Is that why you don't have any in your fridge." Cal chuckled. He settled back onto the couch, and popped open the tab of his can.

Cavanaugh chuckled at the disappointment in his friend's voice. "I promise I'll have a couple of cans for you the next time you visit."

"Does Marty know about this?"

"The accident, no. But in a way, my mother is the reason we broke up to begin with."

"Is she alive?" Cal asked.

"Yeah, she's alive. But the night of the accident I thought she would die."

Cavanaugh paused. "Wanna hear something crazy?" He needed to share with this casual acquaintance something he'd never shared with another human being.

"What's that?"

"I used to ask God to take her out of my life. I mean, I used to actually pray that something would . . . happen to her. So I'd be free of her. But, when I saw her lying unconscious at the bottom of those stairs, I was sure she was dead. I thought God was punishing me for my thoughts."

The weight of the confession hung in the air like a black cloud. Neither man had any words to add to it.

Finally Cavanaugh spoke again. "I guess the accident with J. J. must've triggered the memory."

"Why didn't you just tell Marty that?"

"I didn't know she heard anything until just now."

"So, what you gonna do?"

"What can I do? You were there, man, you heard her. She doesn't love me."

Cal sat back on the couch looking at Cavanaugh as if he'd completely lost his mind. "That woman sat by your side day and night for seven days. Cared for you like a loving mother caring for a helpless child. Not to mention worried me and everyone else to death with the little food and sleep she allowed herself, just so she could stay with you. And you got the nerve to sit here and make a statement like that?"

Cavanaugh was too dumbfounded to speak. So instead, he simply sipped his soda until the tension in the air passed. Luckily, Cal didn't hold his grudge for long, and the two men spent part of the afternoon playing foosball until Candice arrived, and Cal excused himself.

When Candice left two hours later, Cavanaugh was still thinking about the things Cal had said. He resolved to find a way to reach the woman he loved, the beautiful, loving woman she buried deep inside her heart. But first, he had to get past the hellcat she wore on the outside.

Cavanaugh was staying close to home at the behest of the police, who were planning to pick up Harwood Dowel for questioning that morning. However, the whole situation was making him feel like something of a coward.

His initial instinct had been to go to the law firm and take care of Dowel in a completely different way. But both he and J. J. had come to believe Harwood was only an errand boy for someone much more dangerous. The phone rang, startling him.

"Hello?"

"I understand you recently made a withdrawal?" The muffled voice of a man came through the line. Cavanaugh felt his jaw tighten. He'd been waiting for this call.

"Maybe."

"If you ever want to see your friend again you'll decide for certain right now."

"What are you talking about?"

The phone went silent for several seconds. "Cavanaugh, don't do it, man. They're gonna kill me anyway. Don't do it."

The phone was suddenly snatched away, and Cavanaugh felt his heart sink to his toes. They had J. J.

"I've got your money," Cavanaugh confessed.

"Smart man. Stay by the phone, and I'll contact you with a place and time we'll make the exchange."

Cavanaugh returned the cordless phone to its base, and began pacing the room. How could he have not seen this coming? He should have known the embezzler would turn into a kidnapper, holding J. J. to ensure Cavanaugh's cooperation. *So much for having the upper hand,* he thought. He could only be grateful that they left Marty alone. He tried to recognize the voice, making mental comparisons to everyone he knew. No matches. He needed backup but didn't completely trust the police; he still remembered the two men who'd approached him.

He picked up the phone again and started to call the one person he could trust, then slammed it back down.

If anything happened to her he couldn't live with himself. He went into his bedroom and pulled out the box containing the small revolver. He checked the chamber, then tucked it into his jeans. He went back to the living room and did the only thing he could do. He waited.

Marty lay with her head resting on her folded arms, staring at the elegant glass vase of white roses sitting on her small side table. They'd arrived that morning with a note that read:

"I know what you heard, but it's not what you think.
I was having a nightmare, not a dream.
Please let me explain."

The sounds of laughter and music outside her door drifted in, which only added to her depressed state. Cal and Andrea had arrived earlier that evening announcing their engagement, and an impromptu engagement party quickly followed.

Dwight made a call to Angelo's Pizzeria, Tommy made a beverage run to the liquor store, and shortly after that someone turned on the stereo. Soon the sweet smells of good food and the sound of party music had drawn a crowd.

Marty was happy for her friends, but their newfound status only reminded her of just how far away she was from spending her life with the man she loved. She turned over and began counting the many, tiny water spots on the ceiling of her bedroom.

Hearing a knock on the door, she sat upright. "Come in."

"Hey, girl, you all right?" Dina Johnston stuck her

head in the door. "I asked Dwight where you were, and he said no one's seen you in days."

"Yeah, I'm fine. What are you doing here?" She tried to smile at her friend.

"You know Helpless can't wash his own clothes."

"You are too good to him," Marty said, shaking her head and standing.

"I know," Dina said. "Are you sure you're okay?"

"Yeah, I'm fine." She stretched and yawned. She was unsure how long she'd been lying in the small bed, but apparently long enough to become stiff.

"All right," Dina said, reluctant to leave. She stepped through the doorway and started to pull the door closed, then paused. "Marty, what happened between you and Cavanaugh . . ."

"Yeah?"

"That wasn't because of what I told you, was it?"

"No," Marty said, seeing the hurt in her friend's eyes. "No, what happened between Cavanaugh and me, was because of Cavanaugh and me, nothing anyone else said or did."

Dina's eyes narrowed. She was still unsure she accepted that.

"Dina, really, it wasn't you," Marty tried to reassure her friend.

Dina nodded her head, deciding to accept the answer. As she left, she pulled the door, but intentionally left it cracked open, hoping the festive mood would draw the hermit out of her cave.

Marty pulled the small scrapbook of pictures she had collected over the past year out of the bottom of her closet, and crawled into the center of the bed. Pictures of a dream, she'd come to think of them. Pages and pages of happy memories. In almost every one, Cavanaugh was smiling in that brilliant way of his. She let her hand rub over his one-dimensional image, caressing every line of his handsome face. The sound of Rick James's "Ebony Eyes" coming from the other room was too much, and once again she felt the waterworks coming on.

Quickly she stumbled to the door and slammed it shut, as if blocking out the sound would somehow stop the throbbing ache in her chest. She started at the noise of someone tapping on the door. She cracked it to see Andrea's smiling face. Her eyes were filled with compassion.

"Is everything okay?"

"Yes," Marty lied, moving aside to let her newest girlfriend in.

"Sure it is, liar," Andrea said, flopping down onto the bed. "Want me to fix you a plate of food? There's plenty. Dwight ordered like he was feeding an army," she chuckled, but it did nothing to hide the true concern still written on her face.

"No, thanks, I'm fine." Marty sat down on the little bunk beside her.

"Well, I just wanted to say thanks." She touched Marty's shoulder. "For everything. You know, with Cal."

"Don't thank me just yet." Marty laughed fully for the first time all day. "You've never had to live with him."

Andrea just smiled, thoughtfully. "I mean it, Marty. He's a terrific guy, but I would've given up long ago if it hadn't been for you."

"A lot of women would've, Andrea. You just knew he was the guy for you. That had nothing to do with me."

"Well, thanks anyway," Andrea said, hugging Marty tightly. "Although knowing Cal"—she held up her one-carat, solitaire diamond engagement ring, admiring it in the light—"we'll probably be engaged for the next five years."

"At least," Marty added. The two women fell into a fit of laughter, realizing how well they both knew him.

"What's this?" Andrea said, having just noticed the scrapbook.

"Just pictures I've collected," Marty said, embarrassed to be caught with her one-woman fan club spread open on the bed.

"I know it's none of my business . . ." Andrea's eyes drifted briefly to the bouquet of roses. "But if you could've seen the look on his face when he woke up in the hospital room alone . . ."

Marty quickly looked away, refusing to feel any guilt for leaving him so abruptly. She never could have stayed, not after what she heard.

"Andrea—don't," Marty said, putting up her hand to still her friend. She turned her back to the other woman, and Andrea understood the silent request. She stood and quietly crept out of the room. Marty fell back into her pool of self-pity, curling up on her side in the fetal position as she pulled her scrapbook close to her.

She carefully unfolded one of the many newspaper articles she had collected. Since she met Cavanaugh, Marty had begun reading the business section of the paper, something that had, up until then, only served as a carpet protector while emptying the vacuum cleaner bag. The name Saint John appeared often, and given his camera-friendly image, there was usually a picture to accompany the words. She studied a picture of him beside Harwood Dowel. Something struck her as odd. She sat up in bed, studying the picture carefully. Suddenly, she hopped out of the bed, threw open her bedroom door, and went in search of Dina.

The firehouse was ablaze with activity. With so many people living in such a small space, there was always a dispute that needed to be settled or a card game missing a fourth man. The remote to the big-screen TV disappeared and reappeared constantly. Noise and chaos were standard living conditions, and Marty loved every bit of it.

She finally found Dina in the kitchen with Dwight, trying to acquaint him with the new microwave. Marty was certain he already knew how to work it, but who was she to say anything?

"Dina?"

"Yeah." Dina Johnston turned around, pleased to see the interest in her friend's eyes. When she had left her a while ago, the girl had looked so impassive it was scary.

Marty showed her the picture. "Didn't you once say you went to college with Harwood Dowel?"

"No," Dina said, cutting up several eggs for salad. Despite the boxes and boxes of pizza scattered throughout the building, Dwight had talked her into fixing him her specialty chicken salad, before he conveniently disappeared.

"I went to college with Kenneth Stanton," she said, glancing at the picture. "Yeah, that's him." She returned to her task.

Marty's brown eyes widened in amazement. "No, this is Harwood Dowel."

"No," Dina said, patiently. "That's Kenneth Stanton. Trust me, I went to school with him for seven years, I know the man's face when I see him."

Marty took the knife from her friend and forced the paper into her hand. "Dina, read the caption on the picture. Are you sure?"

Dina read the caption, looking only slightly surprised. "Humph, I guess they made a mistake, because this is most certainly Kenneth Stanton. I just saw him at an association meeting a few weeks ago."

Marty's mind was reeling. What did this mean? If the man in the picture was Kenneth Stanton, who was supposedly shot and killed, then where was the real Harwood Dowel? She rushed back to the phone on the wall, and only one thought entered her mind. Cavanaugh was in far more danger than even he realized.

Thirty

The rented sedan slowly pulled alongside the warehouse. Cavanaugh was taking the time to look over the building. Every nerve in his body was alert. According to the man on the phone, J. J. was inside that building. He got out of the car and quietly closed the door, although he knew his caution was pointless. Whoever arranged this meeting was probably aware of his arrival from the moment he pulled up.

He walked over to the large, metal door, looking in both directions, up and down the deserted street. He pushed hard against the door, and it gave, just like the man on the phone said it would. He stepped inside and found a scene that both startled and frightened him. There, seated in identical wood chairs bound and gagged, was J. J. alongside the woman Cavanaugh knew as Beth Stanton.

Standing just beyond the chairs was the man he knew as Harwood Dowel and the two men, Officers Brown and Pulaski, who had accosted Cavanaugh outside his office building. He took note that although Dowel held no weapon, both the henchmen were heavily armed.

"Aren't you supposed to be in jail?" Cavanaugh said, directing his attention toward Harwood and trying to hide the terror coursing threw his veins.

"Cavanaugh, Cavanaugh, Cavanaugh," Harwood said,

coming toward him. "Things could've been so different between us."

"You're right. I could've been dead already."

Harwood threw back his head in laughter. "You know, I liked you the moment I met you, but by then it was too late." He stopped just behind the two chairs.

Cavanaugh cocked his right eyebrow. "Too late for what?"

"It doesn't matter." Harwood shrugged. "Did you bring my money?" He cast a quick glance at the small, black briefcase held tightly in Cavanaugh's left hand.

"What do you think?"

Harwood tipped his head to the side, his blue eyes considering the question. "I don't think so. At least not all of it."

A sinister smile crossed Cavanaugh's lips. "I'm not an idiot. If I hand you all the money at once, who's to say you won't kill all three of us?"

"You're right." Harwood gestured over his shoulder to his two companions. The men came forward and began untying both prisoners.

"I'll tell you what." Harwood came around the chairs and noticed the gun tucked in Cavanaugh's pants for the first time. "Let's make a goodwill gesture, shall we?"

"And what would that be?"

"I'll give you one of the prisoners in exchange for what you have in that briefcase."

"And the other?"

"Once you bring the rest of my money to me, I'll turn the other over to you," he said. "All I want is my money."

As soon as the gag was removed, J. J. called out, "Don't trust him."

Brown brought the butt of a handgun down on the back of J. J.'s head, driving him to his knees. Cavanaugh pulled his pistol, but Brown pointed his firearm directly at him.

"Let's not be rash, gentleman," Harwood said, placing his hand on his sidekick's weapon. "We're reasonable men."

Cavanaugh considered the odds, then tucked his weapon back into his pants. Brown lowered his, and took a more relaxed stance at the command of his employer.

"Why, Harwood?" Cavanaugh asked. "Why go through all the trouble of imitating me to embezzle money from my company? You have clients much bigger than Genesis."

"Is that what you think?" Harwood laughed openly. "This had nothing to do with you or Genesis. In fact, Genesis was bankrupted long before your father died, but what a nice little cover it provided."

Cavanaugh's eyes narrowed as the last piece of the puzzle fell into place. "This money doesn't belong to SJT, does it?"

"Not at all. In fact, it doesn't even belong to me or my associates."

Cavanaugh's eyes darted around as his mind tried to calculate this new information. He had known there was someone behind Dowel, but he'd assumed they were embezzling *his* money. Instead, he now understood they were just using Genesis as a cover to launder dirty money from some other source.

Cavanaugh felt his heart speed up as he considered the possibility. "Is this drug money?"

"Of course it is." Harwood laughed again. "You couldn't possibly think Genesis was bringing in that kind of capital, did you?"

"You know, I'm kinda disappointed in you, Cavanaugh," Harwood added, taking custody of Beth Stanton. "I would've thought you'd put the pieces together long ago.

In fact, I thought you already had, which is why I tried to kill you."

Cavanaugh was amazed at the pleasant tone of the man's voice. He could have been speaking about the weather. Harwood tossed Beth Stanton toward Cavanaugh, and gestured for the briefcase. Cavanaugh looked past the man at J. J.

"Un-uh." Harwood shook his head. "You don't get him until I get the rest of my money. Now pass the briefcase."

Cavanaugh hesitated, knowing there was still a good possibility Harwood would kill them all, once he had what was in the briefcase, and forget about the rest.

As if reading his thoughts, Harwood smiled. "Don't worry, I'm far too greedy to kill you before I have all my money."

Cavanaugh bent slowly, and slid the briefcase across the floor. Within seconds, the henchman known as Pulaski picked up the briefcase and rifled through it.

"There's about fourteen mill and some change," he said, still counting through the stacks of currency.

Harwood pouted. "Oh, well. I guess I'll be seeing you again soon."

Brown pushed his pistol against J. J.'s ribs and nudged him in the direction of the door. J. J. cast one last glance at Cavanaugh before moving out the door. Pulaski stayed with his boss, his gun still trained on Cavanaugh.

"Cavanaugh, I can appreciate your caution. Quite frankly, I'm impressed that you showed that kind of forethought. But make no mistake, you try it again and I will kill your friend."

Harwood Dowel turned, moving toward the back entrance, "I'll call you in three hours for the next drop site," he called over his shoulder before disappearing out the door just in front of his guard, who went out the door with his back to it.

Cavanaugh stood alone in the large warehouse with a still-trembling Beth Stanton. "Are you all right?" He realized how terrified the woman was, and understandably so.

"I guess so." She looked up at him, her green eyes wide with horror. "For a woman who was kidnapped by her own husband."

Noel leaned against the wall with his arms crossed over his chest, watching Marty tear through the folders on his desk like a madwoman. She had stormed into the office, demanding to see the files, without offering the slightest explanation. Had it not been for the crazed look in her eyes, he might have questioned her, but wisely decided against it. Besides, he reasoned, hadn't she already seen everything there was to see in the files?

"What are you looking for?" he finally asked, in exasperation.

"Those bank receipts with Cavanaugh's signature on them. Where are they?" She never turned from her task of opening and closing files.

"There somewhere. What do you need them for?"

"I think I know who's been embezzling."

"Who?" Noel asked, standing straight up. His curiosity was peeked.

"Kenneth Stanton."

"What?"

"You heard me," she said, knowing how insane her theory was. But on the other hand, it was the only thing that made sense.

"It's kind of hard for a dead man to embezzle money," Noel said, wondering if she had lost her mind.

"He's not dead."

"What do you mean?"

She finally paused long enough to face him. "Dina, Dwight's wife, went to school with Kenneth Stanton." She pulled the folded article from her pocket and handed it to him. "Is that the man you met as Harwood Dowel?"

"Yeah, that's him," Noel said, still trying to understand.

"According to Dina, that's Kenneth Stanton."

"How's that possible?"

"I've got an idea, but I need proof."

"What idea?"

"Look, I don't have time to explain right now," she said, fighting to hold her temper. "Are you going to help me or not?"

"Yeah, anything. Just tell me what you need," he said, still carefully reviewing the picture.

Cavanaugh came back from his kitchen with two warm mugs cradled in his hands. He offered one to Beth Stanton, and she accepted it eagerly. He had waited patiently during the short ride back to his condominium for her to speak, clearly seeing she was far too traumatized. But now, he needed answers.

"Beth, I know this whole thing has been upsetting to you. But why would you say Harwood Dowel was your husband?"

"That wasn't Harwood Dowel," she said, into the mug. "That was Kenneth."

"What do you mean?"

"When Kenneth was supposedly killed at the office I never viewed the body. We'd discussed our desires regarding burial, and he'd left strict instructions that his body was to be incinerated immediately. Not even a memorial service was to be held. It was even stated in his will. I thought nothing of it. He always had very strange beliefs regarding religion. And quite frankly, I was still too angry about discovering his affair to care much about how his remains were disposed of."

She paused long enough to take a sip of the warm tea. Her hands were trembling, so she spilled more on her lap than down her throat. Finally she gave up, and set the mug down on the table.

"I probably never would've thought anything of it until that day you came to see me. I could've sworn I saw him, Kenneth, watching the house earlier that day. I just dismissed it as my over-stressed imagination." She cut her eyes to Cavanaugh, then looked away in shame. "I'm sorry I lied to you. Harwood hadn't come for his files, but with everything that was happening, and then you showing up out of the blue like that, I just didn't trust you."

"I understand," Cavanaugh said.

"Do you think it was Harwood Dowel who was killed at the office?" She shot up out of her seat. "Oh, my God. Do you think it's possible that Harwood was cremated? But why? What does it all mean?"

"Beth, I know this is all very upsetting, but I need you to try to stay focused," he said, taking her hands, and pulling her back down beside him on the sofa. "The files at your house, are they still there?"

"Maybe. No . . . I don't know," she said, shaking her head in confusion. "Someone broke in a couple of months ago. They stole some small pieces of jewelry and a TV, and ransacked Kenneth's office."

Her water-filled eyes took on a faraway look. "I guess that was Kenneth; maybe he was looking for something he'd left behind."

Cavanaugh said nothing, but he'd already reasoned that. "Come on," he said, taking her by the hand. "We've got to get to your house and try to find what he was looking for."

She pulled back. "Why don't you just give him the money?" She was trembling again.

Cavanaugh turned to face her. "Even if I give him the money, do you think he'll leave three witnesses?" He spoke as if talking to a five-year-old. "Beth, why do you think he kidnapped you in the first place? With all we know, do you honestly think he can afford to leave us alive?"

She stood for several seconds before answering. "No, I guess I don't."

Marty stared at the dashboard of the small convertible. She was certain Noel was flooring it, yet they were still being left in the dust of smaller economy cars. She gritted her teeth, hating her ex for his obsession with jalopies.

"Can't this thing go any faster?" It was a rhetorical question. Of course it couldn't.

Noel cast her a shy glance. "I'm doing the best I can," he muttered.

She took a deep breath and tried to regain her composure. "I'm sorry. I do appreciate your help," she said, feeling more like herself. She cursed fate for allowing this to be the day the starter on her Jetta died. She was just glad it happened at Noel's firehouse and not somewhere else.

"It's okay." He turned on his signal to change lanes, then turned his head to visually verify the lane was clear. "I know you're upset."

She felt her heart speed up. She could see the precinct just ahead. She began to tap her foot nervously when they were forced to stop at a red light. They were less than a block away. Marty opened the door.

"What are you doing?" Noel asked, panicked by the traffic rushing on both sides of them.

"I can run from here," she said. Stepping out, she quickly slammed the door closed, then leaned in the window. "Thanks again, Noel. I really owe you one."

Noel scanned her pretty face. "I just hope Saint John knows what a lucky man he is."

Marty knew the sentiment was expressed with genuine love. She felt her heartstrings tug, wondering why he couldn't have shown that kind of tenderness when they were together. But then again, had she stayed with Noel she would have never fallen in love with Cavanaugh. And Marty knew in her heart Cavanaugh was her destiny.

She just smiled, and mouthed another silent "thank you." Turning quickly, she ran across the intersection toward 1300 Beubien, the Detroit Police Headquarters.

Cavanaugh and Beth Stanton scrutinized every inch of Kenneth Stanton's office. They opened every box, emptied every drawer, and turned everything into a chaotic mess. Cavanaugh looked at his watch again. They only had one hour left before the second call would come. They hadn't so much as found a single trace of evidence leading to any possible motive.

Cavanaugh turned and grabbed Beth by the shoulders, forcing her to face him. She had been in an almost dreamlike state from the minute she'd been turned over to him.

"Beth, are you sure he never said anything about Genesis? Nothing at all?" He knew questioning the befuddled woman was pointless, but considering their limited options, he had to give it one more try in hopes she would remember something, anything, no matter how seemingly small or inconsequential.

"No," she screeched. "I told you before, Kenneth

never spoke of his work. Never. I wish I could tell you something but I can't." Finally the tears came as the events of the day came down hard on her. She crumpled against Cavanaugh in a heap.

He braced her against his strong chest and held her. "Shhh," he cooed. "It's okay, I'm sorry. It's just, we're running out of time."

She stood straight again and wiped at her tears. "I understand. I wish I could be more help, but I don't know anything. It's actually quite embarrassing to be married to a man for thirteen years and know so little about him." Suddenly her whole body stiffened.

"Wait." She rushed over to the desktop computer and turned it on. "Once, about a year ago, I came downstairs in the middle of the night and was surprised to find Kenneth up working so late. It was so unusual for him; he was always in bed by ten, and slept like a log." She spoke to Cavanaugh over her shoulder.

"When I came into the room it startled him. He rushed to shut down the program he was working on, but not before I saw a single word: the password to open and close the program."

Her fingers tapped away at the keys until she found the familiar icon. She opened it quickly to reveal a password box. "Cross your fingers," she whispered, more to herself than Cavanaugh. Then sighing heavily, she entered the word: ORIGIN.

The soft humming of the internal computer brain working was the only noise as the pair stood like stone statues, waiting. Finally, after several test screens quickly flashed across the monitor, the page opened, revealing rows and rows of digits and words.

"Does any of this make sense to you?" She looked to Cavanaugh, seeing nothing more than odd combinations of letters and numbers that were completely unintelligible to her.

Cavanaugh moved past Beth to stare at the screen, his dark eyes running back and forth, taking in the mass of information. Slowly, his face began to widen into a brilliant smile. "We've got him."

The young officer behind the desk stood looking at Marty as if she'd just sprung a second head. The shiny gold badge that read Officer Finnigan looked like something out of a Cracker Jack® box.

"Please, just let me talk to a detective. I'm sure once they hear me out, they'll understand." She glanced anxiously at the clock on the wall. She'd been there almost thirty minutes, and hadn't so much as gotten past the front lobby.

"Oh? As if I can't," Officer Finnigan said, with slight disdain. He was far too embarrassed to admit that his lack of understanding was exactly the problem. He looked down at the papers spread across the counter once more, still unable to make heads or tails of the issue. "Okay, what's the *nature* of the complaint?" He scratched his head.

The nature of the complaint is that you're an idiot, she thought. But she held her peace. Marty could feel a pounding headache coming on. Every minute she wasted trying to make this rookie understand was another minute Cavanaugh was in danger.

"Okay," she started again, trying to sound calm, "let me try to explain this in a way even *you* can understand."

The young rookie reared back as if he'd just been slapped. "Excuse me?"

"*Is* there an excuse for you?" she said, through clenched teeth.

Officer Finnigan may have had only four months on the job, but he felt he deserved the same respect as any veteran cop. He represented the entire Detroit police department, and she was a single, private citizen.

He was still unsure as to when he lost control of the situation, but he was certain he had. He braced his arms against the counter, about to let into her in a way that would surely remind her of exactly who was wearing the badge here.

"Who do you think you're talking to, lady?"

"Don't get an attitude with me." She planted one hand against her hip, and the other flailed in the air as Marty finally felt her temper explode. "If your IQ was greater than your shoe size, maybe you could—"

"Hold on."

"No, *you* hold on—"

"Is there a problem here, Officer Finnigan?" A baritone voice sounded behind Marty, startling her and the rookie officer.

She turned to find herself staring up at a tall, white officer with sandy blond hair and cheerful blue eyes.

"This lady has a complaint, but won't fill out the proper paperwork." Officer Finnigan lifted the thick stack of papers while working to rein in his temper. The last thing he needed was for Sarge to see him arguing with the irate woman.

"I've told you twelve times, this is a matter of life and death! I don't have time to fill out paperwork." Marty was yelling at the top of her voice. Her nerves were shot.

"Calm down, miss." The senior officer came up behind her, and placed his hands on her shoulders. "I understand you've explained it twelve times, but please, take the time to explain it once more to me."

Marty began spewing out everything she had discovered about the case, completely oblivious to the stares of curious passersby. After hearing her out, the sergeant rubbed his chin thoughtfully for several seconds.

"Come with me," the older officer said, then turned to lead her down a long corridor.

Marty found herself sitting in a room she assumed would normally be used for interrogations. She was calm and a bit more relaxed now that she was dealing with the more experienced officer. Listening to her, he checked the computer and saw the open case file. He had told her that they had planned to have the man known as Harwood Dowel, a.k.a. Kenneth Stanton, in custody by now, but that he'd disappeared along with Cavanaugh.

He asked her to wait while he ran a bulletin for the man known as Harwood Dowel/Kenneth Stanton. The sergeant planned to pick him up and have him brought in for questioning. Marty nervously bit her nails and looked around the room while waiting for his return. She wondered if the long glass that ran the length on the south wall was a two-way reflected mirror used to spy on suspects. The door opened and the officer came into the room holding a long manila file.

"Okay, we've got an APB out for Dowel or Stanton or whoever he is. Soon as he's brought in, I'll let you know. But I want you to wait here until then."

"I can't do that." She shot up out of the chair. "What about Cavanaugh?"

"Look." He came around the table and pushed her back down into the chair. "We've got a maniac loose out there. We already have one witness missing, we don't need two."

Reluctantly, Marty sank back down into the chair, and tried to relax, telling herself that the police knew what they were doing. The officer turned toward the door, preparing to leave. "Can I get you something to eat or drink?" He paused in the doorway.

"No, thanks." Marty's response held the liveliness of an automaton. Her mind was too distracted by the horrifying images in her head. Where was Cavanaugh? What if something awful had happened to him already? How was she supposed to go on without him?

"Okay," he said. "I'll let you know as soon as I have an update."

"Wait," she called to the man who'd helped restore her peace of mind. "What's your name?"

"Pulaski," the officer said. "If you need anything just ask for me or my partner, Officer Brown." He paused as his pleasant face became solemn. "Don't speak to anyone else. You never know whom you can trust."

Marty nodded, remembering what Cavanaugh had told her about the two men who approached him. He thought they were real cops.

The door slid shut and Marty sat back, confident that Stanton would be behind bars soon, and that Cavanaugh was alive out there, somewhere.

Thirty-one

Cavanaugh returned the phone to the cradle slowly, his face seemingly drained of all color.

"Well?" Beth stood over his shoulder, anxiously awaiting an answer to the most important phone call they'd made so far.

"He's dead," Cavanaugh said. "According to the warden, he was killed in the prison exercise yard three months ago."

"That bastard," Beth cried. "How could he frame an innocent man?"

"The same way he could kill his own partner," Cavanaugh said.

They had spent the last hour reviewing the files they found in the computer. Everything finally made sense, and they had the proof they needed to bring the crooked lawyer down. But Stanton and his cronies still had J. J., and until they could get him back, the police could not be trusted. Cavanaugh checked his watch. The call would be made any minute now.

Suddenly, as if willed by his thoughts, the phone rang. "Hello?" Cavanaugh said, fighting to sound more confident that he was.

"Are you ready?" This time the man on the other end made no attempt to disguise his voice.

"Where?"

* * *

Kenneth Stanton gave very precise instructions on the meeting conditions, although Cavanaugh found his choice of meeting place a bit odd. Cavanaugh had insisted Beth stay behind but she'd refused. The pair arrived at the small building at the appointed time, and as expected, they were greeted by complete silence. The elegant foyer of the legal office was empty, not surprising for a Sunday afternoon.

Cavanaugh had a bad feeling. He wasn't sure whether it was that he knew this would be their last chance, or something more. But whatever it was had the hairs on the back of his neck standing up. He and Beth walked the length of the hall together, coming to the partially opened door.

"Come in," Kenneth Stanton called around the door, hearing them in the hallway.

The pair entered to find him sitting at his desk with a pistol firmly trained on them. J. J. sat bound and gagged in the manner in which he'd been that morning. Stanton's two goons were conspicuously absent.

"Put the briefcase on the desk," Kenneth said, carefully watching both. His eyes briefly met his wife's. She stood staring at him coldly. "What's the matter, dear?" he teased, "cat got your tongue? Now, that would be a first."

"Why, Kenneth?" Beth finally asked the question that had plagued her from the moment she discovered her captor was her husband. "Why?"

"Let me see." He leaned back in the chair, his pistol still firmly trained on them. "Retire as a millionaire on a tropical island surrounded by exotic beauties, or grow old and useless with a tired old bag like you?"

"Was it that bad?" she said, with tears in her eyes.

Cavanaugh realized these were not the same tears she

had cried that morning. There was no pain or hurt, only pure fury behind her green eyes now.

"Worse," he said, smugly. "Where's my mon—". He spun around in the chair just in time to see Cavanaugh moving up behind him. "Tsk, tsk, tsk." Stanton shook his head in mock disappointment, then motioned with the pistol toward the other side of the table. "Back over there," he said to Cavanaugh. All the humor was gone from his voice. Stanton realized his wife was intentionally distracting him, so that Cavanaugh could move into a better position and gain the upper hand. It had almost worked.

"So, whose idea was that?" He was looking at his wife a little differently. He would never have suspected her of being party to such a sneaky trick. Maybe he'd underestimated the old girl.

"Mine," Cavanaugh answered quickly, fearing what would happen to Beth if he didn't. He knew that as long as he had the briefcase full of money handcuffed to his wrist, he was protected. But Beth was nothing more than a liability at this point.

"Come on, let's get this over with." Stanton stood and came around behind J. J.'s chair. "I'm sure your friend's anxious to get home to his lovely wife, and I've got a plane to catch."

"There's nowhere on earth for you to hide, Stanton." Cavanaugh spoke in raw defiance.

Kenneth shrugged. "We'll just have to see about that, won't we?" Somehow he'd missed the threat in Cavanaugh's words.

"There's nowhere to run. Especially not," Cavanaugh paused, "when we tell your friends how you've been chipping off their block of cheese."

Kenneth Stanton's face turned to solid rock. "What are you talking about?"

"We got into your little diary, sweetheart." Beth was enjoying her husband's trepidation. She was suddenly feeling better than she had all day, deciding that the pained expression on his face was enough satisfaction for the day's events. "Remember 'Origin'?"

"I copied all your files," Cavanaugh interjected. "I gave them to someone I trust completely, with strict instructions that if I'm not back in an hour, he is to forward all the information to that e-mail address we found under the heading 'Alpha'."

Beth Stanton was smiling sweetly. "Technology is a wonderful thing, wouldn't you say, dear?"

Cavanaugh held his silence. He wouldn't have stolen these moments from her for anything in the world.

"I must admit, you gangsters have come a long way. But some of the old ways still exist." Beth turned and spoke to Cavanaugh in a matter-of-fact tone. "You know, like making people disappear."

Cavanaugh nodded in agreement. "That is true," he mocked sympathetically, "and they do it in the most unpleasant ways."

Kenneth Stanton looked from one to the other, his mouth set in a tight line, his eyes blazing with rage. He was worried now, genuinely worried. They could be bluffing to scare him, but if they weren't . . .

He began pacing, still keeping his weapon trained on the people in front of him. His boss was not the forgiving type. Any man willing to kill his own relatives for greed was not someone you wanted to cross. He'd only skimmed a little of their profits off the top, but what if his boss felt that little was too much? Kenneth looked at his hostages again. He needed a Plan B.

Cavanaugh cut his eyes to J. J. and signaled him to be ready. He wasn't sure what Kenneth was planning, but he knew it didn't involve the three of them walking out of there alive.

"Just hand over the money." Kenneth turned and suddenly grabbed at the briefcase. His eyes widened in horror to discover it was attached to Cavanaugh's wrist. "What the hell—"

Cavanaugh's mouth twisted in a snarl as Kenneth's blue eyes met his midnight-black ones. "You want it? Take it." Cavanaugh rammed the briefcase hard against his chest. Stanton stumbled, but quickly found his footing. Although it was attached to Cavanaugh's wrist, the two men struggled over the case. Kenneth was perfectly willing to rip Cavanaugh's arm off to get it.

As soon as that happened, J. J. started rocking in the chair, attempting to knock it over. Beth Stanton came up behind her husband, who was so busy struggling with Cavanaugh, he never saw the silver paper tray coming down on his back.

Beth was never more thankful for her husband's partiality toward heavy metals. Kenneth Stanton fell to his knees, dragging the desk blotter and all the contents onto the floor with him.

Cavanaugh grabbed Beth's arm and ran. Together they worked to release J. J., untying his hands and feet. Then the three raced toward the front entrance.

They froze dead in their tracks at the sight of Officer Pulaski standing with his back to the closed front door. He was holding Marty close against his side with one hand, while the other held his pistol firmly pressed against her temple.

The trio turned at the sound of Officer Brown coming from the back entrance, carrying two empty gasoline canisters. "Okay, I've covered everything in gasoline." he moved past the group of startled people. "Where's Stanton?"

"Check the office." Pulaski's eyes narrowed as he studied Cavanaugh.

Brown rushed through the open doorway. Shortly afterward, he came stumbling back to the foyer with his injured boss under his arm. A small cut on Kenneth Stanton's forehead was bleeding. He lifted his head, just long enough to glare at the three standing together.

"Kill them all." Kenneth nodded toward Cavanaugh. "Cut off his hand and get the briefcase."

"That won't be necessary." A deep voice resounded from the top of the one-flight staircase. Every head turned up, to see Justin Saint John standing on the upper landing.

"He'll give you the case, won't you, Cavanaugh?"

Cavanaugh stood flabbergasted, staring up at the stern face of his cousin. Everything he thought he knew no longer made any sense.

"I'm sorry you had to find out this way," Justin said. His voice held a note of sincerity.

Cavanaugh was beginning to recover from the shock, but he was still paralyzed with confusion. "We're blood," he said, still not believing what he was seeing.

Justin just looked at him as if he'd spoken in Latin. He was wondering how his cousin could be so naïve. After being raised by that witch, how had he managed to remain so trusting? Deciding it didn't matter, he shook off whatever guilt may have affected his decision to go ahead with the plan.

"You just wouldn't leave well enough alone." He started slowly down the stairs. "And now, look what you've done," he said, gesturing toward Pulaski. "You've gotten Marty involved." Justin paused, long enough to laugh. "I'll tell you, man." Justin shook his head from side to side. "You have the lousiest luck with women."

Marty felt a chill, realizing how much his laughter

sounded like Cavanaugh's. She was the only person not surprised by the man's sudden appearance. This was the idea that had come to mind when she saw the newspaper clipping with Stanton and a man she first thought was Cavanaugh.

It was only after studying the picture carefully that she realized it was not Cavanaugh, but Justin standing beside the lawyer for a press photo at a charity gala earlier that year. The caption had only read: "Dowel and Saint John."

When she went to Noel, she'd been seeking any connection between the law firm and Justin, knowing Justin was the perfect person to imitate Cavanaugh. Only someone who looked and sounded like and knew so much about Cavanaugh, could become him so easily. Other than the difference in age, the two men could have been twins. This was also the information she'd so willingly given to the helpful police officer standing behind her with his pistol trained on her temple.

"What do you want us to do?" Stanton asked Justin, who was still standing on the stairs.

"Finish what you should've done ten months ago," he said, glowering at his incompetent flunky. He bounded down the few remaining stairs, pausing only a moment to look into the face of his cousin. Everyone watched in silence as the mirrored reflections studied each other with disdain.

"Believe it or not, I'm really sorry it had to end this way," Justin said, before walking across the room to the front door. He opened it and paused before going out. "And this time, Kenneth," he called over his shoulder, "get it right." The door closed softly behind him.

"You heard the man," Kenneth snapped at his accomplices, "let's finish—"

"I wasn't bluffing, Stanton," Cavanaugh interrupted in a low but deadly tone. "If I don't speak to my friend within the hour, all the information in those files will go back to the people whose money you've been laundering."

As much as he hated to, Stanton had to consider the possible threat. If Cavanaugh and Beth were telling the truth, and Justin found out about his theft, he was as good as dead.

He nodded toward Cavanaugh. "Lock *him* up in my office and shoot the others." Despite what Justin wanted, Kenneth knew he needed Cavanaugh alive until he could get his hands on those files.

Pulaski and Brown exchanged confused looks. "I thought the boss wanted us to torch the place like we did last time."

"Yes, that would've been perfect." Kenneth was smiling again. "You see, Saint John, the police already believe you tried to burn the evidence of your crimes once before. But this time, they would've found you and your friends amongst the ashes. Can't you imagine the headline: 'Millionaire Arsonist Killed by His Own Fire while Trying to Hide Evidence of Embezzlement.'"

As the smell of gasoline permeated the air, Marty's heart was pounding. They had this all planned from the start. It was no accident that they all ended up here together. Justin had orchestrated this whole thing, making it all seem like random events, and now, they would all die to satisfy his greedy ambition.

She stared hard at Cavanaugh, trying to will him to look at her. Maybe she could tell him with her eyes what she had not with words. How much she loved him, how much she needed him. There was so much she needed to say to him, and it seemed their time had run out.

Cavanaugh could feel Marty's eyes on him, feel her desperation, but ignored it for the moment. He had to stay focused on the three men who held them captive, looking for even the slightest crack in their controlled behavior. "But you can't do that, now. Can you?"

Stanton sighed. "Unfortunately, I can't take a chance that you are lying."

"What about the boss?" Pulaski insisted.

"Do you want him to find out we've been helping ourselves to his money?" Stanton snapped at his cohort.

Brown rubbed his chin. "I see your point. Come on." He grabbed Cavanaugh by the arm to lead him away.

"Locking me away won't change anything," Cavanaugh said as he was led away.

"No, but after we take care of your friends, you're going to make that phone call to your contact."

Cavanaugh jerked free of Brown and swung around to Stanton. "And *why* would I do that?"

Stanton pointed his gun at Marty. "To make her death quick and painless, of course." He leered disgustingly. "Otherwise, it could be long, painful, and very ugly."

Cavanaugh's eyes flashed on Marty only for a moment, but so much was said in just that one moment. He loved her. He would never let anything happen to her. One way or the other, he would make sure they survived this nightmare. A silent promise was made, and Marty felt her hope renewed. They had too much to live for to die here this way.

Then his eyes went to J. J. and Beth, both of whom he now trusted completely. If they were going to get out of this alive, they would have to work together. And the faith he put in them was reciprocated tenfold.

Stanton was so caught up in what he felt was a brilliant scheme, he never noticed the interaction. "Afterwards, I'll disappear with my money, and your cousin will never find me." Stanton didn't feel nearly as confident as he sounded, but letting the foursome go was not an option.

Brown led Cavanaugh past the others toward the open

office. J. J. and Beth watched Cavanaugh's every movement, waiting for a signal, believing he would find a way to deliver them from their seemingly obvious fate. All it took was the slight nod of his head. J. J. swung out and hit Brown squarely in the face. Beth struggled to twist the gun from her husband, who easily pushed her down.

Cavanaugh charged straight for Pulaski, ducking out of harm's way just as a bullet came whizzing past his head. He leapt into the air, grabbing the man, and the two went tumbling across the floor in a mass of limbs.

Stanton could see all his well-laid plans going bad before his eyes. If any one of them escaped, Justin would be sure to discover the truth. He reached in his pocket for a book of matches. Seeing his intent, Marty charged across the room, but she reached him too late. Her hands closed across his arm just as the lit match hit the floor.

The room was almost instantly engulfed in flames. Flashes of red, yellow, and orange charged across the open foyer encircling the group. The white-hot heat was proof of how quickly it was spreading. A stray flame leapt across the air and landed on the back of Brown's jacket. Brown threw himself down, his cries of agony filling the room as he flailed around on the floor, trying to beat out the fire that had already burned through to his skin.

Cavanaugh and Pulaski struggled on the floor, wrestling back and forth. Pulaski was using his large size to pin the other man to the ground. Cavanaugh brought his knee up to the other man's abdomen, and quickly evened the odds. Everyone seemed too consumed by their personal battles to notice the fire blazing around them.

Marty looked around frantically for something to help in the attack. She finally found what she was looking for in the form of an antique, Victorian-styled armchair. She lifted the chair over her head and brought it down in the center of Pulaski's shoulder blade. At first, she was certain the chair had had no effect, until the man fell forward, slumping heavily over Cavanaugh.

Cavanaugh flipped the limp body over and stood quickly to see J. J. desperately struggling with Stanton. The two men wrestled, both holding to the small pistol, neither showing any sign of releasing their hold.

The pistol went off in the air and everyone ducked. Given the smoky haze of the room, no one was certain in which direction the bullets were flying. Cavanaugh jumped on top of Stanton's back, struggling to pull him up off of J. J.

Lead by some savage rage, Stanton became invincibly strong. He flipped Cavanaugh off his back, and seeing whom it was, turned his fury on him. He was no longer interested in J. J. *This* was the man he wanted to kill with his bare hands. *This* was the man who had ruined everything! Cavanaugh struggled to get out from under him, but he had fallen on his back trapping his own bent leg beneath him and making it almost impossible to maneuver.

J. J. and Marty both pulled and punched Stanton, but the blows fell off the man like rubber, given his deranged state. He grabbed Cavanaugh's neck tightly with both hands, squeezing with everything in him. Kenneth Stanton knew his dreams had died, but he wanted to make sure this man died with them.

Cavanaugh was finding it difficult to breathe, trying to pull his leg from beneath him and fight off his assailant at the same time. He felt himself becoming faint, and could only barely make out the frantic shapes of J. J. and Marty behind the man.

Suddenly Stanton's whole body went completely stiff as his horrified eyes looked up to see his wife standing with a smoking gun only inches from him. She clutched the pistol with both hands, trembling from her toes to the tips of her graying hair.

Stanton touched the small place on his chest where he blood had begun to seep through. Only then did Caanaugh realize what had happened.

"Consider that your divorce," Beth said, her paralyzed ngers still gripping the gun.

Kenneth Stanton looked down into Cavanaugh's surrised face as his hate-filled eyes focused on him one last me. Then the villain's dead body fell to the side.

The foursome were the only conscious survivors of the urning building. Just then, a patch of the flowery print overing the walls exploded in a shower of electrical parks, and one by one the electrical outlets began to op and sizzle, while simultaneously a large beam fell, locking the entrance. They were trapped.

"This way." Cavanaugh grabbed Marty's hand and harged toward the back entrance. The others followed lose behind, J. J. guiding Beth over the scattered debris. lready, their clothes were sticking to their skin with weat from the intense heat. Despite their slippery, 'ater-covered hands, Cavanaugh held on to Marty for ear life. Another large explosion shattered a window, cattering shards of glass in every direction.

"Stay low," Marty called to the pair behind them. "Stay lose to the ground." The firefighter in her took charge.

Cavanaugh swore loudly, realizing the back entrance 'as also blocked by falling supports. The building was rumbling around them, and there seemed to be no 'ay out.

"Up there!" Marty pointed to a small, high window ver the toilet, visible through the open bathroom door. 'he group hurried into the bathroom. Cavanaugh tried) force Marty up onto the closed toilet seat, but she reised to go.

"Beth first, then J. J.," she insisted.

Cavanaugh wanted her safe and didn't care how selfish

that need was, but they could not afford to waste one sec ond arguing over the matter. So instead, he helped J. J. lif Beth up to the window.

Beth quickly unlatched the locked window and looke out. She practically laughed in joy, realizing how easy i was. She quickly crawled through and turned to awai the others.

Marty turned to help J. J. He exchanged a quick loo with Cavanaugh and then the two men wrestled her u to the window without the slightest bit of gentleness. Nei ther man had any intention of leaving her behind. Wit brute force, her long legs were forced through the open ing. She landed on her bottom.

Realizing what had happened, she jumped to her fee "Damn him!" She rushed back to the opening just as J. J came over the ledge.

A loud, thunderous explosion shook the earth an tossed the three people flat on their backs. When Mart opened her eyes, she realized the building had erupte in a ball of flames.

"Nooo!" She charged toward the building but J. J grabbed her around the waist and wrestled her to th ground. "No. No. Let me go!" She fought with all he strength, but J. J. was just as determined not to sacrific *two* friends today.

Tears filled J. J.'s eyes as he accepted that he could d nothing more for Cavanaugh, except protect his woman "No, Marty," he whispered through the rivulet of wate coursing down his face. "He's gone, he's gone."

Thirty-two

Marty was so caught up in her grief, she never heard ne fire engine pull into the parking lot. J. J. and Beth sat ilent on the sidewalk, exhausted and distressed as the iremen dismounted and raced toward the burning uilding.

"Marty," Cal called.

Marty swung around in the direction of the voice. She elt the sweet taste of salvation course through her body as ne realized her own engine team had answered the call. he *knew* how good these guys were; there was still hope.

"Cavanaugh's in there. Near the back entrance." She ointed toward the remains of the window frame she'd limbed through only moments before. "In the bathoom."

Cal tapped a couple of men on the shoulder and aced in the direction she'd indicated. Marty took off n the other direction, toward the engine. Her team embers ran in every direction. A group of five carried e heavy hose as close as they could possibly get to the ferno and began dousing the flame. The men with Cal ere pounding away at the back door, working without eing conscious of damage or danger.

Yellow, rubber-suited men clambered over every inch of e burning building like industrious ants, tearing away anks, smashing windows, doing whatever was necessary to contain and eventually extinguish the blaze. There was only one united focus, one goal: rescue.

Within seconds, Marty was in turnout gear and racing back to the building. She'd lost track of J. J. and Beth in the chaos, but it didn't matter. They were safe; Cavanaugh was not. She charged the falling wall like an enraged banshee. Her axe held high, she swung into the wood frame with every ounce of her strength. Soon working together, the group made an opening large enough to allow one small man through—or, as they all turned to look at Marty, a woman.

Without hesitation, she was climbing through the opening. The smoke and fire made it impossible to see through the flames, so she was forced to guide herself from memory. Moving through the inferno with a wear restraint, she struggled to hear even the faintest cry for help. She occasionally called out to him, knowing he would never understand the words through her breathing apparatus, but he would recognize the sound a human, and if able, he would respond.

Marty felt her heart pounding in her throat. *Please God. Please, don't take him from me. Not now! Not like this* The smoke was becoming dangerous. She had been in the building for several minutes. Finally, she came to th opening of what she believed was the bathroom, but in the blanket of smoke and haze that covered every inch of air she could not see anything that resembled human body.

Maybe he had managed to get back out of the room before the explosion. She spun around and peere hard, trying to make out something, anything through the noxious cloud.

She heard Cal in the distance. He was calling her, probably trying to pull her back out of the building. *Not yet.* Sh moved along the hallway, feeling her way along the wal

He had to be in here somewhere. She coughed, and her eyes widened in understanding. The fumes were seeping nto her mask. In her profession, it was the kiss of death. She should've turned back long ago, but how could she when . . . no, not yet. He had to be in here somewhere. Even if he didn't survive, at least his—his . . . his body hould. . . .

Marty slumped against the wall as the weight of her grief came down on her. "NOOOOO!" She howled behind her nask. Her head began to pound as she struggled with the trange concept of living without Cavanaugh. Marty ought to stay on her feet, when all she wanted to do was ie down and die. Right here, right now. There was no point in leaving the building without him.

Marty had never considered herself a coward or a quitter, but in that moment, her will to fight was drained rom her very soul. Then something happened, something that she would later describe as the strangest ensation she would ever experience.

She felt a large hand clamp around her upper arm, at he exact same moment another hand clamped onto her nkle. Through the smoke, she could not see whom either hand belonged to until Cal moved into her line of ision. Suddenly, he was there standing beside her.

"Let's go," he shouted through his mask, "it's too late, Marty. We have to get out of here."

Marty looked at her friend in confusion. If he was tanding beside her, upright, then who was holding er—

She hunched down so quickly, she dragged Cal with er. There was Cavanaugh lying nearly unconscious at er feet. His ash-overed arm extended and gripped her eg. The two firefighters lifted his weight between them nd quickly moved toward the back door. There was no time to check for vital signs, not a millisecond to waste. Dead or alive, they had to get him out of there—now.

In the time they were inside the building, the crew had been working on enlarging the opening, so the trio was able to move through the breach together. As soon as they cleared the entrance, Marty guided Cavanaugh's unconscious body to a grassy area and stretched him out.

The paramedics moved in to care for the man, but they were forced to literally pull Marty off his body, a task they soon found was not as easy as it sounded. Finally the two men were able to pry her free with the threat that she was endangering his life. She released her viselike hold on the man she loved and fell back on the grass. She lay flat, still covered head to toe in her gear, staring up at the blue sky over head. It was all right. She had found what she was looking for, a pulse. Everything would be all right now.

The noise and bustle of a busy metropolitan hospital emergency unit surrounded Marty as she entered. She had rushed across town, after spending almost four hours going over everything she knew about the case with a very patient Officer Donovan at the police station. She wondered only briefly where he'd been that morning when she strolled ever so confidently into the arms of the enemy.

He had informed her that the building had burned to the ground, along with the three men inside. But given the evidence Noel recovered from the safe, the records found on Stanton's computer, and their eyewitness reports, they would have no problem making a case against Justin, who unfortunately, they believed, may have boarded an airplane bound for Brazil.

Marty flashed her sweetest smile and Officer Donovan

continued, telling far more than he should have. They were almost certain Justin was working with someone in South America to smuggle drug money in, launder it through the law firm of Stanton and Dowel, and hide it under Genesis. Justin believed this was the perfect cover. Because the small company had gone unmanaged by the family for so long, he never thought anyone would notice.

Only fate had put Cavanaugh on the trail, leading him to the law firm, as he unwittingly investigated a crime that never happened. As it turned out, the *real* Harwood Dowel had caught on to his partner's part in the scheme and planned to turn him in. Kenneth Stanton, being aware of this, slowly began poisoning his partner in an attempt to make his death look natural.

Late one evening Dowel confronted his partner, and in a rage, Stanton murdered him and exchanged identities. Given the unusual specification of his own will, he knew no one would ever see the body or question the cause of death.

The only loose end had been their legal clerk Greg Toberson, whose bad timing caused him to witness the murder. Stanton created the fictitious story about a jealous spouse and framed the man for the murder. Toberson had been so distraught after witnessing the murder of his boss that by the time the police picked him up for questioning he was almost deranged. His deteriorating mental state played right into the hands of the man who turned him in. With no one to corroborate his story, and two veteran officers testifying against him, Greg Toberson was quickly and quietly convicted for the murder. But fearing that someone might someday put it all together, Stanton arranged to have him murdered in the courtyard at the prison.

His neat little plan allowed him to continue to practice law as Harwood Dowel without the scandal of murder. Since all their clients were large corporations with whom they had no direct contact, no one would be the wiser.

Officer Donovan finished by telling Marty that Kenneth Stanton and Justin Saint John would have gotten away with it, had they not made one simple mistake: attempting to kill Cavanaugh. That mistake had shined a light on the whole scheme, causing Cavanaugh to question things that would have otherwise remained unknown.

After hearing all she wanted, Marty told Officer Donovan that she wanted to get something to drink and stepped out of the small room. Instead of stopping at the pop machine, she continued out the front entrance to her car in the parking lot. She couldn't go another minute without seeing Cavanaugh; she just needed to know he was safe.

Now, she was forced to wait several impatient moments at the counter for one of the busy nurses to acknowledge her, but between the insistent telephone and steady stream of interruptions, no one ever did. She glanced around the crowded emergency room, and realized she could be waiting there all day.

Finally, she gave up on seeking assistance, and went in search of him. She rounded the corner leading into the main corridor. Marty walked along slowly, looking into each room. Cavanaugh was nowhere to be found. She noticed a couple of curious glances from the hospital personnel who were moving back and forth in the hallway, but no one said anything to her. After several minutes and several more rooms, she gave up trying to find him on her own and decided to return to the front desk for guidance.

She crossed the doorway leading to the lobby and stopped at the sight of a brown-haired man sitting in a wheelchair near the window. She started across the lobby toward him, then paused when another woman came up and touched him on the shoulder and the man turned. Marty's heart sank. It wasn't him.

"Looking for someone?" The sultry voice was only inches from her ear. Every nerve in her body came alive with those three simple words.

"As a matter of fact, I am," she said without turning. She wanted to enjoy the feeling of relief that swept over her. He was so close, she could feel his body heat and smell his sweet cologne.

"Anyone I know?" He was almost nipping at her earlobe. Marty held to the wall, feeling her knees weaken.

"Maybe," she said, with a half smile, content to play his game for now.

"Describe him, maybe I've seen him."

"Well, he's five-foot-eleven, with a killer smile." She could feel him blush, which only inspired her. "And he happens to be the sweetest piece of chocolate I've ever tasted."

His laughter exploded behind her ear, just before he bent to kiss her neck. "Well, I don't know anyone who fits *that* description, but maybe I'll do." He turned her to face him.

Instantly her arms came up around his neck, as his mouth descended on hers. She didn't care that they were standing in the middle of a hospital lobby, or that Officer Donovan was waiting for her to return to the police station; in that moment nothing else mattered but the man in her arms. She broke free of the passionate kiss only long enough to tell him something she had feared she wouldn't have a chance to again.

"I love you," she blurted, still mesmerized by his sparkling black eyes.

"I know," he said, and then covered her mouth again.

* * *

Two hours later the couple entered Cavanaugh's waterfront condominium, Cavanaugh leaning heavily on Marty for support. Cavanaugh was still extremely sore from his attempts to escape the fire. After the explosion, he had tried to dig out the back entrance and was struck across the back by falling debris in the attempt. Luckily all he had to show for the effort was a bruised and battered backbone.

"Ca-re-ful," she sounded the word out over each of his slow steps down the carpeted hall. Cavanaugh bit his bottom lip, refusing to acknowledge the difficulty he was having in forcing his body parts to move.

Reaching the door to Cavanaugh's condominium, the couple paused on the threshold and gave each other a knowing look. Using his key, she unlocked the door and guided him inside. "Here we are." She forced a cheerful note into her voice. As soon as the pair cleared the entrance, the large wood door slammed shut behind them.

Marty spun around taking Cavanaugh with her, his arm still draped over her shoulder. Neither were surprised to find that they were not alone.

"Well, isn't this touching." Justin leaned against the door, directing a small revolver on the pair. He sneered, "Makes me almost hate having to kill you." He chuckled. "Well, almost."

Cavanaugh forced himself to stand up straight, despite the sharp shooting pain down his spine. "You should've been long gone by now."

Justin smiled in a way that reminded Marty of why he'd been able to impersonate Cavanaugh so easily. "And leave all this *unfinished* business?" He shook his head.

"It doesn't matter, Justin," Marty spat angrily, "the police know who you are."

"You know," Justin studied Marty through narrow eyes,

you have been nothing but a thorn in my side from the moment Cavanaugh met you. If you hadn't pulled him from the fire eight months ago, this would've ended here." His mouth twisted in a snarl. "I think I'll shoot you first."

Marty and Cavanaugh exchanged a quick glance, and Justin felt the hairs on his neck stand up. Something wasn't right.

"Over there," Justin motioned to the sofa.

Marty guided Cavanaugh over to the sofa and Justin followed, his back to the front door. He never took his eyes off the couple. Justin knew he risked everything by coming back just for them; the police believed he'd boarded a plane hours ago. But he hated loose ends. If left unattended, they almost always unraveled and caused a mess.

"You'll never get away with this," Cavanaugh winced as Marty lowered him onto the sofa.

"Justin chuckled, "I already have. According to the police bulletin, I'm on an airplane bound for South America. No one would expect me to come back just for you."

"No one except me," a weak, gravelly voice spoke from the entranceway.

Justin spun in that direction and his eyes widened in amazement. "Aunt Reline?"

Reline Saint John sat in the shadow of the hallway, with something small in her hand directed at Justin's chest. From her vantage point, one clean shot would kill him.

"What—wh—" A sound from the front entrance caused him to spin around one hundred and eighty degrees.

"Drop your weapon," someone called out in a gruff voice.

Justin stood stunned as the front door burst open and in poured two Detroit police officers. One crouched low to the ground and the other moved off to the side of the door frame. Both men were in full uniform, including the two weapons they had trained on him.

"Drop your weapon, now." The officer in the stooped position demanded.

Justin froze. Left with no alternative, he dropped his weapon. The police officer closest to him grabbed him and forced him face down on the floor.

"Are you two all right?" the other officer asked, and only then noticed the woman in the background.

Seeing the direction of the man's eyes, Cavanaugh spoke up. "It's all right, officer. She's my mother."

"Ma'am, I need you to drop your weapon," he called to her.

Without hesitation, Reline dropped the pistol she'd been clinging to. Her frail fingers spasmed in relief.

Marty reached her before Cavanaugh. "Are you all right?"

"Mother?" Cavanaugh came to stand next to her.

Reline simply shook her head in the affirmative; it was all she could do given the frayed state of her nerves.

Despite his own pain, Cavanaugh squatted down beside the wheelchair. "What are you doing here? I told you to call the police and stay out of sight. You could've been killed."

Her rheumy gray eyes focused on her only child. Then, as if a dam broke inside her, she threw her arms around his neck as the water coursed down her cheeks. "So could you," she whispered through her tears, "so could you."

"Are you the person who made the 911 call, ma'am?" the police officer asked, opening his small notebook.

"Yes." Reline sighed in great relief, sitting back in her chair.

He scribbled madly on his pad. "Did you recognize the assailant?"

"Of course, he's my nephew. I knew immediately why he'd come," she began.

Justin listened in horror as his aunt recounted his dirty dealings to the police in vivid detail. He watched with obvious confusion and bewilderment as he was led from the apartment in handcuffs. She'd been in the apartment all along. And not only had she managed to call Cavanaugh to warn him, she placed an emergency call to the police as well.

In all his planning and conniving, Justin believed he'd prepared for every possible contingency. Except one. Never did he imagine that while he was scheming to kill Cavanaugh and cover his embezzlement plot, his elderly aunt was conducting her own investigation into the strange financial activities of Genesis.

Suddenly, he remembered a conversation he'd had with Cavanaugh shortly after he'd been rescued from the first fire. He'd walked in on Cavanaugh, while he was working in his father's study . . .

"What are you doing there?" Justin asked.

"Mother wanted me to look over the last quarter reports."

"Why?"

"She seems to think there's some inconsistencies."

"Did you find anything?"

"No, everything looks fine to me," Cavanaugh said, "just Mother's way of trying to keep me here a day longer. Another one of the infamous Reline Saint John mind control games. But I don't care if she's convulsing on the foyer floor, I'm leaving tonight."

Justin felt his head pounding with tension—regret—realization. His aunt had known all along. He had underestimated a crippled old woman, and that one mistake had cost him everything.

Thirty-three

It was almost four hours later when the police officers finally vacated the apartment. Cavanaugh had gotten his mother settled into bed, and all evidence of the eventful evening was wiped away.

Marty stood looking out over the balcony. "Is it really over?"

Cavanaugh moved from his position of leaning against the glass door. He winced in pain before coming up behind her. "Yes, it's really over."

She turned into his arms. "I love you." Marty felt the need to repeat the statement every few seconds, realizing how close she'd come to never being able to tell him that again. "I thought I lost you."

He smiled in his special way. "You can't get rid of me that easy."

She knew he was still in a great deal of pain, but she couldn't resist the urge to hug him, to touch him. She needed to feel his solid presence beneath her hands. He stifled a cry of pain, and Marty tried to release him, but he held on to her, pulling her tightly against his battered body.

"No, baby," he whispered against her hair. "If anything can heal me, it's this."

After a moment's hesitation, Marty relaxed into his

arms. She leaned back to look into his face. "I'm sorry it was Justin."

He set his jaw. "No more than I am."

"Why do you think he did it?"

"Greed, I would guess. My father provided nicely for all his nieces and nephews, but apparently it wasn't enough for him."

Her mouth twisted in a smirk. "I never thought your mother would be the one to figure it all out."

"She had her suspicions from the beginning. When she approached me with it, I thought she was just being paranoid. She called an emergency board meeting some months ago with all the stockholders *except* Justin. That's when all the unusual financial activity came to light. Things Justin had been covering up, or making excuses for."

"She loves you—in her own way."

"I know," he sighed. "I just wish that way was less torturous."

"So, what now?"

His dark eyes twinkled with mischief. "Now, we go to bed."

She tilted her head and studied him with doubt. She knew he was still in a great deal of pain from the fire, but at that moment he didn't look like a man in pain. In fact, he looked exactly like a man bent on pleasure. "To sleep, right?"

He shrugged. "Eventually."

"Cavanaugh," she said, warningly. "Surely, you can't want to—you know."

He chuckled. "Why not?"

"Aren't you still in pain?"

"Your loving is the best painkiller I know." He led her away from the balcony toward the bed.

"But," was all she managed to get out before she felt

the firm mattress coming up against her back, and the even firmer man coming down on top of her.

He propped his elbows on the bed, looking down into her surprised face.

"You move pretty good for an invalid."

He nibbled at her neck. "I was strongly motivated."

"Cavanaugh, I can't let you—"

His mouth covered hers as his tongue pushed its way inside. He sucked her up, reveling in the sweet taste he'd missed for too long. "Shh." He cooed against the soft skin of her cheek and neck, working his way up behind her ear. "I need this. I need you."

Marty needed little encouragement to wrap her arms around his neck. She tried to be conscious of his soreness, but the more she touched him the more she wanted to, until soon their clothing was stripped away and they lay in each other's arms as natural as the original man and woman.

"I seem to remember asking you a question the last time we were in this position." Cavanaugh spoke while placing gentle kisses wherever his mouth could reach.

"Mmmm," was her official answer.

Cavanaugh considered it for only a moment. He could probably easily seduce another "yes" out of her. But that was not what he wanted. He sat back on his haunches.

"Marty, open your eyes."

She was still so caught up in the bliss of his touch, the statement did not register until the cool night air finally reached her skin.

"Huh?"

Taking both her hands in his, he pulled her up. "Sit up, we have to talk."

She frowned in confusion. "Now?"

"Yes, now." Once he had her sitting facing him, he continued. "From the moment I met you, I knew you were sent to save me. Now it's time to fulfill that destiny. Marry me, Marty. Save me from a life full of pain and regret for things I can never change. Save me from an existence without love—without you."

Marty could have sworn she actually felt her heart swelling with happiness and pride. He still wanted her. She had secretly wondered if she were simply a life raft. That after all his troubles had passed, his feelings for her would pass as well. But here they were—and he still wanted her. Their love had weathered a terrible storm, but it was still standing. *They* were still *one.*

She threw her arms around his neck and hugged tightly, oblivious to the intense pain she was causing him. "Yes! Yes, I'll marry you." She smiled. "And you were right, by the way. June is a great month for weddings."

Cavanaugh returned her tight hug, and gently guided her down to the bed. He had his declaration of love, and a promise for the future. He was free to pursue his original goal. He quickly donned a protective sheath and guided himself into her warm center.

This was the only real home he'd ever known, he thought. Feeling the flames of passion as her heat consumed him, Cavanaugh gave himself over to the inferno of her love.

Tiny Kendra, dressed in a white, lace smock with a single white rose wound in her curly hair, waddled down the aisle on her short, chubby bow legs. The basket of orchids hanging from her tiny arm dangled casually. Every once in a while, it occurred to her to toss one out, but for the most part the basket remained intact. She was far more fascinated with the people watching her from both sides of the aisle.

Seeing her father seated near the front, she dropped

her basket without hesitation and ran into his arms, still almost ten rows from the front. Erv caught the toddler up in his arms and shook his head. So much for the flower girl.

The wind was blowing lightly, moving the thin, linen material around Cavanaugh's legs. He stood at the end of the orchid-lined path, waiting and watching.

He cast a small smile to the man standing to the left of him. J. J. smiled in return, and touched his shoulder for reassurance. He was looking very dapper, and very out of place in his snappy black tuxedo, fully equipped with cumberbund.

Cavanaugh had to admit he felt a little ridiculous in his own outfit. Standing there barefoot, in linen slacks and a crème and beige silk dashiki. But it was what she'd asked of him, a very informal wedding. When he informed J. J., the man had only scoffed and said enough with this New-Age stuff, a wedding is a wedding.

Across the aisle stood Candice and Dina, dressed in matching crème-colored linen dresses, handpicked by Marty. He couldn't help thinking how much like her the dresses were. Elegant yet casual. Stylish yet traditional. Candice winked at him, looking very lovely, tiny baby's breath intertwined in her hair. Just like everyone else in the wedding party, she held a single white rose. Marty said each rose represented the beauty and love that person had brought into her life. Starting with the very first one, given to her by Cavanaugh the day they met.

All the attention shifted to the end of the aisle where a very pregnant Shoshana stood, her rounded belly almost concealing the man and woman standing behind her.

After several tense moments, Shoshana began moving down the aisle, conscious of every step. Her additional weight was making it difficult to stay on top of the sand.

Her dress was a rush job, but looked every bit as well-tailored as the others.

They'd known she was pregnant when she was measured, but nobody expected her to explode, growing almost three times her original size in less than three months.

Cavanaugh bent to the side, trying to see behind her but it was useless. He could tell from the smiles and aaahing sounds of their small audience of friends that Marty was every bit as beautiful as he imagined. He stood tall and waited, knowing he'd stand there for eternity if necessary.

Marty's heart was pounding against her chest. She tightly clutched the muscular arm entwined with hers. She looked up at the man who was the closest thing to a brother she had, and Cal smiled. Taking a deep breath, the couple began moving down the aisle, then suddenly Marty stopped, frozen in her tracks.

Realizing what had happened, Shoshana paused and glanced back over her shoulder, noting the look of terror on her sister's face. She exchanged a worried glance with Cal.

"You okay?" Cal whispered back. His question was met with a blank stare. Looking at the petrified bride-to-be on his arm, Cal knew he was out of his depth. He made a subtle hand gesture to Shoshana, asking for help.

Shoshana smiled nervously at the group of people, who were even now beginning to realize something was wrong.

Standing at the beginning of a path that would forever change her life, Marty felt like her legs could not support her weight, let alone guide her down the aisle. What was she doing here? Was she truly worthy of this man, this—gift? What kind of wife would she be to him? God knows, she would try her best, but was that good enough? Cavanaugh deserved the very best, only the best. What if she could not live up to his expectations? He was so elegant, so refined, and she was so—not.

The words of a familiar song drifted into Marty's ears. Sung so softly, no one but she and Cal could hear the quiet melody. It was the same song she and Shoshana had sung together as children on stormy nights when the wind outside their bedroom window would howl eerily, making the girls edgy. They would snuggle under the covers together and comfort each other with the words to a silly, made-up song.

You're my sister,
You're my friend,
Rock solid 'til the end.

Shoshana continued to repeat the refrain. Marty smiled, remembering that the original ten-year-old's version of the song had included a rousing chorus of "shake your groove thang," to which the girls would dance around their room. Wisely, Shoshana decided to skip that part.

Cal frowned in confusion at the back of Shoshana's head. Marty patted his arm lovingly. He didn't understand, but that's okay, Marty thought. The message was for her, anyway. As little girls they'd sung and danced their way through their doubts and fears.

Keep moving, Shoshana was saying, *and your fears will subside.*

Marty took a deep breath sucking in the salty air. Then letting out a heavy sigh, she whispered to Cal. "I'm ready."

Together the small procession began to move. Marty was amazed at the number of people willing to fly to Puerto Rico to witness their nuptials. The engine team of Firehouse Fifteen alone took up four rows. Dwight and Tommy were forced to stay behind as part of the skeleton crew. She'd hugged and kissed them both tightly before she left, telling them that they would both be with her in heart and mind. Two seconds later, she spun around and socked Dwight in the arm, when he said Cavanaugh was making her all soft and girly.

The Saint Johns covered the other side, including Reline Saint John, who'd been making impressive strides toward mending the wedge between her and her son since Justin was arrested. Although thirty-plus years of neglect was no easy hurdle to conquer, Cavanaugh seemed willing to give her a chance to try.

Marty smiled as her eyes fell on Beth Stanton, sitting near the aisle, close to the front. The woman reached out and squeezed Marty's hand. Marty knew they were bonded for life, the way survivors often are. All the people she loved, new friends and old, gathered together on a sandy beach near the ocean. *How incredibly blessed I am.*

Soon Shoshana was stepping to the side, and Marty found herself face to face with her beloved. She was pleased with her appearance; she'd dressed in a beautiful, soft white linen dress that perfectly accentuated her long, lean form. Her curly hair was sprinkled with baby's breath also, and her makeup was flawless. But the look of love in his eyes told her she could have shown up in a garbage bag, and his reaction would've been the same.

Cal nodded to Cavanaugh. With a tiny kiss on her cheek, Calvin Brown gave his best friend in marriage, turning her life, her heart, and her future over to a man he trusted, knowing she was in good hands.

The couple stood eye to eye as the minister began reciting the vows that would bind their souls forever. Marty closed her eyes briefly, letting the soft breeze drift over her face. What a perfect June day for a wedding.

Dear Reader:

Thank you for taking a few of your precious hours of leisure to spend with *Love's Inferno.* I hope you have enjoyed meeting Marty and Cavanaugh, their story has been a part of me for some time. I have always been fascinated by firefighters, those men and women who put it on the line every day to rescue complete strangers.

Like everyone else in America, I was left standing in awe of the selfless bravery and uncommon courage displayed on 9/11. In the most tragic of circumstances, we witnessed boundless compassion and incomparable professionalism.

In my own way, Marty and the men of the fictional Firehouse Fifteen are a tribute to these everyday heroes and *she*roes. My way of saying thanks for being there when the call comes in.

I would also like to apologize for the liberties taken in the descriptions of the lifestyle and work environment of firefighters. Needless to say, their truly unique culture is designed for efficiency, not romance.

I am very excited about my first endeavor in the world of romance writing, and would love to hear your comments. Please feel free to contact me at eoverton03@yahoo.com.

About the Author

Elaine Overton resides in Detroit, where she was raised and attended a local business college. A Gulf War vet as the result of her short stint in the Army, she is currently working as an administrative assistant.

Her love of reading is second only to her love of writing. The mother of a nine-year-old son, she can be found most Saturday afternoons traipsing through the woods with her pack of Cub Scouts.